The Chronicles of Tearha

The Number 139

Aden Ng

ISBN (E-book): 978-981-11-5652-6

ISBN (Paperback): 978-981-11-5651-9

To the end of all things and those who face them.

Prologue
The Watcher

"Extinction is the rule. Survival is the exception."
- Carl Edward Sagan

Red lights blared alongside the emergency sirens. Engineers in leather jackets and goggles frantically ran up and down the corridor as bursts of steam shot out from the copper pipings embedded in the walls. Coat wearing scientists stood at each of the valves, taking readings from the pressure meters, shouting out orders for the engineers to execute. The smell of rust was drastically enhanced by the spitting steam while the entire corridor further reeked with the stench of sweat from the working men and women.

A long, shining, silver pony-tailed hair trailed behind her. A sharp, golden eyed view on the front shining brighter than her tanned skin. The femme fatale, with her thigh high boots, short curving blue skirt, tight corset, and a leather jacket one size too small, walked with a wide, confidently swinging gait. She did not duck when the steam pipes shot their hot vapour nor blinked when the men around her shot her their wanting gazes.

"Lady Nora." A scientist ran up to her, brimming with nervous energy. "We weren't expecting you."

Nora Phemtelle, with a steady, monotonous voice, replied, "The Lord Light have requests of this matter to be resolved under his indirect supervision."

The scientists nodded, his ease evaporating, his shoulders tensing as his eyes widened and understood the magnitude of the situation.

Nora asked, "Where is Nadier?"

"The Wanderer? He's out on the Grassplains. We've sent words for him but even then, it will take him at least a day to reach us."

She clicked her tongue. "Walk with me," she ordered and started walking forward with the nervous scientist following seven steps later. "What about The Long Arm? I was told they would be returning today."

The scientist struggled to keep up with her long strides and made sure to keep at least an arm's length away from her. "They are being held up by Adelaide Wiltkins at the southern gates," he told her. "They won't be in for another half-day."

Another tongue click. The pair turned another busy corner which led down a short hallway ending with a heavy steel door. "Damn that Demon Eyes," she said. "Always giving us trouble."

She stepped back. Like a servant, the meek scientist crossed forward. He heaved and turned the handwheel in her stead. With a loud *clunk*, the door swung inwards and opened. The scientist stepped aside and Nora passed him.

The portal lab was a wide, field-sized space separated into two rooms by a large reinforced glass pane that had lines of reinforced copper wires running through the glass. The glass ran the entire 10-meter length and 20-meter height of the wall. Two pairs of scientists and engineers were working a control panel with knobs, levers, pressure gauges, and valves. The control panel stretched from one end of the glass to the other but ending just short at an even larger and thicker steel door on the far right that led into the field-sized chamber.

Nora stepped to the panel and the group of scientists and engineers stopped their work, turning their attentions to her. She asked, "How long has he been in there?"

An engineer took off his goggles in graveness. "Almost a day now. We've sent the first guards in but they were nearly wiped out. Only three survivors." Beyond the glass pane, dozens of bodies were strewn across the next room, most congregated near the door in their futile attempts to escape. "If Lord Akaras isn't stopped soon, the portal will stabilise."

Nora asked, "And that's a bad thing?" At the end of the portal room, a mass of purple seither swirled around a clear, metallic bubble – housing the image of an upside-down swamp – with a massive metal ring suspending it. Wires and pipes ran through the construct, sparking off arcs of electricity at sparse given moments. "Is that not what we have been trying to accomplish for the past decade? Stabilise the portal?"

The scientist who followed her in answered, "Yes, but Lord Akaras is forcing the matter. If it is done his way, there will be a feedback of seither that will level all of Everwind."

"Have you tried cutting off the power to the portal room?"

The engineer looked at the controls as if it had cue cards for him to get through the conversation with her. "We have, but he had switched to grid it internally and is powering it himself. He's using his magic circuits to directly fuel the machine."

Nora set a finger to her chin and contemplated. To the scientist behind her, she ordered, "Get the Second Mage Platoon down here."

"But Lady Nora," the scientist said, "Lord Akaras is the strongest Spellblade in Everwind! The Second Mage Platoon will get slaughtered in there. We need The Lord Light or–"

She closed the gap between them in a blink. Her boots shot up towards his neck as she flexibly bent her body to do so. She notched the scientist's chin below her heel and pushed his head against the wall. With little effort, she angled and lifted the man off his feet as he held onto her for dear life. Despite the sensual pose and the sudden playful tone that gripped her voice, the room was caught up in fear.

"Are you asking The Lord Light to personally come down and clean up your mess?" she asked with a smile. The scientist, held in a grip tighter than her corset, could not even shake his head. She continued, "If the mage platoon can't even handle a dark elf with half his circuits used up, then they deserve to die, just like everyone who questions The Penultima Council." With that, her leg swung down towards the ground like a guillotine, smashing the scientist's head onto the floor.

The man laid there, blood flowing from his head and pooling along his corpse. Nora turned her attention to the nearest engineer who watched her, wide-eyed and shivering. With a tender smile, she asked, "Would you kindly get the Second Mage Platoon for me?"

The engineer nodded and sprinted out of the room.

Akaras Spaedruiner watched the spectacle from the safety of his portal room. He shook his head, not in disappointment, but expectant. Nora always had a sadistic streak to her and it was one that he had detested. His onyx hair short, his skin dark and grey, his overcoat black, the dark elf was almost a shadow in the room with his crimson eyes staring out like a demon lurking in the darkness. The long, sharp ears of his species picked up every single word uttered from beyond the glass. He welcomed the challenge of the Second Mage Platoon. They would prove an interesting break from the task at hand. If they could get there in time.

On the wall opposite him, a large, 2-meter high copper battery wheezed, the needle of the pressure gauge on it swinging into red.

Akaras opened his left palm towards it. A glow shone within his coat sleeve. Then, large arcs of electricity shot out from his hand to the battery. The wheezing stopped. The needle on the gauge slowly retreated back to the whites. He then pulled a lever on the wall closest to him, sending another surge of electricity into the machine.

"Almost there," he mumbled. He looked into the whirling mass of energy. Months of planning had led him to that point. Soon, he would have Everwind wiped from the continent of Eltar. "*Escraeh Tae Lofs,*" he ended unconvincingly.

From within the portal, he could faintly hear the voice of a man shouting incoherently. He ignored the sound and turned away from the portal.

Before him stood a man. A human. Akaras looked on, stunned, having not heard the door opened or even sensed the man's presence. From beyond the glass, Nora and her group also looked on in shock, the appearance of the man a similar surprise to them.

From beneath his coat, Akaras pulled out a long barrelled pistol. The gun had a stock that doubled as a pressurised-steampack and a clip of nails loaded into the barrel. The handle and frame were decorated with bronze depictions of dragons and the copper barrel shone brightly in the light. Though not as powerful as a black powder firearm, Akaras could supercharge the gun to fire paralysing nails as fast as any bullet.

"Who are you?" the Lord demanded.

The man wore a dark grey cotton coat over a steamed white shirt. His pants were black denim, but in a smooth and expertly tailored stitching he had never seen before. His cave-dark hair seemed to be magically held up, styled messily in a fashion that Akaras would define as a bird's nest. The man seemingly ignored Akaras's question and looked up to see the portal.

An excited glint formed in his eyes as he rushed past Akaras and towards the swirling phenomenon, pointing excitedly, "That's a portal! Man, have you caused us a load of problem on the other side." He turned to Akaras to say more. But seemingly noticing the dark elf for the first time, he instead blurted out, "Woah! You're a drow!"

At the comment, Akaras pulled the trigger. The nail blasted out of the barrel, enveloped and followed by an arching line of electricity. It hit its target.

The nail fell to the floor.

"Woah!" The man danced on the spot as the shock coursed through him, though not as potent as it should have been. "D-don't d-do that!"

But Akaras focused on the nail on the ground. An anti-physical shield only meant one thing. "You're a mage?"

However, he had never seen a shield as powerful as the one the man had. Most shields would collapse when even the slightest charge of magic was placed through them. However, the man's physical shield held strong, only letting the magic pass.

"W-well I-I-I don't know about-about–" The man paused, took a breath, and violently shook off the last of the shock. "–that. I am a Hymn though."

"A what?"

"A Hymn," he stated matter-of-factly. They stared at each other quizzically. Then, the man asked, "So... can you put down your gun?"

"No!"

"Please?"

"No!"

"Pretty please?"

"What?" Akaras looked on in confused frustration. "Why would you make a beautiful plea? What does that even mean?"

"Ah!" The man snapped his fingers in understanding. "Cultural differences. Sorry."

"Who are you?" Akaras asked, intending to divert the conversation back to his control.

As if digging through his memory, the man slowly announced, "I... am... The Watcher!" he exclaimed his title excitedly. "Yes! That's the name I was told to use. I am The Watcher. I watch stuff." He blinked. "What? That makes no sense."

Akaras just stared at him before announcing, "You're insane."

"No I'm not!" The Watcher replied. "I got myself tested just last year. Eccentric, maybe, but not crazy." He then looked around the room. The gleam in his eyes as he took in the sight was like a child's who had just opened a present. He turned back to Akaras. "So... can you close the portal?"

Akaras punctuated, "No." Whoever this Watcher was, if he wanted to close the portal, he was an enemy.

"Is there anything you *can* do?" The Watcher threw his hands up, paused, pulled his hair and spun on his feet in a frustrated groan before settling down. "What about not shooting me with that thing again? It really stings."

The dark elf smiled slyly and slowly lowered his gun. "Sure." To his left hand, he sent a powerful charge of electricity. He caught the Watcher staring at his charged hand. His trick was exposed. No matter. Like a gunslinger, he brought his charged hand up towards The Watcher.

But The Watcher was quicker, raising his own hand in a signal to stop. Akaras remembered thinking that a stop signal would affect his electricity as much as a blade of grass would a stampeding army. However, he found himself flying across the field-sized room at the speed of a bullet. Before his brain could even properly register the event, he had skidded off the ceiling and smashed through the top of the 20-meter high reinforced glass, before finally having his body punched and embedded into the metal wall behind it.

Nora Phemtelle took a step back in fear as she watched the most powerful Spellblade in the land get thrown across the room as easily as a dart to a board. No. Easier than even that. It was a feat faster and more powerful than the shot of a bullet. She had not feared anything in over a decade. Now, she stood with teeth clenched, a twitch in a balled fists. Shaking and terrified.

A squad of the Second Mage Platoon rushed into the room and Nora halted them with the same hand signal The Watcher had used, but without the violent aftermath.

Shaking, trying to calm her voice and losing her playful tone, she pointed at the anomaly before them and demanded, "Bring that man in. Alive."

Without Akaras to power the battery, the portal machine powered down and the swirl of purple seither dispersed slowly with puffs. The rooms fell silent.

The Watcher, now looking at his own hand in shock, questioned, "What have I done? What's happening to me?"

His questions echoed throughout the chamber.

Chapter 1
Demon Eyes

Black bricked walls surrounded the cell. A small electric lamp in the corridor outside the bars flitted as the only source of light. The Watcher sat on the right of two opposing metal beds, staring at the clock face of a silver pocket watch.

Adelaide Wiltkins sat opposite him, tracing the movements of his deep brown eyes as they followed the tick of the watch. From the moment they were brought together, the human had not so much as glanced in her direction. But she was used to treatments like that. It was the humans' way.

Nonetheless curious, she asked, "What are you doing?"

Without taking his eyes off the watch, he replied, "I'm looking for any anomaly or offset in the chronological order of the space-time continuum."

"Am I suppose to understand what that means?"

"Not unless you have an innate ability to sense and interpret spatial and chronological temperaments on a subatomic level."

"You humans get crazier every time I see you." She leaned into the wall. Adjusting atop the metal contraption they called a bed, snuggling into her knees and giving a bored yawn.

He finally closed the watch and slid it back in his coat pocket. "I'm not actually insane. I'm just–" He looked up, his eyes shot wide in surprise and a grin spread wide across his face. "You! You're an elf!"

Her messy short hair was as green as the leaves of the forest she lived in, still riddled with specks of the same dirt. Light freckles littered her cheeks like pebbles on the earth. Her build was lithe and tall, her skin the shade of paper. A tattered and patched green tunic covered her upper body. A pair of muddied grey trousers, a small leather belt, and knee length brown leather boots were worn below. Adelaide Wiltkins looked fit to blend into a forest should one sprout up around them. But the most outstanding of her features were not her long, sharp ears or rugged dressing. It was her eyes, whose irises were leaf green while the sclera, the whites of her eyes, were blood red. It was as if she had ruptured a vessel that bled into her stare.

Rolling those crimson eyes, she replied, "Yes, I'm an elf. Don't have to be so surprised. I know you humans only ever get to see us elves in those slums you call Antipods, but we're not some animals for you to gawk at." Her tone snapped with distaste at having to talk with a human. "Inbred apes."

"Alright, alright! No need to get hostile. Sheesh. You're almost worse than the drow that shot me."

"I would shoot you too if you use that language again."

"What language? 'Hostile'?"

"You can't be that stupid." She looked on in confused frustration.

Sensing the enmity she was starting to emit, The Watcher put his hands up in peace. "Look, I'm not from around here. I don't really understand your culture all that much."

"Really?" Her tone betrayed her believe. "You don't know what *d'raow* means?"

Eyes wide, lips pursed, The Watcher shook his head with his best impression of a dog without a bone. She thought he just looked constipated. She scanned his face. Though hard to read, she felt he was telling the truth, which was odd to her. How foreign was he to have no idea of one of the most offencive words to use to a dark elf?

She explained, "*D'raow* is derogatory. It means 'death skin', or 'rotten people'."

He stared at her blankly before commenting, "That's bad."

"Yeah. It's bad."

"Wow, then I really made a mistake there. I hope that Avalas Speedrunner or whatever his name is makes it." He sat back in solemn contemplation.

She processed the name, running it through her list of known dark elves and only one was even a remote match to the butchering The Watcher gave. "Akaras Spaedruiner?" She knew that if anyone was locked in that cell with her, it was for something drastic, though she never expected her cellmate to survive an encounter with Akaras.

"Yeah. That guy." He swiped his hand across her view like a biplane. "Sent him flying into a wall."

"You defeated Akaras Spaedruiner?" She stood to her feet in surprise. "Not possible. He's the best Spellblade in Eltar. How?"

"Well, I sort of held my hand up like this. And focused really hard." The Watcher raised his hand and squinted really hard. He then snapped back into a jovial, casual pose, flailing his arms in excited explanation. "And I tried to wrap him in a temporal stasis. But the laws of physics in this universe might be slightly different so I accidentally sent him shooting off through space without any gravitational suppression. So he went splat!"

A male, matter-of-fact tone came from the corridor outside. "That is what the reports says, though without such childish details." The pair turned to the voice. Outside the cell, leaning against the wall opposite, having slipped into their area like a ghost, a dark elf stayed still near the shadows with his arms crossed. "Like a bullet."

The newcomer wore a leather vest over a black shirt tied by belt straps across his chest, all covered by a night darkened collared trench coat. A pair of thick black pants and maroon strapped boots completed the rugged-clandestine ensemble. A hood further shadowed his face.

Adelaide walked up to the newcomer with a rascally smile and waved lazily at him through the bars of the cell. "Hey, Nadier. Nads. You getting me out of here? Nads?"

The dark elf ignored her, instead addressing The Watcher directly. "Akaras Spaedruiner is my brother."

A solemn fog sunk between the three, with Adelaide losing all playful intents, and The Watcher slowly getting to his feet in sober respect. The latter looked at Nadier and said, "You used 'is'."

"For now," Nadier nonchalantly replied.

"Are you here to kill me?"

Without skipping a beat, Nadier replied, "No." He pushed away from the wall and stepped towards the cell, removing his hood. "If I had been there, I would have killed him myself." Like his brother, Nadier's irises were blood red, a trait shared amongst most of the dark elves. His hair was also jet black, messy and swept over his right eye.

However, unlike his brother, his chin was sharper, his cheeks wider, giving him a more human-like face than the sleek, curved elven ones of Akaras and Adelaide. Flatter. More heavy and boned. An faded orange mark like a tatoo – a sharp seven with a line slashing across, intricately decorated at the edges – covered his left face and cutting through the eye.

Feeling the tension lifting, Adelaide let out a breath of relief, before cheekily telling Nadier, "You know Akaras would have geared you."

"Nice seeing you too, Adelle. But you..." He turned to her cellmate. "Your name. The Watcher."

"What about it?"

"I just came back from a summons from the Overseers." He looked to Adelaide with furrowed brows and a stern stare. She shot up like an animal ready to hunt and Nadier continued, "They announced a new epitaph. The Watcher."

She asked, "What's the name?"

"There is no name."

The Watcher cut in, "Ooo, that's a scary tone. This sounds bad. Is this bad?"

With tone uncertain and bordering on fear, she noted, "That's impossible." She turned and stared at The Watcher, wide-eyed. "You're impossible."

"No." The Watcher grinned. "I'm Batman!"

"I don't know what that means, human, but I am very tempted to punch you for it." She shot him a look normally reserved for a piece of furniture after stumping a toe.

Nadier said, "The Overseers are a 'group' with the ability to see certain aspects of the future. They sometimes assign Epitaphs to individuals who they predict will be influential on the world. They would announce a name and an Epitaph. But you, Watcher, did not get a name. Just an Epitaph. I wonder why." He reached back to beneath his coat and pulled out two hand axes. Adelaide's eyes lit up as he passed the weapons to her through the bars. "It's not always accurate, and some do slip through their sights. But when they mark you, you become someone to watch. The Double Edged Prince, the current king of Aleynonlia. Akaras 'The Bolted Arm' Spaedruiner, the strongest Spellblade of Eltar. Generally, they are pretty accurate." He stepped away from the cell and began walking away.

Adelaide casually called out, "You're not going to help me escape?" She was weighing the axes within her hand as she asked the question.

Nadier replied, "You don't need my help."

The Watcher added, "But you are helping. Why?"

The dark elf stopped in his tracks, a glimpse of his back just before he faded into the shadows of the hallway. He replied, "Lady Nora Phemtelle is eager to put your head to the guillotine. Says you're too powerful to keep alive." He looked over his shoulder, his red eye a piercing stare in the dark. "My brother tried to destroy Everwind. And there's a good chance he might die for it, from you. As far as I'm concerned, you owe me twice, one for his injuries, and another for helping you. In return, I will use your powers to find out who placed my brother in a position to get killed." A glint of mad anger shone in his eyes as the lamp flitted. "And that *aelan dae* will die at my hands."

The dark elf stepped into the shadows, melting into it, and all was silent. Not the sound of footsteps. Not the pant of breath.

Adelaide had ignored the conversation. She had no intentions of getting dragged into a battle that had nothing for her. Instead, she sheathed the two axes into her belt. "It's been my truest displeasure meeting you, Watcher. But it's time for me to leave."

She stood before the bars, closed her eyes, breathed in deep, and took a step forward. When she opened her eyes again, she was in the corridor outside, facing just an inch away from the brick wall in front of her cell. A successful teleportation, as expected.

"Woah!" She heard The Watcher exclaim. "How did you do that?"

She smirked proudly. It was an ability that made her special, unique. A step away from the tedious human breed. "No idea. Maybe it's magic, but I don't have any magic circuits that I know of so–" She turned around and the cell was empty. Instead, The Watcher stood beside her, somehow having escaped the confines of the prison himself, excitedly examining her like a curious child.

"You just poofed! And here you are! Fascinating! Did you you step out of time? No, I would have felt that. So what? You just stepped through space? Folded it like a wormhole? Or did you cut through dimensions?" He blabbered on, though his questions were seemingly more directed to himself than her. He took a whiff of the air. "What's that smell?"

"How did you–" She looked to the bars of the cell, none of which were tempered or moved, the gap too narrow for even her slim frame to fit through. Even though her abilities to teleport had always been a mystery to her, the idea that someone else was capable of such a feat boggled her mind. "What kind of mage are you?"

Seemingly having decided to leave the mystery of her teleportation for later, The Watcher stood to height, adjusting the collar of his coat and sweeping specks of dust off his shoulder. "I guess I'm what you would call a, um... time mage?"

"A chronomancer?"

"Yes! A chronomancer." He snapped his fingers, kindled by energy. With a playful smile, he said, "Now, let's do ourselves a jailbreak."

Chapter 2
The Wanderer

Thick limestone walls surrounded the wooden framed hospital bed. The clean white bedsheets were offset by the respirator – a large tubed one meter tall chrome cased pump – rising and falling with each breath, steadily pumping oxygen into the patient as sure as the Twins would rise and fall each day.

The human nurse, in her white dress, khaki trousers, and a brown apron with a red cross stitched to the centre of the breasts, removed the copper oxygen mask and took the temperature of Akaras, who lay on the bed unmoving, body wrapped in bandage from head to toe, right arm and leg in a cast. After doing a quick check of his injuries, she pulled the thermometer from his lips and shook her head disappointingly. She pocketed the tool in her apron and turned to leave.

"Don't be alarmed," Nadier warned from his dark corner next to the door.

The nurse jumped, her eyes wide in shock, but she did not scream or show signs of fear. "Wanderer," she greeted. "I didn't hear you come in."

"Sorry to startle you," he politely apologised. "I would like to spend some time alone with my brother, if you will allow it."

The nurse gave a slight bow in respect. "I'm sorry, but I've been given strict instructions not to allow anyone else near Lord–um... former Lord, Akaras."

"I understand. But could you make an exception on this? We *are* family."

He could see her eyes shifting in thought before finally settling with, "Okay. But do close the door on your way out." She smiled softly and gave another bow before leaving the room.

Nadier stepped out of the shadows and he scanned the room for any hidden traps or assassins in hiding, doing so in part of habit, but also due to the situation he found himself in. Dark elf assassins were not out of the realm of possibility when the strongest Spellblade in Eltar was at his weakest. When he was sure there were no other souls in the room with him, he went to his brother's side.

With his right index finger, he reached down to his thigh and hooked onto the finger ring of his dagger. With a gentle pull, the dagger popped out of its sheathe without resistance and he flipped the weapon into the grip of his palm. With his left, he reached for one of the many metallic vials hidden behind his belt, hooking onto its finger ring with his other index, pulled, flipped the vial to grip, and loaded it into the empty chamber within the handle of the dagger, like a magazine into a gun.

He moved the blade over his brother's chest, an inch above his heart. He aimed the point just between the ribs and slowly pushed the dagger in. Through the skin, the muscles, and scrapping past the bone. Nadier navigated solely with the sense of touch against the rhythmic breathing and the steady rise and fall of the chest. Then, he felt the gentle walls of the heart. He placed free hand on his brother's chest and sunk just the tip of the blade into the beating muscle.

Akaras eyes shot opened and his body jerked back as the adrenaline rushed through him, but his chest was held in place by Nadier to prevent any damage from the sudden movement. In one swift motion, he removed the dagger with surgical precision, pulled his scarf off, and pushed the cloth against the new wound and staunched the blood.

He watched as Akaras's eyes flitted frantically around the room, taking in his surroundings as quickly as his suddenly awoken brain could. His eyes then landed on Nadier and realisation dawned in them as the wounded dark elf slowly sank back into the bed. His breathing slowed but his heart continued to pump fast through the makeshift dressing.

With a coarse, tired voice, the former Lord greeted, "Nads." He split his brother a gentle smile.

"Hey 'Karas." Nadier nodded stoically in acknowledgement.

Akaras let out a pained laugh. "Always so serious." Though his neck could not move, his eyes scanned the room again. He came to the conclusion, "I lost, didn't I? That man. The Watcher. Where is he?"

"Probably escaping the prison in a few minutes."

15

"Good, good." He closed his eyes in peace at the thought, not questioning the hows or whys of the situation. "A man as powerful as him should not fall into the hands of The Forum."

"Why did you do it?" Nadier asked without hesitation, skipping all other formalities and chit-chat. "Was that why you sent me to the Grassplains? So I wouldn't be caught in the eye of the storm when you destroy Everwind?"

Akaras tried to breathe in deep, only to wince from the pain of his collapsed lung. "If you knew all that, why are you asking me 'why'?"

Nadier got to his knees so that he was at face level with Akaras and could look him in the eye. "I want to know why you want to destroy Everwind." His gaze was steady, unfaltering, a slightly bent brow that hid a blaze of anger. "You and I, we are mercenaries. We go where the prize is most worthwhile. Who paid you? And just what could they have paid you with that would make you go on a suicide mission?"

He let out a pained breath and closed his eyes. "When I found you in your first cycle at the gates of *Ta'Kalenyilgah*, not a memory to your soul, not even a name, I never expected the page would turn to here." He opened his eyes and sized up his sworn brother. "Akaras 'The Bolted Arm' Spaedruiner and Nadier 'The Wanderer'. Banished from *Ta'Galadul*, storming the world of the humans. Gun and blade for hire. Even you, with all your meticulous planning could not have seen this coming."

"I'm not a seer. I can't see the future."

"Be a little poetic, my little brother." His eyes rest on the two daggers Nadier carried and the vials of chemicals he hid. "Take a step out of your shadow and your toys and poisons for once. Join the world."

"We're dark elves, 'Karas. All our time we've lived in the shadows."

Akaras replied, "If after almost two hundred years of banishment and that is still your thinking, then I have failed as a brother." Nadier stayed quietly in contemplation, having always respected his brother's view. Akaras sighed. The quiet pulled on and, growing impatient, he continued, "The *Ta'Galadul* had passed judgement on your actions. You are to be executed."

Nadier's fingers twitched towards his weapons. An execution by the dark elves meant an assassination, and dark elf assassins were known to be the best in the world. Biologically, they were a lighter, swifter race. Their natural abilities, from night-vision to being capable of holding their breaths for longer periods, made them adapt at the art of stealth. Even with his earlier precaution, it was still entirely possible there was an assassin with them, right then and there, and he would not have noticed it. In corners he had not checked. Maybe hiding under the bed, like a nightmare ready to strike.

Likely sensing his brother's uneasiness, Akaras reassured, "Don't worry. Even dark elf assassins needs time to travel." Once Nadier had calmed down, Akaras continued, "They offered to spare you of your execution, so long as I did as they asked."

"And you agreed to destroy Everwind? For my sake?" Nadier wore a rare look of shock.

"Like you said, we are mercenaries. We go where the prize is most worthwhile."

With a heavy heart, Nadier got to his feet. He could think of no other questions to ask, knowing that there was nothing left for his brother to give him. If the Dark Citadel had indeed sent the order to Akaras with such a prize, they would not have told him more.

He went straight to the point. "Any request?" The adrenaline he gave his brother would dissipate soon. But with his belt of drugs, Nadier could easily find one to put Akaras back to sleep. "I could ease the pain. Maybe numb the body."

Without hesitation, Akaras replied, "You could kill me."

"What?" He thought his brother must have gone mad. Even if he was bedridden, an elf's enhanced rate of healing meant he would be back on his feet before the next season. "I can't do such a thing. You are my brother." Though good at hiding his emotions, even Nadier could not sound casual at the request.

Akaras began explaining, "I'm not making out of this alive. I either get executed by Everwind, or assassinated by the *Ta'Galadul* assassins. Look at me. I'm in no position to move, let alone fight back." He looked down at his bandaged body and grunted as the aches started to seep in, a sign that the drug was wearing off. In just a few minutes, the pain would be unbearable. Akaras looked to Nadier with a conviction he usually reserved for battles. "I would rather my killer be someone I know, than a masked executioner or a dagger from the shadows."

Indecisiveness was not a familiar feeling to Nadier. He was a mercenary. A man of the blade. Hesitation in his way of life was often fatal. He had assassinated Lords and Ladies, brought down monstrous beasts and massacred entire bandit camps. He had killed for money. He had killed for favours. Never once had he questioned taking a life on command, at least not since his banishment. But now, his brother's request had brought him to a screeching halt.

Akaras sighed again. "No hesitations, my brother. You are Nadier, the lowest point. So no matter what you do, the only way left to you is up."

To others, the words may have sounded insulting. But to Nadier, they were phrases of clarity. Removing his scarf from the original wound, he pulled out his unloaded dagger and held the blade above his brother's heart. They stared at each other without breaking gaze and Nadier plunged the blade in.

Even to his end, Akaras held his stare. Even when the blade penetrated his skin, his look did not falter. Even when Nadier pulled the dagger out of his heart, he did not blink or flinch. Blood pooled around the wound, and Nadier was unsettled by his brother's firm eyes, which held the will of the dark elf he had come to know and care for, even after life left them.

It was the way of the dark elves. Kill or be killed. Nadier wiped the blood off his dagger with his scarf and turned away. But as he reached the door, his eyes clouded and he stopped in his tracks.

His breathing increased, his fingers twitched. "Dark elves don't cry," he said to himself like a mantra. If they could, eternity would last a painful lot longer.

Chapter 3
The Twin Stars

'The Watcher', like many that came before, was not a name he chose. They were names thrust onto him with expectations, hopes, and to a certain extent, destiny. Destiny was what he felt was dragging him as he ran behind the green haired elf, jogging through a long, pipes-lined copper hallway. It had been a long time since he ran with the main cast of a story, and the feeling of being back in the thick of the action was exhilarating. For centuries, he had just been standing at the sidelines, watching events unfold.

He let out an, "Oh..."

Adelaide stopped at a junction and asked in hushed tones, "What?"

"I just figured out why I'm called 'The Watcher'," he replied with a chuckle, catching up to her.

"Is it important right now?"

He seriously considered the question, with Adelaide glancing back, looking progressively annoyed by the second.

Finally, he replied, "Nope."

"Then shut the gear up." She peeked out of the corner to scout ahead.

The level smelled of despair and alcohol. Hot steam wheezed out from the pipes at random intervals, though cooled quickly into mist so that he had no need to dodge them. Despite having just stepped out of prison, they had not run into a single guard throughout the entire floor. Aside from one of the cells they passed being occupied by a single man, there were no other signs of life.

The Watcher asked, "Where is everyone?"

"We're on the top floor of a thirty storeys metal tower. It's a special prison for 'unique' individuals. Political prisoners, powerful mages, and beings with unique abilities," she explained. She held up her axes at the ready. "The walls here are thicker than a Titan, nothing gets through. Not even my teleportation."

He interrupted, "I'm sure you could if you tried."

She ignored him and continued, "So there's no need for guards in the cell area. They're all out at the entrance. It's easier to funnel prisoners out of one pathway than to chase around an open area."

"How do you know so much?"

She sighed and, knowing the coast was clear, stepped out of the corner boisterously. Axes still drawn, she walked down the last corridor that ended with a steel vault door.

Her tone raised with confidence. "When you live a life like mine, you need to learn of the places you might end up at. Preparation is the key to survival."

"Huh. You're smarter than you look."

"I will put an axe in your face."

The Watcher had a set idea of what elves were like. From all the movies he had watched and books he had read across all of time, they had almost always been depicted as wispy, eloquent, intellectual creatures. But Adelaide Wiltkins was rough, vulgar, and in the half an hour that they had spent navigating the prison labyrinth, she had told him to 'gear off' over a dozen times, which he assumed was the equivalent of being told to 'fuck off'.

They reached the door and Adelaide leaned against it with her ears. The Watcher asked, "What now?"

She turned her back to the door and twirled her axes. "Wait here," she commanded sternly.

Like before, she took a step backwards. But just before her feet touched the ground, her body seemed to vibrate, leaving clear after-images of three, before soundlessly disappearing in a thin puff of brown smoke.

He was mystified by the act. It had been hundreds of years since he had seen another person capable of teleportation, and the fact that the process seemed so vastly different than any he had witnessed before had his curiosity lighting up in joy. Wafting his hand through the smoke left behind, he determined it to not be aether. He brought his palm up and sniffed. Rust. The metallic tang touched his tongue and he made a face.

Just as he was deducing where the rust could have come from, the steel door swung outwards, opening up to a large and wide lobby.

Wooden floor, copper walls, and two security cages made up the layout of the large, mostly empty room. An opening in the wall opposite led to a balcony. Another door to the far left marked the exit. Eight security guards, wearing leather armour, bowler hats, and carrying maces, made up the obstacles of the room. Or they would have, were they not slumped against the walls and collapsed on the ground, bleeding from the open wounds in their back. Adelaide's axes dripping with blood told him all he needed of what happened.

The Watcher ran up to the nearest victim on the ground and exclaimed, "You killed them?"

"Yeah. Either that or we stay stuck here. Lucky for us, they were mostly out for lunch. Well, I did wait for lunch time to escape, so there wasn't much luck there, I guess. Except for Nads coming with the axes. Didn't know he was going to do that." Her reply was nonchalant, as if mass murder was the most daily of her routine.

He turned back to the security. He could staunch the blood, maybe even reverse the cut and restart the heart. He put his hands over the wound, preparing to use his powers, but the image of Akaras flying across the room stopped him in his tracks. It was one thing to teleport out of the jail cell. That was easy. Just a state of chronological suppression and phasing while the world rotated for a fraction of a millisecond. He didn't have to interact with gravity or even hold in atmosphere.

But without proper control of his powers, if he misjudged the gravitational strength of this new world he was in, or failed to properly keep in the atmosphere, the victim could end up spontaneously combusting, or worst, have the spine ripped away from the body at terminal velocity.

He paused for what seemed like an eternity in his endless life, before pulling back his hands in defeat. "I'm sorry," he said to the lifeless body. "I'm so sorry." He got to his feet and turned to Adelaide with a fierce glare.

She stepped back, a flash of fear in her eyes, as she stammered out, "W-what?"

"No more killing."

Regaining some confidence, she replied, "As if. If you haven't noticed, *human*," she punctuated with the same disdain given to cockroaches that starts flying. "We're in the most heavily defended building in Everwind. I don't know what magical world you live in, but if we want to survive, we're going to have to fight our way out."

He clicked his tongue and looked out towards the balcony. An idea formed in his head and he jogged towards the light. A stupid idea, sure, but all of his ideas were stupid until he tried, and continued to be stupid until he succeeded.

"Where are you going?" Adelaide called out, her footsteps following closely behind.

He ignored her, overtaken by the plan that ran through his head, drowning out all other coherent thoughts. He neared the balcony, the light outside blinding. He stepped into the shining gateway, feeling as if he had stepped into the afterlife. But what he stepped on was not a fluffy cloud or molten lava, but the hard and jagged steel grated platform. His hands reached out instinctively to stop himself just as his body hit the rails.

"No way." The words left him like air out of a balloon.

He was a time traveller and he had lived a life longer than anyone physically should. He had seen civilisations fall. Looked on as mass extinctions happened before his eyes. He had participated in end of the world scenarios, not once, but six times. Still, he was both surprised and relieved that he could continue to be amazed by the universe.

The world unfolded before him as if he was in a video game and it needed time to load. But it was more likely that his brain simply needed time to take in just how foreign the new world was to him.

Towers around ten storeys high stood sparse across the entire city of Everwind, numbering like blades of grass in a field. Bricked, wooded, chimneyed, and coppered, the metal frames glimmered in the afternoon light with Victorian shaping, the stone spouts spitting out fluffs of smoke. A wall of stone surrounded the edge of the city, and beyond that, a wide grassland extended into the mountains after, tiny settlements dotting across the stretching landscape. A copper blimp floated past his view. But above all of that, shining light down onto them, were two Suns that hung overhead. One was the size of the Sun back on Earth, and the other, just half that.

"You have two S–" he was about to say 'Sun', but realised that they were in a different solar system, in a different universe, and Sun was probably not their names. "Stars. You have two stars."

Having caught up to him, Adelaide took the tone of an annoyed teacher and replied sarcastically, "You mean Rykka and Cirus? How old are you? Have you never seen the Twins before?"

"No," he replied blankly. "I haven't."

The sound of stampeding feet came from the corridor beyond the entrance. It pulled him back to the situation at hand. He would have time to marvel at the new planet later, but for now, he needed to focus. He eyed the blimp and gauged the distance. A little far and somewhat difficult, but not impossible.

Adelaide turned to the door and spun her axes in her hands. "If you don't have a plan, I'm going to go take care of this."

He grabbed her wrist before she could step away and warned, "Hang on."

"What are you–! Waaaah!"

He wrapped themselves in a time bubble like he did with Akaras. From any other point of view, it would seem as if they had launched away from the balcony like they were fired from a catapult. But he had instead stopped time within their space, retaining just the momentum and gravitational pull of the galaxy and the universe but not the planet. As the planet continued to spin and orbit around the Twin stars, they were left behind. They were not moving. Everything else was. The city grew distant beneath their feet, the time bubble prevented wind from reaching them, making their flight silent save for Adelaide's scream as they flew through the sky.

But he knew something was wrong the moment the process started. His confidence shrunk, not due to the lack of it, but because he started blacking out. The blimp closed in on them, but he knew he did not have enough power to reach it. His arm burned as his magic circuit fought to give him the energy needed to complete the task. But he was running on fumes. The process stopped, the time bubble dispersed. They slowed down in the air, arched, and began to fall to the pull of gravity.

Adelaide shouted, "Watcher!"

He did not reply. Could not. His eyes slowly closed shut as the ground grew before him. Then, silence. Followed by darkness.

His eyes flew open to the sight of trees and chirps of birds.

Chapter 4
Guardian Demon

Fall had come and gone and the trees had since shed their leaves. Soft beds of snow covered the once dried earth and footprints trailed in the blanket of white into the leafless Valendra Forest. Below the white canopy through the unthreaded paths between the sparse spread trees, the coated man walked, sword drawn, fear following close behind. And he should be afraid. The news of the Demon of Valendra having been captured had been circling the towns for almost half a season, yet not a single person till then had dared test the rumours until the treasure hunter below.

Adelaide smiled at the idea of proving the gossips wrong, and chuckled a little at the look of surprise she imagined the man would have when she dropped in. Literally. No one ever looked up. They never expect it. After over a hundred years, humans should have learnt by then. But the problem with living such short lifespans was that there were no real ways to pass and inherit more volumes of information than time permitted.

So she jumped away from the top of the tree, pushing away from the trunk. Her axe reached out to the next tree, hooked onto the trunk, and she wound around it until she slowed enough to land on a thick branch.

"My forest," she whispered to herself. She spun her axes in her hands and threw the offhand weapon into the tree opposite the man. The weapon punched into the tree with a resounding thud.

The man flinched and turned with sword pointed at the ready in the wrong direction, towards the embedded axe. She launched herself off the tree, axe in hand, ready to plunge it into the back of the man's skull as she free-falled. The treasure hunter must have heard her for he turned and pulled his sword to his waist, ready to thrust.

She teleported behind the man, her crouched landing softened by the snow. Her leg stretched out, swept back, and hooked the man by the ankle, forcing him to spin and fall to his back. Before he could retaliate, she mounted him with the dexterity of a master gymnast. Her free hand lunged towards his sword arm, grabbed the wrist, and slammed it to the ground. Her weapon arm pulled back, raising the axe overhead, and swung it down.

No more killing.

The blade thumped into the ground beside his head. She breathed hard, partially due to the cold and adrenaline of the fight, but also from the tinge of fear in the back of her mind. She glared at her victim and his eyes widened in fear. Her red and green eyes, the basis of the tale of the Demon, would usually be the last things her victims saw alive. But not that day.

She hissed, "You're in luck. Go. And tell them Demon Eyes have returned."

With one swift motion, she pulled the sword out of his hand, dismounted him, and spun to her feet. With the sword, she pointed the way out of the forest. The man scrambled to his feet and ran towards the exit, never once looking back.

A breeze blew through, carrying with it a small gust of fresh snow. Once she was certain the man would not return, she sheathed the sword on a small leather strap at her thigh, worn expressly as an all purpose holster. She went to her axe in the tree and with a heave, pulled the weapon out and returned her axes to their sheaths at the back of her belt.

She took one last look at the man in the far distance. With her elven eyesight, she saw him continue his desperate sprint, stumbling, and getting back up to run again.

No more killing.

Adelaide did not scare easily but those words from The Watcher remained with her ever since she returned from Everwind. And every time she remembered them, the image of The Watcher standing before her in defiance flashed across her mind. The steely gaze, the menacing stare, the overwhelming confidence that emitted from him, as if telling her he could snuff out her life as easily as she did the guards.

Shivers ran down her spine and she told herself it was just the cold. Probably. She turned away from the battleground and headed back into the deep forest. Passed a toppled tree. Passed a hill of leafless bushes. Another toppled tree. A small frozen creak. Another toppled tree. To anyone else, the snow-covered landscape would look identical at every turn. But she had grown up in Valendra Forest, and had lived there for nearly a cycle, over a hundred and sixty years. Every corner was memorised. Every change in terrain jutted at her. Landmarks known only to her littered the land. An overturned rock. A misplaced porthole. A tree with weird, twisted branches.

She reached a small creek that was still flowing in the cold next to a small cave made of stacked rocks that looked like jutting cards, the entrance a perfect height for a person. A small campfire burned just outside the shelter next to a large wooden log and the unconscious body of The Watcher.

Ignoring the man, she went into her cave, removed her belt, and dropped her axes and new sword unceremoniously on a makeshift wooden table of planks and vines. She went to the long wooden chest at the end of the cave – a piece of furniture that fell off from a passing caravan – and opened it. Rummaging through her possessions which amounted to everything within, she pulled out a grey fur coat which was another trophy from the same caravan.

The coat was mostly used to keep warm but she occasionally used it to hunt animals. Humans were too stupid for it. Without the heavy coat, she could more easily outmanoeuvre them from the treetops, thus negating the need to hide. Animals, on the other hand, had better senses. They could smell her and see her green outfit before she even got close.

Back at the table, she grabbed a drakfruit from a handwoven basket. She hated the fruit. It was too sour and too sweet at the same time and the scaly red skin was hard to peel off. But she was tired from her fight earlier and was not particularly motivated to go out hunting or gathering. Outside, she grabbed the largest firewood from a pile of other precut ones, too lazy to make two trips. She threw it into the campfire, sat on the log, and began peeling the fruit.

Midway through, she heard the a voice. "Where am I?"

She looked up and The Watcher started sitting up. She noticed immediately that the ground underneath his body still had grass as green as the day she set him down there.

She finished peeling the fruit. "You really ask a lot of questions, you know that?" She paused, waited for him to reply, but he just reached into his coat and took out his pocket watch. Adelaide continued, "You're in Valendra Forest. My home." She took a bite of the crunchy fruit and stuck her tongue out at the tangy taste.

The Watcher looked quizzically over the clock before closing and pocketing the trinket. "How long was I out for?"

"Twenty three days."

"Did you take care of me all that time?" he said with a sly smile. "Feeding and bathing me?"

"Don't be a gear head. I wouldn't even touch you with a pole." She gestured to the green patch of grass he had lain on. "Tried to kick you a few times, but it was as if there was a bubble around you. Couldn't even..." She searched for the word. "Connect."

Muttering to himself something about 'chrono suspension' and 'life support', he got to his feet to stretch. He continued questioning as if his immobility was an everyday event. "So what happened? How did I get here."

The tang of the fruit soured her mood further and his ceaseless questions did not help either. But she put up with it, not just because she had questions of her own, but also a request that she had been thinking about since she brought him with her. "Don't you remember? We were falling out of the sky, thanks to your stupidity."

He glared at her. "Hey! I got us out of there, didn't I?"

"No, *I* got us out of there. You passed out." She pointed to a snow covered cart, which remained untouched during the twenty-three days encampment. "Had to teleport both us out and drag your geared ass through two states. Do you have any idea how much energy that takes?"

He casually remarked in hushed tones, "Surprisingly less."

"What's that suppose to mean?"

He must not have known about elven senses, which was slightly better than a humans', including their hearing. Shocked that she heard him, he nervously defended with, "Nothing! Not calling you impaired or anything."

Adelaide instinctively reached for her axe, but found none after realising she had left them on the table. *Lucky gear head.* Instead of murdering the man, she decided to try Nadier's way and 'talk things out' first.

She asked, "So, who are you?"

"I told you, I'm The Watcher." He sat back down on the green patch of grass, a part of nature taken out of time and space. Silence fell between them as he took in their surroundings with wonder. He looked up to the sky and noted, "Oh, the smaller star is gone."

She had never met a human like The Watcher before. Someone who did not know who she was, or more precisely, cared little about it. Not only that, she had never met a common living being who could swagger in and out of the strange and dangerous as The Watcher did. Someone who experienced her teleportation and reacted in curiosity, not fear. Someone who casually made a plan to launch themselves across the skies and onto a blimp. Yet, someone who did not even know of The Twin stars in their skies or the meaning of d'raow.

No more killing.

Someone who managed to scare her.

Continuing from his train of thoughts on the Twins, The Watcher deduced, "Must have gone behind the big one. That's why it's winter, I'm guessing?" His question was not directed to anyone. "Cool. A planet's season that depends on the positioning of the stars."

She remembered her request of him and cut straight to the point. "There's something I want you to help me do. Since I–"

"I'll do it," he replied without hesitation.

"–did save your life, you owe me for–wait, what did you say?"

"I'll do it."

Stunned, she struggled to form a sentence. Her mouth opened and closed a couple of times. All the while, The Watcher continued to examine the area and made inane comments to himself.

Finally, after gathering her thoughts, she asked, "No questions? Don't you even want to hear what it is?"

"As long as nobody dies, I don't really care. I'll help you. You seem nice."

"But you saw me kill all those guards."

A sombre look settled in his features and he appeared to age almost instantly. "Everybody do stupid things until they are smart. And if you go wrong, I'll just put a stop to you." He smiled at her, though without any menace, as if there was an in-joke between the two of them that contradictorily only he knew of. "Besides, you don't seem like that bad a person. Annoying and immature, sure, and you could also learn to control that temper. But you can teleport and have cool green-red eyes. I'd like to see where you end up in a year from now. But seriously, no more killing unless someone else's life is on the line."

She had never attended a schoo, and never had any older figures to guide her. But she was sure that at that moment, she was feeling the same as a kid being lectured by their parents or teachers.

Speechlessly, she looked at her feet in contemplation. The Watcher rambled on about the cold and how he wished he wore a thicker coat like hers. She ignored him and took another bite of the drakfruit. It didn't taste as sour as before.

Chapter 5

Triage Diplomat

For as long as he had lived, The Watcher had always followed. Never once was he allowed to set his own path. At least, not when the fate of the world was at stake. Not when his brother died. Not when the war started. Not when the world ended. Even now, he was trotting behind Adelaide as she led him through the white forest, crossing creeks and hills that looked all too similar to him, but apparently were familiar enough to the green-haired elf that she needed no second glance to find her direction.

They reached a cliff edge that led down into a small basin. Adelaide peered over the edge, seemingly with half a mind to simply jump down, but decided to circle around to a slope for him to walk. The pond in the middle of the depression was clear, the water rippling from the landing of gentle snow and dust.

He slid down the last of the slope, skidding to a stop by her side. "What are we doing here?"

She pointed to the pond. "Look in there."

He did so, squinting into the deep of the water. It was deeper than he had expected and darkness engulfed it before he could see the bottom. "I don't see anything. There are a few fishes though."

"Look closer, moron."

He snapped her an irate look before turning back to the pond. He squatted by the water-side and tilted his head away from the light. And then he saw it. The figure in the water was huge, the size of the entire pond. Part of it stuck into the dirt, extending into the earth below.

"It's a giant... hand?"

The hand made of brown marble-like stone was easily a hundred times his size. Each phalanx of the finger was the size and height of his body. He shivered at the thought of what creature the hand could have been attached to. It would have rivalled mountains and skyscrapers. A single finger could crush his body if he was ever caught by such a monster.

Adelaide commented, "It's the hand of a sentient." He turned to her with a confused look and she sighed as she tried to simplify her explanation. "A sentient is a class of Titan. Titans are basically extremely large creatures. Giants, dragons, mechs, golems. Those are Titans."

He did not understand half of the phrases she used. Gist of it, sure. And he definitely heard giants and dragons. "So basically, a very large creature..." He turned back to the hand. Eyes still on the pond, he got to his feet. "What does this have to do with this favour you wanted?"

She found a large rock and settled down on it. "Humans have been trespassing into my forest for decades. Usually I'd chase them off. Sometimes, when they fight back, I kill them. All because they want that hand."

The Watcher turned to her and asked, "Why? What's so special about a rocky appendage?"

"It's made of titanium."

"So?" He took out his pocket watch. "My watch is made of titanium too."

"Then you better hold onto it. Titanium is rare, away from Katoki. The amount in your watch is enough to buy a new carriage."

"You're kidding."

"Eltar has some of the best metallurgists in the world. A team of master blacksmith and Enhancer could use it to create weapons that slices through any other metal like paper." She drew her axe out of boredom and twirled it in her hands. She had apparently come used to explaining her world to him. "And because most metals rust, they use titanium for blimps that travels across the oceans. A load like this one here could buy an entire district in Everwind."

Where he came from, titanium was questionably useful. It was expensive and hard to work with, but was still stronger and lighter than steel. But it was by no means flawless. Unless this fantasy world had a workaround for it's downside of being hard to harden, shape, and handle. And there was only one thing he heard during the explanation that could have made that difference.

"What's an Enhancer?"

She almost dropped her axe. Looking to him, her eyes almost screamed, *How could you not know what that is?* But she held back. "They are basically material magicians. They work with materials to enhance them. They create enchantments for anything from machines, to swords, or even trinkets. Some of them are blacksmiths or even alchemist."

"Sciency," he joyously noted. They sounded as near to a scientist as there were, and he wondered if he should find one to help with the problems he had with his powers.

Adelaide cleared her throat, annoyed at having been pulled off track. "As I was saying, there's a group in the south-west called Titan Rangers. They formed during the last decade. Their job is to protect and preserve ancient Titans, like the sentients." She glazed over to the pond. "They have quite some influence in Eltar and can invoke laws to mark places as protected archaeological sites. I want you to go there, bring them over, and have them mark the forest for protection. That will stop people from coming in and trampling all over the place."

"So..." The Watcher built up the joke. "You're a hippie."

She looked down to her waist. "What's wrong with my hip?"

Disappointed, he shook his head. "Nothing. Forget I said anything." The lack of appreciation for his wit in this universe saddened him. In the back of his mind though, he could hear his brother berating him. *You don't have any wit.* He asked Adelaide, "Why can't you go yourself?"

From elsewhere, "Because she's an elf."

They turned to the source of the voice.

Leaning against a tree at the edge of the basin's cliff, Nadier stood out like a rotting thumb, his black ensemble a blot in the snow covered trees. He jumped down from the high ledge, landing soundlessly next to the water's edge. The dark elf stretched, yawn, and walked towards them.

Nadier pulled back his coat, revealing a copper badge engraved with the shape of a bird and the words 'EVERWIND HIRED' pinned below. "Unless she has one of these or is part of some politically relevant group, the moment she steps into a human town, she'll likely be attacked by slavers and thrown to the Antipods."

Adelaide puffed, "I could handle some geared up slavers." Surprisingly, she did not fight back further. Instead, she asked, "How did you find us?"

"Adelle, Adelle, Adelle. Tracking is part of my job," he said derisively, though in more of a friendly jab than insult. "Two hundred years old and still not using your brain."

"Screw you. We're the same age."

"I'm a hundred years older," Nadier corrected.

"You have amnesia for those hundred years. It doesn't count."

The Watcher stepped in, waving away the argument. "People! People! I think we should all just agree that I am the oldest one here."

Nadier cocked his brow. "You?" Adelaide let out a snorting laugh to the side.

The Watcher nodded, smirking. "I'm nine-hundred and six."

The two elves stared at him, in frustration, irritation, or annoyance, he could not read. Any of those ways would be bad, when he thought more into it. After a moment of silence, Adelaide turned her attention away from him as if he was never there, and asked Nadier, "What are you doing here?"

"Hey... I really am that old," The Watcher muttered.

The dark elf replied to Adelaide, ignoring him, "I need your help."

Her eyes widened in surprised. "The great Wanderer, asking me for aid. What brought this on?"

"I need to go to Ta'Galadul to find out who ordered my brother to his death." His eyes darted for a second to The Watcher. "But I can't do that since I'm banished, so I want you to go in my stead."

"Wow," she replied sarcastically. "Flattering. But no. I'm not going to risk the Undercity. Not even for you, Nads."

Nadier smiled slyly and half turned to The Watcher. Though looking at the man, he spoke to Adelaide. "I thought you might say that. I guess I'll just go back to Everwind and check in on the lab. Maybe find out more about that portal research. Looks like some interesting diversion."

The Watcher almost growled, "You know about the portal?"

"No," Nadier replied. "But I can access the apparently extremely interesting information." The dark elf smiled thinly.

The Watcher considered the price, took a deep breath to steady his personality, and turned to Adelaide. "Help him."

She exclaimed, jumping to her feet. "What?"

"Help him," he insisted. "Or you won't get your Titan Rangers."

She stepped angrily towards him, pointing her axe to his neck, her face twisted with anger. "You said no questions asked! You said you would help me!"

The Watcher replied, "Things have changed."

"Why you kow licking shi–!" She was about to raise her weapon when her eyes shot wider than he thought eyes were possible of widening. In a fluid step, she turned to Nadier and threw her weapon at the ground between his feet. The dark elf did not flinch or blink. "You schemed this! You waited for me to tell him and you jumped in with your stupid plan!"

Calmly, Nadier said, "Think about this, Adelle. You'll likely never meet another human who's willing to help you. This might be your only chance of contacting the Titan Rangers."

She looked ready to massacre them, there and then. From what The Watcher had seen of her, and if Nadier was anything like his brother, it would be a bloody battle.

Somehow, despite her hotheaded personality, Adelaide managed to turn away. Taking a deep breath, she swivelled back to Nadier with a glare of disappointment and rage.

The Watcher was almost certain he saw her tear up. "All this time you refused to help me. I should have known. You were just holding that card as leverage." Her teeth was gritted at the end, her fists clenched. She then hissed, "I owe you nothing after this. You and I are squared. And I never want to see your conniving gear in my forest again."

Chapter 6
The Forger

Solar powered flying cars hovered overhead in park. One down the street descended with the press of its driver's remote, a blinking red spotlight shining down from its underside as it did so. The crowd on the pathway parted from the landing zone, allowing the car to touch ground. Hall-walled skyscrapers lined the neighbourhood and zooming cars painted up the further skies.

Coat fluttering, dark brown hair still a waking morning mess, he jogged through the sea of people and pushed out of the crowd to an empty alley. "Tier! Sorry! Sorry!" he called as he neared the man leaning against the alley wall. "Guys took me drinking yesterday and I overslept."

"Oho..." Tier stepped away and towards him. Tier wore a green singlet and muddied cargo pants, his face edged and rugged, his hair dirty and jumbled. "So it's fine for you to be drunk and late but when I do it, it's "irresponsible"." He air-quoted.

"I said I was sorry." He pretended to scratch his neck to prevent Tier from seeing his face. "Besides, I only do this once a year or something. You do it every other week."

Tier clicked his tongue and exclaimed, "Bah, whatever. Here!" He tossed a small brown bag.

"Is this drugs?" he replied uncertainly, slowly opening the gift. "I'm not trafficking for you."

"Don't be a fucking smartass, kid. It's just your birthday present."

From within, he pulled out a pocket watch. Engraved on the sleek titanium case were the symbols of the language he made up for his tabletop role-playing game nights. "It's my name." He looked up to Tier, as he had done his whole life. "You learnt my language."

Tier ruffled his hair. "I love you too, nerd. Now be a good little brother and bugger off. I've got work to do."

Eyes fluttering open, The Watcher ran his vision across the orange dawned sky that filtered through the branches. Gentle snowfall had happened through the night and his teeth were clattering from the cold. A layer of snow covered his face and he shivered and shook it off. He found his hand within his coat, holding onto his pocket watch. His thumb ran over the engraving, reading it like Braille. Sitting up, he swung his legs over the log he slept on. The campfire before him was but embers and Nadier was nowhere to be seen. He breathed a breath of white mist, body shaking from being frozen.

From his side, he picked up the last of the prepared firewood and threw it unceremoniously into the flame. He stretched his hand towards the ember and focused, preparing to wrap the campfire in a time bubble, but without the shell that prevented friction. With a light twitch, the wood spontaneously combusted, flame-tails spiralleing up three meters into the air, twirling and dancing with the sun – no, *twin*rise – before dying back down to a steady fire.

"Too much oomph there," The Watcher criticised himself.

"Neat trick." He turned to see Nadier coming in from the forest, three grey furred rabbits with horns dangled from his belt. "Breakfast?" He pointed to the animals. The elf had obviously gone hunting.

"Sure. Never had those before though." The Watcher asked, "I'm guessing jackalopes?"

"Yeah. How did you know?" He untied the prizes of his hunt and settled down in the snow opposite. "I thought you didn't know anything about this world?"

"Guess some things just translates."

"I've been meaning to ask you about that." Nadier pulled out his dagger, rolled up his sleeves, and casually began skinning the animal, blood dripping to the ground. "How are you able to speak modern tongue so well?"

"Probably like the jackalope. Just translates from world to world, I guess." He got to his feet and stretched. He looked to his palm and realised he had subconsciously took out his watch. He returned the accessory to his coat. "Where I come from, it's called English."

"Ink... klish. Weird. Doesn't exactly roll off the tongue." He masterfully finished peeling off the fur and threw it atop the pool of blood in the snow in front of him. He got up and kicked a fresh layer of dirt over the red. From behind his coat, where he apparently kept an endless pocket, the dark elf pulled out a metal canteen and began washing off the blood from his hands. "Are you really nine-hundred and six?"

"What?" The Watcher asked, unsure of his question.

"Your age."

"Oh." He laughed, surprised the elf even remembered or even took him somewhat seriously. "No. I'm not. I'm uh... probably over a thousand years old now."

Nadier looked up from preparing the skewers and racks from sticks he had gathered earlier. "You're not joking."

"Nope. Completely serious here... for once." He walked around the fire to offer a hand, but Nadier turned him down with a wave. "Nine-hundred and six is just the last age I remembered to count. I don't even remember how old I am, that's how old I am. Did Adelaide tell you about what happened after she brought me here?"

Nadier nodded. "I don't quite understand it." He fixed the meat over the fire and sat back down. "Something about 'frozen in time' and stuff."

The Watcher settled back into his log seat, feeling the age in his bones. He explained, "Whenever my body is dealt a fatal wound, my survival instincts kicks in. Seals me in a time bubble to protect me while my body repairs its damage. And when I grow old, my power regress my age, making me young again. As far as I know, I can't die. At least not without being disintegrated," he sighed dejectedly. "Even then, the amount of power I have, I wonder what kind of impact can even pierce me."

A yawn echoed from Adelaide's home and they turned to the cave to see her stretching in her hammock, the makeshift bed strung across the walls and covered by her fur coat for warmth.

The Watcher asked, "What are you going to do about her? You two were friends, right?"

"I hope we still are," Nadier absentmindedly twirled the three sticks of meat, now a nice roasted brown. "It's just, I need that information. I didn't mean to hurt her for it."

The man punctuated, "You're a liar."

"Excuse me?"

"Don't get me wrong. I'm not saying you're lying about what you just said. You're just a liar, and a coward, in general." Nadier glared at him with eyes as thin as the ice he was threading. He waved for the elf to calm down. "No offence, but that's just the vibe I get from you. You lie in conflict and run in danger, never getting into the fight. After all, fighters don't carry daggers, poisons, and blackmails. Nothing to be ashamed of. I do it all the time. Lying, I mean."

Seemingly satisfied with the apology and criticism, Nadier looked into the fire in contemplation. The Watcher worried he might burn their breakfast with his concentrated stare. Adelaide stepped out of the cave, already dressed, with a simple leather pack slung over her shoulders and her axes strapped firmly at the back of her waist. The sword she disarmed from the treasure hunter the day before was in her hand.

Nadier held the more well done of the meat to her, a painfully obvious bribery for peace. "Jackalope?"

She swiped the stick without a word and tossed the sword to The Watcher who clumsily caught the weapon just before it hit him in the face.

He asked, "What am I suppose to do with this?"

If he had any illusion that she was starting to warm up to him, he was corrected then and there. Her voice was lower than a growl. "You still can't properly use all your magic. So if you die before reaching the Titan Hunters, I'll kill you." She ripped at the meat and walked away from the pair, heading south into the forest.

Nadier asked before she was out of earshot, "Where are you going?"

Stopping just short of the edge of the encampment, she snapped back, "What? You need me to hold your stinking hands? We're going in different directions. I've no need to be burdened by your two gearing asses." Picking up pace, she continued on her way as the two stared at her receding back.

The dark elf sighed and turned back to the fire. He passed one of the meat to The Watcher and dug into his own meal. "Finish up. Once we're good, I'll walk you to Consortia's highway."

He set the sword aside and took the food. Biting into it, the fantasy meat was tangy, and had the texture of gum but the ripping feel of beef. "This is weird," he said with a mouth full of food.

"You'll get used to it."

"No, I mean Adelaide. You said she's going to the dark elf capitol. But her skin is so..."

"White?"

"I was going to say fair."

The dark elf sighed again and The Watcher wondered if the elf did that a lot. Nadier held out his arm with its rolled up sleeve and scratched at the grey 'skin' with the tip of the stick. A line of white trailed after the cut. Like shadows, the grey seemingly wrapped itself back a moment later, a thin layer of gas that surrounded the body.

Nadier explained, "We're just as white as any other of the elves. But our skin are sensitive to light, so we coat ourselves in this gas called *aetherized aeronium*. Once in the undercity, it's so dark that there's no need for it. We look just like any other elves."

The Watcher nodded thoughtfully. Learning new things everyday. He loved it. The world had been amazing for him, travelling through all of time on his own planet. The exchange with Nadier inadvertently brought a smile to his face. The feeling of having new adventures on a new planet and new things to discover again hit him like a wave. He started laughing.

Nadier asked, "What's so funny?"

He burst out uncontrollably, fully embracing the madman he was. "She hates your guts now. She'll probably kill us if she ever sees us again!" He didn't know why he found that train of random thoughts funny. He just did.

Madness must be contagious, for Nadier chuckled, "Yes, she probably will."

Chapter 7
Time Bandit

Kathleen sat still within the carriage with her hands on her knees, legs pulled back defensively. Her fingers pinched at her white frilled skirt, her head downcast as she counted the buttons on her maroon shirt. A strand of her long blonde hair had gotten itself stuck on her lips but she dared not to even blow it away, instead choosing to bite it and suck on the yellow.

The bandit sat opposite, eyeing her in all the inappropriate places. Even through the scarf that covered his mouth and with the light from outside blocked by the curtains of the carriage, even when she wasn't looking at him directly, she could tell he was grinning.

"Just sit tight, ma' Lae," his voice croaked, a frog trapped in his throat. The melanist man reached over and touched her lap. She jumped in her seat, body shivering as she started a silent panic, screaming in her head. "Don't worry though, I can keep you company all day long."

She wanted to scream. To shout. But her jaws were clenched so tight that she could taste blood. The man had a knife. She had seen knives before, but for some reason, that one looked unusually long and sharp, as if the edge was refined to a point of solitude.

"Don't worry. I'll be gentle." He moved closer.

A small whimper escaped her. "Help."

A new voice immediately asked, "Did someone say, 'Help'?"

It was the bandit's turn to be shocked. His knife instinctively slashed backwards towards the once empty seat to the right of him but was stopped by the calm and steady hand of the man in the grey coat with a longsword strapped to his back. The man smiled, an action that made the faded scars of his face stretch and disappear. His onyx-brown bed hair were as carefree as his movements. He closed his hand around the fist of the stunned bandit and slowly pushed the weapon back to him.

The new man turned to Kathleen, "Hi! I'm The Watcher. Nice to meet you." He extended his hand.

Moving without her permission, her body reached out to shake the outstretched hand. She realised she was no longer trembling. "Hi," she greeted back, all the fear that had taken her the moments before vanished as instantaneously as the man appeared. The world seemed to have gotten insurmountably safer in the seconds since his arrival. "I'm Kathleen Ambershey." She did not know why she used her full name when The Watcher only used a title. It just felt appropriate somehow.

"Nice to meet you, Kathleen Ambershey." He sat back and smiled and she could not help but smile back. His relaxed and happy personality felt addictive.

The bandit regained his composure. Sitting straight up, he readied his knife at them. "What? Do ya' two gearheads think tis' some joke?"

The carriage door opened behind him and he once again swung the knife in reflex. And once again, it was stopped, this time, by a calm wrist, for the hand held a dagger of its own. The dark elf casually disarmed the knife with his free hand and stepped into the carriage.

The bandit's eyes grew wide as he realised who he faced. "The Wanderer!"

"Good to see you," Nadier greeted. He looked over to The Watcher, "Your 'no killing' rule is troublesome, to say the least."

"But you did it?"

"Of course. They are all tied up and ready for the patrol to carry them off."

"Good. Great. Fantastic! Now..." He put one arm over the shoulders of the now defenceless bandit. "What are we to do with you?"

Nadier sheathed his main-hand dagger, pulled out his off-hand weapon, and ejected the empty vial from the latter. From his belt, he took a new one and loaded it in. "I ran out of anaesthetics. Now, this one is extracted mixture diluted from multiple snake venoms and will paralyse you temporarily. But it will hurt a lot more, so you might want to choose wisely." He waved his dagger to the bandit.

The bandit looked to his left at the elf and to the right at The Watcher before finally relenting and raising his arms in surrender. "Ya'll got me."

The Watcher padded his head. "Good boy."

It felt as if she had been held hostage in the carriage for weeks. When she stepped out, the light from the noon Twins blinded her and she had to squint to get her bearings. She shivered slightly in the cold weather. The Watcher stepped out behind her and Nadier exited opposite with his new prisoner in tow.

The Watcher asked his companion, "So, the patrol will come by when?"

"In maybe half an hour," Nadier replied. She heard the rustling of ropes. "We can just leave them here."

Then, her vision returned, and she could see all the blood of her guards splattered and spilt across the dirt road. The bodies of her men and driver laid slumped against the carriage or sprawled across the path. Her stomach churned. She gripped it to no avail and she vomited over the ground. Nadier and The Watcher continued their conversation as if her emptying her stomach through her mouth was the most normal thing in the world.

The elf spoke, "This is me. Up north is Everwind. Are you sure you will be able to find Ra'Kalen?"

"Follow the south-east road and it's the first town next to a mountain. I'm crazy, not stupid."

"You could pass for both."

The two exchanged a few more pleasantly disguised insults before Nadier bid his goodbyes after making sure The Watcher could handle things.

Her stomach had emptied out and she was now just coughing for air. She felt like retching again even though there was nothing left. A warm, large hand placed itself on her back and she instantly felt relieved.

"Are you okay?" The Watcher asked.

She breathed in deep and her mind cleared slightly, though her throat continued to burn. But she remembered her position and forced herself to stand up straight and face him. "I'm uh..." She cleared her throat. "I'm Lae Kathleen Ambershey of the House of Amber. I thank you for your assistance." She gave a small bow. Speaking her title and name had become ritualistic for her and she could feel herself calming down just from it.

"House of Amber..." he looked at her quizzically. "Nice. Sounds nice. Like a fast food joint." He turned on the spot to survey the scene.

On the opposite side of the road, the bandits of nine were tied up against each other, with only the one from the carriage still awake, though having given up on struggling against much tighter bindings. To the far north, beyond Nadier's fading back, the city of Everwind glimmered in all its bronze reflection. The Tower of Light stood high, piercing into the heavens, glows bouncing off its copper finish like a beacon shining halfway across the continent. Plains stretched to the east and Valendra's forest peeked out from the west. To the south, the mountain ridge extended to the horizons on both sides.

"Um..." she started unsteadily, looking to the ground, suddenly not daring to meet his gaze. "What do I do now?"

"Well, Nads said the highway patrol passes by here near noon. You could wait around here for them. I'm sure they would be more than happy to take you to wherever you wanted to go."

That was true. As a Lae of the land, officials of the States were obligated to see to her protection and would likely have taken over for her convoy.

The Watcher continued, "Or..." She looked up, hopeful. The Watcher ran through his thoughts. "Where are you headed?"

"Sher–" she stopped herself. Her mind raced fast. "Ra'Kalen. I am headed for Ra'Kalen," she lied through her teeth.

The man beamed with a smile. "That's where I'm headed for! Would you like to come with me?"

"Yes!" She almost jumped.

She was sure she must be grinning from ear-to-ear but could not care less about her appearance. She wanted to shout, yell, and exclaim freedom to pursue her lifelong dream of travel, away from her family and all the pompous nonsense being there entailed. There was so much to do. She needed to pack a bag. Get a change of clothes. Ready the horses. She turned to the carriage and was again brought back to the present by the sight of the dead, stopping her in her tracks, her happiness washed away like a grain of sand against a rapid.

"I can't..." she was almost whimpering again. She had not known her guards and convoy. Never thought there was need to. They were always just there, and she had always assumed there would have been another day to get to know them. But even then, even for strangers, she could not leave them the way they were.

With a soft voice, The Watcher asked, "What do you want to do?"

"I... I don't know. But I can't... leave them like this. Not for the scavengers or passers-by to ogle and glare."

The man walked past her and to the body of the nearest guards. With an underarm carry, he pulled the corpse away from the carriage it slouched against and onto an empty part of the road. He did the same thing again for each of the victims, passing each minute with grunts and sweat and a soft smile that never left his face until all the dead were lined side-by-side. Once readied, he closed the eyes of each one that were still opened, and muttered an unheard prayer under his breath. He went back into the carriage, sounds of ripping cloth following after. When he stepped back out, he had the white curtains rolled up in his hand.

He walked up to her and handed her one end of the cloth. "Here."

She stared sombrely at the cloth. She had never done something like this before. Being sombre. The only funeral she had ever been to involved food and drinks and music and dances. Beautiful dresses and well steamed suits were the norm for her. Bodies were buried with celebrations for the deceased, and frivolous gifts were exchanged with impunity for the living. Looking up, she met The Watcher's eyes, and somehow, she found the strength to nod in conviction.

Together, they stretched the makeshift blanket over the row of bodies. The cloth fluttered over and down onto them like waves, settling and taking the form of the bodies below. Whatever blood was left on the surface pooled quickly through the white, grimly outlining each wound. Somehow, she found that sight much harder to look at than the bodies themselves, and turned away, stumbling back to the carriage to lean against.

Footsteps crunched behind her as The Watcher approached. From the horizon, the highway patrol took form. A squad of a dozen figures closing in.

"If you want," The Watcher placed his gentle hand on her shoulder. She turned to him. "We can still go to Ra'Kalen together." He offered his right hand, palms opened to her.

She looked to it, and with another breath to steady herself, she took it. "Just let me get my things."

Chapter 8
The Storyteller

"If I am understanding this correctly," Kathleen asked. "You are a time traveller?"

The Watcher replied, "That's what I'm saying."

The campfire crackled between them, sparks and ember gently drifting away with the breeze of the plains. Dots of lights freckled the west, the town and villages of Dane and the Grassplains filled the earth like the stars did in the clear night sky. A single hot-air balloon floated slowly across the backdrop, its flame a soft flicker in the background of space. Their destination was Ra'Kalen, the town which stretched the base of the mountain ridges to the south. To the north, Everwind continued to shine bright, the capitol a beacon even at night.

"But you are not able to time travel right now?" She bit into her piece of bread.

He stopped mid bite, thinking of a reply, "Boy, you sure ask tough questions, don't you?"

"I am not a boy," she snapped back, lacking in finesse more than she would like. She scratched at her hair, not having been used to sweating and not showering as much as for the two days they had been on the road. Aside from the few scrubs from a wet cloth, she was starting to feel the need for a good bath. From the looks of it, they would reach Ra'Kalen as early as the next noon and she could not wait to find an inn for a hot wash. She continued, "You really should see someone about that. Maybe an Enhancer can fix your 'condition'? There's one in Ra'Kalen, actually."

The Watcher looked back quizzically in a way she wanted to say was a manner of distrust. He asked, "Aren't you even the least bit sceptical of what I said?"

She smiled back, "My family is the head of the State of Consortia." She looked down to the fire sombrely, flames dancing within her ember eyes. With a deep breath, she forced herself to cheer up her tone. "They held lavish parties almost every other week, inviting performers from across the country with amazing talents, and nothing much surprises me any more. We once had a mage who could turn water into wine."

"Was his name Jesus by any chance?"

"Yes! How did you know?"

"Lucky guess," he nonchalantly replied. "But I am getting the hang of how this universe-multiverse thing works."

Even after travelling with him for two days, she could not fully comprehend the man. Sometimes, he would ask questions so fundamental that she felt akin to tutoring her nephew when she answered. Yet, at other moments, he had a worldly aura, emitting the sense of wisdom in spades and an intellect that seemed to dwarf any known mortal alive.

She leaned closer to the fire, putting her face in the light. Curious, she asked, "What is your world like?"

"Sorry?"

"You keep saying you're from this other universe. Other planet. What is it like?"

He raised a brow, "What is what like?"

"Your home. This other place."

She watched as his smile widened. A grin that spread from ear to ear. A glint shone in his eyes not from the reflection of the campfire. "Oh..." he started with an ecstatic groan. "Oh... my world... is amazing. We had cars–um... carriages, that could fly. Planes the size of trains and faster than ships. We could make food by the millions of barrels with the flick of a switch. We built towers that reached out into space, and ungodly sized domes for games and sports. And holograms! Oh! Those were amazing things. Light that gives a three dimensional image. You would have loved it."

Kathleen could only smile as he reminiscence his home. Campfire stories. One of the things she had looked forward to in her dreams of travels.

"It sounds amazing."

"Oh, it is."

She queried further, "What about the people?'

Then, The Watcher trailed off. "We had... great people. Men and women capable of amazing feats. I knew a man who could fuse with anything he touched. And I knew a thief, oh, she was a thief alright. Stole the throne of a kingdom. A little girl who brought hope to an entire nation. A boy who could snipe off a target from a quarter a continent away. Then there's that kid who could see the end of the world and the old man who stopped it." She listened, attention enraptured to his tales. "Stuff of legends they were. Battled gods and took down monsters of all kind. Tales that get sung off to the end of all time. And for a thousand shining moments, they were truly happy in a world that tried to beat misery into them. The strongest of souls for the harshest of war."

Her heart skipped a beat when a thought crossed her and she nervously asked, "Can I go? To your world?"

The Watcher gave her a gentle smile, his eyes soft with regret. "I would love to take you. But I can't. Not any longer at least."

She had not meant to pry, but her words came faster than her mind could process. "Why not?"

He answered with the casualness that came with having expected the question and none of the hesitation that should have been with how personal it was. "There are rules to being a time traveller. You can't go back to places you've already been. You can't see the same thing twice, unless you are supposed to."

"Sounds complex."

"Is complex. Technically, I am the last of my kind." The mood swung to a deep low, and the campfire flickered almost in a reaction to the atmosphere. She felt a chill ran down her spine and the air seemed to dip. "I can't go back to see any of the people I loved. Can't even go back to visit my own species. As far as I am concerned, I am the last of my kind. There will never be any kind like me again. The last of the Hymns."

"Last of the what?"

He snapped out of his memories, looking to her with clear eyes that twinkled. "Sorry! I must be getting old, remembering the years before like an aged man. Now I just need a rocker and a lawn to yell at people from."

She smiled back. "I'm fine with it, hearing about your stories. I grew up in a strict household. Wasn't even allowed to leave the estate until I was fourteen. Stories are how I grew up. Books that explored the world in my presence. Experiences and recollections from my parents and serv–peers."

Through the light of the flames, she could see him look at her with a sad smile. For some reason, she felt pitied. Yes, her life had not been the most adventurous of all but she had safety, wealth, and stability. Things that many people would gladly hand over their freedom to have. Still, when The Watcher looked at her, she felt like a child again, being gently reprimanded by her mother for deciding to go for a ride on the family steed before her feet could even reach the stirrup, and crying after having fallen off said same horse.

The Watcher shot up from his seat with a loud shout. "Oh!"

Kathleen turned around in fear, expecting an ambush by bandits or hunters, only to be faced with the continued darkness of the night.

"What in the Titans–?" she turned back to her companion and yelled, "Watcher! What did I say about scaring me like that?"

Ignoring her, he rambled on, "Why don't we go travelling?"

"Um... we are travelling, aren't we?"

"No! I mean, yes, we are now. But I'm talking about real travelling after all this is over! After I find out what one-three-nine is and get my powers fixed. You and me," He circled the campfire and extended his hand to her, "All of time and... and... what's the name of this planet?"

The offer rang in her ears and she struggled to answer her question. Elation built up in her. She was being offered to travel, not just the world, but all of history and the future. She needed to answer. Her throat was caught. She forced herself to croak, "Tearha."

"With an 'H'?" He drew back his hand, confused at the pronunciation. "Ter-rha?"

"With an 'H'," she confirmed.

"Weird. But okay." He extended his hand again with a smile so wide and toothy he looked like a court jester. "You and me. All of Tearha that ever existed. Ever will. What d'you say?"

She could only nod. Slowly she raised her hand to his. Like a knight in the heroic tales from her childhood, he brought her daintily to her feet. With a toothy grin, he broke the refined silence with a cheer and a fist pump, pulling her into a spinning hug as he excitedly rambled on of all the things they would do and see. The history they could learn. The legends and stories they would meet.

But she could not focus. In two days, her nightmare of a bandit ambush had turned into the possibility of achieving her dreams of travel in the most amazing way possible. Slowly, the realisation set in.

As the smile returned to her face, she grabbed The Watcher by the arm and pulled the man into a dance lighted by the campfire under the stars of the endless plains of Eltar.

Chapter 9
Omnikid

Adelaide's vision blurred and her head hurt from the world spinning under her back. The bed she was laid in had its mattress removed, leaving just the hard wooden board underneath. She remembered a fight. She got ambushed by a group of hunter. What happened? She strained to sit up, but a furious flare shot through her abdomen and she crashed back onto the bed with a thud.

Her breathing was heavy. Though her breath was turning to mist in the cold air, her body burned hotter than the heat of summer and seared. She reached down to her waist and felt the cooled blood that had dried around the bandages wrapped there.

"I wouldn't get up if I were you."

She meekly turned her head towards the voice.

The hut they were in was smaller than her cave. She could probably cross the length of it in two or three steps, provided she could stand first. The wooden walls were old, blackened with cracks and age, but looked otherwise strong. A single gas lamp hung overhead. In the dark corner opposite, the dark elf sat with his head against the corner of the walls, eyes closed, fighting to sleep against the winter cold. His short sleeved shirt seemed to be an ill choice of clothing for the weather.

Then, she looked down and found her body covered in a slightly over-sized black coat. Annoyed, she croaked out, "I... don't need you... to keep me... warm."

Without hesitation or even a look in her direction, The Wanderer replied, "Yes, you do. Now keep it down, I'm trying to get some sleep."

Clattering of wheels on stone pulled the elf out of her nap. Adelaide sat behind one of the larger boulders, hiding herself from sight of the main road. The stone way up to Ta'Kalenyilgah, the Dark

Gate of Kings, had sparse travellers. Most of them were dark elves returning home. Very little traders went to Ta'Galadul, the Dark Citadel, and those who do were either of questionable morality or very stupid and brave.

She shot to attention, peeking to the side of her hiding spot at the covered wagon that was rolling up towards the gate. The entrance was embedded into the side of a large quarry. The gates were a monolithic arc the height of five storeys with its pillars acting as watchtowers, built by the long lost dwarfs. The structure was intricately detailed with artworks of ancient dwarven heroes and stories, tales which she had always found too boring and generic to warrant interest. No other mortals knew how to build the grand constructions they did, but no others needed to, for the ones that existed had withstood the test of time for countless cycles. Years and seasons had passed but the darven structures continued to stand.

Two humans, a white haired man and a white haired woman, led the horse and its wagon up to the gate. The stone arc towered over them and everything else within the sight of the landscape.

A pair of dark elf warriors came out of the small door that swung out from the bottom of the larger gate. In their hands were pairs of *hiljekts*, a dark elf multi-handed sword that terrified Adelaide. Even in the hand of a novice dark elf warrior, they were fearsome weapons due to their versatility. She had only fought one once before and she subconsciously reached to her abdomen to feel the scar from the battle.

As one of the warriors stayed at the front to question the humans, another circled around back. He pulled apart the canvas that covered the trailer. He poked his head inside and scanned the cargo before stepping back and signalling to his partner that all was fine.

His partner nodded back before signalling for one of the riders to follow him. The woman got off her seat and, along with the two warriors, went into the gate.

Dark elves and their paranoia. The only race mistrusting enough to have a law that required a living person to be temporarily imprisoned as a toll for entrance to the city. It was because of this law that trades between Ta'Galadul and the rest of Eltar were limited.

She waited until the main gate started to open. Despite its large size, the stone door swung inward without so much as a creak to welcome the wagon.

She stepped out of her hiding place and with left foot forward, teleported into the darkness of the trailer. Landing on her feet, she held onto a nearby barrel to stable herself. Turning to face the opening behind her, she held her breath, eyes fixated on the cracks of light from the fluttering canvas, hopeful that none of the guards would be diligent enough to do a second check.

Slowly, they began to move. The transport started forward with a jerk and the clatter of horses feet came from the front. As they entered the shadows of the gates, the light from beyond the canvas shone blindingly, before gently dissipating, and finally vanishing in a quiet blip as the gate closed completely behind them.

Breathing a sigh of relief, she turned around to survey her surroundings, her elven eyes quickly adjusting the the darkness. Crates were stacked up like a wall to her right and barrels to her left. In the middle, directly in front of her, on a wooden bench installed into the base of the trailer, sat a little girl with shining strawberry blonde hair and light brown eyes that sparkled even in the darkness. No older than eight, she wore a tattered brown one piece dress. A pair of patched sandals dangling from her feet too short to even reach the floor.

The girl greeted, "Hello."

"Hello," Adelaide greeted back.

A kid. Why did it had to be a kid? Even she did not kill children. She needed to make sure the girl did not call for help. If she was caught before reaching the city, she would be in trouble. Dark elves did not take kindly to the other races of elves. Especially not after the Exseed War.

However, the girl merely scooted over in her seat and patted the empty spot beside her. "My name's Stella. Stella Barber."

Adelaide blinked blankly, unsure of how to react. But the girl did not seem afraid or worried, instead giving off a gentle smile. She was tired, and the journey through the underground highway to the Dark Citadel would take some time. She did not feel particularly like getting out and walking and the girl did not seem hostile.

Still, wearily, she took a seat beside the girl. Stella asked, "What's your name?"

"A-Adelaide," she replied. "Adelaide Wiltkins."

Smiling, Stella struck up a conversation as if they were long time friends. "I have a friend named Leila." The girl placed her hands together for a faint clap. "She's an elf too. It was hard to play hide and seek with her since she could see in the dark."

An elf? Humans did not live with elves on Eltar. It was an unprecedented thing. Aside from the rare wood elves and the dark elves, the only other races of elves were the class elves and hume. The last two did not have their own citadels and are relegated to lower class citizens in Everwind, with the class elves especially being pushed to the slums known as Antipods.

Adelaide wanted to call the girl out on her lie, but managed to control her temper enough to do it gently. "Humans don't live with elves."

"They do where I come from."

"And where is that?"

"Joan and Milton's orphanage!" she replied excitedly.

"Orphanage?"

"Yes! I used to help out there! But our family moved to Muscoh last year," Stella rambled through the conversation, denying Adelaide a chance to reply. "We went to Valent to deliver some clothes and we're on our way home now! We're just making a stop here for resupply. Sis is a little lazy sometimes and doesn't come with us. All she wants to do is play with Tim, but I guess I can't blame her for that. She's had a rough century."

What's a century? Adelaide wanted to ask. Instead, she chose, "Where is the orphanage?"

"The Outer District."

The Outer District. Just a step away from the Antipods. "And elves are allowed there? In the Outer District?"

"Oh, no. If you get caught, you'd get thrown in jail. But we at the orphanage stuck together. We hid the elves in the basement and attic whenever The Forum people came."

She had never heard of such a thing. Humans and elves, living together. And what was more, humans that protected elves. Usually, independent elves were caught and sold as slaves, regardless of age.

Confused and uncertain, Adelaide looked over and asked, "And you're okay with it? Living with elves?" The wagon began to slow.

"Why wouldn't I be?" Stella caught her stare and smiled. She reached for the older hand and Adelaide drew it back instinctively. The girl smiled again, this time, her lips were warmly parted, her eyes calmer. Soothing. Slowly, Stella took Adelaide's hand in hers and laid their palms against each other. "See. We're not so different. Just like in Tarzan!"

"Tarzan?" They came to a final stop, the axles of the wheels screeching a little as they did.

"Oh, it's a cartoon back from Earth. You wouldn't understand."

The rider had gotten off the horse and Adelaide could hear his footsteps circling towards the rear. "Car... tune?" She knew of only one other person who spoke so cryptically.

Stella let go of her hand. The little girl smiled and waved, "Say hello to The Watcher for me!"

"What?" Before Adelaide could question further, the canvas started to draw open and she had no choice but to teleport out of the wagon.

Chapter 10
Light

Cave walls reached up and around the Dark Citadel. Ores, droplets of waters, and traces of metallic impurities within the stone reflected the light from luminescence moss and the rare torches carried by humans. The stones sparkled and swirled like stars and galaxies littering the sky. The cave moss also helped circulate the air. Four large stone pillars set at the four cardinal sectors of the city supported the ceiling. Within each pillar housed thousands of dwarven built apartments. A long and tall dwarven stone wall and gate guarded the only entrance into Ta'Galadul in the north. It was kept open in times of peace, with citizens strolling in and out of the tunnel, going about their day.

Adelaide sauntered confidently into the city, walking side-by-side with a group of dark elf miners, pickaxe slung over their shoulders. She had always liked coming into the Dark Citadel, once she managed to get pass the main gate, that was. Though as the Demon Eyes she was a wanted criminal, in the dark elf capitol she could blend in, looking just like any of the locals without the judgemental glare of humans.

"You have been called for the plan?" one of the miner asked his companion. "An honour."

"To be given a chance to be a *Rondia'Aelan* is truly humbling."

Her ears pricked to listen, but almost as if knowing she was eavesdropping, the group's conversation degraded into banal chattering.

She knew the rough layout of the city, and knew where best to head to for information. While humans had their inns and taverns, dark elves had the aeronium pond.

The streets were relatively empty. She could have taken a pole and twirled it around without hitting anyone. Dark elves were never known for their active social lives. She continued down the path, following behind the miners that had overtaken her. Between the polished square dwarven houses were a few buildings that came after the age of dwarfs. Placed beside the architectural masterpieces, the dark elf buildings of cobbled stone and wood looked barbaric in comparison.

Splitting away from the group of miners at the next junction, she cut across the north-eastern ordinal street. Over her shoulder at the centre of the city, the boxed shaped Council Chambers stood towering and watchful over the city. She had always admired dwarven architectures. Though not as magnificent as the creation of nature, the mortal-made buildings had always looked aesthetically part of the backdrop of the caves and mountains they were built. Unlike the slobs of human towns and cities pasted haphazardly onto a field of green that felt more akin to vomit on a canvas.

She exited the street and onto the border road. More dwarven houses were built into the walls of the caves. Heading south along the walls, she saw the open area of the Aeronium Pond come into view. The pond was the liveliest spot in all of Ta'Galadul. Though given the dark elves' seclusive nature, it wasn't more pack than a common human tavern. Even so, if she stayed near the gatherings, she was bound to overhear something.

She muttered to herself, "I wonder what this plan is." She noted on the miners' conversation earlier.

"Do you want to find out?"

She spun to face the figure that appeared beside her, her hand reaching behind for her axe. Then it stopped. She could not move. Her body was frozen when the sudden wave of emotion washed over her. She did not know how and she did not know why. All she knew was that the man that stood with her was responsible for the hair that stood on the back of her neck.

His hair shone even brighter in the dark of the cave. Locks of gold and white that sparkled on their own accord. His face was smooth and bubbled with a cheerful smile. And his ears, human ears, poked out of his short, ruffled hair. With golden, cat-like eyes that seemed to stare into her soul, he wore an esteemed white suit that was clear to her even in the darkness. Silver embroidery lined the hem of the outfit. A blackened and polished leather boots was the only dark colour on his person. Even an elf like her found the man handsome.

With a gentle tone, a forgiving smile, and a light-hearted stare, the man warned, "I wouldn't do that if I were you."

Fear. Fear was what caused her to freeze. The man before her was not an ordinary human. She would go so far as to call him a monster. Even without magic circuits, she could feel the power that was emanating from him. Overwhelming. Suffocating.

Slowly, she moved her hand away from her weapon. The smile on the man widened and he commented, "Good. Good. Now, shall we walk and talk, Miss Wiltkins?"

He knew who she was from appearance, which was uncommon. The man was not just physically and magically powerful, but connected. She had a feeling that even if she tried to teleport away, she would undoubtedly be caught in an instant. Relenting to her situation, she puffed up her chest and lead the way forward, refusing to let the man be in full control.

The man did not seem to mind, following just a step behind her with a confident gait. He continued, "I had wished for The Watcher or The Wanderer to be here. The coward or the traitor. But I guess the killer will do."

They approached the pond. The pool of black aeronium floated like fog in a canyon. Aeronium was a gas that was half solid from an innate attraction to itself, making it flow like water but act as air. When scooped or bathed in, it coagulated like goo. The pond reflected nothing, and staring into it was akin to looking at shadows.

Adelaide asked, "Who are you?"

Looking around, she realised how empty the shoreline was and how empty the entire surrounding seemed to be. At the edge of the pool between the middle of the two shores, a stone archway stood. Within it, the aeronium from the pool is aetherised like a pane of glassy air, allowing people to walk through it and cover themselves in the grey coat the dark elves are known for. The *Kalen-Ta'Rae*. Gate of Dark Light. On most days, the gate would have a queue of elves looking to either remove the coat or get a new one.

But it was becoming painfully obvious that that day was not most days. They had expected, if not her, at least one of the three of them. The Wanderer. The Watcher. Demon Eyes. Three epitaph holders who suddenly became the centre of events were bound to attract attention and she should have been more stealthy.

The man stopped at a bench and she turned back to him. He took a seat and patted the empty spot next to him.

She had to resist the temptation to customarily stick out her tongue. Instead, she gristly replied, "I'd really rather stand." Something about the situation with the man felt strange. Strange but important. She had the feeling if she could just figure out what it was, it would give away the man's identity.

He smiled again. "You're here to find out the reason for Lord Akaras's unfortunate demise, are you not?" The man was unrivalled in looks. Even though she was not interested in males, let alone a human man, she could not help but find him attractive.

"Are you here for that information as well?" she asked.

"Oh, no!" He waved off the notion with a laugh. "I'm here strictly on business. But I know the reason why Akaras had to die."

"Which is?" The nagging part of her was intense. *Run,* it screamed. *Open your eyes and figure this out!*

"War." His smile lopped to one side and he almost seem to glow sinisterly in the shadows. "The dark elves seeks to take over the land above. Of course, once Everwind learnt of it, they sent me here for a little peace talk."

"You're an envoy?" she said disbelievingly. He did not have the air of one. He felt much more... more. Then, a question popped into her head. "Why did you want Nadier and The Watcher here?"

"As a gift of good faith, of course." He yawned again, seemingly bored with the conversation yet managing to keep his polite tone. "But I guess the girl who helped in The Watcher's escape would have to do."

"What in the Titans are you talking about?" She was off edge, her main hand's axe flew out of its holster and into her hand. "A gift?"

He looked forward to the Gate of Dark Light. "Do you know the Gate was made by an ancient race called the sentinels?" He crossed his legs and stretched his arms with a yawn. "Ancient elves with unparallelled command of science and technology. Do you know what happened to them?"

A part of her, a primal part, wanted to stab the man. An unexplainable sudden urge to draw her other axe and send it into his stupidly good looking face. Her hands clenched against her weapons' grips and she gritted out, "What happened?"

The man gave a toothy grin, and suddenly, the beautiful visage fell apart. His catlike eyes narrowed into slits and creases of madness broke across his face. His skin had not been damaged, but the insanity of the man broke out nonetheless.

Then the answer hit her. Why she had been afraid. Why she had been uneasy. The man was a human. A human with normal eyesight, walking, staring, looking in the complete darkness of the cave. A human who could see in the dark. An envoy of Everwind. Only one person came to mind.

A whisper escaped her. "Lord Light." The leader of The Forum States. Head of Everwind. Possibly one the most powerful photomancer to have ever lived who had rarely ever been seen in public. Legends said of him having absolute control over all elements of light itself.

She needed to run. There was no way she would be able to fight such a powerful figure. She took a step back and teleported as far as she could, landing onto the roof of a nearby building. Like a dream, the illusion of light faded, and dozens of dark elf warriors surrounded the pond. He hid them in a light mirage. All of them then turned to her, bows and swords drawn.

From behind, the Lord Light voiced, "No escape."

She spun around and swung her axe at where the voice came from, only to watch as her blade went right through his face as if it was all just a hallucination. But she knew it was not. Especially when he raised a finger to her chest. A bright light flashed, blinding her. As darkness settled back, the pain continued the blindness.

Her offhand axe clattered to the floor as she reached for her injured shoulder. She had managed to dodge just enough for the attack to miss her heart. She made a step to the left and before the second flash of light grew bright enough to daze her, she teleported across the roof.

Another step. Another teleportation. And a third. A fourth. She popped out from roof to roof, pushed by adrenaline and fear. She saw the main gate before her. A caravan was on its way out. She could smell blood. She had to breathe through her mouth for her nose was bleeding. Another step forward. Her head rang with pain. Blackness.

Chapter 11
Cold Fusion

The Watcher made it up the gentle slope and was greeted by the town of Ra'Kalen that sat on the flat lands before them. A long lined town made of stone houses and wooden huts in four neat rows, they faced the plains to the north and based the extremely steep mountains behind. In the east was a dancing farmland, thick bushels of yellow wheat swayed in the wind. At the west end, primitive stone steps ran up the side of the mountains, zigzagging all the way to the peak.

From behind, Kathleen asked, "Are we there?"

"We're here," he replied. He turned with an extended hand and helped her up the final climb of the hill. "Sleepy little place, isn't it?" He could hear the sound of children laughing in the distance, but the echo from the mountain side distorted his sense of hearing.

"Peaceful," she replied, scanning the landscape before pointing across him. "There's the inn!"

The road they were on lead straight through the centre of the town, a wooden sign planted into the dirt welcomed weary travellers with a 'Welcome to Ra'Kalen'. She had pointed to the first building on the left after the sign. It was a modest two storey wood house with copper lining the supports and edges. The back of it stretched out a different colour, likely an extension of the main structure. Like all the other structures of the town, it had a single diagonal roof. A slanted board above the double doors had the word 'Inn' painted haphazardly in black.

"That seems a little shady," he noted the rundown sign on the relatively clean building.

Kathleen had already started walking, stating, "It's naught of concern at this point. I just want a nice hot bath."

He could not help but smile. The girl was obviously not used to the travel. On the way over, she had more than once claimed both of them of starting to smell like rotting fish. He followed her to the inn and noted how there were no horses that he could see within the stables behind the inn. They stepped out from the light of the day into the cool dim of the building.

Lighted by lanterns that hung from the ceiling, the floors were plates of wood chequered with slabs of copper. Carved stone tables and chairs were set rather permanently on the metal plates, and the interior walls were of a cool red brick. To their right, a flight of stairs led up with a door installed under it beside the landing. A woman in a flowery dress with the curled white hair of movie grandmothers stood behind the bar, cleaning out a mug while a patron slumped asleep at the far stool of the tavern.

"Welcome to Ra'kalen Inn!" the innkeeper greeted.

The Watcher immediately asked, "What's with the cheap sign outside? This place looks beautiful."

"Why thank ya. Sadly, we 'ave got some vandals 'ere lately. Took a wack to the old board. Kids get bored when 'em season changes slow with da tourists," the innkeeper explained. "So, what can I get ya for?"

Kathleen approached her with a smile, "Hello, we'd like rooms please."

"'Course, we've got a nice couple room for you two."

Together, they replied, "We're not a couple."

The innkeeper grinned. "Really? Could 'ave fooled me. Da way ya grinnin' as ya walked in." She laughed as the two felt their cheeks blushed red. Putting down the mug she was cleaning, she reached under the counter and took out two keys. "Rooms are down da corridor 'hind the stairs. Communal baths ta ya left."

Kathleen stammered, "C-communal?"

"That's right hon', boys and girls." The innkeeper's smile was sly, as if she had witnessed the same reaction dozens of times and could never get tired of it. "We a' got 'em baths while back. Back not 'nough finance to put up to."

Kathleen looked to The Watcher pleadingly, her face redder than the brick on the wall. Laughing himself, he told her, "Don't worry, you can go first. I want to check out this Enhancer that I've been told so much of."

She let out a breath of relief. "T-then, I'll settle our rooms and meet up with you later."

The innkeeper clicked her tongue in disappointment at the outcome, but said, "Da Enhancer? You must be lookin' 'fer Master Hildergard. She's down west. Last store before da mountain steps."

The Watcher thanked the innkeeper for her information and nodded Kathleen goodbye. He headed for the door as Kathleen haggled for the price of accommodations. "Is twenty quints a night fair?" he heard as he exited the inn.

Following the old woman's instructions, he walked down the main street of the town. It was a quiet place and the few villagers on the streets greeted him happily with welcoming messages and warm smiles. He passed by a small park where a group of children ran around and played. The smell of freshly baked bread floated from a nearby bakery and the sound of a woman bargaining for the price of meat at a passing butcher echoed to great effect.

He loved the town, but hated himself being there.

Being in a place of such peace and quiet had never been good for him. People with his kind of background always seemed to attract trouble, which was the reason why he preferred to be on the road of travel, away from settlements like this that would suffer the worst of any misfortune he brought along. He hoped to finish everything he needed to do before the end of the next day. To visit the Enhancer and the Titan Rangers were his order of tasks.

Nevertheless, he enjoyed the atmosphere. Perhaps one day, when the annals of history stops its calling, and the shadow of danger leaves him, he would be able to settle down in a small, quaint, unassuming town somewhere.

It did not take long for him to traverse the small town and it surprised him that such a place was considered the capital of a state. According to Kathleen, the state of South Marika was the least developed of the City States of The Forum. Because of the protection of the mountain granted to the Titan Hunters, they were not allowed to heavily mine their surroundings for stones, unlike the city of Yogai. They did not produce wood like the Rao'Alliance and was not a port town. They did not have the means of mass production of food like the Grassplains, and had only the town of Dane and the city of Valent connected by road. The people of Ra'Kalen thus lead a quiet life. But they had the slight advantage of having one of the four master Enhancers of Eltar setting up shop there, receiving a large portion of their income from exporting crystals.

The shop was not hard to find. It was the only building made entirely of red bricks, sticking out sorely at the edge of town against the green plains beyond. Its glass display window was painted with the simple word, 'Enhancer'. The Watcher stepped inside.

The store was lined with two aisles. In the middle, spread out over two long wooden tables were weapons and armours of all kinds. At first glance, the equipments looked normal. Closer inspection showed each piece to have a crystal embedded into a part of it and The Watcher could feel power emanating from each of them. Though not to the extend of power that a living being could produce, it was enough to send an intoxicating shiver through his body.

At the side of the shops against the walls in glass display cases were the same crystals embedded in the weapons, but put out individually on padded stands. Some were the size of fingernails, while others were that of his palm. The energy coming from the crystals were much stronger than those from the equipments, and each had a tint of colour and feel that differed, from fire red to leaf green.

"Ah! A customer!" He turned to the counter to see a woman walk out of the back room with a small crate in hand. "Welcome to Hilde's. Looking for something to enhance your magic? I'm your girl!" She placed the crate on the counter.

The Enhancer called Hildergard looked no older than thirty. Her long, shining blonde hair was tied into a neat braid and she had the soft, smooth face of a model. Her smile was something he could only describe as innocent and cute. Yet, her body, especially arms, were well toned with the sign of years of work. Wearing a leather workshop apron over long white sleeved shirt, she could have been on a poster for women engineers back on Earth.

He smiled back and said, "I'm looking for something to help stabilise my magic." He walked up to the counter and, from his coat, retrieved a pouch of quints that Kathleen gave him. "What can I get for these?"

She counted the metal tags and her smile broke away. "Is this a joke? You can't even afford a tier two crystal with this, let alone equipments." She looked up to him, visibly annoyed. "What kind of crystals are you looking for? Pyro? Hydro? Terra?"

"Chrono," he stated, deadpan.

Her facade disappeared completely. With none of her previous charm or happiness, she cursed under her breath. "Gearing sod." Her brows twisted down. "Look, I don't have time for your delusions. If you want to play a mage, go pick out one of those tier one aether crystals from the junk barrel." She pointed to a barrel at the corner of the room, away from the front of the store.

"Hildergard!" The two turned to the voice from the door that led to the back of the store.

They had not heard the door opening, but standing under the archway at the back of the shop was a caramel skinned man blocking the door with his 1.8 meters tall and leaned body. He had a denim apron on over white shirt and brown linen trousers. Dusts were visibly puffing out from his body, showing that he had just walked out from a workshop behind. His eyes were a deep forest green and his hair was short, spiked, and a deep navy blue. His ears were sharp like an elf but small like a human and he had the same sharp chin that Adelaide and Nadier had, but with a rugged face akin to a man.

A half elf? The Watcher first thought.

Hilde exclaimed, "Grandmaster Miguel!"

Miguel reprimanded, "What did I tell you about treating people without judgement before knowing their abilities?"

"But Grandmaster, this man claims to be a chronomancer."

"Does it matter?" Miguel stepped out from the doorway, around the counter, and approached The Watcher. They sized each other up before the Enhancer replied to Hilde, "Can you not sense the magic pouring out of this man? Or were you so blinded by your title that you forgot the basics of your training?"

Hilde turned to The Watcher and squinted. He could feel a sense of energy run over his body as she analysed him and he sent out a pulse of energy back to her. Her eyes widened in surprise soon after and she lowered her head in shame.

Miguel said, "I apologise for my apprentice. She only gained the title of master last year. She is talented, but young and hot-headed." He extended his hand in greetings. "Miguel Vallertes, Grandmaster Enhancer of the Kingdom of Aleynonlia."

"Watcher," The Watcher replied with a shake. "And there's no trouble at all." He liked the vibe that Miguel gave off. It was familiar, and almost familial.

"That said, I cannot argue that you do not have enough money to purchase one of her better products as a matter of fair trade. And the fact is, there are only two recorded chronomancers on Tearha, and I happen to personally know both of them." The Watcher smiled, but nodded in understanding. His tact and elegance never leaving, Miguel continued, "Be that as it may, I will not prod you on the reason for hiding your magical element. Perhaps I can make up for my apprentice's rudeness by helping you select an aether crystal best suited for you? Though they are only tier one, they are still magical items of power." He gestured the way to the barrel.

"Thank you," The Watcher smiled and replied. He headed for the barrel of crystals. He looked to Hilde who was still stunned and sulking. He added, "And don't be too hard on the poor girl. After all, 'Every instrument requires to be made by experience'."

"Leonardo da Vinci. Good quote."

Miguel picked up a crystal from the barrel filled to the brim with them. He examined it briefly and placed it back in the pile, apparently able to discern its quality and compatibility with ease. They continued sifting through the barrel in silence, Miguel picking up each crystal and putting them back in seconds while The Watcher only looked at the one in his own hand in entranced curiosity, unable to discern anything more about them aside from being some form of energy battery.

Then, The Watcher dropped his crystal and took a quick step away from Miguel. The Enhancer materialised a pair of long, curved, reverse daggers in a cloud of frozen air. The Watcher reached for his sword, but before his hand even gripped the handle, the blades of the daggers were already on his neck but they did not move further into the skin. Miguel held them in steady place. The Watcher could feel a drying cold emitting from the blades and the inside of his throat parched from the freeze.

"Grandmaster!" Hilde exclaimed.

The two ignored her, eyes locked in their stance.

Miguel noted, "You just quoted Leonardo da Vinci."

The Watcher replied, "And you know who Leonardo da Vinci is."

"Well, Watcher, you now have my undivided attention."

Chapter 12
The Phantom Light

The back room of the Enhancer establishment looked no more than a normal workshop. Workbenches lined the two walls, with cracked and dusted remnants of leftover crystals littered across them. A small compact forge was set in the rear of the room with pipes running out of it and through the walls to the outside to get vented. Next to it was a shining new anvil and hammer. The workbenches had varying tools. From the common clamps and wrenches, to scholastic books on Enhancement, fine jewellery tools, and what looked to be a set of scientific instruments ranging from beakers, burners, and even a copper shelled microscope.

Miguel let the way in, saying, "Step into my office."

"Actually, Grandmaster," Hilde voiced from behind. "It's my workshop."

"Hilde," Miguel replied with a gentle stern, "Do watch the store."

"Ah... um... yes, Grandmaster," she was meekly heard saying before the door closed behind them. Miguel respected how direct the girl was, but wished she knew how to read social cues better.

"Now, where were we?" Miguel pulled out a chair for The Watcher and another one for himself. He sat next to the workbench of scientific instruments. "Ah, yes, you're from Earth."

The Watcher scanned the room and Miguel gave him the chance to survey the location. It was common for people who were experienced in danger to take in their immediate surroundings. He did not know why, but he thought The Watcher felt like one of those experienced few. There was an aura of age around The Watcher that transcended physical appearances and a shadow of a long past that dragged behind the steps of his feet. Yet, alongside it was a glint of barrelling energy.

"We might not be from the same Earth," The Watcher admitted, finally taking the seat offered and turning back to Miguel. "I mean, have you read comic books? They have enough Earths to put wind and fire out of business."

"What makes you think the Earth we're talking about is different?"

"Well, for starters, I'm a pretty awesome character in my world. If someone like you existed, I would know," The Watcher bragged with a grin. He leaned back in his seat. "Have you seen me? I'm awesome, right?"

"I don't know if you're awesome or not. I just met you." Even by his standard, Miguel thought the man was somewhat odd, and he had met many odd people in his life. He pushed to regain his composure. "But you're right. You're right. Chances are, you are not from the same Earth. Let's do a checklist. What year are you from."

"Hah! I'm a time traveller. I come from wherever I want."

Sceptical, Miguel leaned back in his seat. "You really are a chronomancer?"

"That's what I said out there, and that's what I'm sticking to in here."

"Time travel requires an enormous amount of power. Almost inordinately so."

"I know that."

Miguel was still not fully convinced. "What's the first rule of time travel?" From his knowledge, there was one rule that time travellers inherently knew. Like how pyromancers become resistant to heat, this knowledge was something instinctual and necessary for survival. "There's one rule all chronomancers abide by the moment they jump time. What is it?"

The Watcher folded his arms and raised a brow in suspicion. Without any joking tone, he answered, "I must never reveal who I was before I started travelling. Otherwise, someone could go back and me before, stop me from travelling and collapse my entire timeline in a loop."

"Hm..." The Grandmaster rubbed his chin in thought. "Interesting. All chronomancers seems to have the same answer. I should study more into this..." he trailed off.

The Watcher cleared his throat, bringing Miguel's attention back. "Checklist? Different Earth?"

"Right. Different Earth." Miguel shook his head away from the train of thought. There were a lot of questions he wanted to ask The Watcher, but he guessed most of them will have to wait until the situation has been discerned. "So, let's start with major events. Tabulate the timeline. World War Two victor?"

"Allied."

"Okay. Albert Einstein?"

"E equals M-C square."

"So far similar. How about something more recent? The twenty twenty-two climate crisis–"

"Woah, hang on," The Watcher stopped him. "We didn't get that far. A giant portal to another universe appeared at the turn of the century, killed off eighty percent of the world's population. With the poison gas after that further pushing that number down. That's why I'm here in the first place. I want to figure out what's causing those portals."

"Guess that settles that. Different Earths. But portals?" He knew of only two naturally occurring methods of crossing dimensions. Gates, and tears, which were physically unmistakable in name. "What did these 'portals' look like?"

The Watcher gestured with his hands, spinning them around as if he was caressing a ball. "Just a round, spinning, whirlpool of aeth–I mean, seither energy. And there's an upside-down image of a random location in the middle. Can be a swamp or a building, or a tree on a hill. Like a refraction of space-time."

The portal sounded nothing like the other methods of travels he knew of. Though they had some similarities, particularly in the distorted images, they did not resemble the gates or tears. There was only one logical conclusion. Either someone had created a new form of dimensional travel, or there was a new natural phenomenon happening. Given The Watcher's account, he was willing to bet it was the former.

The Enhancer stood to his feet and went to the workbench on the far end. He pulled open a drawer and took out a small, black leather box and returned to The Watcher.

The Watcher took a look at the box and asked, "Are you proposing? I'm flattered, but I'm already married."

"You wanted a crystal, am I right?" The Watcher slowly stood up, another look of suspicion drew across his face. Miguel opened the box, revealing the content within. A single, clear coloured crystal no bigger than the size of the tip of their thumbs rested gently within. "This is a tier seven chrono crystal. The only chrono crystal in existence. I came to Eltar to use their batteries specifically for this purpose. A chronomancer friend of mine requested for it, but I think we can all agree you need it more."

The traveller eyed the crystal, then switched his gaze to Miguel. "What's the catch?" But even as he said so with distrust, his hand reached for the jewel.

Miguel slapped the outreach hand away as one would do a child reaching for a jar of cookie. "Consider it a commission. If you really are investigating these 'portals', then on behalf of the Kingdom of Aleynonlia, and as Enhancer Council to the king, we are officially interested." He snapped the box shut and placed it on the nearest workbench. "Since I am here on an official pass, I can't do any investigating myself. If I were to find myself in any form of danger, I would not be able to fight back without it being a declaration of war."

The Watcher laughed, "So you want me to be a spy? To poke the hornet's nest for you? And in return, I get the crystal?" Miguel nodded, and The Watcher snorted in derision. "How do I even know the crystal will even work? You said so yourself that there's only one of it, so I'm guessing that there's never been any test of quality."

Miguel picked up one of the half-worked crystals from a workbench. He held it up to the light of the lamp, which flickered through the gem and danced off his face.

The Grandmaster asked, "I assume you know what magic circuits are?" He looked over to The Watcher who gave a quick nod. He continued his explanation, "Crystals are just that. They are magic circuits embedded into gems. The magic circuits within each mage is limited, and you can only have so many in your body. A crystal adds to that, like a magazine extension for a gun. It's guaranteed to work since all magic circuits convert seither into energy. The different elements just help to attune to the base elements of mages."

"But my circuits aren't working," The Watcher waved his hand in an exaggerated 'no'. "At least, not properly."

"Seither is a little different from universe to universe. It's to accommodate to some physical differences within each plane. Changes in the laws of physics, that sort of stuff. There are different names for it. Mana, fae energy, dark matter..."

The Watcher added, "Mist and aether?"

"Exactly," Miguel confirmed. "But they are basically the same thing. It'll take some time before your body can properly convert seither on Tearha. It might be a few days, or even years, depending on your abilities. But for now, crystals will help provide a replacement source of energy for you. Think of it as a backup generator."

The Watcher spread his arms wide acceptingly. "Okay then. What do I have to do?"

"Nothing. I just need to calibrate the crystal to your circuits."

They were interrupted when a knock came from the door and Hilde's voice rang through. "Grandmaster, there's a lady here who is looking for The Watcher. She says they have to leave soon if they want to make it to the Titan Rangers and back by twilight." There was a notable excitement in her voice at the notion of The Watcher leaving.

"Thank you, Hilde," Miguel replied. To The Watcher, he asked, "Somewhere you need to be?"

"It's fine. I'll push it to tomorrow."

"Don't worry about it. You don't need to be here for the calibration. You can go up to the Valley of Titans and by the time you're back, the crystal should be ready for you." Miguel explained. He held his arm out. "I just need you to take off your coat and shirt, and give me your hand."

The Watcher did as he was told, setting his clothes aside on the chair and putting his right hand in both of Miguel's. The Enhancer could not take his eyes off the man's body. It was slightly toned and nothing special, save for the multiple bullet sized scars that littered his torso. At first count, there were at least two dozens, maybe more. It was a shivering sight. Unlike the cuts and rips made from blades and falls, or even normal bullet wounds that sometimes nicked and tore, the scars The Watcher had were all clean and perfectly rounded, as if someone had carefully seared the end of a pipe into his skin and through his body.

Kathleen's voice called out, "Watcher?" Miguel was pulled out of his fixation.

The Watcher yelled back, "Don't come in here! I'm naked!" His words were immediately followed by the sound of crashing metal and an agonised scream from Hilde.

The Enhancer's right forearm started to glow. Cyan lines of light pulsed brightly through the vein-like markings that appeared on the back of his hand. The pattern extended, showing the magic circuit that reached up through his forearm, growing all the way to his shoulders.

The circuits roughly divided into three sections at each joint of his arm – wrist and elbow.

Miguel briefed, "I'm going to send a pulse of energy to light up your circuits. I need to see what I'm working with."

"Better make it a really big pulse."

He sent the energy through. He felt as the power flowed from his arms and punched into The Watcher's hand. The Watcher's magic circuit lit up purple. But unlike Miguel's vein-shaped ones, his actually resembled an electrical circuit. The pattern angled and turned sharply, the branches spreading at ninety and forty-five degree angles. Continuing to grow in a single, uninterrupted sequence, the light meandered its way up his arm, past his shoulder, joining up into a point as it triangulated above his heart.

Surprised, the Grandmaster Enhancer let out, "What in the world?"

The Watcher gripped Miguel by the wrist. Looking him straight in the eye, The Watcher said, "A little bit more."

Miguel did as he was told, pushing another pulse into the body. He watched as the second wave relit the arm, moving blindingly up to the chest and to the heart only to spread further instead of stopping. Like an infection exploding from his heart, the light spread into countless more circuits. Up his neck and face. Down the body to his legs. Across the chest to his other arm. The Watcher lit up like a phantom of the light.

He was the Grandmaster Enhancer. The best in his field between the two worlds of Tearha and Earth. He had seen a man with twelve sets of magic circuit that covered his upper torso. He married a woman whose circuits resided entirely in her eyes. Yet, he had never seen a magic circuit as astounding as The Watcher's.

"I can see you're confused," The Watcher ginned, his teeth eerily reflecting the neon purple glow of the rest of his body. "See, I'm not a real 'mage'," he air quoted. He then pointed to the point of origin of the circuits at his heart. "Artificial. I'm a Hymn. H-Y-M-N. Humans-Yielding-Mutating-Nanites."

The number of sets of circuits within an individual determined the adaptability of magic within a mage. The more sets a person has, the more varied tiered spells they could cast. The length of the circuits within each set determined how strong those spells could be. Despite having just one set of circuit, the sheer length of The Watcher's circuit convinced Miguel that if The Watcher ever had access to his full power, the man would be one of the strongest individual in all the universes, able to take a simple fireball spell and channel it to destroy the planet. Even with just a hint of chronomancy in him, The Watcher could use the most basic time manipulation spell to an unthinkable extreme. The man could have powers equal to a god.

"You..." Miguel huffed out, astonishment hiding his fears. "You're really a chronomancer." He finally, fully believed.

The Watcher rolled his eyes, exasperated. "That's what I've been trying to tell everybody!"

Chapter 13

Lady Fatal

"And do you, Nadier, admit guilty to the crime of treason, and be sentenced to death?"

The voice of the Ha'Lof, the high elf of the dark council, echoed through the circular chamber. Standing in the middle of the arena of judgemental stares, wrist and feet shackled, naked with marks of lashes across his body, Nadier looked up to the council with a steadied glare.

Defiantly, Nadier replied, "What happens if I admit my guilt?"

Haeswahl Nunderberg, commander of the dark elf army, stood from her bench. An elf as muscular as a troll, Haeswahl wore the black coat of Grandmaster Commander over the black bodysuit of her trait. Her hair was a disturbing short grey and her eyes had cat-like irises with the red of dark elves. She emitted a fearful presence that silenced the rest of the room into bated breath.

Haeswahl commented, "Once your guilt is admitted, your death will be carried out, post-haste."

"And should I refute?"

"A much, slower, execution," Haeswahl replied with a grin.

The large double doors of the council chamber swung opened and Akaras Spaedruiner walked in with a confident, high-held gait. His coat fluttering behind him bore the arms of the House of Speedrunner, two daggers crossed over a buckler.

"*Aegai* Spaedruiner," the Ha'Lof greeted. "I am to assume there is a good reason for this intrusion?"

Akaras glanced over to his brother and gave a reassuring nod before stepping forward into the centre of the stage. "Yes, my *Hae* Lord. I would like to plead on the behalf of my brother?"

"Objection!" Haeswahl slammed her clenched fists against the table, the sound echoing throughout the chamber like a clap of thunder.

Most of the council members slunk back in their seats but the Ha'Lof stood to his feet and raised an opened hand to halt Haeswahl. Turning to Akaras, he asked, "And what is the condition of your argument?"

"The name of the House of Speedrunner, in return for the life and banishment of Nadier," Akaras's voice rang clear through the chamber.

The Ha'Lof asked, "And should we refute?"

"Should such a path occur, the House will declare war on the chamber."

Haeswahl shouted, "Blaspheme!"

The Ha'Lof silenced her with another raise of his hand. "Very well. The council will now adjourn to convene and discuss the terms and desolation of the House."

"Wanderer. Wanderer!"

Nadier's eyes flickered open to the call of his epitaph. The sound of the streets of the lower city of Everwind slowly waved into his ears and the light of the warm noon Twins wrapped his body in a blanket of comfort, attempting to lure him back to sleep. He took in a deep, hard breath. The stench of the gutter and blood from the butcher's knocked through his sinus and into his brain, immediately setting him straight on the bench, fully awaken by the smell of iron.

The woman before him, dressed in a ragged dress and dirt splattered apron, held out the paper-wrapped bundle to him. "Sorry for the wait." Her short onyx hair shone and glimmered in the light. "Here's your order of brown jaeger leaves."

He stood to his feet and took the small package from her, keeping it inside his coat. "Thanks, Joan. I know it's hard to find jaeger, and there's not really much use for them in a shop like yours," he noted the rustic floristry establishment they stood outside of. "I apologise for the trouble."

"Nonsense, Wanderer. You're one of my best customers. And the medicines you bring have been very helpful for the orphanage." The young woman who was just the height of his chest patted him on the head as if he was a child. "Milton's always hoping you'd one day sit down for dinner with us. You've helped us so much. And you have to teach me more of your alchemical knowledge."

"Perhaps next time, Joan. It's a busy season for me." He took three vials of antiseptic from his waist pouch and handed them over as payment. He left the florist with a wave goodbye.

The lower city streets were narrow and filled with potholes and the stench of tension. Those that littered out on the streets were either rugged mercenaries and travellers who were armed and ready for a riot, or lower class citizens in ragged clothes going about their day with an air of solemnity forever hanging around them. The drains at the sides were littered and clogged, sending a constant odour of rotting eggs into the air. Doors of the five floor apartments were closed, though Nadier knew what laid beyond them. Rooms barely the size of the back of a trade caravan housing families and groups of five or more with corridors strewn of the homeless. The few shops that were opened were filled with hagglers. The poverty stricken district, with the lack of monetary flow, often resulted to trading for food and daily necessities.

He caught a glimpse of the flutter of a cloak from the corner of his eyes and he sighed. A group of city guards were headed his way from down the street and he turned into a small dark alley to avoid them.

The dark elf continued down the narrow path until he was sure they were both hidden by the shadows before saying, "You can come out now."

From behind her 'hiding spot' of a small pile of rubbish, the young girl stood up into view with a wide grin on her face. "How did you know I was here?"

"Tina, if you want to follow someone you know, wear a mask." Nadier pulled up his scarf to demonstrate.

Tinarya Twainrae wore an old, stained, hooded brown coat that was too small for an adult and too large for a child like her. Reaching down to her shin, the coat practically covered the whole of her body like a raincoat. The girl, just a head shorter than his chest, looked akin to a dress that had left its coat rack behind and decided to grow a pair of legs to go out for a walk on its own.

She ran up to Nadier in hops and skips. Taking off her hood, she revealed her sharp elven ears, medium-cut dirt hair, and deep leaf-green eyes. Her smile pulled her otherwise sharp elven face into a bubble and the scar that rested across her nose was barely visible compared to the red stroke that it was the last time Nadier had saw her.

He knelt down to face her, dusting off her shoulders gently. "What are you doing here? If the guards catches you, they'll throw you back into the Antipods," he reprimanded.

"Pfft!" Tina waved the idea away. "I'm a Gutter Rat! I'm not afraid of 'em guards!"

The Gutter Rats were a self-proclaimed rebel group that was really just a bunch of kids that liked to congregate and play in the tunnels under the city. Most of them were homeless, a small sum from poverty stricken families, and a fraction were from the orphanage. Occasionally, one or two runaways from the wealthier districts sneak their way into the assembly.

He ruffled her hair and sighed. "Right, right. Now go back to the sewage tunnels, little Gutter Rat, or I'll tell Mister Jones you sneaked out of the orphanage again."

Tina's eyes widened in worry. "Please don't! We're having noodles for dinner today. I don't want to miss that!"

"Well, we'll have to get going, won't we?" He stood up and turned to face the way out to the streets, only to stop in his tracks.

Silhouetted by light, a figure stood at the entrance of the alley. The slender woman wearing her tight clothing ensemble of a red leather skirt, black corset, buttoned brown leather jacket, and knee length heeled boots, greeted them. Upon noticing the woman, Tina immediately turned away to hide behind Nadier, who covered her with an outstretched arm while his left hand reached for his dagger.

Nora Phemtelle greeted, "Wanderer. Nice to see you again."

"You too, Lady Nora," he monotonously replied. "Is there something I can help you with?"

Tina gripped tightly to the hem of his coat. He could feel her burning a stare at the woman. She whispered to him, "I don't like her."

Nora looked to Tina, who shook back in shock at being overheard from that distance. "I'm sorry, little girl. Maybe you'll like me more if you're dead?" Nora smiled, not a trace of menace on her face.

The girl stood her ground, though Nadier could feel her shaking in fear from just the touch of his coat. He was quite proud of how brave she was. In the end though, she whimpered for protection. "Nads..."

"Don't worry," he said to Tina, placing a reassuring hand on her head without turning away from Nora. To the Lady, he asked, "Again, why are you here?"

Nora turned her attention back to Nadier. "The Lord Light wants to see you."

He had been a hired hand of Everwind for nearly a hundred years. During that whole time, he had not met either the previous or the present Lord Light once. The fact that he was being called now while on his way to investigate the portal for The Watcher was more than a little suspect. But he had a more pressing question to ask.

"What about the girl?" he noted about Tina.

Nora replied, "She can go. No point in wasting energy on a child."

He nodded in understanding. Squatting down and turning back to Tina, he instructed, "Go back home, alright? I'll come visit you later."

She had held back her tears and her eyes glistened with them and was red from nearly crying. But still, she managed to ask, "What about you?"

He gave a small smile. His face felt slightly stiff. It was not often he smiled. "I'll be fine. And remember to open room forty-two for me."

The girl's lips pursed and she nodded. He helped her pull her hood back up and sent her scampering down the alley. He watched as she disappeared into the shadows before standing and turning back to the Lady who had, within the time he was talking to Tina, closed the gap between them without him noticing. A feat that was impressive for a human to do to an dark elf on edge.

He looked down to her high heel boots. On appearance, the footwear looked uninspiring and normal. However, he knew the truth. The heels were made of titanium that were painted black. And the conical tips, which Nora had attributed to long-term wear and tear, were actually by design. It hooked onto any limps that she could grab with her feet, allowing her to break and slam the bones at her leisure with no easy escape. It was a pair of weapon that was terrifyingly simple and sent shivers down his spine whenever he saw them. After all, no one would ever confiscate footwear. Her expert usage of the boots, stealth skills, and early years spent as a spy made her one of the most feared assassin in all of Eltar, even by dark elf standards.

She smiled at Nadier with a beautifully sculpted face. "Shall we leave?"

Hiding his fears, he answered, "Lead the way."

They stepped out onto the streets where a carriage awaited. He stepped forward to open the door for her, never letting it be said that he was anything but polite. He turned for one last look down the dark alley where Tina had ran off and another long look to The Tower in the distance of the central district. He closed the door behind him.

Chapter 14
The Double Edged Prince

The Tower was built by the first Lord Light as the official building of the ruling government. Steam pipes ran throughout the structure, powering the many generators within with heat from the underground lava pool they've tapped. Within the thirty storeys tall tower – which included ten more levels underground – varied types and amount of activities took place. Government officials were housed. Scientific researches were carried out. Political prisoners were held. And even magic was trained. On the tenth floor was the Commission Assembly of The Forum, where the leaders of the country gathered to discuss on all issues. The twentieth floor held the Chamber of the Overseers, where the Overseers charged with the prediction and handling of epitaphs lived.

Because of that, the first floor bustled with activity. Workers travelled in and out with lamp light continually flickering off the copper walls and steel floor. The large level was pillared by two spiralling flights of stairs that led up and through to the top floor. A manned reception counter was positioned to the right of the entrance with an open-space canteen. The area to the left was filled with chairs and space for gatherings and relaxation. Four doorless elevators were set into the wall at the end of the room. Nadier followed Nora through the crowd, heading for the leftmost private elevator used by high rankers amongst them.

"Where are we going?" Nadier asked, stepping into the steel grate box, the shaft that led underground was lid dimly by torches embedded in the walls.

"The Commission Assembly," the spy answered.

While the main elevator only operated every six floors, the private one had access to all. This was to prevent unwanted individuals from accessing the Assembly and Chamber levels. Though Nadier had rode the private elevator before with his brother, he did not actually have the key for it.

From between her cleavage, Nora took out a silver key and slotted it into the control panel. She selected a level and the steam engine ten floors below began to chug. The gears of the machine started turning and the mechanism began pulling the elevator up, the walls of the shaft rushing past by their sides. Nadier had always resisted the inner childish temptation to reach out over the railings to touch the walls that were grinding by. The ride was punctuated by Nora's humming of the travelling tune, *The Road is Long*.

Annoyed, Nadier asked, "Why are you humming?"

"I thought it would help stave off the boredom. You know how we have travelling music? Well, now we have elevator music."

"That's stupid," Nadier replied. "It's less than a minute of travel. What's the point?"

Before Nora could reply, they had reached the tenth floor and the elevator came to a stop. They stepped out and Nadier followed Nora's lead down the corridor towards the Assembly room. She led him through the double doors and into the round chamber.

Shaped like an arena, the Assembly featured hundreds of chairs surrounding a raised platform in the middle. The path to the entrance was embedded into the south end of the room. It was eerily similar to the dark elf council chamber, save for the perpetual darkness. The chairs all had backs taller than the elf himself, and during the gatherings, the Commission discussed issues amongst each other in equal height, while looking down on any outsiders in the literal sense. But the room was emptied now, and the only other person in it was the Lord Light, who stood on the central podium in a gleaming white robe, shining so ridiculous bright that Nadier could swear his skin itched even underneath the aeronium layer.

The man turned and with a gracious smile and opened arm. "Wanderer! Good to finally meet you, after all these years."

Nora left Nadier and proceeded to Light's side.

Nadier bowed his head in greeting. "Lord Light. It is an honour."

"Please, the honour is mine," Light replied, waving the notion away. "The services you provided for Everwind and the United States of The Forum have been invaluable. We are forever in your debt, both you and your brother."

"My brother?" Nadier raised a brow in question.

"Yes. I would like to offer you condolence for his death. I'm sure you've realised this by now, but your brother was coerced into his final acts due to blackmail from the dark elves of Ta'Galadul," Light explained. "In light of this information, the Committee has decreed that he shall be given full honours in death, and his crime as pardoned."

Though the information of his brother's name being cleared did not particularly warranted any feelings from Nadier, he nodded back anyway. "Thank you for your graciousness, Lord Light."

Light continued, "But we do have ill tidings. Our agents have discovered a plot by the dark elves to lay siege to Everwind. As such, I had personally visited their capitol to negotiate."

That was the information Nadier had needed for Adelle to gather. If the dark elves were waging war, it made sense for their culture to send their first wave as an infiltration. And who better to infiltrate Everwind than one of them who had been ingrained into the high society of the city. Now, Nadier knew his target with clarity. Someone like his brother. The Ta'Galadul will pay for the death of Akaras Spaeruiner. His brother was not a pawn in their conflicts.

Light dropped his formalities suddenly, his eyes lighting up with excitement as he clapped his hands together like a child. "In any case, you will never guess who I ran into there. The Demon of Valendria. 'Demon Eye's' Adelaide Wiltkins."

Nadier's heart pounded but he maintained his outward stoical composure. "I hope you had not much trouble with her."

"Oh, do not worry, I am unharmed," Light replied. Nadier could see Nora's lips part slightly in a barely noticeable smile. "But that girl is as elusive as the reports says. She had managed to escape my grasp, just by the hair on the nape of her neck. Not without injury, of course. Though I was surprised by her teleportation abilities. None of the reports before mentioned it. You've faced her before yourself, have you not?"

"Yes," Nadier admitted, but then lied. "But I did not experience this teleportation you mention."

Light nodded in understanding. "Just as expected, given how long we have tried to capture her to little success." The man folded his arms in thoughts before continuing, "But we have a greater issue. The negotiation with the dark elves did not go as plan, and they continue to mount their forces. While I focus my energy and attention on that front, I would like to personally employ you to hunt down The Watcher. As he is your brother's killer, I'm sure you would like to have his head for yourself. It's best if we take him down as soon as possible. A time traveller as powerful as The Watcher would definitely be dangerous to the security of the nation."

"Ah..." Nadier let out in surprise. He tried to not let the information and change in tone get to him. "Of course. But I don't see how I could fight someone that managed to defeat my brother. From what I understand, he is a mage." He knew denying the job would draw suspicion, but Nadier hoped to walk away without taking the mission.

Light explained, "I heard you dark elves have developed a chemical capable of cutting through seither. If so, you should be able to assassinate the man, even if he has an innate magic shield. Even one such as The Watcher needs to sleep."

Nadier reached for the ring from his belt and pulled out one of his vial. He held it up to them. "Neverite. Negates seither based phenomenon."

Light clapped his hands together joyously. "Fantastic. I assume it to be safe to leave the matters to you?"

Acknowledging he could no longer get out of the assignment, Nadier quickly nodded and bowed, "Of course, my Lord. Then, if there is nothing more, I should take my leave and prepare for this mission." He hastened to leave.

"Very well," Light's mouth twitched into a smile. "I await your good news."

Nadier turned and headed for the exit. Just as he reached the door, the sound of chuckling rang out within the empty chamber, stopping Nadier in his tracks with the door half opened. He turned back to face the duo, only to see Light breaking out into a fit of laughter.

Nora exclaimed, "Lord Light!"

"I'm sorry, Nora. I can't hold it in any longer." Light hunched over in laughter as Nora tried to calm him down.

The Lady said, "Weren't you the one who said we have to keep a straight face until Nadier left?"

But Light kept laughing. While the two were distracted, Nadier reached for his dagger. A ray of light shot out towards the elf, slicing off a lock off the side of his hair. Light, still laughing, had a glowing white finger pointed at Nadier.

"Hah... hah!" Light finally calmed down, but a grin was still etched across his face. "I'm sorry. We were suppose to let you leave and follow you to The Watcher and Demon Eyes. I'm sure you would've told them this new information about us going after them directly. But since I gave out our bluff I doubt that would happen now. It'll be much easier to get their locations from you, preferably through torture or magic."

Nadier stood to height, taking his hand off his dagger. "I'm sorry my Lord, but I don't know what you're talking about," he lied again.

"Oh, no use playing dumb. I could see the change in your eyes long before. Before I send you to the intelligence agency, would you kindly let me know how you figured it out?" Light aimed his finger at Nadier's head as if holding a gun. "Consider it a gift to satisfy my curiosity."

As the elf listened to the man, he could not help but grit his teeth, thinking the man conceited. He raised his hands in surrender, the vial still dangling in his palm. He explained, "No one ever said The Watcher was a time traveller. And if you knew that, you probably know of my involvement."

"Hah! I guess I should be more careful with my words." Light laughed loudly. Nadier could see the man's eyes flit to the vial in his hand. Light then said, "I know what you are thinking. You're thinking of using the Neverite to negate my next attack. While I doubt even you will be fast enough to accomplish such a feat, I'll not take my chances. Drop the vial."

The elf asked menacingly, "You want me to drop the vial?"

Gripping the vial itself, he pulled the ring with his index finger. The pin popped out and smoke shot from the tip. He let the vial go, the cannister leaving a trail of smokescreen as it dropped to the ground. Nadier spun and jumped backwards just as a beam of light shot through the cloud. He landed on his arms, rolled, stabled himself in a kneel, before finally pushing up and bashing through the double doors as his smoke grenade continued to cover his escape. Another beam of light blasted out of the room behind him and pierced into the wall just as he turned into the corridor. There was a second of delay before the point of impact exploded, chunks of copper and bricks blasting outward and littering the corridor.

The blast knocked Nadier off balance and he stumbled but he quickly regained his steps. He followed the path to the elevator shaft, only to find the elevator had left and was proceeding up to the floors above. But the machine that pulled the elevator was located in the basement, with the pulley at the top floor, meaning that the rope at the end of the shaft was still descending. He jumped for the rope, grabbed onto it, and began the journey down. It was by the time he had reached the fifth basement that the elevator had stopped. He still had five floors to climb before reaching the lowest level.

"I'll cut the rope," he heard Light's voice echo calmly from above.

Nadier jumped for the walls just as a bright flash of light preceded a loud snap from above. He landed against the wall and slid down it three levels. The rope flailed, snapped and slapped against the shaft with enough force to knock out a chunk of brick. He pushed away from the wall, launching himself towards the final exit at the bottom, grabbed the top of the archway, and swung himself into the tunnel just as the elevator came crashing down behind him, kicking up dust and shaking the ground.

Though panting from fatigue and arms burning from the dangerous journey down, he quickly ran down the empty, pipes-lined corridor of the maintenance level as dust filled the elevator entrance. He stopped at a door with a sign that read 'Sewage Section 42'. He entered and was immediately caught in a waist-level hug from the girl.

"Nads!" Tinarya Twainrae exclaimed. "I got your message! Room forty-two! Aren't I smart?"

He ruffled the girl's hair. "Good work, Gutter Rat." One of the copper plates that covered the sewage line was opened, leading into the underground tunnels. "Let's get out of here."

Nora stood at the edge of the elevator, surveying the crash at the bottom. The lack of blood splatters in the crash suggested that Nadier had escaped. "It seems we might have lost him, my Lord. I will start a search of the building immediately."

Light smiled at the news before saying to himself, "Oh, Watcher. Your friends never ceases to amaze. The people you gather always manages to escape my grasp."

She did not understand her Lord's connection to The Watcher, but it was not her place to question the man who had given her everything. But it was obvious that ever since The Watcher arrived, the Lord's behaviour had taken a drastic change, with more fits of laughter and mania than he was normally known for. His actions within the committee had also pushed more towards hostile resolutions with the dark elves and his meetings with the Overseers had increased.

"Nora," the man passed her a handful of hair. It was Nadier's hair that got shot off during the attack. "Leave the search of The Tower to the security. Get a group of tracking hounds and circle the city walls. If The Wanderer leaves, we will most definitely be able to follow his scent."

Chapter 15
The Walker

Dark clouds covered the sky till the horizon but not a single drop of rainwater touched the dry and desolate lands across his field of vision. The tower on the edge of the horizon was made of piles of junks and jutting metal struts that overlooked the plains, its spotlights sweeping across the landscape. Explosions rocked in from the west with plumes of smoke bellowing out from the sites of devastation.

The warrior sat on the edge of the dirt ledge, hands by his sides, legs swinging away on air. There was still a long walk ahead of them and the brief respite from the fighting and violence of the war was something he had much needed.

A voice from behind asked, "What are you doing?" He turned to see the young man his age, a blond haired, thin built, sharp faced teenager, who took a seat beside him.

"Hey, Luviet," he greeted, before turning back forward to face the tower in the distance. "Just enjoying a little quiet."

"Isn't that a little hard in a war zone?" Luviet asked, swinging his legs in tandem with his friend.

"I take what I can get. You should too. Stay awhile, relax. Who knows when we'll get the chance again."

They spoke at length. Even though the battleground was just a eyesight away, they were, for the moment, safe. The friends spoke of life before the war, and how they see life after. Seconds ticked into minutes and minutes into the hour.

From his coat, the warrior took out a pocket watch, the circular engraving on the titanium frame had been kept unscratched, even throughout all the battles.

Luviet asked, "What's that?"

"A gift. From my big brother. It's got my real name on it. I might never see him again."

"See who? Your brother? Or your real name?"

"Both, I guess."

Luviet slapped his friend across the back. "Well, you've got a brother, right here. And when you're ready, you can tell me your real name too." The pair looked out towards the tower as another explosion echoed from place unseen. "When this whole thing is over, you, me, and everyone, we're going to live happily ever after."

"Watcher?"

"Yeah?" He broke out of his daydream, head shaking.

"Is something wrong?"

"No."

He stood before the last flight of steps before the peak of the ridge. The Twins were setting over the horizon to their west with the double stars lighting the sky in a dizzying array of red and orange that contrailed to the far horizon. The Watcher looked out over the rope rails of the mountain path to the glowing Tower in the north.

"I'm just remembering better days." He turned back to face Kathleen, who had already made it halfway up the last flight.

She had changed into a pair of long brown pants and sleeveless shirt for the climb, long hair tied tight into a bun. "Well, we're almost at the top," she said, panting hard as she did so. "Let's be quick about this. I want to head back and rest my legs."

He quipped back, "You don't exercise much, do you?" He continued the walk up.

"What's that suppose to mean? I exercise plenty, I'll have you know."

"Taking a stroll around the house does not count as exercise."

"It's a really big house!"

They continued their banter on the way up. He had grown to like Kathleen's company. She was definitely a person of noble descent, as stereotypical in physical capabilities as nobles were. But she had a lust for adventure that he had not seen in a while. A want to not just see more, but to know more. She had plenty of knowledge from books she had read through her life and was not afraid expand on them and challenge their ideas. A drive for exploration that reminded him of his own youth.

As if to prove his point, she stopped mid-climb to pick up a blue, rose-like flower. "Prigmatia," she explained the plant. "They use these for blue dyes. I thought they'd be much nicer to touch though. It's a little sticky."

She continued to explain the floras of Tearha to him, always being a few steps ahead, as if to fight the notion of her cushioned heritage by challenging him in speed. He let her set the pace and she reached the peak before him. When she turned away from The Watcher to face the Valley of Titans, she stopped in her tracks and silence fell on her.

The Watcher raised a brow at her lack of motion and noise, asking, "What's wrong?" Worried, he jogged the last few steps up to her side. The moment the Valley of Titans came into his view, he braked to a stop and let out, "Oh Leana... I wish you could see this right now."

The valley extended and circled into a giant basin below with plains of dirt and sparse grass littering the dry landscape. But the creatures that swayed and stood within the basin were the focus of their attention. Four human-shaped Titans stood height-to-height with the peaks of the mountain ridges over a thousand meters in height and almost two hundred meters shoulder-to-shoulder. Giants that towered over them, theirs heads just a stone's throw away from the height at which they stood and the name of the valley rang true. These were not simply giants. They were Titans, in every sense of the word.

Kathleen let out, "Sentients..." Before losing breath again.

Rock personages, their bodies were made of grey marble that shimmered in the dimming light. With legs and arms as thick as buildings and bodies thrice that, The Watcher would have thought of them as nothing more than stone statues had their mouth-less, sharp octagonal heads, with a single dark glass sphere eye, not been turning at an excruciatingly slow pace to survey the surroundings. At each of their joints under the armour of stone seen through sparse gaps were gigantic titanium gears and a rigid metal frame that held the internal skeletal structure of the creatures. There was a single set of giant dirt footprint visible in the middle of the field of grass behind one of the Titans, suggesting it had moved a step forward some time in the past. The print had long since grown over with shorter grass, the one small step lasting weeks, maybe even months.

Kathleen pointed across him and exclaimed, "Look!"

He traced her finger's direction. The line of the ridge had been dirt trudged, sided by grass. The path to their left followed along the ridge until another set of steps cut it off. At the bottom of the steps, a stone hut was built into the side of the land, held horizontal by a wooden balcony and platform that overlooked the basin like tiny guardian watchtower that protected the enormous marvels.

He asked, "You think that's where the Titan Ranger lives?"

"Most likely," she replied. "I don't really see why anyone else would want to live up here."

"Well," he stated as he started their walk towards the building, never taking his eyes off the magnificent giants of the valley. "The view *is* terrific."

The walk was short and before they knew it, the wooden planks of the makeshift path was creaking beneath their feet as they stepped up to the door of the hut.

Kathleen said, "Maybe I should do the talking."

"What?" The Watcher exclaimed. "Why? Aren't I the leader?"

"Since when?" They crossed glares for a moment before she sighed in defeat. "Fine, but don't say anything weird or stupid." She knocked the door on his behalf.

A short moment of silence fell before them and he felt a chill ran down his spine as he thought of how the sentients that were the size of mountains behind them were not making a single noticeable sound. *How could such huge things make so little noise?* He thought, before laughing internally as he realised he had made an unintentional dick joke.

Then, a female voice called out from the opposite of the door. "Who's there?"

Kathleen shot him a stern glance. "Don't say anything stupid!" she reminded.

"Don't worry, I got this." He cleared his throat and, through the door, raised his voice slightly. "Hi! Have you heard about our lord and saviour, the Flying Spaghetti Monster?"

Immediately, his companion sent a hard slap to the nape of his neck. He stumbled a steps forward, only to find his foot caught in a gap between the planks. He reached out to stop the fall against the door, but, as if luck choreographed the world against him, it swung opened and he fell forward, grasping thin air. In the end he landed face first across the threshold.

"Ouch," he understated. "That really hurt my pride."

Kathleen said, "I don't think you have any left."

The female from the hut said, "And I don't know what a spaghetti is, but it sounds disgusting."

He defended, "Oh, you'll love it." Slowly, muscles tensed from age, he got to his feet. He stretched his back with a crack, ignoring the stinging pain on his bruised nose. "It's this little stringy noodle. A little slippery but you top it with sauce. It's fantastic. I'll make you some next time."

The young woman crossed her arms. She wore a plain, long-sleeved white buttoned shirt, mossy green leather pants, and brown leather boots. A crimson red scarf was wrapped around her neck and reached to her waist, dancing around her lean figure and gymnast body. Her long hair with shades of ash brown and gold was tied neatly in a ponytail. With opal eyes, freckled cheeks, sharp chin and scar-free skin, she had a face five years younger than the rest of her body.

She held a long barrelled rifle in her hand with what appeared to be a lance head attached to a grenade launcher. "What are you doing here?" she asked.

Kathleen stepped between the two to address her. "I'm sorry to bother you. My name's Kathleen Ambershey, and this is my companion, The Watcher. We're looking for a Titan Ranger who lives here." She extended her a hand.

The woman took the handshake. "Luce. Lucinda Baerrinska. But I'm afraid you're out of luck. There had never been Titan Rangers living on the ridge. Just me."

"Baerrinska?" Kathleen said, confused. "Isn't that the name of 'The Walker'?"

The Watcher asked, "Who's that?"

Kathleen explained, "She's the first person to ever cross the Leviathan's Helm from Katoki to Eltar. She also took the mantle of the leader of the Titan Rangers after helping to bring the organisation into the modern cycle."

"Former leader," Luce corrected. "I'm retired."

"Retired?" The Watcher exclaimed. "How? You don't look a day over thirty?"

Luce glared angrily back, fingers twitching towards the trigger of her rifle. "That's because I'm only twenty-three."

"Oh! Uh... that's um... great! And um..." He turned to Kathleen for help, only to see her with a hand over her mouth, suppressing her giggles. He cleared his throat loudly, "Anyway, I'm here on behalf of a resident of Valendra. There's a Titan buried underneath the forest there and she would like to have the site marked for protection."

"A buried Titan?" The look of annoyance on Luce's face disappeared almost entirely, replaced with a hint of curiosity. She closed her eyes in contemplation before nodding, "Very well. I will send a letter to the Rangers at The Yard. I will have them meet with the residence of Valent to discuss this."

"Wait a second–!" The Watcher stopped her. Adelaide had not said anything about having to meet with the citizens, and he doubt she wanted her life in the forest disturbed further by humans from the town. "There's a little situation here. Is there any other way to–"

A gunshot echoed through the valley and his eyes went white in shock. For a moment, he thought Luce might have shot at them, but the woman had the same look on her face as he did.

Kathleen jumped with a shout, screaming, "What in the Titans was that?"

The Watcher turned towards the valley and the wandering sentient. "It sounded like it came from the south."

"No," Luce corrected. "That was an echo. The shot came from the north. The town–!" She pushed past them and ran out of her house.

They followed her as she hurriedly climbed the steps up to the line of the ridge. The trio looked down towards the plains and, with smoke tails whisking behind, a lone rider galloped towards Ra'Kalen on horseback. Even from his far away perch, the dark figure was unmistakable.

The Watcher let out, "Nadier."

Behind the dark elf, a line of people followed from such a distance that they were no more than dots on a map. A small spark of light, bright in the final shadows of daylight, emitted from all but one of the figures.

Luce noted, "Muzzle flash."

A second after she said that, a volley of gunshot rang throughout the landscape, echoing into far behind and beyond the valley.

Kathleen's voice was almost a whisper of fear, "The Long Arm."

The figure of Nadier fell off his horse at the foot of the town.

Chapter 16
Bolted Arm

The earth felt wet and warm. His blood formed a small pool on the ground, mixing with the grass to give off a perverted variation of morning's dew. The twin stars had set and only the faint light of early evening illuminated the ground, turning the blood a deep brown. Nadier tried to reach for his dagger but a shot of pain ran through his right shoulder. He touched the point that burned and found the bullet hole in it. It did not feel like the ammunition went through and it was probably still stuck inside his body. Gritting his teeth, he pushed himself to stand on his one good arm. His back gave a loud and painful crack, but aside from a wince, the shock of bones setting itself back into position after the fall from his horse was bearable.

Nora rode in behind, getting off her steed once she was close. "It's funny isn't it?"

Gripping his shoulder, he turned to face her. The two dozen snipers from The Long Arm stood in line behind her atop the rolling hill, and he alone stood between the platoon of snipers, the lady assassin, and the town of Ra'Kalen behind.

To her question, he asked, "What is?"

"You." She walked towards him, her feet snaking around the front leg, setting themselves before each other in a perfectly straight, practised line. "You've never gotten yourself involved in large events before. That's why Akaras made Lord before you did. You never had a vision. Yet here you are, frantically searching for answers in what may be the greatest turning point in the history of the country."

"Well, my brother never died before."

"That is true." She stopped just within kicking distance of him. "I suppose something like that must bring perspective to life."

He warily eyed her deadly boots. When he was sure she had no intention of attacking at the moment, he looked her in the eyes and asked, "Why are you doing this? Why target me?"

"I don't understand what you mean," she replied with a genuine but playful smile. "If you're asking me why I'm hunting you down, it is simply because of orders. Why you, specifically, however? Well, don't flatter yourself. The Lord Light keeps a close tab on all the Epitaph holders in the world, even me. We are great assets, but most of us are also powerful and unpredictable."

Nadier took the moment of calm to remove his scarf. "You speak as if we are merely pieces on a board." With the cloth, he tied a makeshift bandage around his wound with a grunt.

Nora took a moment of thought to consider his statement before answering, "I suppose we are. But so long as our movements and actions does not obstruct the path Lord Light has deemed, I see no issues in being used." She turned to look back at the snipers, all of whom had their barrels trained on Nadier. She turned back to him and said with a sigh, "Truth be told, I don't wish to kill you. Despite your lack of combat strength, I know how terrifying a trained assassin like yourself can be to enemies. And I do hope that terror of yours could be on our side."

"You want me to join you? I don't even know what you're trying to do," Nadier admitted to his lack of information. "The dark elves want to attack Everwind. You're building a portal to another universe, and you're hunting The Watcher, Demon Eyes, and now me. None of that makes a lick of sense to me."

Like a salesperson, Nora merely grinned and answered, "Join us and you'll find out."

He could see no down side to the offer. If the dark elves were truly about to start a war with Everwind, allying himself on the side of The Forum would guarantee a chance to settle his vengeance against those who gave the orders that led Akaras to his death. It would also keep Nora and The Long Arm off his tail, and he would be in a better position to negotiate for Adelle's safety. He had no obligation to The Watcher either, and he would gain answers to all the questions he sought. There was only one logical response.

"No," he replied. "I sell my service, not my loyalty."

The heel of the boot raised to the level of his chin in a blink of an eye. Having expected the attack, Nadier jumped back, drawing a single dagger out in a reverse grip with his left hand. His wound throbbed as adrenaline pumped blood through his body. He brought his right hand up to put pressure on his injury while settling his weapon arm towards Nora.

Despite the situation, or because of it, Nora's smile twisted into that of excitement, though her temptress looks hid most of the malice. "Too bad," she said to him. "I still won't kill you... yet. I need as many hostages as I can to lure out The Watcher."

"Hah!" Nadier got into fighting position, left leg forward, right leg back. "Aren't you getting a bit too full of yourself? I'm not strong, but you're not great a fighter either."

"Oh, I think you're mistaken, Wanderer," she replied with a further sly grin. She pointed a finger gun at the base of his feet. "I'm not fighting you. They are." She pinched her thumb.

Almost immediately, a bullet clacked off the dirt at the base of his foot. Wide-eyed, Nadier stared at the bullet mark left on the ground before looking up to The Long Arm he had momentarily forgotten through his injury and adrenaline. Smoke rose from the barrel of a rifle from the far left, a far enough distance away that the shooter was just a line on the horizon. With that aim and him being stationary, they could have cleanly killed him off if they wanted to.

Nora asked, "So, what's it going to be?"

He shot her a dirty glare.

The Watcher, Kathleen, and Lucinda Baerrinska made it into town just after the complete cover of night had taken them.

Kathleen noted, "Why aren't there any lights on?"

Ra'Kalen was bathed in darkness, with only the faint flickers of missed candles and the lights of the stars to shine the way. To the north, away from the Valley of Titans, the light from The Tower of Everwind radiated like a beacon in the dark.

Luce explained, "It's harder to shoot in the dark. Someone must have realised that and got the townsfolk to snuff out as much light as they could."

The trio turned into the streets, careful to avoid the openings between the buildings that led into direct line of sight for the snipers.

"Luce," The Watcher started. "You've got a gun. Can't you just, I don't know, provide some covering fire?"

"They are too far out of range, even for me. I'm guessing they are using scopes and longer barrelled rifles."

They continued their journey, heading towards the centre of town. Kathleen said, "Where is everybody?"

Luce replied, "They've probably evacuated the town."

"Then we should leave too," Kathleen suggested. "I'll go to the inn to grab our bags."

The Watcher said, "Okay, but be careful. We'll meet up at the western side."

Kathleen gave a smiling thumbs up before separating from them. The Watcher felt his heart warmed a little at the sight of her gaining her independence, capable of acting in the face of the unknown was a far way away from the girl he first met on the highway. Even though it had only been a few days, she had really gotten into playing the role of an adventurer.

Once Kathleen was out of earshot, Luce asked, "What about you?"

"I need to find out what's going on, and what happened to Nadier. Either the town's mayor or that Grandmaster Enhancer should have the information I need."

"Wait!" she stopped him in his tracks with a halting wave. "Do you hear that?"

His raised his ears to the wind and the nightly music of crickets were the first noise he picked up. He was quite surprised that aside from horses, there were other types of faunas that their worlds shared. Then, he heard the soft grumble and chattering distinct to huddled refugees. It was a sound he was all too familiar with from a time long past.

Luce pointed, "Over there!" She began leading the way through another maze of alley.

He followed her through the winding town, her confidence in the road likely stemmed from having oversaw the town from her high perch. A right turn into a small alley. A left on the main streets. Past the open square of the town centre. Another right.

The pair stepped out into a football field-sized park. Hundreds of townsfolk huddled under blankets, trees, and around dimly lit candles. Adults sat nervously within families and groups while the older children gathered solemnly and the younger ones emitted quiet sobs. Individuals wearing poor fitting, cracking leather armour, and holding rusted spears sheepishly patrolled the area, no doubt the town militia, though the negligible numbers did not incite hope of a counter attack.

"Like I've told you, Mayor Geraldine, I cannot interfere in combat," came Miguel's voice.

The pair turned to see three figures walking towards them. In the middle was the Grandmaster Enhancer in a full navy blue cloak. To his left, still in her work clothes, Hidergard stood vigilant, a sabre sheathed at her side. Following behind them was a short and slightly round woman. She wore a plain brown dress that was just a step slicker than the dressing of the rest of the town. Her black hair was tied into a large bun. The Watcher immediately wondered if a potato could walk and talk, would it look like the woman before them.

The mayor continued her plea, "But Grandmaster, surely a man of your abilities would be able to save us from such an assault?"

With a tone of annoyance The Watcher had not heard from the learned man, Miguel replied, "It is not a question of my capabilities, Miss Mayor. I am here on behalf of the king. If I so much as flick a toothpick in the direction of Everwind and its soldiers, it can be taken as an act of aggression and be used as a signal for war. Without any probable cause, I cannot interfere in a country's internal strife." He turned back to focus on the road ahead and saw the pair. "Ah, Watcher, just who I was looking for."

The mayor turned to The Watcher and scrunched. "Watcher?" She stepped around Miguel and Hildergard, making a beeline for the time traveller. With a finger stabbing into his chest, she accused, "You! You're the reason this is happening! You troublemaker, turn yourself into the custody of The Forum immediately or I will summon the militia!"

"What?" The Watcher stepped away from the mad woman. He looked towards the approaching Enhancers. "What's going on here? And why hasn't the town been evacuated."

Miguel calmly walked to them, explaining, "They came for you. They want us to hand you over before midnight or they'll attack the town." He looked around at the scared townsfolk. "They are putting the town under siege and the female spy asked me to tell you they have The Wanderer as a hostage as well. I assume you know the elf?"

"He is my companion," The Watcher admitted. But something more serious weighed on his mind. "Why is everyone gathered this far in? If they are not attacking before midnight, shouldn't you try to evacuate everyone?"

Hildergard stepped forward, pushing the mayor unceremoniously out of the way. "Anyone who steps out of the perimeter of the town is shot. A farmer tried running for the field and he got a bullet through the knee for it."

Miguel continued, "There are not enough steeds either. If we did, riding out would be our best bet, since it seems they can't shoot riders as accurately. We could try to get everyone up the mountain but there–"

"Wait," The Watcher cut him off with a raised hand. To Hildergard, he asked, "Did you say the perimeter? How far out is that?"

She answered, "Any building within the outer streets is a danger zone. Why?"

Luce let out, "Oh no..." Her being the first to catch onto the implied trouble. "The inn is on the outskirts, isn't it?"

A volley of gunfire rang out through the night, echoing a second time off the ridge face of the mountain as if there was an entire army of riflemen firing instead of the few dozens. The group turned to the north, the bright Tower shining in the distance. But the light felt dim, dark, as if the world had frozen cold. The Watcher felt the familiar creeping touch of forebode and regret creeping up his spine.

He shouted, "Kathleen!"

Without another word, he dashed away from the park and towards the inn. The buildings of the town flashed by him and the footsteps of his companions pattered rapidly behind as they raced to catch up.

Luce shouted, "Left!"

He rocketed out of the alleyway and made a hard skidding turn left on the main streets. Luce continued shouting directions to him as they navigated the town. He remembered looking in from the plains and thinking the town was small. Now, it felt as if he was attempting the travel across the globe while riding a snail.

Dashing straight across the final stretch, he could see the outline of the inn in the distance. He could also see the body that laid in the middle of the streets.

"Kathleen!" he yelled for her.

She did not respond. Not a twitched. Not a groan. Just a lump of meat lying on the ground.

Chapter 17
Dragon of Revolution

What did I get myself into? Luce thought internally.

The Watcher stood stunned before them, the body of Kathleen unmoving on the streets. She noticed the man balling up his fists, arms shaking. Luce saw a muzzle flash in the distance. The Watcher raised his hand forward, palms opened. The gunshot reached their ears. The Watcher lowered his hand and reopened his palm. The lead bullet clunked to the ground.

Catching bullets. Great.

From her side, Miguel exclaimed, "Hilde!"

"Yes, Grandmaster." The female Enhancer rushed forward, sabre blade flashing out of its sheathe.

Hildergard stopped between the party and The Long Arm, stabbing her sabre straight into the ground. Her two hands glowed yellow, lines of magic circuits shining. She thrust her arms out together and arcs of electricity danced from the tips of her fingers towards the two ends of the coil. Another muzzle flash. Another ring of gunshot. From the sabres' copper hand-guard, an arc of lightning shot out to seemingly thin air. The lead round combusted upon contact with the electricity.

Lightning Coil magic. Wonderful. Luce was internally chiding. It seemed she had somehow gotten herself involved with a group of powerful, dangerous, and incredible people. She was starting to miss her hut.

Miguel said, "Lady Ranger." She turned to him. The man continued, "As powerful as my apprentice is, we do not have much time." He tilted his head in gesture to Kathleen.

She nodded back in understanding, "Right."

They rushed to The Watcher who knelt beside his fallen companion.

Miguel instructed, "Let's move her round the corner."

The trio worked quickly. Luce carried Kathleen by the legs while the men held under each arm. They shuffled their way back into town, turning the corner and gently laying Kathleen onto the ground beside the inn. Once behind the cover of the walls, Hildergard ran back to the group as two more shots rang out behind with bullets whizzing by.

Kathleen's body was riddled with half a dozen bullet wounds with one in the thigh. Blood drenched her shirt and their hands. Miguel set his hands over the two wounds that looked the most crucial, over her left lung and stomach. His circuits glowed, sending a pulse of blue light to his hands that resonated softly.

Miguel worriedly explained, "She's still alive. Barely. I'll try to stabilise her but I'm not great with healing magic."

The Watcher asked, "Will she make it?" His face creased into the most devastated frown Luce had ever seen. Guilt, sadness, anger, all mixed into a single pained expression.

Miguel did not look up to him, focusing his gaze on Kathleen instead. "If we don't get professional medical help soon, she might not make it."

Hildergard exclaimed, "The town's doctor should be in the park." Without another word, she took off without anyone's complain from the group.

"Luce," Miguel began. "I need you to take a perch in the inn and give us some covering fire with you rifle."

"I can't hit anything from this range," she explained, hugging her gun closer to her chest. Despite the firearm, she had never actually killed a person, and the only life she had ever took had already been on the verge of death.

"I don't need you to hit anything. I just need you to make sure they don't come near us." He finally looked up to The Watcher. "I believe someone is going to take care of them up front."

She looked to the traveller. The Watcher had his back turned to them, standing straight and tall. The man looked larger than she remembered, his presence seemingly tripling and emanating from him in spades.

Miguel said, "Watcher." The Watcher half-turned back. With his hand still bloodied, Miguel reached into his pocket and took out a small crystal. "It's ready. Just feel for the power and cast as you normally would."

The Watcher took the crystal and Luce watched as the man's eyes light up from feeling the extra energy for the first time. Her late fiancee, a terramancer, had the same expression when she first held a tuned crystal.

"Thank you," The Watcher mouthed.

"Don't thank me yet," Miguel replied. "The way I calculate it, that crystal only has about five percent of the power you're used to, so don't overdo it. Madness, I'm telling you. A tier seven crystal not even halving up to a body's circuits is unheard of," he ended in a rant.

Luce got to her feet and her eyes met The Watcher's. "I'll cover you," she said.

The Watcher nodded and turned to leave.

"Watcher..." A voiced croaked out. All three turned to the woman lying on the ground. Kathleen's eyes flickered open slightly, enough for her to look to the man she followed, her ember iris seemingly burning. "Don't... change. No... killing."

Her eyelids lowered shut again, her peace said.

The three left standing exchanged glances. Miguel then promised him, "I'll do my best."

The Watcher nodded one last time before he turned out the corner.

He could barely hear anything. Half his face was pressed against the ground and Nadier struggled to breathe under the lock of Nora's right boot, which was gripped around his neck. The only consolation he had was having his injured arm pinned under him, which slowed his bleeding considerably. He did not like having his hands and feet tied though, but the situation did not seem to be open to other possibilities.

To their south was the town of Ra'Kalen, while the Long Arm lined themselves neatly apart westward. The Long Arm wore bandoleers of ammunitions over leather vests and black shirts. Navy blue pants were held up by pouch filled belts, each containing a fair amount of reserve gunpowder. Some wore brown greatcoats over everything else. The group was Everwind's greatest military strength. Firearms and, more specifically, gunpowder, were rare in Eltar, and the Long Arm had the largest stock in the land. Though small, they were able to overwhelm most of their bows and swords wielding counterparts with sheer range and accuracy.

"This concoction of yours," Nora began, twirling a vial of his Neverite on her finger before his face, the rest of his vials and daggers unceremoniously thrown on the floor. "It's really amazing, negating seither and magic. Why do you only have one vial though?"

He coughed out, "It's not easy to make." He resisted the urge to add an insult.

"Pity it's not enough to coat our bullets in," she noted.

"Lady Nora!" one of the snipers shouted. "We've spotted The Watcher. Awaiting firing ord–!"

In less than the blink of an eye, the time mage appeared before them within talking distance, a crystal glowing purple in his right hand. "No need," The Watcher announced after his teleportation.

The snipers all turned to aim their rifles at him and he raised and opened his left hand to meet them. He had tried the same thing with Akaras Spaedruiner when they met. The result of freezing the dark elf in time had sent the late Lord flying to near fatal injuries. But that was when The Watcher had yet to orientate himself to the spin of the planet. It was different now. He could feel Tearha's rotation beneath his feet. He could see the stars in the sky and the slow movements they made across space. He could feel the planet hurtling through space at 86 miles per second. He was once again the God of Time.

"Fi–!" Silence fell.

With their rifles still pointed at him, the snipers froze. Not a breath nor a blink came from them. Every strand of their hair stood unmoving despite the night breeze. The platoon had been completely stopped within the confines of time itself.

He shot a glare at Nora, "I heard you were looking for me." He stretched out his right hand and bowed in a gesture of welcome, making sure to keep his left and power on the snipers. "Here I am."

Nora dug in her heels and dragged Nadier forward by the neck. He held onto the hook of her boots, choking as he was pushed and forcefully rolled to face up, his back scraping against the ground. She presented the dark elf as if he was a prized animal. He wondered how a woman as slender as Nora could have as much leg strength as that. Eyes to the night sky, coughing, he could now see the situation around him. The female assassin kept a playful smile on her face, not at all unnerved by The Watcher's display of power.

"It's good to see you again, Watcher," she greeted with a toothy grin.

"Have we met before?"

"No, I suppose you wouldn't know who I am." She bowed him a curtsy, digging in her heels and pushing Nadier's neck down further. "I am Lady Nora Phemtelle. Master assassin and spy of Everwind. Right hand of Lord Light."

"Do you help him masturbate?" he snarked back.

"Sometimes," she replied matter-of-factly. "If he asks for it, of course."

Nadier coughed, "Highlight of your life, I bet." She pivoted her heels, catching his jaw with the toe of her boots. With a slight manipulative turn, she pushed his neck out and pulled his head inward into an odd angle, causing him to groan in pain.

Still with her cheery smile, she commented, "Quiet you. Mommy's talking with daddy."

"Daddy's not really that interested though," Watcher replied. "But tell me, Lady Nora, what would it take for you to release Nadier and lift the siege off the town?"

"You let me kill you and I'll lift the siege."

The Watcher let out a derisive laugh. "I'm sorry, but you're far too weak to kill me. I'm not saying you can't try, but if you did, my body would just repair itself again. You don't have the firepower to do the deed. There's no bullet in your gun. No water in the straw. No gas in the tank. No–"

Nora stopped his rambling with a raised hand. "I-I get it. You can stop now. Are you always this annoying?" She crossed her arms in contemplation. "Well, I guess you could always come with me to Everwind and have Lord Light kill you there," she spoke of the act of murder as casually as one would ask for the time.

"And Nadier?"

"He dies here," she said again with the same creeping calm and smile. "I have orders for his life too."

"No deal," The Watcher replied. "Everyone lives, and I die. That's the only way out of this."

"That's not a deal I can take either. I guess the only way out is for you to kill me, then." Her smile grew wider and impossibly more innocent looking despite the sinister undertone. "Should be easy for you, since you'll hate me after knowing I ordered them to shoot that girl you tried to save."

The Watcher raised his right hand at her to do the deed. The glow of the crystal dimmed, and a bullet slammed into his shoulder. A second hit his chest. The third and forth made contact with his head. But each ammunition plopped to the grassy earth soundlessly, the impact absorbed by the natural magic shield of a mage. Nadier could see the look of surprise on the snipers' face. One of them had his eyes and brows scrunched, assessing the situation. She turned her gun to Nadier.

Switching targets, The Watcher returned focus to the snipers and once again, froze them in place before a shot could be fired at the dark elf.

"Hahahaha!" Nora laughed, clapping at the spectacle. "Impressive try. Though I'm guessing this is your first time using a magic crystal?" she asked The Watcher.

He dared not take his eyes or concentration off the snipers again. "What's happening?"

"Magic crystals have limits. Seems like yours only have enough power to create a single time bubble."

Nadier was sure that even without his darkvision, he would be able to see the whites of The Watcher's eyes widen in surprise.

The Watcher asked, "How did you know how my power works?"

"The Lord Light told me. He even told me not to be afraid of your threats of killing, as you've got a strict 'no killing' policy, do you not?" She took a step forward with her left leg, her right eating into the nape of Nadier's neck, causing him another grunt in pain.

In a tone of seriousness Nadier had thought impossible for a man as easy going as The Watcher, the time traveller growled, "Who is Lord Light?"

"He's the hero of the world," Nora replied. She spoke softly of that belief, as if asked about a crush. Returning to the situation, she explained, "You don't have much of a choice now. You either kill me, and the snipers kill Nadier, or hold on to the snipers while I kill Nadier. Or, better yet, you follow your rule and don't kill anyone. Keep your hands clean and surrender yourself to your execution. Of course, Nadier will still die, but the casualty would be much lower, would it not?"

Nadier could see the pained expression on The Watcher's face. The man must have had all the solutions to the world before that moment. Over a thousand years of living is twice more than the average elf. All those cycles spent and all the knowledge and powers gathered to not be able to do anything in the time needed most of him must be devastating.

"Just as Lord Light said," Nora continued, her tone a sickened glee. "You are a coward, Watcher. No. Pausa of the Alvet. The one who ran. The man who have no blood on his hands for fear of killing, but still manages to be the bloodiest of us all. If only you had the guts to end a life."

"Don't worry." They turned to the sound of the voice which was also the source of a cloud of rust brown smoke. Behind Nora, the green haired elven girl stood, her clothes still bearing the two charred holes that Light had shot at, underneath which were blood stained bandages. A bow in her hand with arrow notched, the weapon fully drawn and aimed at Nora's head, she declared, "I have plenty of guts to spare."

"Adelle!" Nadier exclaimed, unable to keep in his joy at seeing her alive.

Nora however, was less thrilled, "Demon Eyes..." she said, sounding defeated. "That's not fair."

Adelaide smiled, "I know."

The arrow blasted through Lady Fatal.

Chapter 18
Braveheart

Adelaide strolled through the snow covered forest, her great-white fur coat blending her into the surroundings. From the corner of her eyes, she could see animals scampering in and out of the edges of her range of vision. Glistening icicles hung off the coniferous trees while the cold dried branches of others held out like extended hands in greeting. The snow covered forest was her sanctuary. The cool winter wind that carried the smell of frozen snow hung on wood. The crunch of the rare threaded dirt beneath.

"Yes!" a man yelled from a far corner of the empty woods. "I've got one!"

Her ears picked up the direction of the noise and she turned to face the distance. From her waist, she pulled out her axes and disappeared in a puff of brown smoke.

"Please, Roget, let's get out of here before the Demon shows up!" a second voice, younger and more high pitched, sounded off.

Adelaide reappeared near them behind a tree and slowly lowered herself to a prone.

"Please, Kiril, there's no such thing as a Demon of Valendra Forest." The first man, Roget, told off his companion while holding up the arrow-pierced carcass of a wintersnow hare. "It's just a myth."

"If it's just the myth, why aren't there more hunters in Valent? Even more so since the forest is so near?"

Adelaide jumped out of her hiding place and rushed at Roget. The man turned immediately to the movement but she could see his eyes struggling to make out the form of her camouflage coat against the backdrop of snow. It was obvious the man had no training in battle for he struggled with panic while attempting to load his bow. Her right axe raised and with a flick of her arm, she sent her weapon spinning through the air. With a crunch, the weapon embedded itself between

Roget's eyes. With her offhand axe, she leapt and slammed the weapon into the man's skull for added assurance.

Slowly, she steadied her breaths before turning to look at the second man, Kiril.

Kiril stood, water forming on his pants. "I-I-I-I...!" he stammered incoherently.

"Go," Adelaide said to him. "And don't come back."

The man turned tail and ran, tracing their footsteps out.

With a bone cracking snap, she pulled her weapons out of the body and stood to height, blood dripping from her blades and pooling around the skull onto the white bed of snow. The carcass of the wintersnow hare at their side.

A deafening silence rang through the forest until she had calmed herself enough to regain composure. Birds tweeted and the nearby stream splashed and ran. The forest was her sanctuary.

"You know what?" The Watcher voiced out.

Adelaide was rung from her semi-consciousness from that sentence. Finding herself carried on the back of The Watcher, she felt a sense of embarrassment and defeatism, but was too tired to admit it. Even with the rudimentary bandaging and her fatigue from having been teleporting halfway across the continent in less than a day weighed on, her wounds from Light's onslaught still burned. If the human so much as made one of his wise cracking comments, she was going to shoot him.

The Watcher continued, "If she had not toyed around with me so much, that Nora chick would probably have won."

She was surprised to find that she had somewhat missed the man's strange line of thoughts. "It's quite common," she began explaining. "Even in stories, the villains often revels in the foreplay."

"Great," he replied. "I thought only bad guys in my world were that stupid."

As they neared the light of the town, figures of four jogged out to them. She instinctively tried to reach for her axe, but a shock of pain ran through her.

"Don't move too much, Miss Hero of the Hour," The Watcher told her in a contrastingly mocking and caring tone. "Still can't believe you made it all the way here with that injury."

The group of four reached them and The Watcher made a quick introduction.

With hair of summer fields, the woman named Luce asked, "Where are the enemies?"

The Watcher explained, "One's dead. The others are out at the field. A dark elf is watching over them."

The hume Grandmaster Enchanter nodded to his apprentice, "You go help the elf. I'll go get the militia."

Hildergard gave a quick bow before running off towards the hill. Miguel gave The Watcher a thumbs up as he turned back into Ra'Kalen.

The forth member of the party was a wood elf. His hair was a shining blond, with the generic sharp face and monocled green iris of his kind, though given a slightly sharper chin and longer forehead that made him seem to be constantly looking down at the people around him from a height. He wore a white overcoat and sleek black breeches capped by a pair of black leather boots.

Approaching The Watcher, the wood elf introduced, "Doctor Greene Parker."

The Watcher quickly said, "She's injured." He gestured with a flick of his head to Adelaide on her back.

Greene quickly nodded and motioned for Luce to help bring the elf to the ground. The human woman took over an arm from The Watcher and the man slowly lowered Adelaide to allow her to stand.

Adelaide, recognising the trademark rifle slung on Luce's back, asked, "You're the Titan Ranger?"

"Yes," Luce replied, shifting under the weight. Greene moved under the other arm and with slow steps, the four-legged group of three began walking forward. "Is something the matter?"

From behind them, The Watcher gave a quick, "I'll go help Hilde." His footsteps then pattered away.

To Luce, Adelaide said, "I expected an elf, or at least a hume. Never expected humans to care much about preserving nature."

"Yeah, well, I never expected a wood elf to be so unimposing," Luce snidely replied.

Adelaide wondered if she was losing her touch. First The Watcher, now Luce. Humans used to fear the knowledge of The Demon of Valendra. Internally, she begrudgingly acknowledged the power and experience of The Watcher and wondered if this Luce also had a history of the extraordinary.

They moved to Greene's clinic, which was to their luck, just around the corner. Passing through the reception, they made their way to the small ward. Like the rest of the town, the building exterior were copper lined wood, but the interiors were made of soft white painted bricks. There were only three beds in the room, with one occupied by a breasted body that laid underneath a clean white blanket. Only the blonde hair stuck out from the side and the height told Adelaide she was not human. Luce and Greene made a passing glance over to the other patient before setting Adelaide down on the empty bed beside her. Between each beds were a bedside table with a bowl of water, a set of medical tools, glass bottles of chemicals, and a cloth. Next to those was a child-sized cast iron canister sided by copper pipes that fed into the walls. A sleek copper pump capped the contraption with a leather oxygen mask on top and a tube connecting them.

Adelaide asked of the machine, "What is this?"

He said with an elitist tone, "Oxygen pumps." His words permeated the feeling as if not knowing the machine somehow made Adelaide less of a person. "You don't need it since you're still conscious and breathing on your own." Greene lifted up her tunic and started unwrapping the crude bandage.

She gave a pained grimace. "What about her?" she noted her fellow patient.

He quietly washed his hands within the bowl of water, drying them off with the cloth. Sombrely, he replied, "She doesn't need it either."

She heard Luce swallow hard. The Titan Ranger excused herself. "I'll see if the others are back yet." She then left the room.

Greene continued cleaning Adelaide's wound and once Luce was out of earshot, he said nonchalantly, "She's dead."

He popped opened one of the bottles of clear liquid and unceremoniously poured it onto the wound. Her back taut as the alcohol seeped in, her teeth gritting in pain. She could feel the liquid and blood pouring out through the back of the through-and-through, soaking into the bed. The cool of the chemical overwhelmed by the burning hurt. The doctor started the same procedure on the second hole, causing the same amount of pain and discomfort with the same amount of bedside manners a butcher treats a piece of meat. Once cleaned, he started wrapping a new set of bandage around her body, neater and tighter than the haphazard job she had done for herself. The process was fast and carried out with the skilled hands only time could train.

"Us elves have higher rate of healing, and the attack was clean and missed all vitals" he noted as he tightened the knot. "The wounds should close fully by the season's quarter. Just keep the bandage tight to keep the wounds closed."

She laid in the bed, heart beating fast from the pain of the heartless treatment. Once she had settled, the aches of her muscles displeased her more than the hole in her body. At that moment, she was happy to be born an elf, and not a weak bodied human.

As the doctor began packing up the used instruments, Adelaide asked, "Did you treat her?"

Without turning, the doctor replied, "Who?"

"The human woman."

The doctor ceased all activities. With an unreadable tone, he told her, "Of course I did."

"Why? Don't you know what they do to us elves? Sell us as slaves. Placing us in the Antipods."

"I think the same could be said about you, Demon Eyes."

She stopped talking. Trying to sit up, her wounds tightened and forced her to lay back down with a groan. "How... did you know who I am?"

"You're a wanted criminal with an Epitaph," Greene said. "Not a lot of people, human or elves, can have a status as unique as that. And your eyes, red and green, are a complete giveaway."

She found her teeth gritted, "What are you going to do now?"

"Nothing. I'll treat you, let you heal, and let you go. One last favour for Miguel and I'm officially squared with him." Greene finished packing all the blood soaked tools within the bowl of water. He picked up the bowl and headed for the exit but stopped short of the door. "An advice for you, 'Demon Eyes' Adelaide. The things the humans do to us, the things we do to them, and the things we do to ourselves, are all equally horrible. But it doesn't matter. Be it humans, hume, elves, or animals, at the end of the day, when we cut deep enough, when we bleed long enough, when we age old enough, we're all the same kind of dead."

The doctor closed the door behind him noiselessly. Adelaide looked to the woman beside her, peaceful in death. She thought back to the winter with Roget and Kiril, and wondered if the dead wintersnow hare had the same sleeping look in death.

Chapter 19
One Two Last

"Don't let it be said I never did anything nice for you," Akaras reprimanded, the light of the campfire flickering shadowy contours off his face as he held out the stick of fish to roast.

The sea breeze drove into the beach, the fire danced fiercely before slowly diminishing with the wind. A single crab shimmied across the shore as the sky and ocean were filled with stars and galaxies respectively. Endless horizon of water stretched the east, merging seamlessly with the edge of space.

"I don't understand," Nadier stated, looking confused at the flames. "What is the point of this 'camping'? Why do we need the fire? We dark elves don't feel much cold and we can see in the dark."

"It's a human thing," his brother replied. "You sit around in a group and just have a conversation. I understand that it allows people to bond?"

"Was that last sentence a question or a statement?" Nadier sighed in difference. "And it's not much of a group when there's only two of us."

"Aelan dae, Nads. You kill the pleasure out of everything. You need to be less cynical and more excepting of cultures and ideas. "

Nadier sat quietly in contemplation of the situation before blurting out, "Karas, your fish is getting burnt."

Akaras exclaimed, "What?" he pulled the fish back, the tail having completely caught fire. "Hot! Hot! Hot!" He waved the burning stick around, frantically attempting to put out the flames on his dinner.

Unknowingly, Nadier smiled.

The candle lamp that dangled from the ceiling of the room flickered like the flames from the beach long ago. The white painted brick walls blindingly reflected the light. The first point of detail he strangely noticed was a ventilation shaft in the corner of the room, a visible fan spinning within the grates. An insect crawled out for a brief respite before ducking back into the metal tunnel.

A familiar voice called out, "Nads, you awake?"

He pushed himself to sit and looked down over his feet. Across the room, Adelaide's green hair peeked out from above the foot board of her bed.

He replied, "I am now."

Almost immediately, Adelle accused, "What have you gotten me into, Wanderer?"

He pushed himself further up, careful not to lean into his injured shoulder which had been bandaged by the doctor. His bare skin was revealed as his cumbersome coat and shirt hung over a chair to his right. His daggers and belt were laid over everything else. His fingers traced a large scar across his stomach and another old wound on his left forearm. He noted how he was not as muscular as most fighters, being more lean than buffed, but mentally corrected himself that he was not a warrior, but an assassin.

With a glance to his weapons, he replied, "I wish I knew."

"Hmph," he heard the girl let out. "You're always killing the mood. 'Don't know' this, 'don't know' that. Is there anything you do know?"

He partly ignored her and scanned the room. A third bed was beside Adelle and he tilted his head to get a better view. When he saw the face of the girl, he let out a soft sigh. "Ambershey."

Adelle sat fully up and the two crossed stares. "You know this girl?" she asked.

"Yeah. A little. The Watcher and I saved her from a bandit attack a few days back after we left the forest."

"You're not the hero type."

"I'm not the villain type either."

The pair remained in silence, never breaking gaze. The soft spin of the steam-powered fan and the humming and creaks that occasionally broke the confines of the steam pipes were the only noise that staved off the muteness.He did not know what Adelle was thinking, but he himself was letting his mind wander between plans for the immediate future and the distant one. Most involved killing one person or another. After a long moment, the door to the ward opened, breaking his thoughts. Miguel stepped in first and was followed by Luce and The Watcher.

The Watcher immediately started, "Hilde is out calming down the mayor." The two patients blinked blankly back at the unfamiliar name. The Watcher quickly backtracked, "Right, Hilde's this guy's apprentice." He thumbed to Miguel.

Adelle asked, "And who exactly is 'this guy'?"

The Watcher replied, "Miguel Vuvuzela."

"Valertes," Miguel quickly correct."

"Right, Miguel Valertes, Grandmaster Enhancer-pants of the Kingdom of Alley-oop or something."

"Grandmaster Enhancer of the Kingdom of Aleynonlia," Miguel punctuated. "Are you trying to get me to kill you?"

Adelle added, "He died once, apparently. Did not last very long."

Miguel massaged the nape of his neck. "You people... I'm starting to miss the idiots on my side of the world."

"There are idiots like us on Ciara?" Adelle replied with a cheeky grin.

Simultaneously, The Watcher and Miguel replied, "There are always idiots like us."

The room grew silent again, with everyone exchanging varying stares of confusion, annoyance, and bemusement.

It had been a while since Nadier saw a natural smile from Adelle or the playful side of her personality. Something felt different about the female elf. She was more friendly with this odd group as she would usually be more cautious around humans. Even if Miguel was a hume, she did not often interact openly with the half-bloods.

Luce quickly cleared her throat and entered the fray. "All jokes aside, we need to decide on our next course of action as soon as possible. The Lord Light will make a move once he's found out his right hand has been severed. We have a day, two at most."

"We?" Adelle asked.

"Yes. The Watcher told me of you and the predicament of your forest. I am intrigued by this Titan of yours, but we will need to head to Valent to discuss this further." She crossed her arms, a seriousness drawn into her eyes. "I will send words to the other Titan Rangers, but given what's happening now, I will personally see you to Valent as well."

Adelle shifted uneasily in her bed and Nadier knew the reason. She was still a wanted criminal and did not particularly get along with the humans at Valent, given she had killed almost all the hunters that had stepped into the forest. But the prospect of finally being able to stop the trespassers coming into her home must have been too tempting to overlook.

"In any case," Miguel continued, "I have a plan for our escape."

Nadier asked, "You're coming too?"

"Yes." He immediately followed with his explanation. "My stakes lies within the knowledge that how this event turns out will affect the world." The Grandmaster Enhancer looked to The Watcher. "Especially you, time traveller."

The Watcher placed his hands behind his head and leaned into them, grinning, "I'm important."

The room let out a collective groan.

The dark elf directed the conversation back on track, "And what is this plan of yours."

"We'll leave separately come the next twilight. Those of us who aren't injured will head up to the Valley of Titans and follow the ridge. Adelaide and Nadier will hide here in the clinic for the moment until they are somewhat healed, and they will leave by the main road later." Miguel started rubbing his chin. "I doubt the mayor's happy about having us here, but Hilde should be able to buy her silence for a while. She's half the town's income, after all."

The Watcher noted, "That's a good plan. I think we'll go with that. Split up and make it harder to be chased. And if the first group of us make some noise while we leave, they'll likely ignore Nads and Adelle."

Adelle piped, "Since when did you start calling us Nads and Adelle?"

"Can't I? It's quite catchy. Like a pop group. Nads and Adelle~! Adelle and Nads~!" His body swayed as he sang. As the tolerance of the room dropped, he quickly stopped and wore an expression of gravity. "Fine. Serious time then. I have a request. Since we now have the foundations of a plan, can all those not injured leave the room? We'll continue the rest of the conversation later. I have some personal words I'd like to say to the patients."

Luce and Miguel exchanged quick glances before nodding and taking their exit from the ward. Luce in particular threw a quick glare towards Adelle while Miguel mumbled about everyone being a pain in his ass. Once the door closed behind them, The Watcher took his strides across the floor.

"So?" Adelle chimed. "What is it you want to talk about? If it's about our deal, we've got geared-nothing for you since Light shot both of us."

But the dark elf caught on quickly. The eyes of the man who just a moment ago was playing the court jester had sunk, the smile gone completely from his face. "We're not the ones he wants to talk to," he explained to Adelle.

The human crossed the threshold of their beds and turned into the nook of Adelle's side. He faced the bed where the body of Kathleen lay. He stood quietly, his coat slowing down its sway. Softly, he said, "I'm sorry. I promised you all of time and couldn't deliver. I should have saved you somehow."

Adelle let out a soft sound of surprise, "Watcher..."

The Watcher continued, "I should have known not to take on a companion. It's my fault. After a thousand years and I've still yet to learn my lesson. I should always travel alone."

Nadier could relate. The lives they lived were not only dangerous, but also unpredictable. The friends they made were strong, but not entirely by choice. It was necessity. Had Adelaide or his brother not shown themselves capable of surviving alone, Nadier would not have gotten as close to them as he did. People in their world looked for those who can look out for themselves so they would not have to.

The Watcher turned to the two elves. "But no time to mourn. People in our positions don't get that luxury." Nadier could see the man's fist clenching tightly, shaking with emotions. "The deal between us, it's off."

Adelle exclaimed, "What? Why?"

"Because I want to know everything. All this now is getting personal. Who is this Lord Light? What are the Overseers and why are we hunted? How do magnets work? Everything!" His face lit up as he shook away his moodiness. With a spring, he danced light-footed across the room, taking the a place in the chair at Nadier's bedside. Twirling on a foot of the seat, he spun around until he could see both of them in one field of vision. "It's time we do things people like us do best."

Nadier asked, "And what is that?"

The Watcher smiled. "Be meddling kids."

Chapter 20
Hero of Monsters

"Don't let it be said I never did anything nice for you," Akaras reprimanded, the light of the campfire flickering shadowy contours off his face as he held out the stick of fish to roast.

The sea breeze drove into the beach and the fire danced fiercely before slowly diminishing with the wind. A single crab shimmied across the shore as the sky and ocean were filled with stars and galaxies respectively. Endless horizon of water stretched the east, merging seamlessly with the edge of space.

"I don't understand," Nadier stated, looking confused at the flames. "What is the point of this 'camping'? Why do we need the fire? We dark elves don't feel cold as much and we can see in the dark."

"It's a human thing," his brother replied. "You sit around in a group and just have a conversation. I understand that it allows people to bond?"

"Was that last sentence a question or a statement?" Nadier sighed in difference. "And it's not much of a group when there's only two of us."

"*Aelan dae*, Nads. You kill the pleasure out of everything. You need to be less cynical and more excepting of cultures and ideas. "

Nadier sat quietly in contemplation of the situation before blurting out, "'Karas, your fish is getting burnt."

Akaras exclaimed, "What?" he pulled the fish back, the tail having completely caught fire. "Hot! Hot! Hot!" He waved the burning stick around, frantically attempting to put out the flames on his dinner.

Unknowingly, Nadier smiled.

The female Titan Ranger stood at the edge of the town, watching the blimps and birds float through the sky against Everwind in the distance. Without the dry air for which cooled her on the ridges, she sifted in the heat of noon, though skin dried by the cold winter air.

From behind her, a voice said, "It's not like you to get involved." Luce turned to see Hilde walking up to her. "You always stay up in that hut of yours. Retirement, you called it."

Luce replied, "I know. But there's something that has caught my attention."

"You? Miss Lucinda 'I fight Titans for a living' Baerrinska have her attention caught?" Hilde walked up to the side of her friend.

Luce ignored her, continuing to stare out at the plains before them. After a moment, she said, "Last night, while I was providing covering fire for The Watcher, that elf girl appeared behind them."

"Adelaide?"

"Yes," Luce confirmed. "She did not sneak up on them. She just appeared. One moment that spot was empty, and the next, there she was, in a cloud of brown. As if she teleported. And there's her hair and eyes. I don't think those are rare genetic traits."

Hilde, catching on to the conversation, let out a surprised, "You don't mean..."

"I think Demon Eyes is a sentinel," Luce concluded.

"If she is..."

Luce finished, "She is the last of her kind and one of the most powerful person on the planet."

As Miguel applied the finishing touches to the item, he wondered how he should compensate his apprentice for letting him use her workshop. He shook the idea out of his head for later before raising up the pocket watch for a final quick inspection by the light. The crystal embedded in the back of the case flickered.

He turned to The Watcher who sat waiting patiently on a chair in the corner of the room. Miguel asked, "And this Stella girl is in Muscoh?"

The Watcher replied, "According to Adelle, yes."

"That's all the way to the eastern coast." Miguel passed the man back his pocket watch.

"Which is why I'm getting all this done. I'll be leaving tonight, before all of you." He held up the watch to examine it. The crystal was perfectly fitted into the casing, as if it had always been so. "Looks good. But does this actually work?"

Miguel puffed his chest as the aesthetic was complimented. "The crystal's energy is now part of the watch. As long as you're holding the watch, it'll be connected to your circuits."

"Was this really necessary though? I really liked this watch."

"Which is why I suggested it," Miguel explained. "It's best to embed the crystal to an object that you keep close to you. The crystal itself is small, and you'd be surprised how often people misplace them."

The Watcher nodded in understanding before pocketing the watch. "Thanks for your help."

Miguel nodded back. Then, the question popped into his head. "The engravings on your watch, is that your real name?"

The Watcher's eyes widened. "How did you know?"

"I could read it."

The Watched chuckled nervously, "That's, hah... not possible... hah! It's a language I made up–"

"In Gaia," Miguel cut in. "But on Earth, it's a fictional language for a television series."

"And you can read it?"

"I was bored one night."

"So you're saying I should be worried about nerds from another universe?"

"No, I'm saying you should worry about geeks," Miguel jibbed. "But also, not to show your watch around too much. We don't know if there is a variation of the language on Tearha. There are variations of Mandarin, Latin, and countless other languages from Earth here on Tearha embedded in both modern and ancient tongues. Be careful."

"Right... speaking of multiple worlds," the Watcher began. Miguel could sense a long topic coming up so he leaned against the nearest workbench for support. The Watcher continued, "When I told you about portals before, you didn't know anything about it. But your tone sounded as if you knew *something*."

"Rifts. We call the phenomenon Rifts." The Enhancer began his explanation almost immediately. "These are many forms of gateways between different universes or dimensions. There are only two types we know of. A tear is a naturally occurring cut in a dimension. A gate is where we magically stabilise an opening by poking at the weak points between universes. After the Second Exceed War, the entire continent of Ciara became sensitive to these Rifts. But there have never been Rift activities here on Eltar."

The Watcher chimed in, "That doesn't sound normal." The man's face was lighted up with curiosity and attention.

Miguel continued, "No. It's not. And neither was your description of your 'portals', which is why I am interested in what's happening right now."

"From one genius to another slightly less intelligent genius..." The Watcher pointed first to himself then to Miguel, to the latter's annoyance. "What would be your educated guess on the nature of these portals?"

Skipping the offhanded insult, he replied, "A gate is a stabilised pathway between two universes, like a tunnel with a door. And a rift is a small cut within the edge of our dimension that doesn't reach all the way through. From what you say though, it sounds like these portals are more akin to someone punching a hole through universes using brute force, with energy leaking out like a drain."

The Watcher nodded again as if he was a child being taught an interesting fact in class. He got up and gave a small bow in thanks before heading for the door. It seemed he have all the information he needed. He stopped just short of reaching for the handle before turning to ask, "How much of my name do you know?"

"Just your first."

"Shorten it."

"Dan."

"Shit. That's no good."

Miguel asked, "How many people outside your time stream knows your real full name?"

"Three. And they're all dead."

"Well, let's not make me the fourth one."

Though his hand was on the handle of the door, The Watcher was not yet ready to leave. Something still tugged at his mind. Deciding to continue through the conversation, The Watcher stated, "There's something else that's been bordering me."

"Speak."

He turned back to the Enhancer. "Nadier took slightly more than a full day to ride here from Everwind on a horse, am I correct?" The Watcher asked, to which Miguel nodded to the details. "Say the horse was full tilt sprint the whole way, that meant the distance between Everwind and here is about a thousand kilometers."

"That's about right. Why?"

"When I jumped from The Tower of Everwind, I could have sworn the height was no more than two hundred meters."

"Again, about correct. But what is your point?"

The Watcher asked, "Are you good with mathematics?" To which Miguel nodded affirmatively. The Watcher continued, "When I was at the ridge of the Valley of Titans, I could barely see past the plains. Tell me, given the curvature of the planet, how is it possible we are able to see Everwind at the horizon?"

The Enhancer did a quick, rough mental calculations, fingers dancing as he counted through the formula for viewable distance by height. His eyes slowly grew wider as The Watcher looked on as the hume made a second round of calculations to confirm the theory.

Miguel confirmed, "We should not even be able to see past a quarter of the way to Everwind." The Enhancer looked worryingly to the time traveller. "You're saying Lord Light have the powers to–"

"No. I am saying he *is* bending the light waves of the entire continent so that he could watch over the entire country in one fell sweep." The Watcher's mind churned, the gears of logic piecing themselves together. "It's a very slight change over a long distance. It's not something you would notice if it was done slowly across many, many decades. Maybe even centuries. And unless you're someone specifically looking for such a thing, it's not likely you'll notice it."

"You were looking for it?"

"No. But I'm not just 'someone' either."

"If he has the power to do such a thing, why hasn't he come after us? It should be easy to kill most of us without a fight."

The Watcher finally opened the door. Before stepping out, he glanced gravely back to Miguel. "I think he's doing this for his ego. And an egotistical man with power terrifies me."

"My Lord Light!" the messenger greeted as she stepped onto the balcony of the tower.

The Twins had set and darkness once again took the land. Yet, despite the shadow that had engulfed their half of the world, Light almost glowed with holy brightness. His land stretched out before him. From the port cities of the west to the mines in the east. The glow from each town and municipality dotted North Eltar. The ridge of the Valley of Titans cutting off the unsavoury sight of the undeveloped south.

He turned to the messenger. "What is it?"

"We have received reports that Lady Nora has been killed in her mission, my Lord." The messenger had his right foot in a slight bent step forward as he meekly bowed, head staring to the ground, never meeting Light's gaze. "The Wanderer and his companions are still at large. What are your orders?"

"Leave them. There's been words that the dark elves are making their moves. The heads of those three are no longer required for bargaining now that it has come to this stage," he replied sternly, returning his gaze back to the lay of the land. Unknowingly, a toothy grin spread across his face. "But I want to watch their movements a little longer. They may be of more use to me on the ground."

"Understood, Lord Light." The messenger furthered his bow before turning away and walking back into the tower.

Alone again, Light spoke aloud. "Oh, my dear Danny-boy, what would you do now? A war is brewing. Can you still stand at the sidelines and watch as innocents dies?" Unable to hold back his joy any longer, he let out a short laughter and started humming, *"Who are these monsters knocking at our doors? Whose claws are sharp and teeth bared raw. Draw your swords and take the floor. Blood splatters windward from all to all. I will knock at the wood that is course."*

...For I am the monster at your door...

Chapter 21
The Broken

"Hello, Mister Galloway!" chimed a happy, feminine voice.

The old librarian looked up from his reception computer. Before him stood a fourteen year old girl with long, strawberry blonde hair wearing a loose fitting yellow sundress for the hot summer weather outside.

"Stella Barber! Nice to see you again!" the old man exclaimed excitedly. He had not had much visitors in the library ever since smartphones were popularised. To the girl's side was a gloomy redhead in a white shirt and black jeans ensemble. "And the elusive Timothy Kleve! What a treat!"

From behind the girl, a third teen stepped out. With hair of snow white and skin of dark, he wore a cooling white singlet and pair of shorts.

Galloway clapped his hands together in surprise. "And Clay Barber! Wow! Everyone is here. Such a rare honour."

Clay smiled and waved sheepishly. "Hello, Mister Galloway. We've got summer homework."

"Oh, and what kind of fascinating homework would bring you to a library?" the man replied with a sarcastic joke of a tone.

Seemingly having not picked up the tune, Stella happily answered, "We were asked to write a short story about an alternate universe for English Literature Class. Do you have any nice fantasy books we can take as reference?"

Galloway chuckled back. Turning to his computer, he quickly searched through the database of books. "You three are really taking this seriously."

Simultaneously, Tim and Clay replied, "I'm not."

The old man smiled. "Well, it's good to see all three of you together again." He printed out the search result and handed them the paper of the selection of books. "Let me know once you're done. We can go for some ice-cream later, my treat."

Stella took the paper off his hands, cheerfully replying, "Thanks, Mister Galloway, for everything!"

The trio walked off into the library, chattering about their assignment. The morale for defying the normal gloominess of homework was kept high by Stella's constant intractable spirit.

Once they were out of earshot, Galloway mumbled to himself, "It's the least I could do." His lips sloped into a frown.

The sound of explosions and gunfire continued to ring in his ears. Panting, sweating, eyes staring up at the star littered sky, The Watcher waited patiently for the all too familiar beat of his heart to calm. Light flickered against the edges of his nose and he turned his head to see the campfire still going strong. It was his last camp site before reaching the town of Muscoh where Stella Barber resided, the child whose name and apparent knowledge was shared with a similar person from his world. He had left Ra'Kalen three days ago and took the scenic route to his destination. He can only hope his party of misfit have had the same luck with their exits.

A noise drew his attention and he turned to the sound of shuffling. Though he was alone when he went to sleep, that was no longer the case. Sitting behind the flame was a boy no older than ten, with a buzzcut hair of snow white and dark ebony skin that blended with the night. He poked at the fire with a stick as the ember light flickered contour across his face. A country boy wearing rural white singlet and patched brown pants, he had the tired eyes of an old man that screamed anachronism from the rest of his body.

The boy said, "It's the dreams, isn't it? Don't worry, I used to think they were freaky too. But I got used to it." He readjusted his seating, bringing a knee up to his chin to hug. He started explaining, "It's the Peninsula. That's the name for the outer shell of the universe. On Earth, we know that as the dream world. Here, it's not a stable place so we can only dream of things we know. Our pasts, mostly."

Slowly, The Watcher sat up from the cold, hard ground. Looking around, there was no one else he could see within the reach of the light. To the east, faint sound of waves came from the far off shoreline, sea breeze carried the faint waft of the ocean. The wispy light of the town of Muscoh was a day of riding away. His horse, a brown steed, was lying asleep on the ground not far from them. Tied to the lone tree they were under was the newcomer's black and white.

He turned back to the kid, "It's you."

"It's me," the boy replied, his tone uncaring and stoic.

"Clay Barber."

"That's my name." The boy tossed the stick into the fire. "Nice to see you too, Mister Galloway."

"Mister Galloway..." The Watcher mused. "It's been a while since anyone called me that."

"That's right. Do you prefer 'Watcher' now?"

"A little. It sounds cool. A tiny bit like a superhero." The Watcher stared the boy up and down, making sure his mind was not playing tricks on him as it often did, confirming the boy was indeed there and not just a remnant from his dream. "How did you find me?"

Clay pointed to the town of Muscoh. "Tim had a vision of you. He was singing, 'The librarian is coming to town.'. When I saw the campfire, I guessed it might be you."

The Watcher sized up the child. He had many questions he wanted to ask, but found it hard to prioritise them in a way that would make sense. Clay Barber was a teenager he knew back in his universe. The teen had given up his life to save the world, taking up the mantle of a death god in return for the power to protect the universe. Even though The Watcher knew the Barbers were alive from Adelle's account, seeing the living face of one who was once dead was still a new and stunning experience. The dead don't come back. That was the one rule that even time can't break. Because even if resurrected, that life was not the same as the one before.

He went with his gut on the question. "You look younger."

"That's what happens when you die and gets resurrected. You live, you die, you come back. Rinse and repeat." Clay flourished his hands in a cycle for emphasis. "You die in one universe, you get revived in the next. Usually, you'd come back as some form of life resembling what you were. If you're unlucky, you could just as easily come back as a maggot or a tree."

Even though The Watcher knew the reasons, it was odd seeing a hundred year old former god speaking casually and eloquently about a multi-dimensional phenomenon in the body of a ten year old.

Nonetheless, The Watcher continued his questioning. "And you have memories of Earth? How's that possible?"

"We were gods of death. The bonus to that is we choose when and where to come back to, and whatever we want to bring with us. New bodies, same memories." Clay then sighed and looked towards the flames. "When Stella told me she had notified you of our presence, I nearly blew a gasket. Over a hundred years we served our time as gods of death. We took souls of those that were dying and sent them on. Billions and billions of people, dying by our hands, all just to protect the people we loved. I really thought that when we finally resurrected, we'd get to live a peaceful life."

The boy stood up and dusted off. The Watcher followed the action.

Sombrely, with a croak of regret in his throat, The Watcher said, "I need your help."

"We know. That's why I came here first. I wanted to make things clear to you," Clay replied. He walked over to his horse, untying the creature from the tree. "We watched you fumble around the century, time travelling from one major event to the other, never getting involved, always watching. When we were having the whole portal trouble, when we started dying one-by-one, you could have helped us. If you had just broken your little rule, billions of lives could have been saved."

The Watcher contemplated his position and wondered if he was in any position to argue. He could not have acted in those circumstances. His role as a time traveller meant if he meddled one step out of line, the world could collapse around him. He had to choose between two great evils and disasters. But Clay was right. He was perhaps the most powerful being in his universe and he had done next to nothing but watched the world burn.

Clay continued, "I'm going to help you because my sister wants to. Come to the library once you're ready. We'll be waiting for you there." He climbed onto his horse before turning to face the town. He then punctuated, "But this is the last time. After this, we're officially retired from the whole 'saving the world' business." He clicked the stirrup and the horse broke off for the town, dust rising behind them.

The Watcher stood watching the trail faintly reducing into the distance. Alone again with his thoughts, he thought back to his friends from the war. He thought of the two world-ending catastrophe that had led him to jump into a portal to another universe. He thought of Timothy Kleve. He thought of Clay and Stella. He thought of his brother, Tier. He thought of Luviet. He thought of his Gallena. He thought of Kenji.

At least he wasn't sleepy anymore.

Chapter 22

The Son

Muscoh's library was located next to the port as a single storey brick building that faced the open ocean. A large trading vessel was floating offshore, awaiting the all clear from the port that would allow them to dock. A flock of birds flew overhead, and while The Watcher wanted to akin their cries to that of seagulls, the brown feathered, quadruple winged creatures were nowhere close to their white feathered counterparts.

From his bench, The Watcher pointed up to the birds. "What are they called?" he asked as Clay Barber came walking towards him.

The boy looked to the sky, glancing at the birds. "Northern kuzzards. They must be migrating."

"Kuzzards? That's a stupid name," The Watcher replied while getting to his feat.

"I don't want to hear you say that. Your name is 'Watcher'."

"Hey! Watcher is a coo–" He paused in thought. "You're right, it's kind of stupid. I'm changing my name. I'm McFly from now on."

"That's even worse," Clay snipped back.

The two walked through the single wooden door of the library. Inside, the central area was occupied by a single large rectangular table surrounded by chairs. With a quick count, a dozen shelves lined the sides of the table with the entire back wall of the building being a single bookshelf that stretched from one end of the room to the other. The room was gently lit by soft incandescent lamps accompanied by glimmers of light sifting in through the windows. To their immediate right was a small wooden table with a book and an empty chair. A plaque on the table read 'Reception'. The Watcher paused in front of the table.

Clay asked, "What's wrong?"

"I'm just thinking back."

"You were a librarian when we first met."

"Yeah. It's been what? Nearly two hundred years for me."

Clay looked solemnly to the 'Reception' plaque. "It's been nearly that long for us as well." It was odd hearing the phrase coming from the body of an ten year old, but he thought that must be what others opined of him and his thousand year old age.

Soft, gentle clacks of footsteps echoed through the room. The two of them turned to face the inside of the library. Solely from the sound of her steps, they could hear the elegance of the walk behind it. A smooth, almost whisper of a gait without the dragging of feet or clacking of heels. The little girl walked out from behind a book shelf to their right, hugging a black tome as thick as her body. In skirts of pleated red and a cotton shirt of white, she smiled gently when she saw The Watcher, her strawberry blonde hair waving behind her as she approached.

She greeted with a bow. "Hello, Mister Galloway. It's good to see you again."

"It's good to see you too, Stella." The Watcher could not help but smile back at the wispy girl. He had almost forgotten how alarmingly eloquent her presence was. Even with the body of a child, Stella Barber continued to hold a poise that transcended centuries.

She nodded back, still with the same gentle smile. She gestured to the long table. "I assume you know why you're here?" She took her steps towards the nearest seat, putting her book down and taking a chair.

"You told Adelaide you knew me. You wanted me to find you." The Watcher sat beside her.

Clay left the two to their talks, standing as an uninterested guard at the front door.

Stella replied, "That's right. I would have gone to you, but there's quite a bit of limit on this child body of mine." She looked down to her chest and patted her undeveloped breasts. Clay gave an awkward cough as she did so.

The Watcher said, "I don't know what you're thinking of right now, but it's probably inappropriate for someone your age." He raised a discerned brow.

She gave a cheeky grin. "Why? I'm over a hundred and fifty years old."

"Not physically. It's kind of weird."

Smiling, she quickly changed topics and held the black book out to the man. "This tome contains a compilation of all the information in this world that I think would be useful for you. Information on countries, politics, floras and faunas, cultures, technologies, and a few major mythos."

"And the Rifts? These portals that The Forum are attempting to make? Anything on them?"

"Yes." She flipped opened the book on memory, landing onto the chapter on Rifts. "Muscoh's a trade port, so we've got books from Aleynonlia that comes in with information about Rifts. These portals we deal with are a new phenomenon here, and no one aside from me, my brother, and Joshua knows how they works. Because, you know, we used to be gods and all that."

"It isn't like you to brag."

She replied, "Honestly, I'm not. I'm just being direct."

"Okay, fine. But back on the point of it..." he egged.

"Back on the point," she continued. "Normal Rifts, like the gateways that Aleynonlia employs have a thin layer of pure energy at the entrances. They protect most of the physical energy of one universe from leaking into the others. Imagine a bubble, and if we put a finger through the bubble, the surface tension continues to wrap around it that prevents air from leaking out."

"Like a bubble?" The Watcher repeated for clarity.

"Like a bubble," Stella confirmed.

He still found it a little disconcerting, looking at these century old adults in children bodies. It was as if their physical movement and speech were not exactly matching with their thoughts and youthful expression.

Stella moved on to explaining the portals. "These portals though are more like having a straw poked through them. The rest of the bubble's still intact, but the air inside it can still leak out. The Earth that we came from didn't have any seither, so when one bubble was connected to the other, the seither leaked as the universes tried to balance the amount."

They recalled the crisis that the leaking seither had caused. Since not a single human had evolved enough tolerance against the energy, billions of people died from poisoning amongst other calamitous events. Earth, over the course of two hundred years, became a wasteland, with humans barely surviving. All because two portals appeared over the two centuries.

From the door, Clay chimed, "But we stopped it, didn't we?"

"We did," Stella confirmed. "But I think the first time we did it, we simply got lucky."

The Watcher asked, "How so?"

She explained, "In researching all this, I've found out that to close the portals, we need to do so from both sides, otherwise, we're just cutting the straw short and the path will eventually reopen itself."

"So who closed the portal on this side?"

Stella noted, "You did. Remember?"

The pieces fell into place within his mind almost immediately. Akaras Spaedruiner had manipulated events to force the portal to open faster, attempting to turn the experiment into a weapon of mass destruction. It also coincided with the first portal opening in their universe. He had taken out the dark elf, who had been powering the portal machine with his electrical spells, inadvertently shutting down the gate from Tearha. He had gotten lucky. But there had been two portal phenomenons on Gaia, which meant the second one was either underway, or had not started yet.

A second portal that he had to stop.

The Watcher stood from his seat with Stella watching him with a smile. She said, "I wish I can help more." The girl got to her feet. Facing the older man, she continued, "But I promised my brother this would be the last time."

"I understand," The Watcher replied. She hugged him, and he gently padded her small back. "You've already done more than enough. All of you." He looked to Clay with a smile. The boy acknowledged the silent thanks with a nod.

He left the siblings alone to the quiet peace of the library, stepping out into the afternoon light with Stella's lexicon of a book in hand. The Twin stars glared down from the sky with another flock of kuzzards cutting through a cloud in formation. The ship that had been anchored out at sea had started making its way into the port, sails unfurled against the wind.

The sound of children laughter caught his attention. Looking down the streets, a girl in a white dress ran across the road, her long, light golden-brown hair dancing behind. Following closely, a young boy, hair red and messy, dressed in an oddly paired set of grey pants and green shirt, dashed after her, a smile on their faces as they played their game of cat and mouse. The pair disappeared around a corner as they ran towards the town's centre, their laughs and yelps of joy echoing across the dock. A man walked calmly and slowly after them. Golden haired and comfortably dressed in white, his wife, a red headed woman followed by his side. The familiar man turned and gave The Watcher a glance. The man nodded with a smile.

The Watcher gave a small wave back.

The couple continued their walk after the playful kids.

The time traveller felt his hands clenching into fists. Though he had more answers than before, he was still not fully certain of what was happening within the country, and was unsure of the actual threat that they were facing. But he thought that he owed these smiling people something. He owed them an earnest effort to protect their happiness. And it was a due he desperately wanted to pay.

Chapter 23
Algid Angel

They moved under the cover of the night, coats tied tight around their bodies to prevent even the slightest fluttering. Nadier spun the daggers in his hands out of habit while following closely behind the leader of the assassination squad. They jumped the walls that surrounded the manor and landed at the edge of the garden.

The leader signalled for Nadier with a wave before pointing to a building on the far right. Nadier waved back with two fingers to signify an understanding. His target was in that building.

They split up, with the leader melding into the shadow as she headed for the main hall. Nadier stepped around, circling a small pond as he headed for the far right bedchamber. A steady yellow incandescent light casted a cross from the window onto the ground. Slowly, he peeked around the light and once affirming there was no one else within the room, he slowly lifted the panel open. In a swift motion, he jumped in while holding onto the lintel. Legs first, the dark elf smoothly slid into the room, landing with nary a sound.

Once in, Nadier let out, "What the..."

It was the soft, steady breathing that immediately drew his attention to his surroundings. An arid of colours splashed across the room. Maroon, teal, brown, and green made up the walls of splattered art. Wooden toys littered the floor, with a few copper carriage models thrown into the mix. He was surprised he had not stepped on any of them from his entrance. A copper lamp stood on a nightstand with a bottle of milk. Next to the bottle was a small gas pump spinning the shade of a lamp, casting shadows of animals dancing across the walls.

A wooden crib sat peacefully in the corner of the room on the far side of the door. Gripping his dagger tight, Nadier walked up to the crib and peered into it. Within, the baby not even old enough to have tufts of hair lay asleep.

"It's just a child..." Nadier muttered.

He had not agreed to it. His orders were to kill the Umbersin family, including the heir, but nothing mentioned an infant. It was likely not needed to. Dark elf assassins were meant to follow orders regardless. They must have not thought him independent enough to question. And while he had killed many in his line of work, he had never harmed a child. But it was his mission. His duty. His order.

With knife in hand, the dark elf stood speechless. An untrained line of thoughts ran through his mind. He was bred as assassin. And assassins of the dark elves were as good as a soldier, if not better. An order was the law. Insubordination was met with a trial, and have always ended with death.

He reached for the lamp on the nightstand and with a slight push, sent it breaking into the ground. The baby began to stir, its eyes slowly focusing on the dark figure before.

Nadier muttered, "I'll come back when you're older."

The whispers of guards from outside signalled his exit, and the assassin quietly slipped out the window as the baby began crying.

He woke to the muffled voice of the guards of *Ta'Kalenyilgah* – The Gate of Dark Kings – outside. At first, it was hard to hear what the elven soldiers were saying through the thickness of the walls of the crate he hid in, but as his mind slowly crawled back to life, the words clarified.

"Any undesirables?" the guard asked.

"No, sir," the trader replied. "Just crates of fruits and vegetables."

"Very well. We'll still have to look over your goods. These are just standard procedures."

"Of course," the trader replied. Nadier found the grip of his daggers.

The caravan shook as a guard got onto the trailer. "Are those tinbreroot I smell?"

"Yes. Fresh off the coast."

"Ah. Mind if I buy some off you right now? My daughter loves them."

"Dark elves have children?"

"Of course," the guard replied. "They do not stay young for as long as you humes do, but they are child nonetheless."

A few minutes passed with the guard and the trader bartering through the price of tinbreroot. Nadier's throat itched from the dust within his hiding spot and he held back a cough. Another shift in the trailer as a body clambered onto it. The cover of Nadier's crate opened, and the stoutly trader stared into the box. The dark elf grabbed one of the tinbreroot at his feet, a red, root-shaped fruit, and discreetly handed it over to his guardian. The trader took it and closed the lid back on him.

It did not take long for the caravan to continue its move forward. Even from within his box, Nadier could feel the cool of the underground shade engulfing the surrounding and the smoothness of the ride as they transitioned onto the smooth stones.

He counted the minutes that passed. Then the hours. The steady clattering of wheels on stone rhythmically setting the pace. At the fourth hour, they made it through the underground highway, as evidence by the increased noise from outside indicating they had entered the main city.

Nadier was reminded it was the first time he had returned in over two hundred years.

Readying himself, he shifted in his seat and pushed against the lid of the crate. But the wood did not budge. He tried again, putting force into the corner, yet only a peek of an opening appeared. He had been had. The trader had double-crossed and trapped him.

"That crafty shit..." Nadier cursed. He wondered if there was a bounty for 'The Wanderer' in the capitol.

He squatted uncomfortably, both hands placed at opposite edges of the box. He pushed to the right, then quickly to the left, and immediately right again. The crate tilted rightwards, towards the direction he knew the exit was. His hope was to throw himself out of the trailer and break the wood by crashing onto the ground. Another left and a final right later, the crate toppled over, the dark elf half-crushing a tinbreroot as he landed of his shoulder.

"Don't break anything in there!" the trader shouted. "Just hold your horses. I'll let you out soon."

Nadier was not taking the chances. He set himself up and with another round of pushing and pulling, fell over again.

"Hey!" the trader shouted. "Stop that!"

Nadier spat out a spit full of dust, completely ignoring the trader. He continued with another roll. He could hear the man cursing in frustration and felt the caravan picking up speed. His captor intended to reach their destination quicker and Nadier hastened his escape attempt. Another three toppling ensued. Then, they came to a stopped. The dark elf froze at the action, or lack thereof. He realised the sound of the crowds that should otherwise be on the streets were not heard, and instead, they were surrounded by a wall of silence.

Two distinct sets of footsteps broke the quiet. One from the trader as he walked around to the back and another coming closer from a distance. Then, the footsteps stopped and the crate lid to his right opened, the wooden cover falling to the ground as it did so. Nadier peered over the edge. He had been just one roll away from successfully carrying out his attempted escape.

"As expected of you," a new voice boomed. It was female and carried a lacklustre strength. "Our most infamous child should manage at least this much. Else, I would be sorely disappointed."

He had only seen her face on portraits of papers announcing her coronation. Her long black silk robe covered her body and extended to her shin, leaving her looking as if she floated about on a cloud of shadows. Without the aeronium that covered dark elves from the light, her skin was pale white. Her onyx long hair was tied in a ponytail and her freckled sharp face was brought out by her night-dark sclera and piercing red iris. The Ha'Lof of the current cycle, the newest high elf of the dark council. Nintarin Waynwalker stood paying off the stoutly trader with a bag of quints.

Nadier climbed out of his confines just as the trader finished counting his coins. With a bow to the Ha'Lof and sly grin to Nadier, the hume climbed back onto his horse and left.

The Wanderer looked to his surroundings. In the darkness of Ta'Galadul, his eyes adjusted, but without any source of light, everything was coloured deeper into grey. He partially remembered the decor on the high stone walls and field-wide room. They were in one of the delivery halls of the Council Chambers building in the centre of Ta'Galadul. The trader left from the double doors which closed from the outside after him.

Ha'Lof Nintarin asked, "How does it feel to be back home?" She stared at the walls around them with eyes that shone as if she was looking at a painting.

"I don't know," Nadier replied, wiping off the patch of tinbreroot juice from the shoulder of his coat. "I've been stuck in the box the whole time back."

"Yes, that is true. I apologise for that. But I had hoped to get you here without you being spotted." She circled him and stood back to back. "This is no trap, as I am sure you are wondering of. Perhaps the crate was, but not this."

"So what is this, if not a trap?" He turned to face her back.

"A request. We will be attacking Everwind soon. Our armies will be ready in a few days, and there will be war between the two countries." She turned back and scanned his face carefully before asking, "You don't seem surprised."

"I had my suspicions. What does this have to do with me?"

"Do you know how the dark council members are selected?" Nintarin asked.

Nadier's silence replied a negative.

She continued, "I'm not surprised. The process is highly secretive. Magic circuits in elves are rare. But those with them are often powerful. The strongest of the Spellblade thus become the leader of the army. The same goes for the other roles on the council. The smartest, the bravest, the wisest, the oldest. From one council member down to another. Ha'Lofs like myself, however, are selected on chance. The youngest seer of two hundred age will take the role."

"You're a seer?" Nadier asked. "Is that how you found me?"

"Yes. I am a precognitive telepath. I can read glimpses of minds across all of time and space." She turned to face him, waving her hands across her chest as she explained her powers. "And I heard the outcomes of the events about to unfold. I am not happy with it."

"I'm guessing you lost the war against Everwind?"

Nintarin paced slowly left and right, or as Nadier saw it, glided. "No. We won. As expected. Commander Haeswahl Nunderberg still leads the army. And she is a military genius like none in our history. Our victory was assured from the beginning."

Careful of his next choice of words, Nadier paused, giving it some thought. For some reason he felt he was being tested and that his reply would determine Nintarin's exact response. "So what is worse than war?"

"An endless war," she replied without pause. "We are creatures of the shade. Do you really think we can hold onto the land of light? There will be constant rebellions. Countless dead strewn across the land. Precious aeronium will be lost along with the lives of their hosts."

"And you want me to stop it?"

"Yes."

"If you do not want the war, could you not convince the council out of it?"

"I have tried," she explained. "But aside from the sage, we were overruled by the majority of the council. There is no room back."

"This is not my fight."

"That's what your brother said."

"Why?" That was the next most pressing question, Nadier thought. "Why would the Ha'Lof of the dark elves want to encourage their own defeat?"

She stopped pacing, turning to look him in the eyes. "Each of us represents something. The commander is strength. The adviser is intellect. The sage is wisdom, and so on. I am the visionary. I am responsible for the future of the dark elves." Her tone settled in one borderlining despair. "I wonder, when my predecessor moved to spare you of your execution, did he too saw the future I am seeing now?"

Nintarin looked to the empty walls again, a glimmer of light in her eyes shone as she pictured the future onto the empty canvas. Nadier waited patiently for her reply.

Finally, she continued, "We are a warrior race, Wanderer. The one thing we excel in is killing. But you are different. When you committed your crime of insubordination, you exceeded us. You became more than a *da'raow*, more than death." She walked up to him, close enough that he could see the freckles on her cheeks and the stillness of her eyes. "There is no room for warriors in the coming age. You will represent us dark elves in the new world of gods and heroes, or our race will end in the coming days."

Chapter 24
Sword of the Shadows

With his hood up and scarf covering the bottom half of his face, Nadier followed Nintarin through the streets towards the barracks. He had forgotten much about the culture of dark elves in his time in exile. Unlike the human world above, the elven city was not bustling from minute to minute. No seller of meat constantly screamed for attention; No bright coloured flowers arranged out on stands for effect. The moody grey atmosphere, lit by the glistening cave moss, felt like a perpetual midnight.

Even though they were technically 'buildings', the main construction of the barracks were actually carved into the side of the stone walls. The 'L' shaped structure, with windows within the natural stone, extended out into an open courtyard that was fenced with walls of stone thrice their heights.

Nintarin said, "I suppose you'll be able to enter the compound yourself? I doubt I'll be able to let you in through the gates."

"Of course," Nadier replied. Though he was still wary of the reason for her wanting to bring him to a location potentially crawling with soldiers, he relented to the prospect of information.

"Very well. I will meet you inside." She walked straight off towards the guarded gates.

He turned into the nearest alley beside him where a thick dwarven building was partnered with a wooden elven one. He lined himself at an angle from the stone wall and with a running start, rushed towards it without hesitation. He jumped, kicked against the stone, turned, and grabbed onto a wooden ledge that marked the foundation for the second floor of the elven structure. With the strain of his upper body's muscles, he pulled himself up, kicking off against the wall with his legs, and reached for the window sill above.

With a grip on the sill and a foothold on the ledge, he turned to gauge his path. The dwarven stone work was smooth and without creases, preventing any holds. He would have to make the last jump up to the rooftop in one take.

Taking a peek into the elven building to make sure no one was watching, he reached out and grabbed the head of the frame, climbing fully onto the window with his feet. He squatted, and with a push from his legs and pull from his arm, launched himself further up the elven wall. His feet found a landing on the window head, and using gravity to angle himself back, he launched away from the window and grabbed the edge of the roof of the opposite dwarven building. Taking a short moment to catch his breath, he finally pulled himself onto the empty rooftop.

The elf walked over to the far edge and watched as Nintarin was allowed into the compound without question. The Ha'Lof paused at the door, turned, and seemingly looked towards Nadier's position. Even with their eyesight, with him completely dressed in dark clothes, it should have been impossible for her to have seen him. He felt a chill down his spine as he thought that and Nintarin walked into the compound.

Without wasting time on that shiver, Nadier found a part of the courtyard that was empty. He backed up on the roof as far as he could, aiming to the abandoned spot. Calmly and without hesitation, he sprinted towards the opposite ledge that faced the compound. Launching himself off the parapet, he soared across the street. On his descent, he grabbed the hem of his coat and pulled them open as if they were a pair of wings. He did not glide, but it slowed him enough that when he landed, the momentum did not break his legs. Being elven meant he was lighter and more spry, but that did not excused him from gravity. He rolled forward, redirecting all his momentum away from the ground to the front. He ended with a jump to his feet, still in the pace of a light jog, pushing even more kinetic force up and away from his legs.

As he slowed, he looked up and was brought face-to-face with Nintarin.

She told him, "Impressive."

"How did you know I would land here?" As far as he knew, a seer's ability to predict the future was restricted, and not something that could be activated as-and-when.

She smiled and replied, "I have great instincts."

Despite not having any reason to think so, he felt that she was lying, and he was not afraid to show that thought through a scrunched up face. She shrugged with indifference and led their way through the otherwise empty court where on later hours, combat training would take place.

He asked as they walked through the suspiciously empty land, "Where is everyone?" Even after making their way through the large double archway that led into the barracks dug into the earth, he had only seen three other souls making their rounds as guards.

Nintarin answered, "All the soldiers have been brought to a briefing at the Council Chambers. We're mostly alone here."

"You planned this, didn't you?" Nadier asked.

"I'm a seer, and the Ha'Lof. I can see it, and I ordered it."

He stopped in his track, looking on with worry and surprise. "If they find out about what you did..."

"They will, in a few hours. Not long now." She looked to him with a dire conviction. "Which is why we must hurry. Despite being ready for it, I'm not particularly fond of dying, and would like to escape if possible."

Nadier nodded, part in understanding and part in solemnity. The woman was making a sacrifice, one that he could not comprehend. Not just because he did not have all the pieces of information, but he also thought it was not in his nature to sacrifice himself for someone else. He felt above that line of action.

They went through the empty barracks, stone rooms quiet even by dark elf standards. Through the building, they finally walked out a large archway the size of ten elves and stood facing an open area.

With similar designs to the underground highway, the open area was the size of a field, with ground of spread gravel and walls of smooth stone carved with the ragged artwork of dwarfs. Most of the images that decorated the ancient walls were of squared animals, with a few pictures of different races mixed in. The ceiling curved over itself with stalagmites that hung like fingers reaching down from above. To his far left were *reupenters* – steam powered repeating crossbow-like siege weapons – that were arranged in a line. To the far right wall, a giant wooden door surrounded by gears the size of a mortal was kept close to keep out unwanted attention from the underground highway. They had arrived at the siege arsenal.

However, the sight that caught his attention the most were two towering rock giants that stood unmoving in the middle of the gravel field. At five storeys tall, they were made to half the height of the ceiling, With dark rough rocks for bodies, the giants' shoulders were wide and bulked. But where there should otherwise be a head was instead a stump that curved into the torso. Their hands were two hulking boulders attached to long arms that reached the ground. They stood on four legs of stones like the centaurs of old. Every single part of their bodies had smooth stones reinforced by lines of seither that glowed a faint purple. Even without any magic circuits, Nadier could feel the energy that ran through them.

Nintarin asked, "Do you know what these are?"

Breathless for a moment, Nadier could only softly reply, "Titans."

She added, "Not just any Titan. These are the siege golems, Hulvarks, used by the Seracue Dominion. Their armour of stone can ward off any blade, and the magic linings that marked them can disperse spells up to tier six. It took a long time for us to gather the required knowledge to create one, let alone two. Slow moving, but next to impenetrable. If they reach the walls of Everwind, they would tear their defences down within an hour."

"And you want me to stop them?"

"Yes."

"Are you insane?"

From behind them, a familiar voice replied, "Yes, ma Ha'Lof, are you insane?"

They turned to face the Grandmaster Commander of the dark elf army, Haeswahl Nunderberg. Even after hundreds of years, Nadier remembered the female, the person who had pushed for his execution. Muscularly built, she wore a coat as black as Nintarin's cloak. Her irises were a deep maroon red and feline shaped, her short hair a shivering ashen grey.

Nintarin greeted formally, "Commander Haeswhal."

Haeswahl continued, "I knew it was suspect that you of all of us would call for a war briefing, seeing as you were the one who opposed the plan the most." She looked to Nadier. "And now I find you here conspiring with our most recent traitor."

Nadier skipped the formalities, immediately asking , "Are you alone?"

"Sadly, I had not anticipated your arrival, Wanderer. I had hoped to persuade ma Ha'Lof out of whatever foolishness had gripped her." Haeswahl smirked. "But 'Wanderer', it has been long. Such a fitting human title for one banished."

From under her coat, she drew the multi-bladed sword of dark elf design, a hiljekt. Hers had a light tin of blue, showing the rare traces of mithril that made her blade lighter and stronger than others.

Nadier reached for his dagger but was stopped by Nintarin's outstretched hand.

"I will handle the commander," the seer said. From under her cloak, she pulled out a four-section staff, interconnected by short chains. On both ends attached a blade. With a wisp of a motion, she laid the chained weapon in a circle around her. "Once we begin, I expect you to find your own way out."

He could not see any gathering guards or soldiers behind their opponent, and Nadier deduced that in her rare hope for diplomacy, Haeswahl had not called for protectors.

His theory was proved true when the commander said, "Shame there will be no one to stop you, Wanderer. However, that does not mean I should not try."

The left of her face lit up red as vessels of magic glowed, marking her skin like a growing infection in her blood. Her sword burst into flames and she sent a slash of fire to him.

With a twirl and a whip, Nintarin snapped her chain of staff into the path of the flames, nicking with enough force to dispel the burst of fire.

Nadier took the cue and pulled out a smoke grenade. He threw the vial into what was left of the flames. The contents exploded and gushed into their surroundings, shrouding them in a thick waft of cloud. Concealed, and moving purely on the memory of the layout of the area, the traitorous dark elf made his escape.

In the fog of smoke, Nintarin took a calm step to her right as the blade of fire slashed down where she stood. The sword of her opponent extinguished and vanished into the thick cloud again.

Haeswahl's voice boomed, "Do you really think you can defeat me?"

"No," Nintarin admitted. Despite her powers, or because, due of it, she knew she could not claim victory. With a smirk, she replied, "But I have great instincts. Enough to buy time."

Haeswahl's weapon lit up again as it stabbed towards her. Nintarin spun her main staff around, the chains coming together with the action, locking into place as her four-section weapon turned into a double sided spear. She twirled the polearm upwards, knocking away the thrust. The flaming sword vanished again.

Haeswahl asked, calmer than before, "What do you think Nadier can do? He is but a single elf, banished by the country that raised him, rejected by the one that took him in. What can he do against our unstoppable soldiers? Against our two Titans?"

Nintarin smirked as she deftly stepped away from another slash of fire. "Honestly, while it is true that he will bring about your downfall, the plan to do so would not be his to make. Moreover..." She pointed her spear to a seemingly random direction just as the smoke began to clear. As the gas dissipated, before her stood her opponent, notched squarely into the sights of her weapon. "Neither will he be the one to stop the unstoppable army."

Chapter 25
The Lonely Mercenary

Fire raged across the seaside town. Pillars of flames reached up to the sky from the burning buildings as dancing hands of red and orange destroyed everything they touched. There were screams. Piercing yells of chortling pain and dry gurgles that came only from death unimaginable. Burnt. Cut. Drowned. Eviscerated.

A female voice shouted from out of her field of vision, "Get Adelaide out, now!"

A male yelled in reply, "What about you?"

"I'll hold them back. Get our daughter and run!"

In a puff of brown smoke, the male elf appeared before her. The memory unclear from her years as an infant, she could only make out his green tuft of hair.

"Hey..." he said softly. "Time to go."

She reached out to hold him and the man held onto her tiny fingers gently. She blinked, and the sky was no longer burning, the world no longer shrieking. A peaceful, piercing calm struck into her soul. Before her was the blackness of space littered with uncountable stars. The sound of rustling leaves could be heard off her side.

"Stay here," he told her. "I'm going to get your mother and be right back."

Another puff of brown and the man was gone, leaving her alone to be watched by the light of the stars. By the time the Twins had risen and coloured the sky with a blood red dawn, the man had yet to return.

A croaking voice sounded, "What do we have here?" An unfamiliar face leaned over into her view with a hair that was receding white and eyes that were stretched to be kind. "An elf girl? Aren't you lucky I found you first."

The mumbled voice of Miguel Vallertes continued the lengthy history lesson. "And after the First War of the Gods, the genocide of the two races became the longest lasting dent in the history of Tearha. And–"

The sound of rolling paper echoed through Adelaide's stirring head, waking her in time to see a rolled up piece of newspaper thrown on an approach for her face. She jerked back, jumping away from the attack, leaning back against the spine of her chair. Despite avoiding the hit, she still fell backwards and landed with a crash, the back of her head smacking hard into the ground.

Eyes tearing up, rubbing the nape of her neck in pain, Adelaide cried, "What the fuck are you doing?"

Miguel looked to her, annoyed, "You're suppose to be listening to my lesson." She mumbled about the history remedial being boring and Miguel sighed in defeat. "And where did you learn the word, 'fuck'?"

She got up from her fall, resetting her chair and taking her seat. "The Watcher taught it to me. He said it was a swear word from his home universe. I like how it rolls off the tongue. Fuck. Fuck. Fuckity, fuck, fuck."

Another sigh and an additional palm to the face later, the Enhancer noted that he needed to have a stern word with the time traveller. "In any case, I need you to listen to everything I tell you."

"Why?" Adelaide asked. "What's the point of me learning all these long gone history?"Her irate voice echoed the room.

They were within the town hall of Valent. Save for the large rectangular table that they surrounded and the chairs they sat on, the room they were assigned to by the mayor was empty.

From a corner, Luce, who was half asleep and hugging her rifle, answered, "You'll be meeting a group of people who has a death grudge against you. The least you can do is learn a little of their history to appease them."

Adelaide clicked her tongue in frustration. She had not expected to be dragged into the negotiation. She had expected Luce to do all the talking while she waited aside, but the Titan Ranger had insisted that Adelaide was 'a key to making it work'.

The Demon Eyes' first arrival into the town had sent a wave of panic and murmurs. Guards had rushed out to take her into custody, only to be talked down by Miguel and Luce, both of whom were world known and held a high standing. Had the Enhancer and ranger not been at her side, she would have likely started a bloodbath.

Just as she wanted to start questioning their plans for negotiation, the door to the room swung open and in came the Mayor of Valent. The man was a tall, lanky, human male. With slick, combed-back red hair and a black leather vest over crisp white shirt and deep brown cargo pants and boots, he was a confusing mix of worker and politician in looks.

Following closely behind him were the varying nervous and rugged men and women of the town's militia, totalling twenty numbers in all, attempting to squeeze into the relatively small room.

Miguel asked, "What is this? I thought this was a peaceful negotiation?"

"Forgive me for being careful, Grandmaster," the mayor replied. "I think it'd be best for me to be on my guard when the former head of the Titan Rangers and yourself come into my town with The Demon of Valendra for 'peace talk'."

"If you know it'd be dangerous, you should also know that an attempt to show such strength against us does nothing but provoke." Miguel stepped forward confidently. "I am certain the three of us can handle your town's militia with little problem."

The mayor raised a brow. "Is that a threat? I thought this was a peaceful negotiation."

Luce added, "It is." To which Adelaide let out a soft scoff.

"Barbaric," the mayor spat at Adelaide.

She half stood to her seat but was stopped by a gesture from Miguel.

The Enhancer said, "This is peaceful. But so far, your actions have belittled that. A show of military might through numbers is nothing but provocative."

The mayor gave the statement some thought. After a reluctant minute, he raised his hand and waved a stand-down order. Most of the militia proceeded uncertainly out of the room, with only a male and female guard, both with swords sheathed and donned with better quality armours than the rest remaining behind.

The mayor said, "Then I hope you don't mind I leave at least two for my own protection."

Graciously, Miguel replied, "Of course."

The pair of trios took their seats facing each other across the tables. The mayor looked to Adelaide, a hidden anger drawn into his eyes. He then turned his attention to Luce.

"I understand you are the one who made a request for this meeting?"

Luce replied, "Yes. As I have come to realise, there is a fallen sentient Titan within your borders of Valendra Forest. I would like to discuss the terms of claiming it as a archaeological site under the terms and agreement of the Sentient Preservation Act."

"Wait!" Adelaide chimed in. "Archaeology? I thought we were going to cordon off the forest for protection?"

Luce explained, "Under the protection of the Titan Rangers, we will do our best to make sure the forest is preserved."

"That's not what we agreed to!" Adelaide shouted, slamming her hands on the table and pushing to a rushed stand. "You're betraying me!"

Luce calmly replied, "We agreed to nothing. I merely said I would come discuss the terms of preservation of the forest with regards to the Titans' body."

The mayor, apparently piecing together the puzzle of events, asked, "So why did you ask The Demon to be here?"

"Because I wanted her to hear this." Luce turned to look Adelaide in the eye. "Under the Sentient Preservation Act, the Titan Rangers are not allowed to harbour fugitives within our area of protection. If you continue to dwell within the forest, we will do everything in our power to hunt you down and turn you in."

Adelaide reached behind her back, drawing her axes. Miguel calmly stood to his feet, backing away from the scene as the elf held her weapon to the woman's neck. The others in the room sat back, wide-eyed in surprise and fear at the turn.

Adelaide growled, "You..."

Unfazed and still in her seat, Luce continued, "However, I want to offer all parties involved a compromise." Everyone in the room listened intently to her next words, despite the axe still held to her throat. "Adelaide Wiltkins, I want to conscript you into the Titan Rangers under the Ranger Conscription Agreement with The Forum. In return," she turned to the mayor. "You are to pardon Adelaide of all her crimes."

The man got to his feet as well. "Nonsense!" he exclaimed. "This creature killed dozens of our hunters and countless others from Consortia and Iona. Even if we agree, what makes you think the other two states of the forest will let you get away with this?"

Luce explained, "Because we will be killing three of your birds with one stone. We will remove Demon Eyes from the area either way, and provide all three states with a percentage of agreed compensation of titanium harvested from the Titan. And, the forest will become a preserved ground with the Titan Rangers taking over the job of patrolling, preventing unlawful hunting and gathering."

The mayor, at a lost for words, could only silently contemplate on the offer. Miguel whistled, impressed at Luce's negotiating capabilities. Taking a deep breath, the mayor relented, nodding to the terms.

"That... is not an unfair deal, I would say. If I can speak on behalf of the other leaders, I think they too would agree."

Luce lastly turned to Adelle. "Now, the decision is yours. You can run back to 'your' forest and fight everyone to the death. Or, you can come with me and live."

Chapter 26
The Princess of Blood

Adelaide felt her hands tightening around the handle of her axe, which blade was held close to Luce's throat. She was seething, her muscles trembling with the pain that only unbridled anger could have created and she was not sure why. She looked to Miguel, who stood with an unreadable expression, then to the mayor and his guards.

The elf gave it a second of thought.

Then, she took a step backwards and teleported out of the room.

Reappearing at the town square within the puff of rust-smelling cloud, gasps immediately filled the air as men and women of all age and race stopped mid-action, pots crashing into the ground and crates tumbling off shelves. The busy marketplace stopped abruptly, all eyes on Adelaide who appeared in the centre of the intersection. The crowd dispersed around her, stepping away from the elf with green hair.

Mutters filled the air and slowly, the hushed whispers turned into frustrated grunts. Then, the frustration turned into an angry clattering.

Finally, a man shouted, "Demon Eyes!"

Adelaide turned to the voice and saw an old man, limping towards her with a cane in his hand and a fury in his eyes. He sped up his speed once he was close enough to confirm who she was. Despite her being sure she had not met an elderly human before, something about the man was familiar to her.

He growled, "You monster! How dare you show your face here?" When he was within throwing distance, a young woman ran out of the crowd to him, stopping his advance with gentle force. "You! You! After what you've done! You dare to show your face!"

Adelaide defended, "I've never met you before."

"Of course you haven't!" he yelled, voice cracking. "You don't have to meet the aftermath of your killings. My son, Kiril, you killed his best friend. He was so guilt-ridden with having survived he ran away from the town. I have not seen him in three decades!"

Unconsciously, she took a step back, her heart skipping a beat as a bead of sweat rolled down her temple.

The old man continued, breaking free of the hold of the woman, shakily pointing his cane at her. "You! You ruined our family! Get your geared face away from us!" He bent over to grab a rock from the ground, almost toppling over as he did so.

But he stood back straight with conviction and threw the rock at Adelle. The stone harmlessly fell to the side without strength, the old man falling to his knees in tears after the outburst. Then, a loaf of bread flew past her face. She turned, and the baker had her arms out in post throw. A stalk of vegetable followed, hitting her in the back of her head. Adelaide stumbled slightly from the impact, but otherwise unhurt. Next came a rotten fruit. Another small rock. A bucket that missed. The townspeople gathered in an uproar and soon, a barrage of random objects flew towards her general direction.

She saw the glimmer of the butcher's knife and stepped aside, the blade embedding cleanly into the ground where she once stood. She shot a dirty glare to the man who threw it, but the reply was not the one of fear she had gotten used to from her prey. It was a stare of fury.

"Adelaide!"

She turned towards the voice that called her to see Miguel jogging forward. She squinted in focus, took a step to the side and teleported to the northern edge of the town

Behind her, the town continued in a loud frenzy at her appearance. Before her, just a short walk away, was the edge of Valendra Forest. She breathed in deep, clenched her fist tightly, and began her walk back to her home.

"So that's it?"

She stopped in her tracks, turning to the familiar voice. Nadier was sitting on a bench against the edge-most building of the town.

The dark elf lectured, "Run back to your forest and wait for the next person to kill?"

She gritted her teeth and growled, "Don't you have a brother to avenge? Or a war to stop?Aren't you suppose to be in Ta'Galadul?"

"I do, and, I was." She saw the bags under his eyes. Even for a dark elf, they were considerably shadowed. He must have travelled through the night to reach Valent. Nadier continued, "But those things aside for now, this is more important."

"What is?" she asked.

"Saving you."

She snorted derisively. "I don't need your 'saving'. And don't think I've forgotten how you and Watcher betrayed me."

"I saw an opportunity."

"So you used me."

"I use everyone!" Nadier shouted, smashing his hand against the stone wall behind, dust falling off the shingles of the roof.

Adelaide took a step back in shock. For all the years she had known him, he had never once raised his voice. Before then, she had started to wonder if Nadier could even shout.

The dark elf took a breath for composure. Once he had calmed, he settled into his seat again and continued, "I use everyone. I'm a dark elf. It's what we do. And this is going to be weird, coming from me, but we do have the ability to care. We just don't show it much."

"Is that right?" Adelaide replied, sceptical in her tone. "You expect me to believe you're caring by betraying?"

"Is there any other way?" Nadier asked honestly. "Humans do it all the time. Little white lies for those they care about. We just go a little further. Little white betrayals." His tone was flat and without bravado. He honestly believed a betrayal was no more than a lie. It was the way of the dark elves.

Frustrated at his unbelievable attitude, Adelaide angrily asked, "So how did you help me? You sent me into the Undercity. Had me shot by Light and caught up in a stupid war I wanted no part in. How is that helping me?"

"Because the world moved on without you, I wanted to show you that. The legendary Demon of Valendra. You saw how people reacted to you? The fear is gone. You used to be a legend. Then, they realised you were just another mortal, another elf. Now they know your powers. Everyday, your mystery gets unravelled a little, and you get ever so closer to being caught. You've already been taken in once. Without The Watcher, you'd probably be dead."

"What's your point?" Adelaide asked menacingly, getting tired of his roundabout way of speech.

"I spoke with Luce before leaving Ra'Kalen," Nadier admitted. "She wanted you in the Titan Rangers. I told her what she should do to corner you. I gave you a way out. To clear your name."

"That's not what I wanted."

"You want to say your goal is to protect the forest, am I right?" Though the statement was simple, the tone was overwhelmingly accusing.

She did not reply. Could not. Because he was right.

Nadier continued. "But you and I both know that's not true." He stood up and walked calmly to her. "You want to protect *your* forest. If you want to make that forest yours, go build a damn castle. Take responsibility. Otherwise, sooner or later, you won't be able to run any further."

They stood face-to-face, met eye-to-eye. Adelaide sometimes wondered if all those years ago, were they brought together because of fate or destiny. Even though in all likelihood, it was just because they lived within a rare circle of killers and loners. It was how nobles always met other nobles and how farmers mostly knew other farmers.

Nadier reached out and cupped a hand to her face and her eyes widened in surprise. His expression was unusually stoic, yet eyes held kind. It was a look she had seen only twice, both a long time ago, in a village aflame on the face of a man who held her hands softly, and later on the old man who took her in for the few years he had left to live. She sighed, lowering her head in defeat and leaning her closed eyes into his shoulder, a single awkward hand of a dark elf behind her head.

"I've lost a brother," Nadier said in an almost whisper. "I can't lose a sister too. It's time we grew up, or we're both going to die alone. So please, Adelle, take Luce's offer."

"Alright," she replied without looking up at him. "Just for you, Nads."

A new voice, cold and calculating, sounded, "How sweet."

The pair pushed apart and turned to face the newcomer. Standing before them with the background of the forest behind him and the Tower of Everwind further away on the horizon, Light stood with his bright white robe, practically shining under the Twins' light.

Adelaide drew her axes and Nadier's dagger swung out, the dark elf quickly and swiftly loaded two vials into the hilts.

Light smiled menacingly. "My dear Wanderer, I heard you found something interesting in the dark." His hand clenched and a longsword of pure light burst from within his balled fist. "Let's talk about that, shall we?"

Chapter 27

Ex

"Listen," Light said, pacing left and right before the two elves, a sword of light in his hand. "I don't really want to fight. I just want to know what you've found in the Undercity. And once I know, I'll go~!"

"You're lying," Adelaide replied immediately.

"You're not here to let us go." Nadier added.

The smirk on Light's face broke the handsomeness as a bent would to clay. "I'm not lying. Not entirely. I'm not The Watcher, you know~?" he sang his way with a glee that felt sick. "I don't lie all the time. Just enough to get me by."

A question hit the dark elf, and he asked, "How did you know I was in the Undercity?"

Excitedly, Light exclaimed, "I was watching you, my little monster." He pointed back towards The Tower. "From over there."

"How did you see–?" Nadier paused and looked towards The Tower before staring around at the sky in shock. He turned back to Light with a seriousness in his eyes. "What did you do?"

Light chuckled, "Oh, look, you figured it out." Then, his brow cocked aside as he thought out loud, "But that must mean my dear Watcher has already seen through it a long time ago."

Adelaide asked, "Seen through what?"

"He did something to the sky. Think back, Adelle. A hundred years ago, two hundred even, could we see as far as we could now?"

Light spread opened his arms. "That's right! I 'flattened' the waves of light over Eltar. I can see as far as I need, as far as I want. Nothing escapes my eyes."

Nadier did not move from his spot. Something stirred within his head as he stared blankly ahead while puzzles began to piece themselves together in his mind.

Almost instantly, Light grew angry, his voice growling as he said, "What's with that look? I know The Watcher has that look. He's the only one allowed to have that look!" He pointed his palm forward and charged up a blast of light.

He fired. Adelaide jumped towards Nadier, fingers reaching out towards the dark elf. The tip of her nails scraped him, and she teleported the both of them a step to the left just as the beam of light shot through where they stood, blasting apart the ground behind them in a shower of dirt and mud.

"Nads!" She shouted at him. "Get a grip! Focus!"

Light stepped menacingly towards them. "I grow tired of this. Tell me what you've found out in Ta'Galadul, or my next attack will not be so kind."

Nadier refocused and plainly told Light, "The dark elves are ready for war."

"Is that right? That is not something I wanted to hear." Light mused. He did not question Nadier's statement, somehow knowing it was truth without confirmation. He held the sword of light like a one-handed spear. "I'm afraid you have outlived your usefulness and I tire of playing with you. I have a war to plan."

A grenade arced through the air, thumping into the ground at Light's feet before the spear of light was thrown. The small cannister exploded, sending a rocking blast and shock wave outward, pushing grasses away and sending chunks of dirt flying. Nadier took a quick look back towards the town to see Luce darting away into the cover of an alley wall.

"Adelle!" he shouted, taking a grip of the elf's shoulder.

She teleported them behind Light, the man was still coughing within the cloud of dust. Her axes spun forward, slashing into where the Lord stood. The man raised his arms, blocking the two weapon with the shell of magic that surrounded his body. Nadier stepped around Adelaide and spun a stabbing dagger towards Light. Light reacted with unparallelled reflexes, bringing down Adelaide's weapons with the force of his body as he ducked at Nadier's attack. But the dark elf felt the tip of his blade nick at familiar soft skin, the Neverite tipped blade cutting through the shell of magic. Light gathered another collection of energy within his body. Nadier placed a hand on Adelaide's shoulder and she teleported them away.

They reappeared where they started, but Light still charged his spell. With a roar, the man opened his arms and released the blast, knocking the two elves off their feet. Behind them, the shrapnel of light chipped off parts of the walls of the buildings.

Nadier and Adelaide laid on the ground, bodies aching and cut. The force of the blast had saved them, counter intuitively pushing them away from the shrapnel. But they were still sliced at parts of their skin, clothes tattered and tissues bleeding gently from the wounds.

Adelaide was out cold and Nadier was in no condition to recover. He looked back to the alley and saw Luce ready to charge out. The dark elf softly shook his head and the Titan Ranger reluctantly stood back into hiding.

The sound of footsteps crunched towards them and Nadier turned back to Light who had manoeuvred closer to within a dozen steps away. Somehow, the dark elf managed to get back on his knees but he found no strength to stand. Instead, he redirected his energy for a hate-filled glare.

"Impudent children. So young. So full of hope. So stupid. But I do give you credit for cutting me," Light lectured, his right shoulder bleeding from Nadier's cut. The Lord raised his left hand, palm opened towards the sky. Rays of light started converging above his hand, a ball of light slowly forming. "I'll let your death be spectacular. **Crystal–**"

Nadier braced for the attack.

"Fantasia!"

The orb of light exploded, rays of hard beams pierced through the air in thousands of random directions. Nadier did not blink and kept his eyes opened, determined to face his end without fear. That courage was helpful in witnessing what came next. A triangular wall of ice burst out of the ground before him, the light shards passing through them as they would glass, the beams refracting and hitting everything around them except their bodies. The waves of projectiles lasted a second. Two. A total of ten seconds passed before the barrage stopped. Standing between the elves and the wall of ice was Miguel Vallertes, the Grandmaster Enhancer of Aleynonlia.

The smirk on Light's face widened in deformed cracks through the refracted ice. "Well, well, well. Miguel Vallertes, in the flesh. I'm honoured. You know, I lost track of you after Ra'Kalen."

"The Watcher's smart," Miguel replied. "He left first, and had Nadier leave second. Knew you would keep your attention on them while we left third and that you would not risk following The Wanderer into Ta'Galadul."

"That sounds like him. Always thinking five steps ahead," Light said. He then asked, "Did you throw that grenade?"

Nadier knew then that Light did not know of Luce's involvement and hoped Miguel was smart enough to have caught that.

Miguel replied, "Of course."

Nadier internally whispered a silent thanks.

Light warned, "Attacking me is akin to a declaration of war."

"I didn't attack you. My hand just slipped."

"And the wall of ice?" As Light said that, the wall of ice shattered into sparkling dusts.

Miguel grinned, "My magic just slipped. You know how fickle they can be."

Light continued with a menacing growl, "Well, I suggest you step aside and keep your hands under control. Or I'll have to consider your next move a declaration of war." Light raised his palm again, slowly generating another ball of light. "What do you think your king will say to you dragging an entire continent to battle?"

The Enhancer stood his ground. "You know who I am. Do you really think my king – no, the Clovers, will not move if I decide this was a fight worth entering?"

"Honestly," Light admitted. "I think I can take you all on."

From his hands, Miguel materialised two daggers within shines of icy mists. He held them both in reverse, and brought the hilt of both weapons together, holding them aside the left of his waist.

"Crystal–" Light began.

"Ex–!" Miguel started.

A sword pierced through the air between them, stopping both men in their cast. A second sword fired across like an arrow, closer to Light and slammed point first into the ground at his feet. And a third followed even closer between his legs. A fourth. Fifth. The sixth was aimed and shot directly at the Lord, who in quick steps, seemingly vanished from the spot, reappearing a jump away. Another sword shot at him. Another vanishing step. A barrage of hundreds of swords followed, seemingly without end, Light seamlessly dancing around each and every attack.

Then, as suddenly as they had started, the attacks stopped, a lone sword embedding with a tang into the ground behind the Lord, the hundreds before vanished as if they had never been there, unseen.

Light noted, "It seems The Watcher has arrived." The group looked out to the horizon where the time traveller approached with a confident swagger. Light continued, "As much as I would love to stay. I don't think it's time for me to meet my dear friend just yet." He turned to smile at his enemies and after engulfing himself in a beam of light, vanished from where he stood.

With the immediate threat gone, Miguel knelt down beside Nadier. "Are you alright?"

"Y-yeah..." Nadier turned to Adelaide, who was still unconscious.

Luce ran out to aid the green-haired elf. "She's fine," the Titan Ranger reassured. "Just knocked out, it seems."

Miguel helped Nadier to his feet as The Watcher continued his slow approach. The dark elf sighed, a hand on his wounded right shoulder.

Miguel asked, "What's wrong?"

The dark elf replied, "You, Watcher, Light, you're basically gods."

With a dead seriousness, Miguel replied, "We killed the gods in the last war. You know that, right?"

"Honestly? I can't tell the difference anymore."

Chapter 28
Tactician Grey

"Luviet!" the young man shouted to his friend. "Hurry!"

The young soldier named Luviet charged through the field with six others following desperately by his side. With each step taken, a small explosion rocked through their ears but cut off mid sound like a broken record. Behind each of their tracks, the ground erupted. But the dirt stopped mid detonation, frozen in time like a flower mid bloom.

Luviet shouted back, "Pulse! Fling them away!"

"I can't concentrate enough for that! Just hurry!" Pulse replied. "I can't hold on much longer!"

As he said so, on the opposite end of the minefield, the explosion was released from the hold of time. The blast sent up a pillar of dirt. A second followed closely. And a third. Like a domino in chain, the mines detonated in sequence, chasing after the soldiers as they continued their desperate run. Luviet raced straight towards Pulse, the latter straining all he had to prevent the mines in front of them from continuing their detonation while attempting to hold off the ones behind that had already exploded.

"Get down!" Luviet yelled, diving the last leg towards Pulse.

The time mage was tackled off his feet, falling backwards into the trench. His hold over the mines vanished and the resulting simultaneous blast rocked the very ground they landed on. Five of the other soldiers slid into the trench just as the shockwave blasted dust overhead. The sixth and last member jumped in and used her powers to pull a blanket of earth over their heads just before the sound of shrapnel cuts through the air above them.

The terramancer pulled off her mask and helmet before jumping straight into Pulse's arms. "You were amazing!" She kissed him on the cheeks.

Still panting hard from his exertion, Pulse managed to reply with a smile. "Thanks, Gallena."

His eyes crossed gaze with Luviet. The latter gave Pulse a thumbs up with a tired smile. "Good job, buddy."

Within the cramp makeshift trench of dirt and mud, under a blanket of dust and shrapnel, and surrounded by a field of explosions and gunfire, the group of eight let out a victorious cheer.

The Watcher was awoken from his nap by a tap to his shoulder. His eyes opened to Miguel walking by. He had fallen asleep on the log outside the small cliff-side cave that Adelaide called home. Snow had begun falling again, and, despite having been told that the season was a quarter into winter, it was only the second time he had seen snowfall on Tearha. Both times were within the forest of Valendra. Miguel sat on the edge of the log. The campfire had been restarted and the rest of their motley group of five sat around it. Night was settling, and the only warmth was the burning flame.

Though the deal with Valent had been made, they feared returning as the crowd had continued their rowdiness after Adelaide's sudden appearance in their town square. They had decided to hide in Valendra Forest at Adelaide's old camp-site until the commotion died down.

Nadier had just arrived and took the seat opposite Watcher, positioned to the left of Luce and right of Adelaide. The dark elf noted, "This is the most pathetic army I have ever seen."

The Watcher sat up with a stretch and corrected, "We're not an army."

Adelle asked, "So what are we?" She held a pouch of snow to the back of her head, still nursing the injuries she received from her fight with Light.

Silence caught the group and everyone exchanged uncertain glances.

Miguel leaned closer to the fire to bring the conversation forward. "Let's review what we know. Light is planning something with the portals. We do not know what, but the fate of The Watcher's home world is at stake on that. I think it's safe to assume that aside from Luce, none of us will be allowed back into Everwind to find out more."

Nadier added, "Not to be rude here, but I don't think Watcher's world is of a big concern to us."

Luce commented, "The dark elves are planning a war. And they somehow got their hands on the alchemy formula for siege golems. If they attack Everwind, even with Light at the helm, they'll kill thousands of people."

The group turned to Adelaide, waiting for her to chime in.

"What?" she replied exaggeratedly, setting her snow pouch to the side. She pointed to Luce. "I'll just agree with what she says. She's my boss now, right?"

While the group gave a collective sigh, The Watcher let out a laugh to which Adelle replied with a chuckle. He was glad to have hit a rapport with the elf, despite their relatively rocky beginnings. He found her an interesting individual, and he liked keeping himself in the circle of fascinating people.

Adelaide continued, "Look, seriously though, I don't know what you guys think five of us can do. Sure, we have Miguel, but that's just one Clover. That's not enough to fight two armies, a master spellblade, and the strongest photomancer on Tearha." She leaned back onto her outstretched arms and taut her back in a cracking stretch.

The Watcher asked, "What's a 'Clover'?"

Luce answered, "They are a group of powerful individuals that are either physically, intellectually, or politically strong. Or a combination. They fought the last Exceed War with the gods. It's said that having just one Clover is enough to turn the tides of a war."

The time traveller looked to the Enhancer, eyes wide with reverence. "I don't know what this Exceed War is, but it sounds impressive."

Miguel shook his head uncertainly and replied, "We're really not all that great. Don't count on my powers alone being able to fight this battle. And don't count on the others coming to help. None of them are really within reach right now."

Then, a question returned to The Watcher's mind, and he asked, "I've been meaning to ask this, but what is up with the weather? You said it was winter, but it has only snowed twice so far."

Miguel answered, "The Titan War to the south burnt the atmosphere, so winter has been coming in later for a while now. The full snow season starts around now. I think your world calls it global warming."

The Watcher scratched his head in frustration. "Good to know some stupid never changes."

Luce, realising The Watcher kept going off tangent, added, "Is this relevant?"

"Environment is always relevant when fighting a war."

"And you know this how?"

The Watcher smiled at her. "Oh, I'm very old, my dear ranger. I can lose count of the wars on the fingers of my hands."

Abruptly, The Watcher's eyes opened wide in surprised remembrance of a piece of information. Reaching into his heavy coat, he pulled out the black tome that was given to him by Stella. He began flipping through the pages before stopping on the chapter on the dark elves.

Miguel asked, "What's wrong?"

"Dark elves are allergic to starlight, which is why they have a skin of 'aeronium'." The Watcher read aloud and looked to their resident dark elf.

Nadier pulled up his sleeves and held out his forearm to show his darkened skin. "It's basically a layer of shadow," he explained again. "We wear it to prevent ourselves from being burnt in the light."

The Watcher's eyes darted to-and-fro the corners, as if a wall of information was out before his eyes in thin air. He stopped, looked to the dark elf and asked, "So, the soldiers, they need aeronium as well, right?" Nadier nodded a confirmation. The human continued, "It says in this book that aeronium is limited on Eltar. I'm guessing that means you have to transfer aeronium from one person to another?"

"That's right," Nadier confirmed. "We have a pond of aeronium. The ancients dwarfs built this gate that transfers aeronium from person to pool depending on the direction you walk through the gate."

"Interesting..." The Watcher mumbled, quieting down as he held his chin in thought.

Adelaide's eyes lit up. "The ritual..."

Nadier snapped his fingers as the idea hit him as well. "Oh, that's brilliant." Noticing the confusion on the other three, Nadier leaned closer to the fire and explained, "The dark elves have a ceremony where before a major fight, they are all called back to the pond to return the aeronium for redistribution."

"Everyone?" Luce clarified.

"Yes. Everyone," Nadier confirmed. "If, at the moment the last elf walks through the gate, we destroy it, there will be no redistribution of the coat. No more army."

Luce shifted in her seat. "But the siege golems will still be a problem. Knowing your kind, they'd still attack with the golems, just to even the score." She placed a hand on her chin, her eyes shifted blankly for a second, her voice toning down as if reminiscing on the past. "I'm not eager to have these Titans running around, stomping the land."

Adelaide brought up, "Nads, during the fight with Light, you stopped with that stupid look on your face, like you figured something out."

"Ah!" The dark elf piped up, reminded. "Yes. I figured out why Light wanted you, me, and The Watcher out of the equation so badly."

Save for The Watcher, who continued in his thoughts, the rest of the campfire gathering listened intently, even as the Twins were setting fully and the shadows from the fire fought with the twilight shine. The crackling of firewood continued to uneven the beat of the whispering wind.

Nadier drew one of his daggers and unloaded the vial of cartridge into his palm. "Neverite. It's a substance created by dark elves to cut through mages' shields. They are hard to make, because one of their ingredients is dark elf blood."

"Ah..." Miguel let out, as he himself pieced the puzzle together. "The only dark elf not bound to Ta'Galadul could make neverite to fight mages. And... an elf with the ability to teleport multiple people across a vast amount of space will easily slip through Light's sight."

"And The Watcher," Nadier continued, "Can manipulate time, arguably, the only thing faster than light itself. We're the perfect trio to sneak up on the human."

Without warning, The Watcher jumped to hit feet. "Oh! Oh! Oh!" He got out of the circle and ran around the campfire excitedly, jumping and punching the air. "I got it! I'm so smart! I'm a bloody genius!"

Hopping the gap between Adelaide and Nadier, he stopped between everyone, standing above the flames of the pit, the flickering fire reflecting in his dirt-brown eyes.

Miguel got to his feet with a toothy grin, waving his fingers knowingly at The Watcher. "I think I've got the same plan as you do."

"Of course you do," The Watcher replied with a confident pat on his chest. "You're as smart as I am. And I don't say that often."

Adelaide interrupted, "When you two are done feeling each others' egos, mind telling us the plan?"

The Watcher turned to the rest, and with a smile, said, "Here's what we'll do. We're going to do everything, in one swoop. Stop the war, stop the golems, and infiltrate Everwind. And we'll do it all before winter ends."

Chapter 29
The Forge in Flames

Miguel and Luce were up and ready to go by the fade of midnight. To Nadier, the pair seemed eager to return to Valent, both their faces showing the outlines of a reluctance to spend unneeded time outside of the comforts of settlements. From what the dark elf knew of their stories, he was not surprised that they'd prefer to journey as little as necessary. They must have had enough adventures for their lifetimes.

He asked Luce before she left, "Are you sure about this?"

The Titan Ranger replied, "The plan? No. Not sure at all. There's too little room for error, and not enough people to fix them." She re-tightened her scarf and pulled her long golden-brown hair out from behind.

Nadier crossed his arms in query. "And you are empathic of that?"

"No," she replied straightforwardly, doing a quick check on the sling of her rifle. "But you heard our options. None of them are particularly good in terms of casualty counts and wiggle room. As mad as this one goes, at least no one dies."

Nadier nodded understandingly. "You know that there's no need for you to stay."

"Have you ever fought Titans?" she quickly asked, to which he replied with a gentle shake of his head. Luce continued, "They are sentient, but most don't know they are sentient. These are beings made for being controlled, but have the capacity for individuality."

He theorised, "If they realise they are alive, it's likely they can become dangerous beings of destruction."

"Or they could evolve, become something more. The next breed of life." She looked over his shoulder at The Watcher who sat next to the campfire, engrossed in the Black Tome of information. "That man is terrifying. I think he saw through me. 'Nobody dies,' he said."

"Do you think that meant the Titans as well?" Nadier asked.

"Why else would he come up with such an insane plan? There are much better ways to gain trust. Much better ways to take down golems and infiltrate Everwind."

The two silently contemplated The Watcher, observing him from their distance as the flame flickered shadows of age across the man's face. A circle of dirt from melted snow laid an arena around him, fluffs of white ground away from the heat sparsely spreading. A soft snowfall dotted the air.

Miguel, having packed, walked towards them. "Ready to go?" the Enhancer asked.

"Sure." Luce replied. She turned to Nadier. "Make sure Adelaide doesn't die."

"I don't need you to tell me that," he replied matter-of-factly. He handed her a sealed letter as instructed by The Watcher. He continued, "But why are you so interested in her?"

Luce merely let out a breath of a laugh before turning away with Miguel. The two travellers walked into the forest of darkness. Since Miguel was a hume, his night-vision would guide their way back. Nadier watched them walk further and further until they disappeared behind rows of staggered trees. The dark elf turned and headed back to the camp.

As he stepped in the warmth of the fire, he announced to the time traveller, "They've left."

The Watcher looked up from his book. "Who?" His question was so fuelled with honest confusion that it managed to annoy even Nadier.

He bit back slightly. "Who else? Miguel and Luce."

"Ah, yes. The smart guy and sad girl."

"Sad girl?"

The Watcher closed his book and tucked the tome away under his coat. His tone dropped, "There's something I wanted to talk to you about."

Nadier stopped in his tracks. He was making his way to Adelaide's cave of a home, but if the dark elf had learnt anything the past few days with The Watcher was to always listen at the lowering of a pitch. He stood half-turned, the flame's warmth heating up the left of his cheek.

The Watcher continued, "This plan. Are you okay with it?"

"Of course I am," Nadier replied without skipping a beat.

The Watcher explained, "I'm going to assume you understand what we're trying to do is as close to a genocide as we can get." Nadier kept silent. He stared at Watcher with an unreadable expression. The Watcher decided to continue, "Even if they somehow manage to escape the trap, the moment we destroy the aeronium gate, the dark elves can never see the light of day again."

Nadier took over the exposition. "They'll be able to travel within the reach of the mountains, not a single step more. Yes, I have thought of it. As I comprehend, I will be the last of the dark elves."

"And you are okay with that?"

"It is as the Ha'Lof's prophecy states. I will represent dark elves in the coming age."

"That's a singular phrase."

"I know."

They continued to lock eyes, stares filled with their own kind of convictions.

The Watcher told him, "If you are smart, and wise, and bullheaded, and really lucky, you can change prophecies. I've seen it happen. End of the world stopped by sheer stubbornness."

Nadier contemplated silently, staring down to his feet. He then started, "My brother tried to show me something. Something about this world of the light. I'm not sure what it was, but I want to try to protect it until the day I can find out. This is the path I've decided."

Nodding understandingly, The Watcher returned his focus to his tome. Without looking up, he told Nadier, "Honestly, being the last of your kind is not as great as it seems. I thought I'd finally get some alone time, but our lives are just too long to go unaccompanied for such a length. But at least you won't be the only one who is the last of their kind." The man went silent, his gaze sifting back and forth between the pages of his book.

Nadier knew what he meant. Both Adelaide and The Watcher were the last of their kinds, even if Adelle did not know it yet. The last sentinel, and the last... whatever The Watcher was. A *hymn*? He thought he remembered the man mention it. Soon, Nadier himself will become the last of the dark elves. He made his way into Adelle's cave.

Over the time they had travelled, the fruits Adelle have gathered had gone bad. A strong scent of citrus filled the cold air even without the bowl of fruits left at the table to emit the smell. The green-haired elf sat at the back of the room before her chest of belongings, obliviously packing and planning on what to bring with her. Littered around her were her axes, her great white grey fur coat, a couple of spare clothes, and a small leather pack that was half filled.

She voiced out, "I thought I'd have more stuff than this."

He asked, "Why?" She had apparently heard him coming in.

"I've been living here for over a hundred years."

"You've never done much outside. You lived off your hunt, and you got through day-to-day with a simple fire." He walked forward, looking over her shoulder and into her chest. Only one last thing was left within. "Spiralé."

"I told you, that's a ridiculous name for a bow."

"I made it, so I get to name it," Nadier replied. "Are you going to take it?"

"I'm thinking," she answered. "You know how I don't really like to use bows."

He sarcastically let out, "Yes, yes, you like your axes. You're a great axe wielder." He placed a brotherly hand on the fluff of her head. "But where we're going, we don't need greats. We need the extraordinary."

Flickering beats of flame shone out over the pages of the Black Tome. The Watcher continued to pour through the information, doing his best to remember all that he can. He knew what others thought of him. A mad man. A genius. A child. A savant. In truth, he was perhaps just two of those things. Aside from his powers to control time, he did not possess any more abilities other humans did not possessed. He wasn't good at sports; had no talent in studying; no extraordinary memories, or possessed any greater understanding of the workings of the universe.

But he had time.

Hundreds of years of time to learn. And he had experienced a lot. The internet was really helpful for a period.

He spoke aloud, "I still don't quite know why you are here. Why now? Why not a few days earlier when the pain was more raw?"

The figure of Kathleen Ambershey, ember eyed, blonde haired, all down to the details of her freckles and maroon lips and dressed in a plain brown dress sat beside him.

Kathleen replied, "Maybe it's because you're in a war now. You have issues with wars, after all."

"I never told you about my war experience," The Watcher noted.

"That's why I'm a hallucination," she smiled at him, stretching her non-existent legs towards the fire. "I don't need you to tell me anything. I am just a figment of your brain." He was disconcerted that even his illusions had shadows, which told him how much of the world was simply in his head.

"Right..." he let out a sigh. "Why is it even the part of me that's insane is still smart?"

The silence replied him, the hallucination gone. The flames of the camp fire cracked and popped. His eyes no longer focused on the book in his hands.

Chapter 30

Lord of the Beasts

The woman with short, messy blue hair and a pretty boy face that glistened with sweat stabbed the training spear into the ground. Her sweat stained, tight fitting singlet showed off her slightly built body and the hems of her cargo pants were stained with dirt. She raised her hand to the left in gesture and Luce tossed her a bottle of water from the sidelines.

Luce asked, "Have you seen the new movie?"

After taking a swig of water, she replied, "What movie?"

Luce walked up to her, taking in the surrounding indoor stadium with floodlights shining in from the far corners of the field. Save for a maintenance worker fiddling with a panel on the far end of the track, everyone else had left.

Luce replied, "Jacques, don't act like you don't know what I'm talking about."

"Relax, love." She stepped forward and gave Luce a welcomed kiss. "I know the one. About crossing the Helm, right?"

"Yeah. What do you think of it?" Luce crossed her arms seriously.

"About the movie? I thought it was a little campy. Effects were pretty decent, but they could use a little more Eikly. That man can act."

Luce raised a brow. "I'm talking about them walking The Path. Going across to Eltar. Leaving this sentient forsaken place."

"Are you worried about not killing that Titan?"

"Yes!" Luce shouted back, pacing away from Jacques in frustration. She turned back on her feet. "It's treason, Jacques! I walked away in the middle of a fight! They could lock me up! Put me in front of a firing line!"

"Can I ask you why you did it? Or rather, didn't do it?"

"I don't know? What do you want me to say?" Luce was on the verge of screaming. "That I don't have the guts to kill something that's alive? That I think all living things deserves a chance to try? I'm a coward? I'm a terrible soldier? What?"

Jacques nodded understandingly and walked up to the younger girl, placing two gentle hands on her shoulders for calm. "No one has ever been tried for being a conscientious objector and it's not going to happen to you."

Luce took a deep breath, closing her eyes to take peace in the temporary darkness. She opened back up to Jacques and asked, "What if they do?"

A smile back. "Then we run. As far as we can. To somewhere where, hopefully, there won't be any wars."

Lucinda Baerrinska woke to a cold breeze that floated through the edge of the town. Cirus, the lone of the Twin stars that was left in the sky for the winter was ported to set over the edge of the world in the west. In front of Luce, to the south, the ridges of the Titan Plains ended in a sheer, left-lined by the protruding treeline of the forest and stretched with roads of grass. The silhouettes of a marching line approached the town of Valent.

The bench she sat on was one of the many that lined the outskirts' fences of the town. The quaint but countryside gesture of openness almost overshadowed the events of the previous day, where hundreds of the town's citizens condemned Adelaide with violent prejudice, a prejudice Luce could not fully dissuade against.

Adelaide was a murderer, someone who had killed countless number of people over the years. Defending her actions were next to impossible. But 'next to' was Luce's argument. Adelaide fought against what she saw as an invading force against her home. The same argument used by every war that had ever been fought in the history of the world. What gave so many people before her the leeway to escape judgement but not her?

It was thin.

But Luce wanted to be right. Needed to.

"Luce?"

She looked up. The marching line had reached her and the group of Titan Rangers surrounded her bench with one man who stood directly before her and in front of everyone else. He had the short greying-brown hair and rugged beard of those that had slept on the streets all their life. His gentle hazel eyes scanned her face and a beam of a smile formed from his rugged lips. Light wrinkles shaded his forehead. Before speaking, he pulled together the tattered coat he had worn throughout his life in an attempt to refine, covering up the loose greying singlet underneath.

"Hey you," Joashden Stalewaver greeted. He continued to wear the same leathered cargo pants brought over from the bottom of the world, patched and age-worn as he liked the feel of the fabric.

"Hey yourself, old man," Luce greeted with a smile.

"I'm not that old."

"You are old."

"That's no way to talk to your elders."

"'Elder' is just another word for being old."

He grinned, "It's good to see you again, Luce."

She leaned in for a hug which he readily gave back.

A hume girl jumped out from behind his large back, exclaiming, "I'm here too!"

"Hello to you too, Misti." Luce smiled to her as she left the embrace.

The tomboyish hume danced around Josh. Wearing a set of maroon cotton long-sleeved shirt and dirt stained shorts, she hopped and skipped her way back to the crowd of Titan Rangers, her brown hair blending in with the rebelliously and ruggedly dressed group, all of whom held the poise of survivors, holding in their hands varied weapons. From swords and shields to the rare rifles and nailguns.

Josh smiled back at the hume girl before turning back to Luce to ask, "Where's this Grandmaster Enhancer you wrote about?"

She gestured back into the town. "Trying to talk the mayor into lending us the aid of their militia."

He nodded. "Okay. I'll go help him negotiate something. You brief the squad on what they'll be doing." He gently patted her shoulder and strolled past.

"Hold on!" she turned back and called out to him. "I'm retired!"

Josh kept walking. "So am I!" he stated nonchalantly.

"That's because you're old!"

"I'm only fifty-four!" he shouted back finally as he entered the town.

Luce let out a sigh and turned back to the group. Made up of men and women; elves, humans and humes, the Titan Rangers were unlike any other major organisations in the world. A tightly knit community of people, they were more akin to a mercenary guild than any government or armies. Everyone held similar goals of protecting nature and life along with the preservation of the Titan species, hence, their name. The group consisted mostly of the remnants of the wood elves of Eltar and any hume that left the Antipods of Everwind, though humans made up a small percentage as well.

Luce wondered how long it had been since she was amongst so many of her trade.

She started by asking, "How did you all get here so fast?"

Misti answered, "I intercepted your message for The Holdings. Josh was already at The Yard, so I decided to make my way there and get a group ready to move."

Luce asked, "I got lucky?"

Misti smiled affirmatively and Luce let out another sigh. They had been running too heavily on luck recently. Adelaide's miraculous rescue at Ra'Kalen and The Watcher's timely return to Valent. She wondered if that pool of good fortune would be running out soon.

A male elf from the crowd asked, "What's our move, leader?"

"I'm not your leader anymore," Luce replied.

Impatient, Misti exclaimed, "Nobody cares! Just get your gear on!"

Luce rubbed a thumb against her temple where a headache was building. For some reason, she thought Adelaide and Misti would get on well, with their crass attitudes leading the way. And for a brief moment, she wondered if maybe Jacques and Adelaide would hit it off as well. With another sigh, she braced herself and stepped back into the familiarly uncomfortable shoes of a leader.

"The dark elves are readying for war with Everwind. We have a small infiltration group on their way to Ta'Galadul to stop the main forces," she explained as thinly as she could the plans of The Watcher. "We on the other hand will have to deal with the vanguards. Two siege golems, courtesy from the Seracue Dominion."

Misti dropped her playful persona, asking, "How did they get here?"

"The golems? That's a good question. But I'm afraid we'll have to find out after everything has settled. We're low on manpower, and lower on time." She refocused her briefing back onto the plan, her voice turned grim and her eyes scrunched as the fading light of day glared off the lightly snow dusted fields of the plains. "The golems are currently being controlled by dark elf terramancers. However, once the main dark elf army is cut off, the golems will revert to their base instructions. Destroy Everwind. They'll barrel straight for their target and Valent is in their way."

"We could set up a perimeter and buy time to set up holding spells," Misti suggested. "Trap them between the forest edge and–!"

"No." She was cut off by Luce. "We're going to redirect them around Valendra Forest and away from the town. We'll stop them outside the walls of Everwind."

The Titan Rangers gave her questioning stares, eyebrows raised in surprise. Murmurs quickly flooded the ranks and many were asking, "Why not stop them here?"

Luce continued, "I know this is dangerous, and that this plan puts the lives of the people of Everwind at risk. But there is a greater reason for this, one which I cannot share with you, for your own safety."

She was the trump card. From what Naider had reasoned, Light did not yet know of her involvements. As far as the Lord was concerned, she was a non-player. A neutral party. It had to be kept that way for the plan to work. A distraction party backed by some of the most destructive creatures of war a mere stone's throw away from the walls of the city without the fear of being stabbed in the back. All eyes would be on them, including those of Lord Light. The perfect distraction.

She emphasised again, "I can't tell you the hows and whys, but the fate of not just the people of The Forum, but that of a whole world, depends on the success of this mission." She straightened her back and stood to height, her hand instinctively moving to touch her rifle for strength. "I have never, and will never, force anyone to follow. But know that I will never ask you to go somewhere where I'm not willing to go myself. I ask you now, my friends, will you walk with me?"

Chapter 31
Seven Leafed Clover

"Keep trying," The Watcher egged on from their cover at the edge of the forest.

Frustration hung in the air as Adelaide exclaimed, "I told you, it's not possible!"

Nadier watched patiently from his perch atop the canopy, occasionally glancing south towards the stone gates of Ta'Kalenyilgah. They were waiting for the dark elves to start the Transcendent Ceremony, where they would return their aeronium coating back to the aeronium pond. With his elven sights and using Light's manipulation of the horizon, Nadier could see the stream of dark elves that were slowly returning to the citadel. The gates being fully closed would be the signal for the start of the ceremony and for them to move. Until then, The Watcher focused on training Adelaide for perhaps the most important role in their plan.

"It's possible," The Watcher reiterated. The pair sat on the forest floor, a pile of small rocks between them.

"I have never teleported inanimate objects before!" Adelaide exclaimed as she tossed a rock away in anger. "I can only teleport people."

"And I keep telling you, that's not physically possible!" He raised his voice in equal hair-tearing emotions.

He glanced up to see Nadier shaking his head in amused disappointment. The Watcher took a deep breath. Despite her age, The Watcher sometimes felt that talking with Adelaide was similar to speaking with a teenage girl.

"Listen," he decided to explain his trail of thoughts from the start. "It's literally not possible for you to be able to only teleport living things."

Her attention piqued and she asked, "What do you mean? You keep bloody saying that, though you've yet to actually explain anything."

"Your clothes, your weapons, all of those are inanimate object. Your outer layer of skin, your nails, those are also not fully biological parts of your body. Those are dead skin cells but you teleport them just fine."

"They... they are of the body," she tried to explain the phenomenon away.

"What about me and Nads? We're not part of your body, but you've managed to teleport us before," he referred to their escape from The Tower and their battle with Light. His tone dropped as he said, "It's not possible to teleport selective things, including living things. You teleport areas of space. That's why there's always a cloud of rust after you teleport. You're folding between two points of space."

He straightened his back and with a motion of the wrist, produced the rock that she had thrown away just moments earlier. Extending his palm in a gesture for 'try again', she sighed and took the rock back.

Adelaide muttered, "If only you were an elf..."

"But I'm not. The moment I step into the city, I'll get killed. So it has to be you and Nads."

She let out a breath for calm and The Watcher could not help but think how far she had come. Just a few days ago, she would have likely axed him in frustration. Whatever Nadier said to her at Valent must have had a great impact on her.

"Okay," she continued. "Let's try this again."

"Focus," The Watcher instructed.

He noted how her powers were more similar to the metahumans of his own world. Like himself, hers was a focused, individual ability that could extend uncountably further. Though he had a theory of the workings of her powers, the origin was still shrouded in mystery.

The crunching of leaves had him turning his head. Nadier had landed down beside them. Returning quickly to a trained calm, the dark elf approached with an ominous announcement. "It's time."

The pair nodded back and Adelaide got to her feet. Stretching her shoulders, she said, "I'll scout ahead." She disappeared in a puff of rusty brown smoke.

The Watcher coughed slightly from the gas and mentally noted 'magic farts' as a joke he would use on her later. Left with Nadier, the two men exchanged glances.

Immediately, the dark elf asked, "What do you think are our odds in succeeding?"

"You'll teleport in with Adelle and follow the crowd," The Watcher began the explanation of their plans again. "After that, Adelle will–"

"I know the plan," Nadier interrupted. "But I want a number. What do you think our odds are?"

The Watcher picked up a leaf from the muddied ground. "A seven leafed clover."

"I'm sorry?"

"The chance of finding a four leafed clover is one in ten thousand. A five leafed clover is one in a million," The Watcher said, spinning the leaf on its stem. "Our chances are more along the line of finding a seven leafed clover."

"That's not very good."

"It's not as low as you'd think though."

"Why a seven leafed clover?"

"Seven is a lucky number," The Watcher replied with a grin. "And that's how skilled and lucky we have to be."

Adelaide reappeared in another puff of smoke. "We're clear," she announced on her return. She laid a hand on Nadier's shoulder. "Time to go."

The dark elf looked to The Watcher and said, "Remember to clear our way out."

After a nodded reply, the two elves vanished from the scene. Left alone to his thoughts, the time traveller took to listening to the sounds of nature. The rustling of leaves, the croaks of animals he had yet to read about, and the whispers of the wind. All of which were sounds he had not gotten accustomed to, despite having lived for so long. He was used to the loud honks from cars on the streets. The constant whirring of machineries in cities. The deafening blasts of gunfire in wars. The clashing of steel in battalion skirmishes.

He wondered if it was time he retired from watching over the universe.

"What are you going to do when you retire?" His eyes followed thin air as the hallucination of Kathleen walked out from behind a tree.

He replied with a shrug. "I don't know. Travel around. See the world. Have some adventures. Maybe I'll finally pick up knitting."

"So... exactly the same as what you're doing right now?"

"Except the knitting."

She circled around him and sat back-to-back. "How long have you been travelling?"

"You're in my head, shouldn't you know?"

"So what does the fact that I don't mean to you?"

"That I can't remember?" he replied with honest scepticism.

"And what does the fact that you're hallucinating about me and not, say, Tier, Luviet, or Gallena, says about you?"

The Watcher sat silently, running through the possibilities of answers. However, he already knew what the hallucination was saying about him. It was something he had trouble coming to terms with even though, for as sure as the wars he fought, it was something that happened.

He replied, "It means I can't remember their faces. Can't remember their voices. I catch glimpses of them in passing dreams and that's about it. I've forgotten all of them, save for their names."

"And what about me?"

"I'll probably forget about you too. Hundreds of years of living and you'll need to make some space in your head for the new things."

"Like Adelle and Nads?"

He didn't reply. Did not need to. She wasn't actually there with him. They covered her body under white sheets back at Ra'Kalen. She had probably been sent back home by now. Whoever sat behind him was just a reflection of his own self-questioning.

Kathleen continued, "I wonder why you asked me instead of those two to travel with you?"

It was because he wanted to watch someone react to his life. Have someone, untouched by a heavy past tell him, 'you did good'. Someone fresh and new to share his story with and be reaffirmed that he did the right things all those years ago and the years to come. Someone unburdened with a strong conviction in life to question his motive and reject his premise.

She carried on her questioning. "If I'd lived just a little longer, do you think I would have liked you as much as I did when I died? Knowing all your stories, maybe I'd just hate you a little more."

He pulled his legs into his chest and buried his face in his knees. "I'm sorry. I couldn't save you. Shouldn't have asked you to come along with me. Should have just left you alone on the side of the road."

"You're a smart man. You should have already figured out what my reply should be."

He felt tears build up on the edge of his eyes. "Please, don't say it."

She continued anyway. "Not being able to save people isn't a mistake. Nobody can save everyone, no matter how strong they are." He did not want to hear the next sentence so he covered his ears but the voice of the hallucination echoed through his head. "You didn't do anything wrong."

He let out a silent, internal scream, even as he felt the presence of Kathleen leaving. An irrational physical reaction created by his mind. But he knew that the hallucination was over for now. He remembered the joke of 'magic farts' he had wanted to tell Adelaide. Taking a deep breath, he wiped his face dry with the sleeve of his coat and got to his feet. Bones cracking, back stretching, the world was suddenly more saturated than before. He made his slow way towards the mountain gate.

Chapter 32
Apparition Dragoon

"For too long we have been shunned and buried within the dark of the world," Haeswahl Nunderberg shouted from her stage beside the aeronium pond. Her coating, having been taken off revealed a pale whiteness underneath that was more aglow than most elves. "It is time we reclaim the world that is rightfully ours to rule. It is time to we return the world of the light back to the hands of the shadows!"

The *Kalen-Ta'Rae*, the Gate of Dark Light, a stone archway that acted as the coater for the shadowed skin of dark elves stood still beside her. Twice her height and width, the centre of it was a thin layer of translucent purple hue that danced forebodingly, backed by the absorptive darkness of the aeronium pond behind.

Thousands upon thousands of dark elves had gathered around the aeronium pond till they spilt into the streets and alleyways. Some sat with their feet dangling off seats from rooftops as they listened to Haeswahl's speech from afar. The last few of the dark elves still covered by their black aeronium skin stood in a line of dozens before the Gate of Dark Light. One by one, they knelt before the gate, giving a silent prayer for the success of battle and a hopeful passing on of skills and ideologies back into the pond. With their hopes given, they passed through the gate, shedding their skin of darkness.

Haeswahl drew her sword and punched it into the air, an act that was reciprocated by the crowd with a roar of a huff. "We are the dark elves. The superior race of Tearha! Our ancestors feared us and hid us under the earth. But no more! We will retake what is rightfully ours!"

The last elf in line for the gate stood unmoving, an act which caught Haeswahl's attention, bringing her speech to a grinding halt.

The mysterious elf asked, "Is that the propaganda you have fed them? A tale of superiority?"

The commander, in a confident stride, slowly walked off the stage. The crowd had grown silent as Haeswahl made her way behind the stranger. "I know that voice."

With a fluid hand, Nadier pulled off his hood and downed his scarf, turning to face the commander of the dark elves. The strongest Spellblade of their generation after his brother, Haeswahl Nunderberg was a military genius that had studied and rehearsed the scenarios for war for hundreds of years in anticipation of her moment of glory. And he was about to do something incredibly stupid to her.

He asked, "Where is *ma Ha'Lof*, Nintarin?"

"She has not been your *Ha'Lof* for a long time now, Wanderer." Haeswahl paced before him, a glowing look in her calculating eyes. He knew she was weighing the option of directly attacking him. "Nintarin has been remitted to her chambers. She will remain there until the war is over or she acquiesce to support us."

"I see..." Nadier muttered, slightly disappointed that he would not have the chance to rescue the seer. He took a deep breath before returning his attention to Haeswahl and told her directly, "I challenge you for the council seat of commander."

A wave of murmurs spread through the crowd and Haeswahl cocked an eyebrow in question. "You are not a Spellblade," she noted.

"Commanders are not selected because they are Spellblades," he lied. "Commanders are selected by strength. The strongest of us becomes commanders. It just so happens that the strongest have always been Spellblades."

"Is that a fact?" Haeswahl asked.

"Does it sound disputable?" he replied.

She stopped to contemplate, her eyes scanning his for signs of waver. A hushed mutter in the crowd drew questions of her authority and instigated shaking in rumours of fear. To counteract the dissent, she said aloud, "I should have killed you without an utterance of words." She turned and started walking towards the crowd who parted away in a circle, creating a makeshift arena.

Nadier followed, adding, "If you had killed me without letting me speak, morale would drop. The people would question why you murdered a kin in cold blood."

"You wagered the fate of a continent on my compassion?" She took her place in the arena, drawing her sword which lit up in flames.

"No, I banked on your tactical genius. That you were smart enough to take the bait," he replied, pulling out his daggers. He loaded a cartridge of neverite into his left blade and a red lined vial into his right. Hood up, scarf up, he readied himself for the fight. "But if I did wager on anything else, compassion would not be the worst."

"And now, you get too honourable a death than you deserve."

Sword aflame, she slashed the weapon vertically down, sending a line of fire that twirled and cycled into a ball, hurtling towards Nadier. His main blade, held in a forward bladed grip and seeping in highly combustive liquid, moved to his side. With a fluid step away, he simultaneously slashed at the fireball, the contact between weapon and flame created a backfire explosion, negating the blast of both attacks, flickers of orange ambers fading into the dark like pyreflies.

He charged at Haeswahl who reciprocated with a melee cut from her flaming sword. He slightly dodged, parrying the weapon just off the side with his left dagger before thrusting his right at her face.

She leaned back slightly, his blade just a nail scratch away from the bridge of her nose. She brought her sword up to counter. He brought his explosive dagger down to meet the blade. The weapons met and the blast threw them apart.

Nadier regained his footing almost instantly and charged back in. His offhand dagger, held in a reverse grip with a ring worn around the index, swung out on the finger. He flicked his hand forward and the blade slashed at Haeswahl like a spin of a fan. She dodged. He swung back and charged in close enough that she could not bring her sword in. With another flick, his dagger returned to his palm and sliced back for a thrust. She dodged back again.

Irritated, the commander stabbed her sword into the ground and an explosion blasted out from the penetration point, sending both of them flying back through the air, though they both managed to land on their feet.

With a roar, Haeswahl shouted, "Enough!" The left side of her face lit up red, her circuits running at full. She held out her left palm and snaking flames quickly orbited and gathered into a giant ball of flame the size of a head. "**Escraeh Ra'Yovix!**"

Pellets of flame shot out of the ball of fired towards Nadier in seconds of succession. He started running offside, the pellets flying past him into the ground, blasting apart the earth in small explosions on contact. The crowd behind him dispersed in haste at the manic attack.

Haeswahl's palm followed Nadier in aim. The Wanderer meandered his path, dodging as best as he could as the main sourced fireball shrunk in size with each attack. The commander pushed her palm forward and the remainder of the fireball rocketed towards him. Larger and more destructive, despite sidestepping, the blast from the final attack as it exploded against the ground knocked Nadier off his feet.

He let out a grunt, the pain reverberating through his body as he landed on his chest. He turned over onto his back and was faced with the tip of Haeswahl's blade.

"Well fought, Wanderer. But you are not strong enough to take my seat. Not even remotely close."

He smirked. "I know."

Sensing something amiss, she asked, "So why challenge me?" Rage and scepticism scrunched across Haeswahl's expression.

"I'm a dark elf. Lies are my swords," he added with a laugh, "I'm not the clincher. I'm the distraction."

She turned to the Gate of Dark Light. Beside it, Adelaide stood. With a wink to Haeswahl, she placed a hand on the stone archway and teleported the top half of it away, what remained cutting off cleanly in a cloud of rust. Afar, the other half of the arch could be heard crashing into the ground within the city. With the gate destroyed, no other dark elves could re-coat themselves from the aeronium pond.

Haeswahl turned back to Nadier, her face literally glowing red with rage as her magic circuits burned and her cat-like eyes narrowed. "*Da'roaw!*"

"And don't forget it."

She pulled her sword up, readying to cut his head off. An arrow hit the handle cleanly with such force that the weapon flew out of her hands. She turned to Adelaide who held her custom bow – *Spiralé* – in her hand post-shot. Haeswahl held out her palms, ready to blast her away with another gathered fireball.

Nadier spun on the ground, dancing on his hands and back. With a fluid top-spinning strike, he cut across his opponent's shins with a neverite dipped dagger, slashing through the mana shell that protected the mage. Following the momentum, he kicked upwards, knocking the commander's hand up, the fireball blasting skywards into the ceiling which exploded in a nova of red. With another spin and push, he jumped back onto his feet just as Haeswahl fell to her knees, shins bleeding from the attack.

Adelaide ran up to her companion, grabbed his hand, and before the dark elf commander could react, the two teleported halfway across the city.

From their rooftop afar, Nadier pulled down his hood and scarf and listened to the echoing screams of Haeswahl as she cursed his name. Large chunks of rocks and stalactites fell from the cave's ceiling from her fireball, crashing into a loud, panicking crowd at the aeronium pond. Dust caught within devastation lifted into clouds.

Breathing hard from his fight, Nadier pointed out, "She's not happy about this."

Adelaide patted him on the shoulder and reminded, "We're not done yet."

In the distance, Haeswahl Nunderberg screamed, "Release the Titans!"

Chapter 33
The Long Shot

"Where are we going?" Adelaide asked as they ran down the streets. "We're supposed to be looking for the terramancers controlling the golems!"

Nadier replied, "The fastest way for us to find them is to find the Ha'Lof."

She replied, "You mean Nintarin?" Nadier turned to her with a cocked brow that asked how she knew that name. Adelaide snidely remarked, "I follow the news."

"From your trees?"

"Yes, from my fucking trees."

"What does that word even mean?" Nadier asked of the insult.

"I don't know. The Watcher didn't tell me. But I love how it just sails out the mouth."

The dark elf sighed as they turned the corner on the empty street. With the rest of the city gathered at the aeronium pond and them travelling at the speed of an occasional teleport, they did not expect to have any company. Speeding towards the centre of the city, the Council Chambers could be described simply as a giant stone box. The width and height of a third of the cavern, the building was a towering twenty storeys tall and wide, with cells of windows embedded over the sides like hives.

"There!" Nadier pointed. A sole window on the highest floor had the bright flicker of flames.

"I thought dark elves didn't need light?" Adelaide asked.

"We don't," he confirmed. "It's a signal."

She placed a hand on his shoulder and they teleported towards the glow.

They reappeared within the eloquently polished room. Opaque white drapes surrounded the king-sized bed. An ornate clothes stand stood to the corner with a set of similar looking silk black dresses, each glimmering with dust of gems to make them individually valuable. A marble dresser and silver rimmed mirror was the most extravagant of the furnitures in the room. A single candle stood flickering on the table, casting an almost blinding display of dancing shadows across the night stricken under world.

Adelaide noted, "There's no one here. Maybe she escaped the city?" She pulled apart the drapes to the bed to find an empty frame. Not even the mattress was left.

"That's not possible. Not without an aeronium coating." The dresser he inspected was relatively empty. Save for a comb, a few pieces of jewellery and sparse hairbands were scattered around. "We destroyed the gate, so she can't go anywhere."

"Nads," Adelaide called.

He walked over to her as she picked up a letter stuck under the frame of the bed. She handed it to him.

He unfolded the letter and read the contents before passing the paper back to her. "It's for you."

"What?" she replied in surprise. Taking the letter, she read the contents out. "Demon Eyes, the two terramancers are kept on the third floor of the Eastern Pillar. Third window from the right. Heavily guarded. When the candle runs out, they will step out onto the balcony." She lowered the paper. "Why is she telling me this?"

Nadier stepped to the window which faced the Eastern Pillar. "She must know you're the best archer on Eltar."

"I am not," she replied, taking the letter to the fire after memorising the contents. She joined him at the window.

"Just because you don't like archery, does not mean you're not the best," he insisted. She had been hearing him remind her of her skill with the bow for decades.

Adelaide huffed. "There's another part at the end. It's for you."

"What did it say?"

"Wanderer, when this is over, head north."

"North of the city?" he questioned.

"Doesn't say."

They stood silently for a moment, contemplating the cryptic message. Nadier then instructed, "Forget it. We'll figure that out later. Let's focus on the matter at hand."

Spiralé, her custom bow, hung at her side. A small leather holster on her left waist held the bow tight with a simple notched metal clip.

As she joined Nadier at the window, she unclasped the weapon and held it in her left hand.

The bow had a green reijidium metal cable tied to the nocks that ran the face side of the limbs to the grip. The cable was further tied evenly at eight different points along the spine of the bow. Made of dark caraco wood, the bow had a onyx gleam to it. The cables ran into the grip, the latter of which was wrapped in lined leather, save for the a small port on the right where the arrow would later rest against her fingers. A small rubber roller sat within the port. The long bow was three quarters her height when strung.

She reached for the arrows from her quiver at the right of her waist. Two long arrows with just a finger from the tip at full draw were chosen. One was held dangling between her index and middle fingers while the other by her thumb and the string.

Nadier unloaded the neverite from his dagger, uncapped the vial, and poured the contents onto the sharpened tips of the projectiles. Since they were aiming for mages, it was a needed addition to penetrate their outer magic shells.

Adelaide aligned her first arrow against the string but refrained from pulling. Her thumb was the only limb on the bowstring. The shaft rested on her left thumb and against the rubber piece of the grip, her index notched the arrow from dropping out. The second arrow was held strong between her index and middle fingers. Then, they waited. She took aim without raising the bow, getting a sense for the distance between them and the pillar half a city away. She counted the windows. Third from the right, third floor. Just below the line of sight given by the other buildings with only the top half of the balcony visible over barren rooftops. The cave was cool but breezeless and they could hear the scrambling of thumping steps from the panic across the city.

Then, the candle light was snuffed by darkness. The head of two figures stepped out onto the balcony of the pillar. She raised her bow at a high angle, lifted her left index from the arrow, pulled the bowstring with her right thumb, and released the shot in one quick motion. The stretching of the limbs of the bow pulled the metal cable of the limbs, stretching into the grip. The small coil within the grip revved. On release, it whirled, spinning the rubber piece on the grip, reducing friction of the arrow against the handle and giving it a slight but game changing boost in spin and power.

In a split second after firing, she had slipped the second arrow out from between her fingers and notched against the string and onto her thumb. The first arrow was halfway through the air, now descending from its arc. Again, she waited to pull. Holding onto a draw only reduced the power of the shot.

A fifth of the distance left in the first arrow's journey, she finally drew the second one. The second was aimed straighter than the first without the angle up. She did not need it. She fired. Just as the arrow scraped past her holding arm and the fletch brushed against her left thumb, she focused, and teleported the projectile across the city.

Even from their distance they could see the first arrow with the weight of gravity penetrate the left mage's throat. The second arrow reappeared right before the other target, piercing clean through the skull and exploding out the other end. The two bodies crumpled where they stood.

She turned to Nadier with a grin.

The dark elf asked, "Was that so hard?"

"It's not as fun as a fight." She clipped her bow back onto her waist holder. "There's not much challenge when I'm using a bow. I still prefer my axes." She tapped said weapons which dangled from the back of her waist.

Nadier sighed and shook his head. "You're just like Watcher and Light."

"How so?"

"Monstrously strong." His brows crooked as he noticed. "When could you teleport arrows?"

"First time trying. I had the idea after Watcher told me I could teleport objects," she begun her explanation. "When I teleport, I don't lose any momentum, so I thought the same could go for all cases."

"You bet the future of the continent on a test run?"

Deadpan, she replied, "Yes."

Silently, he ran his hands through his hair and rubbed the nape of his neck. She could almost see Nadier's head exploding at the revelation. Adelle could not help but let out a soft laugh at the dark elf's discomfort.

Nadier exclaimed softly, "You and Watcher are going to kill me."

She placed a hand on his shoulder and affirmed him, "Not today."

They teleported out of the room.

Chapter 34
Trader of Places

The hallucination of Kathleen Ambershey leaned against the wall with arms crossed in annoyance under the arch of *Ta'Kalenyilgah*, the stone gate of the dark elf city which stood towering over them. The Watcher paced up and down the length of the gate, his fingers nervously rubbing away palmy sweat. Moments ago, the gates had been closed after the guards retreated into the dark to join the ceremony. He had managed to use his power to reverse time on the gates to a point where they were opened. He reasoned that he did not break open the door. It simply never closed.

Vexed, Kathleen asked him, "Can you just calm down?"

The Twins were setting. Light was fading quickly and shadows were drawing through the north-eastern flat plains. A large flock of birds burst out of the canopy of the forest to the south, caws echoing through the air as they crossed the clouding skies towards the western twilight.

"Can't help it," The Watcher told her. "Nothing I can do."

"Shouldn't you be used to it by now?" she asked casually. He did not reply and instead continued his steady pacing. She looked around at the guardhouse built into the side of the gate. "Where are the guards?"

"I'm guessing Nadier's distraction worked. They got called back in."

"Lucky for them. You would have killed them." He was uncomfortable with how she noted murder in a way he did not want his subconscious to be thinking.

He corrected, "I wouldn't have killed them."

"Sure..."

The tumbling of rocks echoed through the highway path that led down into the darkness of the citadel.

Squinting into the shadows, The Watcher asked, "Is anyone there?" Silence replied, and he called out again into the dark. "Adelle? Nads?"

Another period of quiet was presented to him. Reaching into his coat, he took out his pocket watch. The crystal glowed slightly violet as he ran a charge of power through it. He raised his left hand and snapped his fingers. A bright ball of light popped out floating before him, a coagulation of slowed and trapped light that pulsed white. With a slight gesture, he sent the makeshift torch floating into the darkness. As the ball crossed into the deeper shadows, growing brighter as it went and lighting up even the ceiling of the tall cavern, red eyes reflected like a pack of wolves waiting to pounce. Hundreds of dark elf soldiers stood in the black of the tunnel, helmets on and armoured up, swords in hands ready for battle.

"Shit," The Watcher let out at the sight of a battalion of warriors. "Not cool."

Kathleen asked the question his body would have asked in a moment, "Why aren't they attacking?"

He took a closer look at the dark elves. "They aren't covered in aeronium. Look, their skins are white. They're probably waiting for night to come."

"Unbelievable. Nadier and Adelaide actually did it. They destroyed the gate."

The Watcher grinned, "I never doubted them for a second."

"If that's true, I would never have said it the way I did."

He was not particularly enjoying the presence of a conscience that could call his bluff. However, he had an even more pressing matter at hand. He had to stop the dark elves from leaving at the end of twilight. He had to hold the line till the siege golems made it out. Examining the light from the Twin stars, The Watcher drew the sword from his back and drew a clean line into the ground just before the gates as if a stick through sand.

He sheathed his weapon and announced to the army of elves. "Hello! I'm the Watcher! How are you all doing?" The soldiers did not reply. He thought that was rude as he felt his greeting was heartfelt and sincere. "Not the speaking kind, eh? Fair enough. Fair enough. Then, just listen and I'll do all the talking. This line here is not for show. Nope. It is for your safety. For this is where you'll continue surviving, so long as you do not–!"

"Enough!" A female voice boomed from within the tunnel, cutting his monologue short. "There is no need for your plans, Watcher. Soldiers, stand down and return to the city!"

Shuffling started within the dark elven ranks as the soldiers immediately and obediently turned away from The Watcher and began their journey back down into the city. The Watcher, with another snap of his finger, dispersed the ball of light in a bright burst. The tunnel walls gained a higher colour tone and contras for a few seconds with streaks of rainbow's hues glaring before the light bounced back and out into their normal routine. The passageway was thrown back into darkness and The Watcher could only watch as a woman dressed in a long black robe stepped out of the blackness into the light shade.

The woman swept back her onyx hair and said, "Greetings, Watcher. I am Nintarin Waynwalker, the *Ha'Lof* of the dark elves." She gave a slight bow.

Kathleen chirped, "I thought she betrayed the dark elves. Why are they still listening to her?"

Nintarin replied, "Because my full actions have yet to be revealed to the people. The commander wants their morale high for the battle."

Stunned, The Watcher stammered, "Are you talking to–? Can you see her? Are you talking to me?" He pointed to Kathleen then to himself.

"A little of both," Nintarin explained. "I am a telepathic seer. I predict the future by reading thoughts across time. The ability to read minds is an extension of that and I can hear her voice in your head. It's very noisy in there but this Kathleen's is undoubtedly the loudest at the moment."

He had dealt with telepaths before and never enjoyed their encounters. Their abilities to dig into ones' minds was deadly when properly honed. Though there were some ways to counter their abilities, telepaths were often powerfully annoying.

Kathleen asked, "What are you doing here?"

Nintarin's hand slipped out from under her robe and swept back towards the dark highway. "I am clearing your path. My last act in this 'war'."

"This is weird," The Watcher noted. "Outside of my head, you must be talking to yourself."

"No. I am conversing with you."

He started, "Why must–"

"Seers be so cryptic?" Nintarin finished for him. "That is a question I doubt anyone can answer."

"Please don't–"

"Do that? I shall try," Nintarin replied with a sly smile.

Daylight was waning and orange bathed the outside of the gate, the light sliced over the side of the mountain in a canvas of burning light. Nintarin stepped out to the edge of the shadow behind the line drawn by The Watcher. The colour of flames baked the ground slowly, angling out towards the line in the ground.

With a sigh, the Ha'Lof looked past him towards the outside sky and said, "The aeronium gate was our lifeblood. Our ancestors built it with help from the dwarfs. It gave us an option to avoid extinction, a chance to once again stand out in the Twins' light." She reached out a bare hand into the twilight. Her pale white skin almost glowed in the gleam. "We were given the chance to feel the warmth of life again. But our blessings we did not take. We let greed seep in and fester. Let it take roots in our hearts. An unavoidable outcome of all living beings to always want more."

Kathleen called out, "Hey..."

Nintarin's hand began to redden in the light. Patches of maroon blood formed on the outstretched palm. The Ha'Lof turned her hand over a few times, baking both side until the reaction painted her pale hand red. Sighing, she finally pulled back her blistered, scorched, and bleeding hand.

A small tremble shook the ground and the group turned back to look into the darkness of the highway.

Nintarin noted, "The Titans are here. I guess that part of your plan is complete." She began walking back into the highway.

"Wait!" The Watcher called out and the dark elf stopped in her tracks. "Come with me. I can get you out."

Nintarin did not return to gaze at him. With a steadied voice she instead warned, "You're in the leagues now, Watcher. The individuals you will face on Tearha will be nothing as weak as the ones you've challenged before. You're no longer the only one with the power to take on gods now." The quakes of the earth grew stronger and louder, rhythmic in steps taken by the Titans that were travelling out from the depth of the dark. Nintarin finished, "I appreciate your concern and offer, and I admire your philosophy of rescue, but I cannot in good conscience say that is an optimal outlook. You cannot save everyone. Not me, not Kathleen. Though I do thank you for trying."

Without another word, she returned to her trek back into the dark home of Ta'Galadul. disappearing into the shadows just as night turned over the last light of twilight disappearing over the far off horizon.

Kathleen piped, "That was weird and oddly helpful."

"Deus ex machina," The Watcher admitted in a melancholic tone. Nintarin's arrival and dispersal of the troops had been an unexpected but welcomed aid.

The trembling ground continued, rising in strength and sound as loud thundering stomps could be heard echoing from within the tunnels. The stars started to litter the sky, grouped in heavy blots. The Watcher noted he had not been able to properly appreciate the night sky until then, not with everything that had happened. Focused entirely on the stars, he did not notice the trembling rise to a deafening mash.

Kathleen noted, "All that noise in your head. The shouts of people you failed to save. It must make it hard for you to focus on the real world."

Just as she finished, the sky was covered by a towering creature. The siege golems, head just barely under the towering Dark Gate of Kings, stomped overhead on centauric legs, stone arms swinging stiffly at their sides. In a single file, the two giants marched down the slope of the mountain, obediently following the final instruction of their former masters. If all had gone to plan, the terramancers controlling the Titans would have been knocked out and left with no control save for their last commands.

In a puff of rust and smoke, Adelaide and Nadier reappeared at the gate beside him. The trio stepped out completely from the cover of the earth and into the winds of Tearha. They stared at the golems wandering off in the direction of Everwind and by extension, Valent.

Adelaide approached The Watcher. "How about that? We fucking did it!"

Nadier reprimanded, "Watcher, you will not teach any other vulgarities to Adelaide."

She replied, "I'm over two hundred, Nads, I can swear what I want to swear. Right, Watcher? Watcher?"

The time traveller had turned away from the Titans and was now facing the gates in silent contemplation and stewed on what he was about to do. Nadier approached the former and placed a reaffirming hand on his shoulder.

You cannot save everyone.

Nintarin's parting words echoed in The Watcher's mind. He held his pocket watch tighter than before and the memory of his brother, Tier, flashed through his mind. From the side, Kathleen gave him a supportive smile. He turned his head over to Nadier who nodded in solemn understanding, and lastly to Adelaide who stood with arms crossed in unfeeling impatience.

With a deep breath out, The Watcher reached out his free hand towards Ta'Kalenyilgah. With a downward swipe, the entirety of the gate and the parts of the mountain behind it crushed down in a heap of dust within the blink of an eye, sealing the entrance to Ta'Galadul with the literal weight of a mountain. The way in and out of the Dark Citadel was buried forever after.

Chapter 35
He Who Marched

Luce could only describe the sensation of seeing a Titan akin to an orgasm. A sense of wonder that overwhelms you. Your body numbs over and freeze as the sight of monstrously towering creatures that should not possibly exists lumbering across the landscape. Despite having faced numerous Titans in her short life, Luce continued to admire the creatures for their sheer sheerness even as the two siege golems started their slow approach from the mountains. From her distance, even from the dark of night, the moving Titans were clearer than a ship on empty ocean waves.

"Hulvarks," Joashden Stalewaver said, walking up and taking a stand beside her at the edge of the town of Valent. "That's the official name for them back on Katoki."

They watched the Titans descent the mountainside, two sore thumbs that poked out of the background. At their foreground, across the field of South Valent, Misti and her group of three other terramancers continued to pull up a long and tall wall of earth with their magic. Stretching half the length of the town, they needed the dirt wall to encompass even the last building. The non-terramancer Titan Rangers and the town's militia reinforced the slanted blockade with gathered spare wood and copper beams, all working feverishly under glowing flickers of lamps.

He said, "I don't think we'll be able to redirect them with just a dirt wall. If only Miguel could help out, I'd guarantee it would work. That guy is ridiculously powerful."

"I told you," Luce repeated, turning to look back at the Tower of Everwind. "We can't let Light find out we're with Miguel and the others. We have to keep neutral for this bluff to work."

"I know. Still don't think the wall will work though," he admitted grimly. "But... now that I've seen them, I think there's another way."

"What's the plan?" Luce asked. "Do they have any weaknesses we can use?"

"They're like the Rankors. Quadrupedal. But theirs is to make sure if they ever lose a set of legs, they'd still be able to move." Josh was an encyclopedia of knowledge on golems and mechs. After his arrival on Eltar, he had also brushed up his extensive information to include sentient Titans. He continued, "Their shells are the toughest of all the basic golems. Lined with onyx, which is why they have that dark glow to them. The general thinner sizes of their bodies makes them more compact, harder to break. "

"Weaknesses?" Luce repeated.

Josh continued, "Their forearms are heat treated with mineral veins as reinforcements. Their command sigil is fused within, so we'll have to drill through the wrecking balls to start the conversion."

"Josh?"

"Yeah, Luce?"

"Weaknesses."

He sighed. "If you take out two of its legs, the Hulvarks will just continue walking on its forearms. They are golems made for siege. They are made to take hits and anything short of an Agarez's cannon would probably graze them."

"We're not killing them, old man."

"I'm not saying that," Josh quickly corrected. He knew how much the talk of killing Titans angered her, and she knew he'd never jeopardise their relationship that way. "I'm just pointing out that these are brute force Titans, made to punch an entire building into the ground while on the front lines of war. Redirecting them to Everwind alone would take considerable amount of power. But good news is, they are slow, so that gives us some time to recover."

Luce noted, "You still haven't told me their weaknesses yet, old man."

"Sure I did," Josh replied with a grin. "Think it through. They are tough. They are slow. They are near unstoppable Titans of brute force."

She blinked, and her mind clicked. She ran down the dirt road out of town, leaving Josh behind. Dashing across the field, she approached the workers building the walls. Misti saw her running towards them and stepped away from her work.

The younger girl greeted enthusiastically, "What's turning, boss?"

"Change of plans. We're going to force the golems out of their path. Brute force it."

Misti's eyes widened in surprise. "Wait? We're going to hurt them?"

"Josh says these golems are some of the most sturdy of their kinds, so it's okay for us to be a little rough. If it fails, we can at least slow them down until the wall is finished."

The girl nodded back, a glint of seriousness in her eyes. "Okay," she replied with unflinching trust.

Luce asked, "What's our strength?"

"There are only sixty of us," Misti recounted the number of rangers with them. "Two water, one wind, two fires, four earths, one lightning, one dark, one light, two nature. Ten impact weapons. The rest are disablers. We've got about eighty strong from the town's militia."

Luce hastily spewed, "I need you and one other earth mage to come with me, as well as the two pyromancers and all rangers with high impact weapons." She quickly ran through the impromptu plan in her head. She added to the list. "Hydromancers with ice spells and aeromancers."

Misti nodded. The girl ran back to the working group, clapping her hands together as she made her call to arms.

"Look at you." Luce turned to the voice too see that Josh had slowly followed her down. "All grown up and leading an army."

"An army's no joke," she told him.

"I know," he replied with a gentle smile. "This? I think they're more like a rescue team. They're not cut out for fighting."

Luce nodded in agreement. No one joined the Titan Rangers to fight. In fact, many of the inhabitants of the two strongholds were deserters of The Forum's army. Men and women too peace loving or scared of death for bloodshed.

Josh added, "They just returned, by the way. That Watcher fellow and the elves."

"Why didn't you say so earlier?" she puffed childishly.

"You ran off before I could tell you!" he exclaimed.

Letting out a derisive sigh, Luce asked, "So, where are they?"

"In town. Once they've rested up and restocked, they'll head to Consortia's side of the forest to wait for the signal. They told me to wish you luck." He paused with a cheeky grin. "The elf girl, what do you think of her?"

Luce exclaimed in surprise, "Adelaide?" Josh nodded in confirmation. "She's hot headed. Vulgar. Completely lacks discipline."

"But she's cute, right?"

"Are you trying to blind date me again?"

"Come on! It definitely won't go like last time. What about the dark elf?"

Perplexed and feeling her cheeks heating up, Luce tried to divert the subject back. "We're in the middle of a mission! This is not the time to talk about my dating life."

"Fine," Josh pouted like a big old bear. "But we're not done with this."

Misti ran back up to them and gave an enthusiastic if not overly dramatic and sarcastic slap-to-the-face salute. She reported, "Ready to go when you are!"

Luce nodded and said, "Right. I'll be with you shortly. Also, can you get someone trusted to head to my cabin and retrieve the spear?"

Before Misti could even nod, Josh piped, "I'll go." The two girls turned to him, confused. He gently explained, "I'm not much use here now. After The Walking Path, my back's not what it used to be." He jokingly patted his spine, much to the worried frowns of the girls. He added with a chuckle, "I'm kidding. I'm fine. I'll go get the spear and be right back."

Luce sighed before giving a nod of understanding and a small smile back. She hugged the man and he rubbed her back gently. Though she would never admit it and though he annoyed her greatly some times, Josh was like a father to him ever since crossing into Eltar. He had taken care of her in the worst days of her life and everyday after.

They parted and Misti stepped up to the plate. The younger girl said, "See you in a bit, pops."

Josh smiled. "See you in a bit."

Father and daughter hugged, and Luce had never seen Josh smile more than when he was with Misti. The man looked to Luce, and his smile widened. Finally, they left the embrace and Josh turned to make his way back into the town and towards the stable. The two girls watched his large back disappear between buildings.

"Fifty-four," Misti said.

"What?" Luce asked.

"That's how old Josh is this year. After everything he has been through, he really should take it easy."

"What's stopping him?"

"Us," Misti replied nonchalantly. "The way we live at least. Every time he hears us in trouble, he comes running."

"That's why I retired early."

Misti chuckled toothily. "Well, you're not retired right now." She gave patted Luce's back. "Come on, sis. Let's go." She led the way to the waiting team of Titan Rangers.

Chapter 36
Planet Breaker

"Hold!" Luce shouted, her throat coarsening from giving directions. She was taught to shout from her lungs when commanding troops during her time as a Titan Hunter, but she had never gotten that trick down pat.

They had rode out into the field and intercepted the golems' path and were facing them from running distance as night engulfed them.

Once more, she yelled, "Ice over!"

The two hydromancers ran forward towards the pair of towering golems, circuits on their arms glowing bright teal. Buoyant snowfall had carpeted the ground in a thin cotton fluff of white, kicked up by the charging rangers in puffs as if dandelion seeds bursting into flight. Light from the stars in the night sky glittered in slight reflection over evening dew. With sweeps of their arms, the hydromancers froze the stretch of ground before the golems in a cold snap.

With each earth pounding, ground shaking, ice shattering step, the golems made their way across the land, breaking apart the frostbitten floor with ease. When all eight of their feet are on the patch of ice, Luce gave the attacking order.

"Cover them!"

Misti and her partner terramancer pulled at the earth, their circuits glowing a dark brown in the black night. With forced jabs at the empty air, large chunks of dirt flew to and slapped themselves over the body of the respectively targeted golems as extra layers of earthen armour. A sole aeromancer stood between the two Titans. With channelled wind, she summoned a spiralling up-draft of strong tornading current.

"Fire!"

She raised her rifle joined by the line of rangers with high impact weapons of hand cannons and grenade launchers. Together, they fired away. They aimed low as their shots angled upwards from the aeromancer's gale, curving through the air. The two pyromancers joined the assault with high explosive fireballs that soared and curved towards their targets, lighting up their surrounding like tiny Twins. The spells hit after the initial firing squad, exploding into dispersing embers and sparks.

Dust cleared, flames vanished, and the night returned to a beating peace drummed by the steps of the siege golems. Knocked off the path of ice from the heavy bombardment, the golems continued their undaunted march as if they had simply been slightly pushed by a passer-by on the streets.

"Luce!" Misti approached with heavy pants. "I don't think we're going to make it."

The leader of the Titan Rangers looked back towards the town, glowing lamps and torches dotting the stretch. The builders of the earth wall was reinforcing the far end of the town, doing their best to secure the last few buildings in the way.

Luce said, "We're almost there."

They had been repeating the freezing and pushing process for three hours, executing the manoeuvre over a countless dozen times, moving just a dozen steps westward each attempt. They had pushed the Titan's two third the way out of the path of the town.

"Just a little more and we can clear the outskirts."

Misti argued, "But the mages are tired." She pointed to the worn out rangers, some bent over against their knees.

The golems were stalking past them. The longer they rested, the less time they had to continue the push and less effective each of their hits were at angling them away. Luce stepped up before her team and the pyromancers intuitively produced two floating balls of flames as sources of light, casting flickers across her face; Shines off her golden hair; Glitters off her sweat.

"We are Titan Rangers. We swore that we would protect the sanctity of life, especially those of Titans, and the ones who can't protect themselves." She held the barrel of her rifle and forcefully jabbed the butt into the ground for emphasis. "But what is the point of protecting just a segment of life?"

She pointed back towards the town. "These buildings are the livelihood of the people that live there and I will not rest until I save all that I can! What say you?"

The rangers roared back, punching their weapons and arms up to the air. She was not sure when she became the effective communicator she was. Luce had always just said what was on her mind and somehow, people tended to follow. Somehow, she ended up leading.

Luce continued, "We'll work in cycles. Mages, take turns where you can. Everyone else, alternate between firing and ammunition runs. Instead of timed attacks, we will fire at will for as long as possible and keep the pressure up."

Another affirmative yell from the group rang through the night. The Titan Rangers reaffirmed to move.

Adelaide hid within the shadows of the vine laden canopies of the northern trees. She looked to the walls of Everwind and pass them to The Tower in the shining distance. Golden light danced around the city, reflecting off bronze pilings and copper beams. Steam rose from the power plant next to The Tower. A blimp slowly ascended from the hoverfield in the far east, tardily floating into the vast void of space.

She said aloud, "I bet I could hit Light from here with my arrows if I tried."

From below, meld within darkness itself, Nadier replied, "He'll see it coming. Unless you can teleport the arrow straight into his face. But even then, he can enter hyperspace and just dodge it then. Also, it's honestly a little far, even for you."

Near them, Miguel slept against the trunk of another tree deeper in the forest. The Watcher sat in a small clearing studying the stars. As recently as a quarter a season ago, she would not have expected to be in the company of a human, hume, and dark elf at the same time.

As she thought of her companions, her mind wandered back to Luncinda. "I wonder how the Titan Rangers are holding up?"

Her ears could pick up the faint sound of explosions in the distance. She was sure Nadier and Miguel could hear them as well, but simply chose not to speak of it.

"It's not like you," the dark elf noted. "To care about people."

She sighed, admitting, "I'm turning into something weird."

"You say that as if we were normal to begin with."

"Let me ask you something," Adelaide let out. "Why are you doing this? Is it really to protect the world?"

Nadier went quiet. She could not hear even his breathing. Years of training to stay hidden in the shadows granted the man an impossible stealth. A deep breath overtook her as she thought of the scenario of an army of dark elf like him creeping into war.

His voice broke, "I'm not sure. It could be I'm still after revenge for my brother. Or maybe, I'm trying to find my own path and the road of a protector seems lighter on the soul than an assassin's." She barely heard him shuffle away. "Get some sleep. Even at their fastest, they'll only reach Everwind by next midnight. Mostly likely the dawn, latest the noon, after. Not much for us to do but wait."

She swung her legs out over the branch she sat on and laid back into the trunk. Light snowfall began dotting the landscape as a long series of continued blasts rocked the faraway field. She fell asleep almost immediately to the midnight light.

Dawn came and the chirps of birds from the forest were abruptly cut off into terrified squawks by the crashing of trees. The Hulvark golems took their first step through the western spine of Valendra Forest, easily bending trunks and crushing barks as they ploughed through the dried winter trees. The Titan Rangers had done the impossible and redirected the monstrous sized creatures out of the town's path. By Miguel's calculation, the forest would slow the Titans considerably, though would not stop them. It was the optimal time to regroup and recuperate.

Luce watched as Misti lifted the rubble from the fallen building of Valent, helping the town recover from the destruction that had barrelled through like a force of nature.

The Mayor of Valent, still in his crisp, neat dressings, approached Luce. "I do not think I can thank you and your Titan Rangers enough."

"Think nothing of it," Luce replied. "Though I would appreciate it if our presence was not announced to The Forum for a few days."

"Of course," the mayor agreed. "I don't know what you and your... friends... are trying to do, but no one goes to such lengths for reasons of unimportance. You have my silence for as long as I can keep them."

"Thank you."

Just three of the outskirts buildings were destroyed by the Hulvarks, and half a roof smashed away in a spell gone awry. Aside from that, every other structure was left intact, and the golems had even miraculously missed the stables. The earth walls had also held much better than Luce had expected, buying them precious minutes for one final run to save the orphanage. Damage was at an absolute minimal.

Luce added to the mayor, "Once we settle the Titans, our rangers will return to aid with reconstructions and repairs."

The mayor nodded a gentle thanks before returning to assess the damages. Misti, after clearing her pile of work, walked over, beats of sweat rolling down her face despite the cool and dry winter air.

Luce instructed, "Once we've settled the arrangements, have everyone rest up for the day. We'll chase down the Hulvarks once twilight comes." Misti nodded and Luce gave her a pat on the shoulder. "Good work. Get some rest when you can."

"You too," Misti chirped with positivity.

Chapter 37
The Historian

Leaves danced in turns, the tiny sapling's stem slowly but surely widened and grew with each passing second. A new leaf unfurled from a fresh branch. A stray root bulged out from the dirt of the ground. The stem slowly turned from green into a light white, on the way to brown.

"This is weird," Tier noted as he shifted his hand in control of the growing plant, the stem bending towards the direction of his palm as if within it held the sun.

"Plant manipulation," his brother replied, a scanner beeping in his hand as he ran the camera over Tier. "The ability to control flora. Quite specific, this ability. I wonder how it works?"

"Doesn't matter," Tier laughed as he stopped playing with the growing sapling. "As long as it works. What does it say about yours?"

He turned the scanner onto himself. After a second of running, the device let out a beep and he turned it back over and read, "Latency: Focal point temporal manipulation."

Tier asked, "What does that mean?"

The brother sat there for a moment, carefully considering the words. "I'm not really sure," he lied.

"You're useless."

"It's not like you're any better."

The siblings continued their insults and banter, chatters continuing under the autumn trees, amber leaves slowly sailing down as a breeze blew through the bustling park.

It was midnight by the time The Watcher woke. He had fallen asleep with the Black Tome in his lap, flipped opened to a page on the culture of the dark elves and marked on the paragraph he was at by a leaf. He had passed literal decades of his life by reading. Countless hours spent staring at ink on pulped wood. He preferred the turn of the page with the touch of faint nature. It reminded him of family.

Miguel sat by the fireside, the flames sheltered by a makeshift roof strung together with the snow-soaked winter vines of the northern trees, preventing the light from being visible from afar. Upon noticing The Watcher waking up, the hume tossed an apple-sized purple fruit over. The Watcher caught it instinctively. After a moment examining the gel-like skin, he bit into the food.

"Juicy. Crunchy," The Watcher reviewed. "Taste like pear."

Stars in the sky shone brightly with faint pockets of galaxies that flickered less. Adelaide's form could barely be seen in a tree on the border of the forest keeping watch with Nadier at the base. A wolf howled in the distance. A late flock of birds faintly flew overhead. He took another bite of the fruit.

Miguel asked, "Had a good dream?"

"Yeah," The Watcher replied. "Is it always like this here? Dreaming about the past?"

"It is. We're not really sure why though. I theorise it has something to do with the universe's connection to time, but I must admit, I prefer this than the kind of dreams Earth has. Random nonsensical stuff. It's too much a workout on the mind if I'm resting."

"I don't think it's random," The Watcher replied. "From what I understand, the dreams are connected to the dimensional structure. Where I come from, we dream about different worlds and different stories, glimpsing the multiverse without ever knowing it exists."

"What about you?" Miguel asked. "Do you have stories?"

The Watcher took another large bite out of the fruit. With his mouth half full, he replied, "Sure. Loads of them. What would you like to hear? *Harry Potter*? *The Old Kingdom*? I even have the complete works of Plato memorised."

"How about the story of The Watcher?"

The time traveller swallowed hard and grinned with purple teeth. "Nah. That's boring. Besides, you're living it right now, aren't you?"

"What about before 'Watcher'? Before Tearha?"

"What is this? Some kind of job interview?"

"Maybe."

Adelaide's laughter could be heard from the treeline, with Nadier's stern but hushed reprimand that she keep her voice down carried over the tone of a whisper on the wind. A light from The Tower in the north flickered off. Lightning flashed in the far west over the ocean.

The Watcher began, "There was a war. Just like any story, there was a war. But this one lasted a little longer than the normal stuff you're used to."

"A hundred years?" Miguel asked.

"Try seven thousand," he replied with a straight face. He watched as the Enhancer's eyes widened at the number. With a sigh, The Watcher kept his black book back under his coat and finished the last of the fruit in one bite and tossing the seeds unceremoniously to the ground. "At first I thought the war lasted just two years. Turned out what I thought was the beginning was just the end. I went back in time chasing the strings to the very first butterfly that started all the fighting, hoping to cut off the tale at the root."

Miguel added, "And you turned out to be the butterfly."

"How did you know that?"

"I watched *Back to the Future*. Ierba introduced it to me. Storyline could use work. Fun movie."

"Heh..." The Watcher let out a laugh, amazed at how pop culture managed to travel across time and space. He continued, "Yeah, well. I became the first butterfly. Bit the bullet. Ate the dust. I started a seven thousand years war, all because I failed to stop the first one. But I wasn't allowed to mess with the things that I knew happened. Rules of time travel meant if I even took a step too far right, I could erase the entire universe from existence. How fun is that? So I had no choice but to watch as everyone died. Some from old age, many from fighting. My brother, my best friend, my mentor, my wife, everyone died. All because I couldn't stop the first butterfly when I had the chance to act. I'm the last of my kind."

Miguel let out a sigh and a disappointed shake of the head. "It's not your fault, you know?" He said it with such clarity that The Watcher looked up with a level of confusion. Miguel explained, "I've heard that story dozens of times. Princess Scarlet, Lady Rubi, King Adam, even my own son. Honestly, I don't know what it is about you people that make you act like this."

"What are you talking about?"

"The lot of you go around saving worlds and protecting everyone you can see. But every time one of the thousands of lives you've saved don't make it, you take it as if you've failed the entire universe."

He tossed a handful of twigs into the dying fire and the ensuing sparks jumped and cracked into smoke. "But I guess that's what makes all of you who you are. People willing to shoulder the whole weight. But you need to remember this, Watcher..." Miguel turned to watch as Adelaide and Nadier approached their camp-site. "You're not alone in this."

With a silent nod of half-hearted understanding and contemplation, The Watcher got to his feet to take his turn at guarding. He passed the two elves as they came into the light. Nadier gave a nod while Adelaide replied to his smile of a greeting with a stuck out tongue. He took one last look back as the pair sat down beside the fire to warm up. Pulling his coat closer together to brace the cold, he headed to the lookout tree.

Adelaide chose the tree. The vines were the thickest amongst all of their surroundings, criss-crossing in hatches and curves. It was also the tallest tree of the nearby bunch, giving them a clean view up to the gates of Everwind and across the plains to the east and back down south. The long scope were only possible using Light's control over the view of the continent to their advantage. Though if he had made that much leeway with the bent light, The Watcher could only shudder to think how much asset Light had pulled with it over the decades. With a sigh, he began his slow climb up the snow littered trunk.

He took each step with a grunt. Though his body was young, he could feel age seeping into his mentality. He wanted to sit down by a warm fireplace with a cup of hot chocolate and a book while shouting at all the kids that trespassed onto his lawn.

Are there hot chocolates on Tearha? He was surprised at how the question came about.

He had not actually thought about it. Somewhere, in the back of his mind, he always imagined that after the whole affair with the portals had been dealt with, he would return back to his universe and do what he always did. Travel back and forth in time, overseeing the universe as it progressed from one calamity to the next. But the thought occurred to him that as long as he did not travel backwards in time again, he would be free from his chronic bonds on Tearha. There would be no need to worry about stepping on any other butterflies. His timeline would once again be straight. He could live normally.

Honestly, I don't know what it is about you people that make you act like this.

Miguel's words rang in his mind, even as he found a comfortable nook within the thick branches of the tree to lie into. The statement echoed deep into his thoughts.

...you people...

He contemplated the idea of a farm in a countryside. He'd spend the rest of his days toiling away in the field. And one day, maybe, when he was finally ready to go, he would pass away on his porch in a rocking chair, a nice book in his lap and a hot cup of chocolate by his side. One day, he would gain enough control over his powers enough to shut off the instinctual survival mechanism that saved him every time he was close to death and healed him of his every fatal injuries. The instincts that made him immortal.

Kathleen's voice rang out in his head. "Look."

He turned to the plains of Eltar. The two giant golems marched across the land as they had been doing for the earlier part of the day. However, behind them, breaking out from the edge of south Valendra Forest was a trail of dust unmistakable as the kickbacks from horses galloping. The Titan Rangers were on the move. By his estimate, their mission would begin just an hour after dawn.

Chapter 38
The Rat

The Watcher looked on from afar as arrowheads glinted and muzzles flashed off the walls of Everwind. Projectiles disappeared before the light of the day while the Titan Rangers closed in from behind. As the bullets found their targets, splotches of dust blotched off the golems that approached the walls with the same effect as a speck of dust hitting a person. He watched as a lone pair of Titan Rangers on horses circled the Hulvarks at full speed, moving between the golems and the wall, likely Luce in an impassioned plea to Everwind for a ceasefire so as to allow them to handle the situation.

"She's got this," Miguel said to him from his side.

"I know," The Watcher replied. "But..."

"You want me to stay here? Just in case Light comes out for a personal visit?"

"Am I that annoying when I do smart mind reading things?"

Miguel shrugged. "No idea. I don't know you well enough yet."

The Watcher patted the hume in the back wordlessly. He left the Enhancer to watch over the Titan Rangers from the edge of the forest. Explosions echoed from across the landscape as the rangers engaged their targets.

He joined his two elven companions at the northern edge. Nadier was taking a check of his utility belt while Adelaide sharpened an arrow. They turned as he walked over and Nadier asked, "Are you ready?"

"Let's go."

Adelaide chimed, "Where to?" She sheathed her arrow back into its quiver.

Nadier pointed across the field to a third of a way from the edge of the eastern wall. "There's a gated sewage outlet in that general area."

They watched as Adelaide did a quick mental calculation before she said, "It's quite far. It's going to take me at least two teleports to reach." She glanced to the two men with her and gave a smile of joking disgust. "Especially since I'm carrying you two dead weights."

The Watcher confidently placed a hand on her right shoulder. "I have full faith in your ability."

Nadier set his on her right. He added, "Try to aim for somewhere where we can hide from The Tower."

She looked to the dark elf in annoyance, her expression universal in teenagers for not wanting people to tell them what to do. Turning back to the plains, she scanned the landscape. Her head stopped at a gentle slope slightly left of the line to their destination. When they reappeared, they would be visible for just a moment, but even with the angled hiding spot, there was a chance The Tower would spot them. They could only hope that the distraction by the Titan Rangers bought them the opening. With a nod of her head, they teleported across the plains, reappearing right before a mount just tall enough to barely block out the line of sight to half of The Tower.

Nadier quickly wrapped his arm under Adelaide's shoulder, gently lowering the girl onto the ground as she wobbled from the stress of long distance teleportations.

"I'm fine," she waved him away. "Just give me a minute."

The Watcher took a prone position and crawled his way to the side of the slope, careful not to give away his location to The Tower. Peeking over the mount, he watched as the Titan Rangers, now off their horses, encircle the two golems. Earth spikes shot out of the ground to the right underside of the nearest golem as explosions from fireballs and grenades flashed at the opposite feet. Iron chains sparkled as they were fired from launchers, snaking through and over the air, strapping across the golems. Another earth spike shot out from the front, and the Hulvark stopped in its tracks against the dirt pillar. Slowly, after nearly a full passing minute of yank, pull, and push, the first golem fell over to its sides, smashing up a cloud of dust.

The Watcher whistled at the sight. It was like watching a pack of mice take down a rhinoceros. People scampered around the creature nearly ten times their height and hundreds of times their size, working in rehearsed unison at disarmament.

"Watcher." He turned to Nadier's voice. Adelaide was back on her feet slightly worn, and Nadier called to him from beside her. "We're ready to go."

He nodded back and shimmied to them. He took Adelaide by the hand and she stood up to get a look at her destination. With another blink of the eye, they reappeared at the wall of the city. A short walk east, they arrived at a grilled hole in the wall that leaked brown sludge down the side of the mossy brick into a puddle of black. The trio went to it.

As they approached, they could see a little girl pressing her face against the dirtied grill. The girl attempted to turn to the corner of her sights.

"Nads?" the girl called out.

"Tinarya," he replied sternly. "I thought I told you to just leave the cover open?"

Unscrewing the cover from the inside, she replied smugly, "As if you could find your way around the city sewers without me." The cover slid open and hung by the side.

"You've got a point," Nadier said. The dark elf ruffled her hair to her giggle as he climbed into the cold damp darkness of the sewage tunnel.

Adelaide followed with a brow ticked questioningly at the young elven girl. "Who's the *lika*?"

"Great question," Tina replied. "Who's this walking broomstick?"

"Walking broomstick?"

"Yeah! You look like you have leaves on your hair."

The Watcher chuckled as he entered last, greeting the girl with, "Hello! I'm The Watcher." To the annoyance of Adelaide, who was calmed by Nadier after her vulgarity filled reply was ignored.

"Hi!" she greeted back happily. "I'm Tinarya Twinrae, leader of the Gutter Rats!"

"Gutter Rats?"

Nadier replied back, "Their play group."

Tina pouted back, "We are rebels!" She said so as she closed the cover behind them.

The Watcher laughed and said, "Alright, my little rebel. Lead the way home." The trio parted way to allow her to pass them.

The group of three adults with a combined age of over a thousand and five hundred years followed the little girl no older than nine.

Light shone in stripes through the sparse bars of drainage from the streets above. Shadows of pedestrians crossed over occasionally like eclipses. While the two grown men and woman had to duck their heads to travel down the tight steel pipes, careful to avoid the puddles of grime and slippery moss, the little girl zipped from one end of the tunnel to the next effortlessly, patiently waiting for the trio at each junction and turn.

Left, right, left, a curve, and a long straight path. Cross a bridge over a torrential sludge and around a bend that split, skipping a forked tunnel that led deep down into the earth.

Tinarya suddenly stopped at a cross under a set of foggy skylight. She held her hand up and the trio ceased moving. A finger to her lips told them to stay quiet. Shadows swayed to-and-fro the grate above.

"I thought the dark elves were attacking," came the voice of a female guard, echoing into their space from the world above. "Where is their army?"

"No idea," came a gruff male. "But the Titan Rangers are dealing with the golems at the walls right now."

"Lucky us, eh?"

Tinarya met eyes with the trio. She patted the air slowly, signalling for them to thread lightly for the moment. Gently, they moved past the section as the guards continued their chat towards after hour plans. Once the guards were out of earshot, they returned to their speed of a fast crawl. The Watcher thought he might be hallucinating again when he saw shadows darting out of the corner of his eyes. However, at a bent, a young boy stood below the light from a drain above. Tina hugged the boy before moving forward, and Nadier gave him a high-five before the kid scampered off into the dark of the tunnels.

Continuing through the underground, he caught more glimpses of the Gutter Rats kids, either from the soft echoes of light steps, faint giggles, long shadows on walls, or the blink from his peripherals. They reached a large main tunnel where sludge torrented through the middle of the sewage pipe sided by dirtied maintenance walkways. He pinched his nose from the stench of raw sewage which he made a snide comparison to the smell of rotting corpses bloated with spoilt milk.

The Watcher asked, "How are we crossing this?"

Adelaide smirked and simply teleported to the other side. She turned back to the ones left behind and grinned playfully. The Watcher chuckled as 'magic farts' went through his head again.

Tinarya smiled back and clapped once. The clap echoed down through the tunnel and the clunking of wood and metal rang back. A moment latter, from the darker depths of the tunnel, a wooden platform floating on empty barrels bobbed down the sludge, a rope tied to its back. Once it neared, the rope taut and the barge stopped just before them, creating a temporary makeshift boat bridge.

With a practised jump, Tina took two hops onto the barge and stepped out the other side. The girl stuck a tongue out at Adelaide, and like a child, the latter returned the gesture. The Watcher laughed and Nadier sighed before crossing the barge after them. With another clap, the rope to the barge shook and tightened before it was slowly pulled back to the darkness it came from.

With another turn into a smaller tunnel, they ended at a dead end with a ladder leading up to a closed manhole cover. Tina climbed up and knocked against the copper. After a few seconds, the manhole popped opened and light shone into the tunnel blindingly.

"Come on!" The girl finally spoke excitedly as she climbed out.

The dark elf followed Tina up the steps.

Adelaide, with visible distress on her face from the confinements of the tunnels, immediately teleported out to the top the moment she was able to see light, an act which brought about a short but shocked yell and an immediate berating rail from Nadier above.

The silhouette of a figure leaned over the manhole and a familiar voice greeted The Watcher as the latter took the first step on the ladder. "Hello." A hand reached down towards him. "Welcome to The End of the World."

Chapter 39
Hero of the Mist

The 'End of the World Orphanage' was so nicknamed because kids who were brought there often thought that was where everything ended. The people at the orphanage though, made sure to prove everyone wrong. The motley group climbed out into the alley behind the three storey house that was in slight disrepair. Copper plated shingles hung lopsided at angles on the roof and steam pipes running the walls were oxidised brown. A window on the third floor had its grill left hanging. A teddy bear dangled from a clothes hangar on the bar.

"Are you sure you don't recognise me?" The Watcher asked, staring at the man who had introduced himself as Milton Jones.

The man who ran the orphanage had red hair messier than a bed in the morning. It was as if he had decided to stick his head down the plumbings of a toilet and flushed. His eyes were a faint sky teal and held an airy glassiness in them that shone brightly in the light. With an evening stubble on his chin and slight bags under his eyes, Milton showed the weary signs from having to take care of as many children as he did. But his smile was sincere, almost as if his heart was light on his conviction. He wore a patched white shirt and string-tied brown cotton pants. Simple, rural garb.

"You're The Watcher, right?" Milton replied with a laugh. He held out an opened letter. "It was in the instructions Nadier sent us."

"That's not what I–"

"We can talk more inside," Nadier approached the two men. The dark elf scanned the neighbouring buildings packed too tightly for his comfort to escape. "It's not as safe out here."

The group marched into the orphanage behind Milton. In a file, they entered through the single wooden back door, half repaired with patchwork planks of wood over holes.

"Did you get burgled?" Adelaide asked, pointing to the damage.

Milton laughed. "No, no. It's the kids. They like playing inside the house."

They walked through the orphanage. The sound of scampering feet knocked through the ceiling with flecks of dust falling. Eager little eyes poked out from doors and around the corners of the stairs. Some of the kids waved to Tinarya as she passed, and she puffed her chest out proudly, leading the guests of honour through the orphanage.

They turned into the living room. Lacquered wooden floor gave off smirked sheens from the flickering incandescent lamp that hung from the ceiling. The couches were set in a circle, the middle of which was filled with scattered toys of dolls and bronze figurines. A woman stood from a lone sofa at the sight of the group. In denim shorts, a clean dirt stained white shirt, Joan Jones's onyx hair sifted with the light as she approached Nadier.

"Wanderer!" she greeted the dark elf happily.

She hugged him, and his body stiffened straight, hands at his side at the uncomfortable display of affection.

Nadier coughed out, "Um... it's nice um... it's nice to see you too, Joan." Milton, Watcher, Adelaide, and even Tinarya, all held back scoffs of laughter. As Joan let away from the embrace, Nadier asked, "I would like to stay, but it's important that we get to The Tower as soon as possible."

"We understand," Joan said, gesturing them to the seats. "But the steam tunnels are depressurising right now. We can't open them even if we wanted to."

Milton took a place on a two seater couch and Joan followed. The Watcher patted Nadier on the back and took the single seater to the left of the couple. Adelaide relaxed by leaning against the wall and Tinarya ran off to parts unknown. With a final sigh, the dark elf relented and took the last chair.

"So," Milton began. "Honestly, we don't want to know too much about what's happening, only that it is happening. But we owe Nadier here quite a bit, and if he says it's important enough to risk his life for, we'll help however we can."

Adelaide chimed, "How did this stickler ended up in the graces of an orphanage?"

"The Wanderer is our primary patron," Joan said. "Most of our funding comes out of his pocket. And he helps with making medicine for the children, for a small trade fee, of course."

The Watcher smiled at Nadier. "I didn't know you liked kids."

The dark elf looked to the wall offside with a scoff. "I don't hate them."

The Watcher laughed and turned back to Milton and Joan. "By the way, how are we getting to The Tower from here?"

Milton explained, "The orphanage was built on an old junction between the steam pipes' maintenance tunnels and the sewers. I don't know much about the underground myself, but the little rats like to run around down there, and they say it connects to practically anywhere in Everwind."

Nadier continued, "We'll take the steam pipe tunnels straight through the middle and upper district towards The Tower."

The Watcher nodded, only to have his eyes dart to the corner as he caught sight of Adelaide's ears picking up. "Adelle, what is it?" he asked.

"Someone's coming," Adelaide replied. "I can hear metallic boots clanking. Where are we?"

Nadier answered, "We're at the outskirts of the Antipods." His statement raised a confused glance from The Watcher, to which he continued to explain, "The Antipods are the slums. It's where the Everwines throw elves and half elves to. It's where they keep us outsiders. Any elves that steps outside of the Antipods without protection or official recognition are arrested."

"That's racist," The Watcher noted.

"That's life."

"Quiet!" Adelaide raised. "I hear something else.... wood... clanking on stone?"

"Spears," Nadier deduced. "Used as walking sticks."

Milton got to his feet. "It's the guards. Why are they patrolling now?" He turned his attention to the seemingly empty hallway. "Tinarya?" he called.

The girl popped her head out from the side of a wall as if she had been waiting all along for her summons. "Yes?" she answered.

"Take everyone down to the steam tunnels." The girl nodded, but the man added a last minute instruction. "And do not go into The Tower, you. Stay safe, and don't get in trouble."

Tinarya stuck her tongue out playfully and showed a crossed finger. She gestured for Nadier to follow and the dark elf got off his seat in response. Adelaide stepped out of the room while The Watcher and Nadier hung back.

"Sorry about this," Nadier told the Jones. "I didn't mean to cause too much trouble."

"Nonsense," Joan gently rubbed his shoulder. Despite the hundreds of years of age difference, Joan seemingly held a motherly grace throughout her existence. "You stay safe, and come back in one piece. It's not the end of the world yet."

A small smile tilted Nadier's lip. "I'm not one of your kids."

"Neither are my kids."

With a final thankful nod, Nadier stepped out after the two girls, leaving The Watcher alone with the couple.

Milton asked, "Is something wrong, Watcher?"

Joan gave a slight bow and left the room, noting she needed to see to the children. Upstairs, the thundering of pattering footsteps were like drops of rain, the children scrambling to hide the elven amongst them as the news of guards spread.

The Watcher asked Milton, "You really don't remember me?"

Milton looked quizzical, his face scrunched in an attempt. "No, I don't think so. Should I?"

With a sigh and a smile, The Watcher replied, "No. It's fine. Have a good life, Milton Jones."

"You too, Watcher." The man smiled, to which The Watcher gave a hearty laugh.

With an understanding nod between them, The Watcher turned and followed the rest of his party out into the hallway. Tinarya waited at the end, waving the man over, before disappearing left through an archway. He followed and found an opened trapdoor with a stairwell that led down into the basement. Making sure to close the door behind him, he walked down into the dimly lid underground, where a faint orange glow below lit the way.

"Is everyone here?" Tinarya asked as he rejoined the three in a small tight chamber.

Copper cannisters of hot water and barrels of stored food littered the cramp storeroom. A single lamp hung above their heads provided the sole lighting.

"Yup," he replied. "Let's go."

"Not yet," the girl said.

They stood above a steel manhole cover. From the gaps, hot steam rose with the nose scorching stench of burning sewage. Sounds of pipes clanking and whirring whistles from bellowing steam shouted from below them.

Nadier said, "We'll have to wait a few minutes more while the pipes depressurise. We go in now and we'll just be hit by boiling steam."

From above, they could hear the knocks on the front door from the guards and Joan's greeting as she answered.

"Ma'am, we need to perform a check to see if you are housing any illegals."

"Of course," Joan replied. The Watcher could sense a slight sarcasm and hidden pride under her tone. "Would you like to start with the upstairs?"

"If possible, we'd prefer to check your basement, if you have one."

The four collectively held their breaths at the notion. Somehow keeping a beatific level of calm, Joan replied, "I won't recommend that. The pipes are depressurising right now. We're next to the sewers, so the smell..."

"Say no more!" A guard quickly added. "We'll check upstairs."

They listened as the guards' clanking boots echoed with each steps from the stairs above. A long hiss from below signalled the end of the depressurisation process. Tinarya took a crowbar from the corner of the room and with Nadier's help, opened the cover to a burst of hot smelly steam.

Chapter 40

Seed

Outside the walls of Everwind on the northern plains, the second golem came down to Tearha crashing. Chains dug into the earth tightened as Luce directed Misti and the other terramancers to lock the Titan down. A gentle rain of white sifted between them. The late snowfall of the season did not stop them from moving in heated formation. The first Hulvark that was restrained had two pyromancers torching surgically through the giant stone arms to reach the control circuit implanted within. Only afterwards could the terramancers begin overwriting the magic that bound the creatures to their former masters' commands.

"Hold it down until we're done with Hully!" Misti yelled over the shifting Titan trying to kick up dust.

While walking backwards and reeling her grappling hook back into her rifle's launcher, Luce asked, "Hully?"

"Yes! I'm calling the other one Varky."

"We're not keeping them," Luce replied.

"Oh, come on!" Misti pouted. "I've been practising the swap-over spell for years!"

As they chatted over the work being done, a rider galloped in from the south. Josh's large build of a silhouette was clear and recognisable, even from a distance.

Misti noted, "You sent dad away so he wouldn't get caught up in the fighting, didn't you?"

"Don't tell him that," Luce defended.

"You're so squishy."

"Shut up."

She left Misti to work on converting the golems and approached Josh just as the latter got off his steed. The man unstrapped the spear-cannon from his back and pushed the weapon out towards Luce with a crooked smiled.

Luce gave a snide greeting. "You're late."

"Bah, I figured if you wanted me here you would have just asked." She snatched the spear away with a chuckle and a shake of her head.

It felt like an every day again for Luce. She would be remiss to say she did not miss spending the time and effort at protecting the majestic creatures. Even more of a lie if she had inked no liking her compatriots. They had good chemistry, the group working together smoothly and happily despite personal differences. She enjoyed that part of them the most.

But a loud clapping followed, breaking the bustling work of the Titan Rangers on the field. Everyone turned to the source. In the middle of the group stood a man dressed in all white, glowing brighter than the Twins, with lines of silver etched into the seams of his bleached white suit.

"Bravo!" Light cheered on. Silence fell on all except the pyromancers, who continued their surgical job of slowly melting away the excess rock from the arms of the Titans as a single mistake could cost the creatures pain. "I saw everything. Impressive. Like a bunch of nercrofants taking down a fox. I am Lord Light, leader of Everwind."

Misti joined her father and Luce in standing together, casually taking the spear-cannon away from the latter. She weighed the weapon in her hand.

Luce stepped forward and said, "Lord Light, I am Lucinda Baerrinska, and I'll represent the Titan Rangers in all official negotiations and discussions."

"Please, Miss Baerrinska," Light waved away the notion with a laugh. "There's no need for all that formal speech and pomp. I'm extremely grateful that you and your band of misfits stopped that possibly horrendous siege from happening."

"Well, we are glad to be of–"

"But that's not what I'm here for," Light interrupted, his tone unfitting of the grimness the words carried. "I want to know where The Watcher went."

Luce fluently lied, "Who?"

"You've never heard of The Watcher?"

"My apologies, Lord Light. But I've been a recluse until just recently. I don't receive much news."

The Lord began pacing in a circle, speaking more to himself than the people around him. "There's a chance that you are telling the truth. That you don't actually know who The Watcher is and that I'm wrong. You were simply in the right place at the right time and my suspicions that this is all part of The Watchers plot is nothing more than proof of my insanity, and that by doing what I'm about to do, I'll be starting an inter-faction war." He stopped walking and scratched his luscious hair as he contemplated the situation. "That would be a crazy thing to do. Utterly mad. The Council might condemn me to the pits!" He then turned to Luce and held up a finger like a gun. "But his disappearance from my view corresponds too closely to the Titans' movements. So it's a good thing I'm insane and don't give two crap."

A beam of light shot out of his finger, the spell aimed at Luce. A wall of ice burst out of the ground and the beam refracted through it. Miguel Vallertes quickly moved between Light and Luce, stepping in with a confident gait within the blink of an eye. He turned to Light, and the two superpowers stared down.

Light smiled. "Did you think I'd fall for that again?"

"Dad!"

"Josh?" Luce exclaimed. The older man fell to his knees, hands on his abdomen, grey shirt slowly being covered blood red. Luce rushed to his side and gently lowered him to the ground. "Don't! Don't! Hey! Stay with me, old man! I'm not losing you too!"

"You asshole!" Misti shouted.

"No!" Miguel reached out his hand and tried to stop her.

But the girl had already launched herself into the air with the catapult of an earth spike. She aimed the spear cannon down at Light and fired a grenade. Light shot another beam perfectly aimed at the explosive, which detonated mid air into a cloud of black smoke. Misti dropped through the dust cover and, with spearhead pointed downwards, aimed for Light's head.

Two beams of light fired at her and she twisted in flight. Her body became a rag doll before dropping to the ground, breaking up a cloud of fresh snow on impact. She laid unmoving in the dirt.

"Misti!" Luce yelled, tears streaming down her eyes. She managed to somehow gather up a breath of courage before shouting, "Healers! Quickly!"

Miguel let out a long, low growl as the twin daggers appeared in his hands in a puff of crystallised cold. Nerve-like tentacles stretched and snaked from the weapons' hilts and blades, reaching out to and fusing with his skin. They separated and reconnected to his forearm with every move of his hand, as if they were worms, wriggling in reach of air. His right arm glowed a bright cyan as his circuits lit up in preparation for the battle to come.

Behind him, Luce shouted orders of aid, the young woman torn between the man she treated like a father and the girl who was as good as a sister. Titan Rangers ran from side-to-side in panic while pyromancers and terramancers pushed through the nerve wrecking atmosphere and continued their delicate work on the Titans. To his front, Miguel's staring match with Light did not waver, and the Lord stood with a cunning grin bordering on pride. The Grandmaster Enhancer placed his left hand on his waist and brought the pommels of his two daggers together. The nerve-tentacles connected between the two weapons, and the ones that were set in his skin stiffened to resemble circuits.

"Ex–" Miguel seethed. A burst of energy emitted out from him. A dome of cold that spread with him at the centre. Cotton snow spiked with fluffs of frost and winter grass froze over in waves of white icing. Lord Light generated a sabre of light in his hand. Miguel yelled, "–SEED!"

Light rushed with sword in hand, stepping into hyperspace, closing the gap between him and Miguel at thirty times the speed. The Enhancer reacted, drawing his weapon at the same speed to meet the attack. His daggers glowed, and when contact was made, they turned into a double bladed polearm with the teal blades of his daggers at both end of the shaft. The double bladed pole hummed with cold and the material gently shifted as if made of living muscles.

Under his breath, Miguel whispered, "Cold Fusion!" The name of his legendary soul arm.

"Exseeder!" Light yelled with a manic grin.

The Lord drew his sword back and struck forward in three successive slashes. Miguel pulled back a step, and with deft controls from the nerve-tentacles, spun Cold Fusion in a discus before him, deftly parrying the attack with the momentum of each turn.

He grabbed the edge of the polearm with both hands as it retracted before bringing the weapon over his head and slashing downward towards Light's. Ligh placed the lightsabre under the path of Miguel's wrist. The latter stopped his attack just before his wrist was sliced off by the caustic weapon. Gymnastically, Miguel's right leg kicked straight up, redirecting Light's arm and weapon. His left feet left the ground as Miguel did a backflip. A spike of ice grew out from where his feet parted and shot straight up for Light's head. The latter sidestepped the attack. Miguel landed on one hand and spun on it, slashing his weapon in a wide arc that generated a wave of spiked ice from the tip of the cut.

Light jumped and dodged the first ice spire, landing on top of the ice itself.

Miguel twisted on his arm, pushed, spun in the air, and delivered three slashes towards Light in float. Each cut generated a new wave of ice spikes upon the previous set. Light repeated the jump twice, before being unable to react to the last attack. The Lord's body broke into glowing fireflies, which separated, flew around, and reformed behind Miguel.

The Lord steadied and generated a sword of light in each hand. He kicked off from where he regenerated and went in for the killing cut, assaulting from Miguel's rear.

The Enhancer stabbed Cold Fusion into the ground. "**Corpse Party**!" he shouted.

All went black.

Hyperspace battles were conducted by individuals of monstrous strength. When one gained the ability to enter hyperspace, their parameters, physical and mental, reflexes and endurance, are all enhanced multiple folds for a short period of time. She could only watch, with tears down her face and Josh's unconscious body in her lap, as Miguel and Light's fight of high-speed proportion unfolded.

Before the hydromancers could reach Josh or Misti to treat their wounds, before she had a chance to breathe again, or blink to dry her eyes of tears, in the span of ten short seconds, the battle was concluded. Flashes of light like neon spun like cars in long exposure pictures, and sudden gales of cold and spires of ice erupted before her within snaps.

She could not make out what Miguel shouted under the booms from their burst of speed, but could feel the power when the black dome suddenly appeared before her. Stretching the size of half a field, the dome was of pure dark, with no colour going in or out. It was as if light itself had been caught within it and failed to escape.

And as suddenly as it appeared, the dome vanished in a burst of colours that temporarily blinded her. After regaining her sight, she noticed that where the dome once was, Light and Miguel had switched places from where she last saw them, both facing away. The mutated polearm of Miguel disappeared in a flash of icy sparkles and Light fell to his knees.

Slowly, the Lord light let out a laugh as blood dripped from his face and body from dozens of cuts. A glow of aura surrounded him as his magic frantically ran to heal his injuries. His laughter grew louder and the man got to his feet, suit ruined red from his wounds. He turned, and Miguel did the same, the two superpowers facing each other exactly as they had started.

Light began, "You win this one." Without another word, the Lord dissipated in a flash of light, leaving just droplets of blood in the snow where he stood.

Luce could visibly see Miguel's shoulders dropped as he let out a sigh relief. He turned to her, and with the circuits in his left arm glowing a bright blue, said, "I'll do the healing."

Chapter 41
The Waiting Girl

Steam pipes hissed and whistled. Humid air smoked the bricked lined walls and misted the small maintenance tunnels. Running along the centre line of the city, The Watcher followed behind Nadier, Adelaide, and Tinarya, walking the mile long final stretch towards The Tower. A familiar wave rushed over his body and The Watcher felt a tingle of energy run down his spine. His hair stood on edge as he whipped his body around to find the source of power, only to be faced with the path he had already walked.

"What's wrong?" Adelaide asked from the front.

"Did you feel that?" he replied.

"Feel what?"

Time. He wanted to say it. The trace of chronal energy had swept over the surrounding in a powerful burst. A much more powerful level of energy than he could summon in one moment. For him, it would take a few seconds to build up that amount of energy.

Instead, The Watcher replied, "Nothing. I'm just imagining things."

They continued down the tunnels for what felt like ages. The walls blended into a single view of brown bricks and grey concrete that shadowed by. The copper and steel pipes started to look like a video running on repeat. Finally, they reached a T-Junction, where a ladder in the centre led straight up into another tunnel to climb. Tinarya led the way up.

He climbed after Nadier. The moss at the corner of each step of the ladder made for slippery grips, so he proceeded slowly. The silhouette of the dark elf above disappeared as he climbed out of the tunnel with the light at the end a flickering yellow. The Watcher ascended into the glow.

Lit by two incandescent lamps at opposite ends of the room, the small space was filled with heater tanks, and pipes that ran around the walls into what looked to be a generator with a whizzing pressure gauge. Clanks and hisses were more prevalent in the room than they were in the tunnels.

Tinarya gleefully announced, "This is generator room thirty seven!"

Nadier added, "We're right next to the portal room. How did you know this was where we wanted to go?"

"I'm smart like that!" The girl danced on her feet laughing. Nadier nodded with a smile and ruffled her hair.

"Alright. We're going to take a look. Stay in the tunnels. If we're not back in half an hour, just leave without us."

Tinarya nodded and gave Nadier a playful salute. The trio of "adults" left the room, stepping out into what seemed to be an empty hallway. The sudden quiet they walked into was almost deafening. The noise of steam pipes clunking and whizzing that was rife in the generator room was muted in the corridor. A clunk of metal echoed from far down the passageway and continued on down a bent.

Adelaide and Watcher looked quizzically to Nadier, who returned the expression with a confused hike of his shoulders. None of the three had expected the abandonment the place held. Nadier held gaze with Adelle, pointing to his eyes and followed by gesturing to the pathway down. Adelle nodded and teleported to the end of the hallway. Peeking around the bend, she paused and surveyed the area before teleporting out of their sights.

Moments went by as the two men stood at where she had left them. The silence was starting to mess with The Watcher. He hated long periods of quiet. They never boded well in movies and were always followed with someone being picked off by a serial killer. Luckily for him, it was usually the black man. The steam pipes hissed again. He wanted to make a fart joke.

Then, Adelaide jogged back from around the corner. "It's empty," she announced confidently. "There's not a single person on the entire level. Are you sure we've got the right place?"

"How's that possible?" Nadier replied in surprise. "This is definitely the location."

The Watcher concurred. "I remember this corridor from when they arrested me. Could it be they've moved the experiment?" The trio shared a period of silence before he continued, "No use standing around here. Let's check the portal chamber and see if we can find some clues."

Proceeding down the hallway Adelaide had checked, they turned left where she had vanished right and walked the short final stretch down to the heavy steel door of the portal. They stopped before the door, looked to the slightly rusted handwheel, and exchanged glances.

Adelle let out, "Well?"

The Watcher insisted, "You two open it. I'll keep watch."

"How about a 'no'?" she replied. "You two muscular people can open it and I'll keep watch."

Nadier added, "How am I muscular?" He pointed to his more lean than meat body. "You've got more skin than I do!"

The Watcher held out his left palm, opened face up. He placed a closed fist on top of it. "You've got this game here?" The elves looked at him and nodded, before taking their positions.

"Break wrap cut!

"Ro sham bo!"

"Break wrap cut."

The two elves looked at The Watcher, who threw a closed fist while they had open palms. "Damn it!" he let out.

Breathing deeply in acceptance of his lost, he set himself by the side of the rusted handwheel and began pushing up. The wheel creaked as it slowly turned. Then, Nadier stepped in and added his strength to the other side, pulling the crank down down. Adelaide grabbed from the front and twisted the wheel. In silence, the three heaved, and the wheel turned with a clank, unlocking, the door swinging slightly inward. They pushed into the room.

Above them, the hole in the reinforced glass where Akaras was thrown through had not been repaired. Nadier and The Watcher both looked at the broken segment and dented metal behind it before turning away and focusing themselves back on the task at hand.

The room had been emptied. The batteries that once lined the walls had been unplugged from their stands with wires now dangling and strewn around the room without meet. Where was once the portal generator was left with an empty space littered with leftover parts. Nadier stepped into the portal room with Adelaide to investigate while The Watcher stayed in the research chamber.

He flipped through the piles of notes and paper that were left of the work desk. Carefully but quickly, he glanced through them, finally landing on a blueprint hidden under a stack of folders.

He called out, "They've moved the portal!"

The two elves came back into the room, with Adelle asking, "What did you say?"

"They've moved the portal project," The Watcher explained, showing her the blueprints. "This is a design for a geothermal generator. I'm guessing they couldn't find a way to power the portal constantly over a long period of time and needed to work from scratch."

Nadier asked, "Where would they move such a thing to?"

"From this design, I'm guessing somewhere higher up the levels. You'd need to be a dozen or two storeys above ground for this to work." The Watcher handed over the blueprints. "What's the date written? Third of Winter. When was that?"

Adelaide answered, "Twelve days ago."

The Watcher continued his deduction. "If all these plans were changed just then, it means there's nothing we can do here. It would take at least thirty days for them to build this new generator. And a year for it to fully power the portal." He picked up one of the folders and handed it to Nadier. Adelaide looked as if she was about to hit something to make the numbers go away. "There's nothing we can do here. Nothing for us to destroy or sabotage."

Nadier set the folders aside and asked, "So, what do we do now? We don't know what happened to the Titan Rangers. We might never have another chance to break into the city again. We can't stay at the orphanage, or anywhere in the city for that matter. The patrols are too tightly packed."

He stood there, thinking, for a time long enough that Adelaide went for a walk inside the field-sized portal room and came back. Finally, he said, "I'm going to wait."

"What?" was their simultaneously shocked reply.

"I'll wait here. In The Tower. For a year. Once they've rebuilt the portal, done their research, got everything working, I'll break everything and force them to either give up the project or start from scratch again, which they probably won't have the resources for."

Adelaide scoffed, "How are you going to survive in The Tower for a year?"

"I'll sleep it off," he said. Looking to her, he continued, "I'll find a corner of The Tower to hide in and put myself in a temporal bubble, just like how I was after we escaped the prison here. A year would go by from the outside, but for me, it would be just a few hours."

They stared at him wide-eyed. He was not surprised at their reactions. After all, he was talking about a form of time travelling. A very basic chrono freeze time travel, yes, but time travel nonetheless.

After having a moment to absorb the information, Nadier finally sighed. "I'll tell Tina to pass a message to Miguel. We'll need them to hold the line outside for a year and do what they can from there."

Surprised, The Watcher asked, "We?"

"Yeah, stupid!" Adelaide slapped him in the back of the head. "We've come this far. I know I don't look it, but I really don't want you to become a light beam pincushion." Before The Watcher could say his thanks, she quickly added, "I want you to become my pincushion." She tapped her quiver of arrows with a smile.

The Watcher looked to Nadier and caught the dark elf glimpsing up at the hole in the glass and the crater in the wall left by Akaras. Their eyes met, and the time traveller sighed. "We'll need a place to hide."

Nadier noted, "I've got just the spot."

Chapter 42
Overseer

Travelling through The Tower was almost laughably easy. The elevator that was damaged when Nadier escaped had yet to be repaired, which made the entire shaft free for their movement. Following Nadier's instruction, Adelaide teleported the trio up to the twentieth floor through the elevator line, which lead them to a long corridor that seemingly circled on itself. The ceiling was three times their height and designed in an arc, making The Watcher feel as if the walls were collapsing in on them.

Guards patrolled the level in random intervals and directions, but with a few well timed temporal manipulation from The Watcher to slow and speed themselves up, they got through the blockade with literal whistling and hands in their pockets. They passed by multiple doors lining the outside walls of the corridor until they reached the opposite end from the elevator where a double wood door stood mirrored on the inside. Nadier stopped with his hand on the knob just before entering.

"What's wrong?" The Watcher asked. "You left the oven on or something?"

The dark elf replied solemnly, "I don't really have great emotional attachments about this room."

Adelaide jabbed sarcastically, "Compared to your normal emotional attachments about people."

Without any further explanation, he pushed opened the door and disappeared within. Adelaide and Watcher shrugged at each other and stepped after the dark elf. Immediately, they understood why Nadier detested the particular chamber.

The room was circular and extensively large, made of pale grey concrete that bled boringness into the corner of their eyes. It was a stark contrast to the otherwise copper and red bricked design of the rest of Everwind. Conical pillars held the five storeys high ceiling up at four corners. Ledges lined the walls at intervals, large enough to be rooms of their own with no way up nor walls to keep out intruders. In the middle of everything, tied to a cylindrical pillar, the scene reminded The Watcher of what he had seen at the New York Stock Exchange. It was information that fed through information, knowledge of the world at the tip for anyone to access and play with at their will, except with less humanity involved.

Half a dozen copper pods were hung around the central pillar. Within them through clear glass were blue liquids that held decrepit sleeping bodies of humans, hume, and elves that were scraggy and hairless.

Rubber and copper tubes ran from each pod to the main attraction that hung in the middle facing the entrance. A female human, whose body was wrapped within a copper shell up to her neck, dangled from a set of bars that held her up like a punching bag. Her face was wrinkled and bony, with grey hairs falling from the seams of her scalp. Despite the shrivelled look, The Watcher knew she was no older than fifteen.

The girl's eyes flickered open, and with a soft musical voice, smiled and said, "Wanderer. Did you bring me something nice to eat?"

Nadier replied, "I'm sorry, Rena. Not today. I had not expected to come here."

"A shame." The withered girl turned to Adelaide. "Demon Eyes. It's been a long time."

Adelaide asked, "Have we met before?" Her voice shook slightly at the grotesque masquerade of a human before her.

"We are meeting now."

The Watcher walked up to the girl and placed a hand on the shell that encased her, looking up and down the machine, to-and-fro the connecting cables. His hands balled into fists and trembled. "Who did this?"

"Watcher," Rena replied gently. "You know very well who. I suspect you have since you got here."

Adelaide bombarded, "What is this room? What's going on? And who are you?"

Nadier began his explanation. "This is Renasque Isvael. She is the Overseer of The Forum. She has the ability to predict the future of individuals by names and a brief description of their power or accomplishment. She's the one who gave us our epitaphs."

The Watcher cut in, "No. That's a half truth. She's a seer. A precog. But I'm guessing her original ability was not to predict the names and epitaph," he corrected grimly, limply moving over to the pods of bodies. He stopped at one where the body inside had decomposed to nearly bones, but still held the pale reddish hue of living skin and the bloodshot glow of faded circuits. The body had degraded to the point where he could not even tell if it was a man or a woman. "I'm guessing that power belongs to this person."

Rena replied unsurprised. "That is correct. My original ability was to view the glimpses of consciousness from the deaths of individuals. I see the death of people."

Nadier asked The Watcher, "How do you know all of this?"

"This machine is a circuitry modification pod. A *Lusus Naturae*. I'd recognise this technology anywhere. It confers the specific ability of one to another. If you placed me in the pod and had another of my species in the shell, you'd be able to give the person the same power over time I have. There was this girl, Emily Young, who... It doesn't matter... It was a long time ago." He drifted away from the memory.

Turning back to Rena, Nadier said, "Rena, I apologise. But we're not here to chat." He explained the plan to hide out within the Overseer Chambers. "The ledges on the walls are high enough that no one can see us from the ground. It's the perfect place to conceal ourselves until the anointed time."

Adelaide added, "Right under their noses."

"I understand," the girl replied with a cramped nod that looked as painful as it was uncomfortable to execute. "It is unlikely that anyone would find you here. It is, as literal as the saying, the last place they will look."

"Thank you, Rena," Nadier told her, which she smiled back in reply.

Adelaide placed a hand on the dark elf's shoulder and reached out to The Watcher. The latter took it and with a blink and the trio teleported to one of the ledges on the walls two and a half storeys above the chamber floor. Post teleportation kicked up a cloud of dust. The floor of the ledge had gathered a thick layer of particulate over the years, perhaps even centuries, from the look of things. Each of their steps left a fresh print on the concrete.

"So," Nadier asked, taking a seat in a discreet corner. "How does this work?"

The Watcher snapped his fingers and Nadier froze in place. But he was not completely immobile. His eyelids were closing at an excruciatingly slow pace.

"Nine hours," The Watcher explained to Adelaide, who watched on with a mixed expression of shock and awe. "He's living one year in nine hours. At that rate, it would take him about five minutes to blink. One thousand times slower than us."

"That is just geared up accelerant," she dropped into a native slang of words as she squatted before Nadier, getting a closer look of the phenomenon. "What about–"

Before she could finish, The Watcher locked her in a time bubble of her own. At that speed, any sound they made would not have enough audio over time to carry any substantial distance, effectively rendering them muted from the world. With a nod of satisfaction at his handiwork, The Watcher decided to take care of one last business. Taking out his pocket watch, the magic crystal embedded within glowed a light lavender. With a slight push of force, he teleported himself back down to ground level, manipulating the spin of the planet and pull of gravity in infinitesimal and instinctual ways to perform the feat.

He approached Rena, who had apparently waited for him. He asked her, "How long have you been connected to that contraption?"

"Should be a year now," she replied with a nonchalant smile, as if her predicament was the most casual of situations.

The Watcher noted, "I can save you."

"I know."

"If you stay there any longer, your magic circuits will be too far damaged to remove from the system."

"I know that too."

"It has to be now." He raised his hand and his pocket watch glowed once more.

"You know you can't do that."

He scoffed. He could feel his power just edging at the tips of his fingers. "I can do whatever I want. I have the power of a god."

"But you're not one. Are you?"

Even as tears welled up in his eyes, he could see his outstretched hand shaking. "I can save you," he repeated the mantra. But if he did, there will be a building wide search and he, Nadier, and Adelaide would be found within hours, even with their exceptional concealment. "I can save everyone."

Rena grinned the innocent smile of a girl her age. "And don't you forget that."

Once, in what had to be ten lifetimes ago, in the early years of his powers, he had seen first-hand the damage the machine that housed Rena could cause. Someone had brought that same machine over from his universe, for he was sure that despite the similarities between the two realms, the technology on Tearha could not replicate the monstrosities of his age.

With apprehension, he lowered his hand and diminished his power, the glow of the crystal subsiding. Without another look to the seer, The Watcher teleported back to the ledge where his companions were frozen on. By then, Nadier had finished his first blink. The Watcher took a seat beside the two, but did not freeze himself. His mind wandered back to his past, and he knew only one person capable of recreating the devious machine. An invention that was more a freak of nature than the mutants it produced. That same person would also be the Lord Light he faced now.

He found it poetic that his first battle in the Endless War was against a Lusus Naturae, and that another one had reappeared again there on Tearha. Over 10,000 years into the future of his world, the Endless War started with him, his brother, and people who saw fit to call themselves 'god'. Now, 10,000 years before and within another universe, he was about to end it, and finally lay the war to rest.

Chapter 43
The Tree of Crossroads

The man encircled the table, left fist pounding repeatedly into the old hard wood, the knocks resounding throughout the otherwise silent room. Each hit shook the table, which in turn shook the lantern on it and disturbed the flame within. Eight others stood around the set, their shadows dancing across the walking in flicks and flickers while the world continued to explode around them, including the young man named Pausa Alvet.

The pacing man stopped before the archway that lead into the area, setting both hands on the flat surface, letting out a sigh. He relented, "I don't see a way out of this."

Pausa replied, "That's what I said when I first tried a condom. Turns out I was wrong back then as well." A woman laughed in the corner and Pausa winked back. "Gal knows what I'm talking about."

"Gallena!" the man yelled in frustration.

She replied, "What? It's funny." She composed herself before continuing, "Look, Luviet, we have to remain composed on this. We can think it through together."

But he ignored her. Instead, he turned to Pausa and reprimanded, "This is not the time for you wise-ass remarks."

"On the contrary," Pausa stepped up to table. "I think it's the perfect time for jokes. Everyone's stressed, the world's coming to an end, and we either become rulers of the universe or die in a suicide attack within the next few hours."

The room fell silent. Pausa felt disappointed. He thought he had teed up the joke with well placed wit and sarcasm. An explosion rang through the night, puffing dusts up from the cracks within the walls. Outside the broken window, fire raged across the landscape in the distance. Wind whistled through the shelled building. Not a single one of them reacted to the fighting outside. They were used to it. It was their everyday.

Luviet broke the silence. "Let's take a vote. Who's still in the fight?"

Gallena and three others raised their hands. She added, "Who thinks we should take the deal?" Luviet and another three agreed. "Pulse?"

The room turned to Pausa, who had yet to pass his ballot. The young man noted, "It doesn't seem right."

"Which side?" Luviet asked.

"Both," Pausa replied. "Fighting makes no sense here. With what we know, there's no guarantee continuing on would stop the war. But taking up the offer..."

"Sacrifice one life to save the world."

Pausa continued, "I have no doubt everyone in this room would volunteer if it came to that. But it does seem too good to be true."

"Why?" Luviet pushed.

"My guts."

The man's laugh hid an underlying tone of frustration. "No offence, my friend. But you're not a precog. Your instincts don't mean much to me." Luviet headed for the exit. "I'll be outside if you need me. Let me know when you've made your decision."

Gallena attempted to go after him, only for Pausa to stop her. "I'll go," he said.

"Okay," she replied without resistance. Leaning in, she gave him a kiss which he reciprocated deeply. She smelled of the sweat from the day. One day, he would miss those small moments of peace within the raging battlefield. One day, he would forget her. They parted and Gallena added, "I trust you."

He smiled to her before following Luviet out. The structure they hid in had been shelled by artillery earlier in the day and the floors above had collapsed onto the apartments opposite him. Miraculously, the room he came out from had avoided the damages from the attacks and settled like a cave within the rubble. He stepped out of the destroyed building and out in the open.

Luviet stood at what might have once been a balconied pathway with a beautiful view. Now, most of the railings had been torn from the battle, and the ledge over had crumbled into a slope of debris. Beyond Luviet, out across the landscape, flashes of gunfire littered the smog filled night. Blood red sky gleamed the horizon like a sunset greeting from hell.

Pausa stepped up to his friend and the latter began talking. "We're almost there," he said, staring at a tower made of protruding scraps of metal. "Just a little more."

Pausa asked, "We all want to end this war. But you've always seemed a little more... eager than the rest of us. Why?"

"My grandfather was born the day the war started," Luviet explained. My whole life has been this. The screaming, the running, the firefights. Not a single day went by where I knew what true peace was." The man let out a sigh.

He was not even in his mid twenties, his face still holding tightly with muscles from his teenage years. A young boyish charm to the light skin. A look of life in his luscious bright hair. His parents consummated old, and he was the youngest of all of them. Yet, Pausa always felt Luviet was on the verge of becoming a senior citizen.

Luviet continued, "What little information I have of peace time, I learnt through books that were left unburned. Through words of mouths not too dead to speak. Many times, through the tales of dying soldiers who wanted my help in listening to their last stories." His eyes sparkled as tears welled, but never felled. "I want this war to end. Not a single generation after me should ever go through this. This war, this endless war, will be the last of the wars. No more fighting, not more dying. I'll make sure of it."

Pausa did not have a reply for he had no consoling words. He was an outsider, a man out of time, thrown into a battle he had never heard of. Because of his situation, he looked up to Luviet. As far as he knew, the two of them were polar opposite in their raising. But somehow, through series of events that happened thousands of years apart, they were brought together in a turning point of time.

Attempting to shift the conversation to something less grim, Pausa asked, "Do you remember when we first me?"

"Yeah," Luviet replied with a much needed chuckle. "I nearly shot you."

He laughed at the memory. "Well, you remember that hill with the tree?"

"Of course. The Tree of Crossroads."

"Do you know why it's called that?"

Luviet shook his head. "Ever since the war began, all our knowledge and information of lores and legends had been shovelled into the fire."

"Well," Pausa began. "Where I come from, The Tree of Crossroads is said to be where people meet. Legend has it that the tree exists throughout all of history, on every world, every universe. All of time and space. Wherever and whenever, a tree like it exists."

"That sounds like a fairytale."

"It is. But it sounds nice, doesn't it? A tree that can bring people together. The legend further says that those who first meet under the tree are bound together by fate itself."

"I'm calling bullshit on that one."

"I know," Pausa ended. They stood in silence for a moment, listening to the ambient of war. Finally, Pausa announced, "I'm going to ask Gallena to marry me."

"I know."

"I want you to be my best man?"

"What's a best man?"

"It's usually a person close to the groom. It's like a sidekick for lifetime commitment. You hold the ring, or whatever you use to propose here, and give it to me. You're also my back-slap commissioner."

"So, if I think you're messing with Gal, I can slap you?"

"Until I die."

"That's a nice thought." They both laughed, their voice carrying off into the echoes of gunfire. Luviet squinted at the horizon and his tone changed. "We should move out soon."

"Why?"

"I see rovers."

Pausa scanned the landscape but could not make out the supposed vehicles. Luviet passed him a binocular and pointed in a seemingly far grey part of the distance. Through the lenses, Pausa could see faint clouds of dust being kicked up by the familiar outline of the small buggy-like vehicles.

"Wow," Pausa said, impressed. "How did you see that?"

"I have good eyesights."

"Similar to how I have good instincts?"

"You have terrible instincts," Luviet jabbed.

"I'm going to warn the others," Pausa said, turning to head back into the ruins.

As he walked, he could have sworn he heard Luviet muttering, "Soon, peace will come."

Tier set a cup of tea down on the table. Embedded sequin made the surface of the furniture reflect a dizzying array of light from the afternoon Solar. He slid a plate of cake over to his brother opposite, who took the small fork provided and dug in with hastened glee.

"Chill, man," Tier berated. "You'll choke yourself to death, eating like that."

The brother slowed his pacing with a muffled laugh. He swallowed the sponge that was in his mouth and washed it down with water from a bottle. "Can't help it. Haven't eaten all day today."

"That's because this is breakfast. Nobody eats before breakfast."

"I do," the brother replied. "Night shift work is killing my body clock."

"Anyway, have you heard? The F.A.C is calling for all Hymns to report in for registration." Tier poured some milk into his tea. A group of bustling morning commuters rushed by the street of the diner in tandem with the changing traffic lights. A car honked far down the road. "Sounds like they're rounding them and tagging them."

"Sucks, that. But I think being a Hymn could be a cool thing."

"Why?"

"Superpowers, man!" he raised his voice slightly in excitement. "Can you imagine? Shooting laser beams. Flying. Stopping bad guys and saving the day?"

"Those are comic books, brother. This is reality."

"Can't hurt to dream. I mean, I know people are generally selfish, but I can see some people doing good with their powers."

"They're more likely to use them to earn money first."

He snorted derisively. "You're too much a pessimist. Mark my words, one day, someone with powers will don a cape and save the world."

"Maybe the 'world saving' part," Tier reluctantly agreed, sipping his tea. "The cape? Not so much."

The Watcher woke to the sudden rush of noise back into his ears. The time bubble had expired and he could sense with the sudden dip in temperature that the times had changed. He had arrived in the future. To his right, Nadier and Adelaide were still stuck in cryo-freeze, both in mid-action of readying their equipments. They would have to spend a while longer with their preparations. Double checking, The Watcher made sure the time bubble surrounding his two companions would last another hour. It should give him time to confront Light and end things while giving the two elves sufficient leeway to escape.

The smell of rust and blood floated to him. Getting to his feet, he carefully edged to the ledge, peeking over to make sure no one else was in the chamber with them. Beneath him, the Lusus Naturae had been broken apart and the damage was akin to the wreckage of a plane crash.

With dried blood surrounding it, the metal casing that held Renasque Isvael was cracked opened like the shell of an egg. The body of the Overseer was unmoving within it.

Chapter 44
The Dead Battalion

The Watcher crossed the Overseer's Chamber, his footsteps a silent echo through the massive rotund room as he approached the destroyed Lusus Naturae. The copper shell had been sliced opened cleanly a quarter into the way. Melted metal coagulated the side as if a lightsaber had cauterised the shell. Laying sprawled within the mess was the dehydrated and decomposed body of Renasque Isvael, her skin dried to the point where her bones lined her frame, her lips forever parted in a stretched smile that bared teeth and peace.

Backing her, the capsules that held the former Overseers had been cut opened and burnt, the bodies within mutilated beyond recognition. It was not an execution. It was torture.

He knelt down beside the body, tears flowing down his cheeks. "I'm sorry, Rena. I'm so, so sorry."

My original ability was to view the glimpses of consciousness from the deaths of individuals.

Her words flashed into his mind like a car accident. Looking around the debris pile, his eyes settled on Rena's left hand which was balled into a fist. A small streak of brown extended out.

Tenderly, he unravelled the closed fist and pulled out the contents, strains of fused skin and dried blood vessel tug and snapped away. A small scroll of brown leather, covered in maroon and grime, was retrieved.

Within it, the words were written in dried and flaking black ink.

18th floor.
Good luck.

For two years, the girl had been trapped within the cage. She must have seen her death come and right before being locked into the copper shell, she wrote those lines for him and held on throughout the ordeal.

He got to his feet, fists trembling from a tumultuous rage of emotions. Without another look, he walked out of the chamber.

The hallway was eerily quiet. Dead silence rang in his ears like the whistle of a far off train.

"There's no one here." Kathleen Ambershey stepped out and around him, scanning the corridor. "Where is everyone?"

The Watcher ignored her, following the rounding path in silence until he reached the elevator. The shaft that was damaged by Nadier and Nora had been long since repaired. He called for the moving platform, which arrived in seconds. Stepping onto the fenced up lift, he could hear a barrage of voices as whispers from far below. The floors above remained stilled in noise.

Kathleen noted, "Nadier said you needed a key."

Again, disregarding her, The Watcher casually pressed the button for the eighteenth floor. After a short seconds of wait, the elevator rumbled and began lowering down.

"What the–?"

"It's Light," The Watcher explained. "He's charismatic, coercive, cunning. The three Cs."

"He lied about the key? Why?"

"Because he can." As the elevator continued it's journey, the voices from the ground floor grew louder. But with each passing level, the silence above simply got more deafening. "It's how he fights. Despite all that physical power, he'll choose to play the game. I think because the old him is still in there, somewhere."

The elevator stopped and he got out onto the floor into a small reception chamber. It was a small rectangular room with two stone tables that lined the pathway leading to a large set of double doors. A large plaque hung arching over the doorway, reading 'Feasting Hall'. With confident treads, he crossed the threshold and forced the doors opened. The two wooden blockades swung away with little resistance, rotating on their hinges and slamming into the walls, the impact reverberating through the large, empty hall.

With a long aisle down carpeted by red with gold seams and four rows of six columns worth of long dining tables at its side, the hall stretched to two empty stages built into the left and right far walls. Red bricks chequered with plates of copper plastered the atmosphere. A high ceiling with four large chandeliers of glowing incandescent bulbs hung overhead.

At the far end, opposite the entrance, another long table was set perpendicular to the rest. Behind the table at dead centre sat Light in a robe of white and streaming gold. Behind the man, the towering opened portal swirled purple, the Mist spinning clockwise and counter-clockwise simultaneously, a dizzying rotation. Within the middle of the spectacle, a clear orb-like image of a desolate landscape sat upside-down.

Light greeted enthusiastically from his seat, "Please! Watcher! No need to be violent with the door. It's not like it made the Star Wars prequel."

"The Skywalkers are an annoying family," The Watcher retorted loudly, taking long strides through towards Light. "Whiny little bitches."

"I agree," Light replied. The man gestured to the long table before him, where a bounty of food of varying colours, freshness, and variety, laid sprawled. "Come, chat with me over a meal. You must be wondering how I got to this world."

The Watcher stopped before the table but did not take a seat. He asked, "What happened to your body?"

What was once a handsome, unblemished face had a scar running across right cheek to chin and diagonal across the nose. Underneath the pristine clothing, glimpses of further scaring could be seen peeking out. There were more wounds than The Watcher could count.

"Oh," the Lord faked surprise. "These? Just a gift your friend gave me. I believe he's the Cold Fusion. Miguel Vallertes? And I thought we were godlike before, you and I. I guess I should have known that he would be strong. They wouldn't be called Godkillers, otherwise."

The Watcher could feel fragments of time within the wounds. Little parts of space out of tandem with the rest of the world around them.

Light continued, "Corpse Party. Miguel's exseed burst. Bastard brings a cold so freezing that it slows time itself. Worst yet, his cuts brings a little of that cold back with it. Practically cripples the body's ability from healing. So even if you survived his initial attack, the injuries don't heal normally. I spent two seasons bleeding to death before time resumed. I was a walking corpse." He pointed to the scar on his face. "Had to cauterise some wounds myself to survive."

The man laughed at his own story before turning his body around to look at the portal behind. Sided by metal towers that fired off electrical currents, there was a power generator the size of a small house hidden within its shadows further back. Pipes from the geothermal venting lead upward behind it.

Light said, "But I have this now. Just a while longer and the portal will be fully connected."

"Stop this," The Watcher plainly retorted. "People are going to die."

"Oh, lighten up, will you? Get it? Lighten?" Light picked up a roasted drumstick and threw it lightly to The Watcher. The latter did not react, instead, he stood still as the food bounced off his chest and dropped to the ground. "Well, that's not very nice, wasting food like that."

"Light..."

Instead, the madman rambled on, "But let me tell you though, it wasn't easy getting here. Not especially after what you did to me. I had to punch a hole through the universe itself! Might have lost a few screws on the way."

"Light, please..."

"Say it," Light blatantly asked.

"What?"

"Say my name."

With a cracking voice of sorrow, The Watcher replied, "I can't."

"Oh, you and your rules," Light waved him with frustration. "Come now, there's no one else here. Honestly, if I wanted to collapse my own timeline, I wouldn't have used 'Light' for two hundred years."

The Watcher stood in contemplation of that logic, and found no loops for it. "So why do you want me to say your real name now?"

A soft smile spread across Light's face, and for a moment, they were back in the good old days of blood and war. "We're the last ones left, aren't we? If you're not going to call me by my name, then there's no one else who can."

The Watcher looked up to the swirling portal once more. He sighed and asked, "Why did you kill Rena?"

"The Overseer? She had served her purpose. And her existence was a threat to my plan," Light explained matter-of-factly. There was no remorse in his tone. It was the voice of the greater good. He had always been the voice for the greater good. Then, his lips cracked into a dented grin. "I also wanted to hear you say my name. So I killed everyone in this building. The country is still running fine. No one even realise their entire government dissolved. Just like Belgium and New Haven."

"Light..."

"With this portal, I can finally finish our mission. Reshape Gaia to a standard of peace. No more wars. No more anything! Our vision will be realised! All you have to do is say my name."

"You can still stop this. We can still stop this."

Light slammed his hands on the table, the food jumping and splaying across the tabletop. He pushed away his seat, the bench knocking backwards as he shot to his feet. "We're the last ones, Watcher! There's no one else! With this, we can bring everyone back! We can save everyone we loved!"

The Watcher screamed back, "At what cost? The death of everyone outside our timeline?"

"SAY MY NAME, PAUSA!"

"LUVIET!"

A blinding burst of light emitted from Light's body, sharp rays shining in all directions, piercing wooden tables and blasting chunks off of walls. The Watcher drew his sword and Light formed a sabre from his element. The Lord leapt over the table, slashing at The Watcher. The time traveller stepped back in tandem with a swift parry. Light spun, raised his sword, an opening between them.

He slashed down.

Chapter 45
Desolate Spectre

Being in a time bubble for as long as they had been was a strange experience for Adelaide, to say the least. She watched as the world flicked by in fractions of seconds, time after time skimping across her vision in a melted array of faded events and leftover colours of blur. To her right, Nadier raised a brow quizzically at her stare.

What is it? he seemed to ask.

She shook her head. Nothing.

Though they moved at the same speed through time, their voices did not travel across clearly, and their world revolved around the whisper of noises that was trapped within their enclosures. To her left, The Watcher was fast asleep, mouth wide opened in uncontrolled snores. His head twitched uncomfortably as his eyes scrunched in sudden soreness, before settling back into a rhythmic breathing.

She sighed, having never sat still in the same place for as long as she did then. Her legs bounced in place, attempting to rid themselves of the pent up vigour. Her hands itched after the nine hours sit, having already slept most of the time off. She drew her bow and did what had to be the hundredth check through her equipments, before settling them back in their holsters. She glanced over to her left and noticed The Watcher was gone.

"What the–?" She stood to her feet in surprise.

Her vision blurred as a rush of light and colours bombarded her sights. Noise returned to her ears like a blaring horn. She was on stable standing, but still disoriented by the sudden restart of time. Beside her, Nadier looked equally confused, staring left at right at the sudden phenomenon. There was a faint dip in the temperature in the air. Barely noticeable, though still managing to tickle her senses. A lighter humidity touched but a change in the density of the cold. She was in the future.

But before she has a chance to marvel, she sounded, "Where's The Watcher?"

The graveness of the situation returned to her.

She heard Nadier let out a dissatisfied huff. "That man still doesn't trust us..."

"Do you trust him?" she asked back.

Nadier did not reply. He casually approached her and allowed her to set a hand on his shoulder. They teleported down to the ground. It was there they noticed the brutality that had occurred from the destruction of the construct that held the Overseer. The dried blood. The cracked metal. The dead bodies.

"Oh no..." Nadier let out, slowly approaching the body of Rena. Adelaide followed behind as the dark elf knelt down beside the corpse. He ran a hand over the dried face. "I really should have been here."

Adelle replied, "You're surprisingly soft with kids."

"We were all kids once. Even if we don't all remember it. Innocence should be given for as long as possible. Before all the negativity of reality clouds the mind, have some hope." He let out a deep breath and his eyes settled on something brown and blood soaked on the floor. He picked up the leather scrap and read its contents before standing to his feet and pocketing the note. "I know where The Watcher is. He's on the eighteenth floor."

Without another word, he began walking towards the door.

"Hold it!" Adelaide shouted behind. "Why do you think The Watcher left us behind?"

"You used to be quite dense..." Nadier replied without turning back. She could not tell if he was being derisive or just stating the obvious. He explained, "He left us behind so we would not get involved."

"So why are you getting involved now? Your revenge is complete, is it not? We've taken out all the dark elves that had ever wronged you and your brother, and added some!"

"What about you?" He asked back. "Your forest is saved. Why did you follow him here? What is worth enough to risk travelling into an uncertain future?"

They stood in silence. Not just the chamber but seemingly the entire building echoed their sentiments. Even with their elven hearings, they could not pick up any distinct noises around them. The Tower had been abandoned. Left behind, just like they had been.

"This discussion is over," Nadier plainly puts it. "You and I both know the reason why we are here and why we're going this far."

She knew. She had known for a while now. But uncertainty was clouding her. She had never stuck with a group for as long as the trio, nor for as dangerous a situation.

She managed one final shot and asked, "What do you see when you look at The Watcher?"

"I see myself," Nadier simply replied.

Grumbling under her breath, she followed the annoyingly inscrutable dark elf out. As they had expected, the corridor was abandoned. Following the way back to the elevator, they called the lift down and entered. Once Adelaide had a line of vision to the eighteenth floor, she teleported them up to the level, where they stepped out onto the reception area.

"Where are we?" she asked. Nadier responded by simply pointing to the sign that hung over the double door which read 'Feasting Hall'. He gave her a disappointed look and she snarled back. "Smart-ass."

Together, side-by-side, they stepped into the gleam of the dining hall, only to stop once they've crossed the threshold. Before them, trapped within what seemed to be a giant glass ball that twisted and squirmed from whichever angle they looked from, was The Watcher and Light, frozen mid battle.

Carefully, the duo approached the phenomenon. The room was an eerie quiet despite the destructiveness of the frozen scene in front of them. Light, with rays of magical hard-light beams ricocheting away from his body, was stuck mid-strike, his blade floating just short of contact to The Watcher's face who was wide opened from head to toe, the latter's sword flung aside post-parry. If the battle had lasted just a split second longer, The Watcher would have been killed.

Behind the battle, equally trapped, was the portal of gas and the equipments that powered it. Every single mist of it was stopped in their swirl. Each arc of electricity caught mid connection from metal to metal. Every refraction of light bended to the curvature of the time bubble, distorting as they stepped to the side and circled the area.

Adelaide reached a hand out to touch the scene.

"Stop!" Nadier yelled at her.

"What?" She replied, annoyed at having been given a command.

He picked up a fork from the disrupted table. With confidence, he threw the utensil at the bubble. The metal seemingly stuck itself onto the globule, almost plastered on like a wanted poster. Adelaide took a step to the side and realised that was not entirely the case. Rather, the fork had flattened itself onto the surface of the time bubble, as if every single microscopic layer of it had been fused into the same spot they came into contact with.

Nadier explained, "This time bubble is a trapped fragment of instance. As the days passes by, layers of dust will probably coagulate onto it, until it one day turns to nothing but an unmovable orb of grey. Everything within it is trapped in the moment The Watcher deemed."

She knew what he was thinking, but asked regardless, "What do we do now?"

"You teleport me in, exactly as I am, in a split moment of time. Whenever this time bubble expires, the battle will end." The dark elf prepared his daggers, loading into them vials of Neverite for battle. He looked to the 3D painting of time, and practised blocking a strike that would come from Light's direction. "Put me right in the middle of the fight. I'll block the hit for The Watcher, and we'll see how it goes from there."

"And what do I do?"

"Live your life," he said, getting into position, taking a stance that fits the frozen scene of conflict. "I have no idea how long this time bubble will hold, or how long The Watcher will take. It could be minutes. It could be cycles."

"That's not–!"

"And don't try to to follow me."

His glare was piercing. Determined. There was no talking him out. Adelaide simply nodded, and once Nadier was ready, she held onto his shoulder in a tight grip before reluctantly teleporting the dark elf as instructed. The Wanderer reappeared within the time bubble, placed between Light's strike and The Watcher's body, surrounded by the teleporting puff of rusty smog.

What do you see when you look at The Watcher?

Adelle let out a sigh, wondering at which point in the past season did she change so dramatically. She looked to the purple portal, frozen in its time, before turning her gaze to her two companions. At what point did her hatred for human died to a gentle simmer?

I see myself.

Muttering under her breath, Adelaide whimpered, "I see myself, too."

She stretched both hands out and vanished in a puff of brown smoke.

Chapter 46
The Lady in Waiting

"From the Endless War to the Solaris War. The Battle of Haven to the Fight for Genesis. Even the Vashmir Pandemic and the War of the Mist." Kathleen Ambershey set the final book, *Years to the End of the World*, down on a table with eight others. "How many times did you actually take part in a story?"

"Just two of them," The Watcher replied. "I was a bystander for the others."

He was in a rotund room. Two storeys tall, the ceiling was lit by dozens of flecks of light that resembled stars. Bookshelves lined the walls, with roundels above each that glowed a soft white acting as sources of light. Four wood doors were poised at each cardinal directions upon an annulus platform of velvet carpet.

The platform led down to the grassy circular 'ground floor', which consisted of a round table bolted to the centre of the room and three swivel chairs surrounding it, despite never having had more than two occupants in the enclosure at once. Piles of books occupied the table mountainously. Above the table, hanging down from a ceiling mount that pivoted was a monitor that showed the world outside his body. The Watcher sat on one of the chairs, writing feverishly into an empty book.

Taking a seat opposite him, Kathleen spun on the chair, admiring the place. "I like this room. It's so much more decorative than all the others."

"I saw the design on a television show once. Thought it looked neat." He did not take his hand away from his frantic scribbling. Despite the speed of his writing, the words seemingly squirmed into a perfected readable font. Noting the lights, he said, "I liked the round things on the wall."

As he set the final period onto the last page, the book he wrote on shrunk to fit the text. He closed it, the title reading *Ulysses*. He sat the book upon the pile, with works ranging from *The Hobbit* to *Don Quixote*. Even one titled, *Height Hack: A Universal Guide on Stretching*.

Kathleen finally caved and asked, "What are you doing?"

"I've read many books in my lifetime." Involuntarily, he taut his back in a stretch. What for he was not sure as he had not felt any physical discomfort since his arrival. "I thought it would be a good way to kill some time to write them from scratch."

"You're joki – no. That look on your face is totally sincere."

He twisted his vision and lopped his tongue out the side of his mouth in comedic response.

"You should take things a little more seriously," she sternly reprimanded.

He looked up at the monitor. In it, Light was frozen midway through a slash down towards his head. At the corner of the screen, he could see Nadier and Adelaide, an image he had recently seen arrive. However, they moved at a speed so slow, you could only tell they were not motionless by comparing minute to minute freeze frames. Or, if you were The Watcher.

"How long do you think they'll stay there?" he asked.

She replied, "I don't know. How long before you leave this placc?"

"Once they realise there's no way out of the time bubble without my say so, they'll give up," he convinced himself.

"Are you sure about that?"

"Of course. They're tenacious, not stupid."

"What's the difference?"

He made a quick calculation as he watched Nadier's eyes slowly closing in a blink. It was off to watch someone blink in slow motion. Without realising, most people have slight ticks, making one eyelid close slower. Nadier's left eye was just less than a fraction of a tenth of a second faster than his right.

Kathleen asked, "What's your plan?" He turned his attention away from the screen and she continued, "You're not going to stay here forever, are you?"

"Of course not."

He had calculated, using what he deduced from Tearha's astrological movements, that in one year of Tearha's time, he would have the opportunity to remove the time lock placed on the gravity of the area. Along with Light, they would be hurled into space, fired through the building at an angle that would not likely see any people in harm's way. It was ironically similar to what happened with Akaras Spaedruiner. Back then, The Watcher had just arrived on Tearha and had not included the planet's spin and orbit into the calculated use of his power, which threw Akaras into the wall at the speed of the rotation of the planet.

Kathleen voiced, "That's a stupid plan."

Even though The Watcher only recapped the formula in his mind, it had never once slipped past the hallucination of the late Kathleen. Just part and parcel of conversing with figments of imaginations inside ones' own mind.

He explained, "The physical matter that had coagulated on the shell of the bubble would experience intense friction upon release. By that time, the force would be equivalent to a supernova. I would have to be flung far out enough into space that the solar system would not be caught in our wake. Until then, I will remain here."

"Why do you have to be awake?" She probably knew why. It was just his mind's way of working through problems. He had gotten so used to bouncing off ideas within his head that it had never occurred to him that his brain could actually bounce those ideas back.

"I need to know when to release. My consciousness is locked in base time. Speed one. Tearha moves at one hundred and thirty nine multiples."

"The number one-three-nine..."

"It's the base time of Tearha's universe. Like how my universe is seven. That's why dreams lasts for such drastically different times in different worlds." He leaned back in his seat, closing his eyes with a sigh of fatigue. "I should have figured it out sooner. Might have saved me the trouble of finding the answer. I could have saved a few lives. Your life."

"It would not have prevented anything."

"I know," he admitted and silence fell between them.

When he reopened his eyes, Kathleen was gone. Instead, Luviet sat on the steps beside him, a book titled *Genesis* in his hands. Flipping through the pages, the man that had come to take on the epitaph of Light chuckled at memories on the paper.

Luviet asked, "How much of us did you try to forget?"

"As much as I can," The Watcher admitted. "Besides, I'm nearly a thousand years old. There are bound to be some things that slips my mind."

"Is that the lie you tell yourself when you say you can't remember the faces of people you've met?"

"It's not a lie," The Watcher replied. "I can't remember anyone's faces."

Luviet scoffed and noted, "One hour have passed on Tearha."

"I know."

"You plan to stay here for one year, Tearha time."

"That's right.

"How long have you been here?"

He paused. It was a question he tried not to bode on. "Five days and nineteen hours." For his plan to work, he would have to stay time-locked for one hundred and thirty-nine years.

Luviet laughed, putting the book down on the floor beside him. He got up and walked to the centre of the room and placed his hand on the mountain of books. The Watcher wasn't sure what was so funny. It was a sacrifice he was willing to make. After all, Luviet, no, Light, was his responsibility. It was his role as the man who won the Endless War to see the final phase through. With a blink, Luviet turned back into Kathleen.

In the voice of a wisp, she said, "You have to stop living in just the past and the future." Her head looked to the monitor, causing The Watcher to follow.

What the monitor actually showed was the world through The Watcher's physical eyes. And where once stood just Light and an impending strike, was further blocked by a body of black.

"Nads..." He had not thought of that possibility.

They knew. Those two idiots had to know that there were no guarantees he would remove the time bubble, or if he did, it would not be any time soon. Nadier must have had Adelaide teleport him in, bypassing the temporal shell. Instantaneous teleportation. In the corner of the screen, Adelle still stood, looking sombrely away. Then, she too vanished in a blink. However, she did not reappear within his line of sight and he scanned the screen for her presence to no avail.

Luviet spoke up, now joined in the same room as Kathleen, pacing around on the circular platform that surrounded the centre table. "They've gone all in on you."

"It's just Nadier. It's one life," The Watcher argued. The last of the dark elves. "A small sacrifice. I won't even remember him in a few years time."

In a sweep of calm anger, Kathleen wiped the table clean of books, sending the novels and guides flying onto the ground. "You don't remember anything? Look at these books you wrote 'just to kill time'!" She picked the nearest copy off the ground. "You wrote the entirety of The Seven's Saga out on a whim! The Lord of the Rings! Grace and Defeat! From memory!"

Luviet added from his high ground. "You remember just fine. You simply don't want to because you're afraid everyone will die and leave you the last man standing."

"I–but..." The Watcher tried to retort.

"No buts."

He spun on his feet at the new voice. Standing at the southern doorway, with rays of sunlight shining at his back was his brother, Tier, leaned against a frame. Short, ruffled hair of brown and eyes of hazel, the man wore his trademark cock-eyed grin. Sharp jawed, deep dimpled, framed cheeks, wearing the blue shirt and black jeans he was last seen in, Tier was a splitting image from the distant past.

In almost a disappointed tone, Tier scolded, "It's time to get off your ass. No more excuses. We didn't leave you. We're just waiting for you at the end of the line."

All four doors to the room opened and an out-pour of people, men and women, old and young, spilt into the room, surrounding The Watcher. He recognised the faces. Faces he had wanted not to recall. Faces he had associated with lost and courage, love and death, happiness and hatred, songs and blood, family and enemies, friends and rivals.

Then, Gallena stepped through the crowd. Green eyes reflecting like a leaf in the sun. Long, curly hazel hair nicking the catches of her shirt. A smile that could melt hearts and thaw ice ages. A musical chuckle escaped her and she gave The Watcher a light kiss, the honeyed taste of her lips lingering for what must be eons.

"Stop pretending you can't remember us," she giggled the words out of her. "It's bad for your health."

Amongst the crowd, Luviet was nowhere to be found.

His brother came to his side. "Alright, little bro." They turned to watch the monitor where time continued to stand still. "I know I sound a little racist here, but that black guy and the hippie elf girl out there? They're your companions for this leg of the race, just like how we were for the earlier parts." He wrapped an arm around The Watcher. Despite being the same height, Tier had always managed to make The Watcher felt like a coddled puppy. "In the future, they will leave you, and others will join. That's just the deal. But at the finish line, I'll have a cup of hot tea waiting for you."

A small boy tugged at the edge of The Watcher's coat. He looked down at the child he thought of as a mentor.

"Stop taking on all the big things by yourself. From the dawn of it, we were bundled together. You're only alone if you think everyone else is together. You're only homeless if you think home is where you were born. You're only the last of your kind if nothing is alive."

Chapter 47

The Ghost of Years

Time returned exponentially slowly. A single second stretched out into seemingly minutes as every action played frame-by-painful-frame. The Watcher watched as Light's sword clashed with the Neverite covered blades of Nadier's daggers. The world glowed brighter with each passing moment as the physical objects of dust and utensils that had accumulated around the time bubble rubbed against each other in an instantaneous moment, creating friction that would have a heat that matched a star. The sound of the explosion happening around them grew in his ears.

His hand stretched out towards the dark elf. He needed to get to Nadier and move both of them out of the explosion radius as quickly as possible. The circuits in his body attempted to charge but they sputtered and burnt as energy left him. His hand reached Nadier's shoulder just as another hand touched his own. The explosive sound cuts away. The bright glow was replaced with a copper ceiling.

As if pulled back by a vacuum, time returned. The explosion rocked across the dining hall, flinging the already stumbling Watcher back through the air from the sheer force of a shock wave. Burning heat grazed his skin and debris warmed his face with bloody cuts.

He landed on his back, followed by two resounding thuds beside him from Nadier and Adelaide as the last of the blast wave washed over the trio. A breeze of warmth blanketed their bodies followed by an instant back draft of cool.

Silence took the room as dust clouds settled slowly like sand in a crystal lake.

For a long while, they laid on their backs, struggling with aching joints and bruised backs, attempting to shake the ringing out of their ears. Adelaide was the first back on her feet. Though she stumbled slightly from the quick use of her teleportation, she nevertheless managed to notch an arrow into the string of her bow and had the weapon drawn to the front. With a helping hand from Nadier, The Watcher got to his own feet. The dark elf stabled his stance before standing forward with his weapons.

The time traveller signalled his companions to halt their attacks with a hand before the dust even settled. They had landed near the door, almost across the room from where the blast had occurred. Bright light streamed in from opposite them as the wall had been blown opened to the outside world, gleaming through speckled fog.

As the room cleared, the damage revealed itself. The wall opposite had all but crumbled with an evenly shaped hole canvassing the scenic view of steady snowfall outside. Two thirds of a crater originated from where Light and The Watcher had once settled as their battleground, with chairs, tables, utensils, and bits of metal from the portal machine strewn in a haphazard debris field. The portal continued to spin, even without any machinations powering it.

After reaffirming the halt signal to Adelle and Nadier, The Watcher approached ground zero with a tired but confident gait. He staggered down the slope. While the thick ceiling and floor between levels were cracking beneath his feet, they remained otherwise supportive.

In the middle of the crater, lying with his clothes tattered, charred and torn, along with patches of seared skin that overlaid cuts and scars, Light twisted his head at the approaching Watcher, his golden hair dusted and blood soaked lumped with each turn.

"Do you remember Captain Lily?" Light choked out. He slumped his head back onto the rough ground as The Watcher sat down beside him. "She was amazing, wasn't she?"

"Yeah," The Watcher replied. "Smart and brave."

"In the twenty-first and second centuries, before things went to shit, I read about great people like Churchill and da Vinci, and I thought that in another time, another place, she could have been a Hullway or Yousafzai."

The Watcher sighed and leaned back into his arms. "We could have been a lot of things if you had not did what you did."

Light gave a blood gargled laugh. "You chased me across time and space. Even now, in another universe, you won't get off my heel?"

"I can't help it. I told you, didn't I? I'm with you until the end."

The Lord's breathing slowed. "Do you think we could have been friends?"

Small, dandelion-like glows of light started emerging from Light's body. The glow-puffs floated off onto the breeze and were carried out the opening in the wall, riding the wind.

The Watcher turned, panicking on his knees. He exclaimed, "What are you doing?"

"Scattering my molecules into light itself. Dispersed into the universe." The small glow-puffs drifted further and further from the body, fading and dispersing into dusted sparkles as they went out into the open. "I'd really rather you not win this time."

"You selfish bastard!" The Watcher screamed. He held out his arm to wrap a time bubble around his former comrade, but his magic circuit simply sparked and faded. He took out his pocket watch only to see that the crystal too had lost its charge and glow. "We're the last ones! Don't you die on me!"

Light cackled, blood overspilling out of his mouth, spitting and spluttering around him. "Look at you, all the power in the world and can't even save a single life." He gave a smile that bordered sadistic and kindness. "You haven't answered me yet... in another time, another place, could we have been friends?"

Tears streaked down The Watcher's face as his fist clenched in anger, frustrated that even to the end, the man known as Luviet fought for his ideals. Light's form began to fade as the glow-puffs doubled in numbers.

The Watcher reminded, "We're family."

Luviet's smile widened and a glimpse of his former self flashed across an aged face right before his body disappeared in a poetic field of firefly ashes.

The dust had mostly settled, and aside from the ominous portal that continued to spin before him, the sky was clear with freckled snow. The city of Everwind sprawled out before him, a couple of buildings on the outskirts seemingly destroyed and a section of the wall to the east having collapsed as if from siege. Aside from those few slightly out of place demolitions, the city was quietly whispering about its day.

Footsteps neared from behind and The Watcher got to his feet to face the two elves that approached.

Nadier asked, "Is it over?"

"Yeah," The Watcher replied, taking a quick look back at the ground where Light once laid. "It's over."

Adelaide asked, "What about the portal?"

He did a quick calculation on the velocity of the portal's rotation and concluded, "It's losing power. It's more stable than the first one I dealt with, but without a power source, it'll simply vanish after a time."

"How sure are you?" the dark elf asked.

"Eighty-seven percent?"

"Well, that's more than what you usually go by." Nadier turned and began walking back to the exit.

Adelaide asked, "Where are you going?"

"*We* are going to find Miguel and Luce. They'll be wondering what happened over the past year. The Watcher can stay and watch the portal, make sure it closes. It's literally his name, after all."

She turned to The Watcher with a look of concern, a relatively new expression for her to wear that he found heart-warming, though unsettling for her personality. Regardless, he gave her a reassuring nod and she reluctantly nodded back in agreement before following Nadier out of the room.

Pocket watch in hand, he noted the returning of power to the trinket and deduced that the proximity to the portal must be speeding up the crystal's charge, though he did not hide the wish of hoping it had just been a few minutes faster. Just then, he noted how familiar the newly destroyed room looked. As he pieced his thoughts together, he heard a thud from the direction of the portal.

Turning around, The Watcher witnessed as the man in dark grey coat and ruffled black mud hair straightened up after landing on the ground in front of the portal, flicking whiffs of dust off the shoulders of his coat.

The newly arrived man attempted to take a step. "Oosh!" He raised his hands to regain balance on the uneven ground. "That was trippy." The newcomer did a quick scan of the room before his eyes rested on The Watcher.

The Watcher greeted, "Sup', Pausa?"

Pausa replied with a satisfied grin, "Well, hello to me too."

"I look good."

"You too."

The two laughed, before Pausa asked, "So, what happened here?" He looked around the emptied and destroyed room. "What did we do?"

"What makes you think we did anything?" The Watcher replied, slightly offended.

"It's because it's us," and The Watcher begrudgingly agreed.

"Oh!" The memory returned to The Watcher like a brick. "You use the name, 'The Watcher', here."

Pausa cocked his head aside. "Huh? Weird. But okay. So, where do I go now? Are there any Mexican food here? I could really go for a taco right about now."

The older man smiled sadly. He held up his fingers, poised to snap them. "Why don't we find out?" With a flick and pluck, Pausa Alvet vanished from where he stood. Muttering under his breath, The Watcher noted, "We end the same way we begin."

The portal seemed to almost sputter before losing its coherency. In a gentle burst of seither energy, it dissipated in a wave of purple, leaving just the limpid winter sky behind, a blimp puttering across the horizon.

Chapter 48
The Wayward

"Was this because we took our time?" Adelaide asked.

"Don't be absurd," Luce replied. "It would have happened either way."

The noise of the room was sang by the soft, gentle breathing of Misti's unconscious body. The girl had grown taller in the year they were locked in time, but the lost of weight from being bedridden had skinned her to a frame of what she once was. Her once short hair had grown out, sprawled across the bed she laid on. Adelle had never met Misti, but according to Luce, the girl was a bubble of excitement that could ricochet from topics to fights with boundless energy. A hard image to picture given her current state.

Josh had moved Misti to Port Llamba, where they benefited from the influx of ships and doctors from across the continent that used the port as a way station to Everwind. Despite the varied medical knowledge that flowed into the growing city, none had been able to cure her. Miguel had a world-renowned healer examined Misti only to determine it a neurological damage.

Luce took a seat by her sister's bedside. Taking the younger girl's hand in hers, she rubbed the creases in the knuckles. To Adelaide, she said, "You should go see them off. We'll talk more about our plans later."

Adelaide wasn't sure how to react. Though sensing the sombre mood, she took the chance and deduced Luce wanted some time alone.

A door out, a flight of stairs down, and a second exit later, she stepped out into a quieting twilight port scene. Stray dock workers, most on breaks, and some carrying crates lingered on the waterside stretch, sparsely littering the place. Half of the docks were empty, with the last ships leaving for their evening journeys and no new vessels coming in till dawn. The last of the winter Twins was lowering over the horizon, half cut off their light by the raised ocean. A cold wind without snow blew through the place.

From northwards down the port street, The Watcher and Nadier approached, their long coats waving behind them, the latter with his hood drawn up.

The Watcher asked, "How is she?"

"Not good," Adelaide replied. "Apparently it's some sort of brain damage. Miguel said she needs a new-row-surgeon."

"Are there even any on Tearha?"

"No. Miguel said he considered bringing one from Earth, but wasn't sure if they'd be able to operate on half-elves," Adelaide replied. Upon noticing the growing look of concern – and slightly worried The Watcher would drag them into another unneeded adventure with his 'solutions' – she added, "But not to worry, Luce has a plan."

Nadier cocked a brow, an act which was almost impossible to discern under the shadow of his hood and the dark of his skin and hair. "A plan?"

"We're going south, to Citi. Their sciences are more advance. Luce thinks she can get a good doctor there."

"Katoki?" Nadier asked, surprised. When she answered with a nod, he sighed and rubbed the migraine he must be getting. "That's not a plan. That's suicide."

Unknowingly, she smiled. "You're the one who said I should go into their employ. Besides, we'll be fine," she laughed off the dangerous idea. "Josh is coming too, and those two are the foremost experts on this."

"They are the only experts on this! No one else have ever made it across alive!" Nadier exclaimed, slightly loudly and very uncharacteristically. He calmed himself before sighing, "How am I suppose to leave if you're just jumping into trouble again?"

The Watcher cut in, "You're leaving?"

Stunned, the dark elf swapped looks between a surprised Watcher and a confused Adelle, unsure of which track of conversation to continue. Finally, he replied, "Yeah. I'm planning on going north."

She asked, "To where? Devara?"

"Alavia," Nadier corrected.

"You can't scold me for a suicide mission if you're going on one yourself," she berated with a grin.

The Watcher simply looked on with confusion before saying, "I don't have a single clue what the two of you are talking about."

Nadier, now used to the lessons in lore, explained, "The south is a burning, tainted war zone and the north is an eternally dark, frozen wasteland. They are both mostly uninhabitable."

"Eternal darkness?" The Watcher questioned. "Are you thinking what I think you're thinking?"

"Probably. If there was any chance of dark elves surviving, it would have to be in places of perpetual darkness. The only geographical area I can think of aside from underground is The Frozen North. It makes sense my people would go there, since daylight never reaches."

The Watcher smiled, "Looks like you two don't need me to get you into trouble. Perfectly fine doing that yourselves."

The elves looked at him quizzically. Adelaide noted, "Sounds like you're not coming with either of us, which is odd. You look like the kind of man who'd run into danger with a smile."

"Hah!" The Watcher grinned. "On most days, you'd be right. But I've been told the Clovers wants to meet with me. Something about having unlimited power over time and space or something. Don't look so disappointed, you two." Despite what he said, the trio wore satisfied smirks. "I'm sure we'll see each other again."

Nadier nodded. "When are you leaving?"

"I've already left." He nudged his head to the direction of a ship travelling out towards the light rise. "I'm not really good with goodbyes, so I have to force myself somehow."

"How...?"

"Time travel. Came forward a little to say my farewells."

"Heh. So we're all landing on our feet?"

Adelaide replied, "Seems like it."

Their shadows stretched along the street and up the wall. A dock worker carrying a long crate huffed past them. Nadier deftly moved his head away as the box made a swipe for his noggin while the worker turned the corner. A long silence dragged between the three and a ship blew its horn loud into the atmosphere. Above them, a slow moving balloon had floated into view.

"We're not very good at this," The Watcher finally said. "The whole 'being friends' thing."

The two elves groaned. Adelaide thought there had been a silent agreement between them that while they considered each other as friends, none of them would ever say it. It was just not in their nature. Nadier had said it best when he pointed out the lonely existence the three shared prior to meeting each other. Letting out a moan of a laugh, the dark elf turned and walked away. With a wave of a hand, The Wanderer began his journey north, following the shore forward.

The Watcher asked, "Is that how he says goodbye? Without a word."

"No," she corrected. "That's how he says 'see you later'."

The Watcher laughed heartily, voice echoing to the emptying docks. Turning away from her, he walked down the nearest pier and out towards the western light. The gleaming Twins' light curved in a crescent twilight with one shining brighter from behind the other.

"Beautiful," his voice rang back clear in the quiet. He stopped at an invisible line drawn between the end of two boats. "A crescent sunrise over a sparkling ocean. Never thought I'd live to see something like this."

She blinked and the man disappeared from her vision, gone back to the point of time he came from. To her right, Nadier had grown to a black thumb in the distant. She could feel her cheeks stretching in a smile. She stepped onto the wooden plank of the pier where The Watcher left and began walking towards the end. Behind, she heard the door of the room Luce had rented close and a following of footsteps after. At the edge of the water, Adelaide watched the boat carrying future-past Watcher hoisted away by winds on its sails. A visible hand waved at her from the deck and she waved back. The dock workers began singing *Last Goodbyes* to end their day. The voices hummed in from all directions as they started the tune of the song in gruff and uneven tones.

Mothers and fathers cry for them, far away they'll go.
Ladies waves and husbands bawls, far away they'll be.

Luce came up beside her and said, "Josh will take care of Misti here for now. We'll have someone come from The Yard to be her guardian on our journey."

She stopped her send-off of the time traveller, lowering her hand to her side. "What do I do now?"

Luce explained, "We're going to train you as a Titan Ranger first. Given your skills, we should be ready to begin our journey south when the first days of sear rolls around."

With the setting of the light, you will leave your past behind.
When it comes time to stand and fight, know your sailors did.

Adelaide thought back on their journey. From the day she met The Watcher when he was thrown into the same cell. And even before that, her quiet life in the trees with occasional visit from Nads and treasure seeking hunters. They had just prevented the extinction of life on a planet in another universe, and stopped two wars from happening in theirs. Yet, the world seemingly rolled on without a blink.

And when your feet steps on waving decks, you will say your last
goodbyes.
At the end of your long lives, say it one more time.

Despite she no longer having a place to call home; for Nadier, not having people to call family; and even The Watcher, who had no present rooted in a history; she was certain none of them had ever felt alone together. She felt home is where you want. Family is what you have. Friends are what you make. Something mushy and awkward along that line.

Epilogue
The Number 139

The lone tree stood atop a small, gentle hill. Shin-length wild grass grew in all directions on the seemingly endless plains, though a single dirt road stretched north-south to his east. At his south, a stone mountain stood overlooking the lands that stretched before it, a citadel hidden at its horizon carved base. To the east and west, farmlands laid for as far as the eyes could see. Straight up to north was where a sky cutting mountain range stood, though at that distance, the heaps were hidden by the curvature of Tearha. Yet, a tall stone spire jutted out from the horizon, piercing the clouds like a needle through the earth itself.

The Watcher stared up into the canopy of the tree, light sparkling through like morning stars. It still felt odd, seeing light-brown leafs as a healthy sign for a plant, but that came with the idea of living in a world where a version of autumn – Leaf – came after winter, and a summer – Sear – would be next. 8 seasons. 49 days each. Nearly a year had passed since the end of Light's reign in Everwind. Or, as those on Tearha called it, 6 seasons.

From what he knew, Luce and Adelaide had headed into Katoki at the start of Fall, earlier than they had planned, and had lost contact since. Nadier's whereabouts in Devara were more precise, though The Watcher had been requested to stay out of the dark elf's way until the storm had passed. As for the continent of Eltar itself, a new parliamentary government had been set up in temporary management. For The Watcher, he had separated from Miguel when he landed on the western continent and had spent the time between exploring the lands. It was not until recently that he regained contact and was asked for a meeting.

Creaking wood and clattering hoofs had him turning away from the tree and back to the east. A cart filled with mostly emptied baskets of vegetables dragged by a bane black mane pulled to a stop at the bottom of the hill. From the steed, a man in khaki coloured pants and dirt brown shirt dismounted. From the cart, a young girl with brown braided hair vaulted off the far side, denim shorts and white singlet muddied from the day. Finally a teenage boy, just slightly taller than the girl, stood to height, with hair of deep navy blue and a receding elf ear. The boy, in a crisp white shirt and black pants, exchanged a glance with The Watcher before nodding. For a moment, The time traveller thought of Miguel.

The man from the horse spoke muffled instructions to the kids before turning to walk up the hill, leaving the young teens to explore the nearby field.

"Hello, Watcher!" the man greeted as he closed.

"King Adam?" The Watcher asked in confusion. The man did not carry the regards of a royal in his eyes, nor did any of his physical cue suggested so.

Laughing it off, the newcomer reached the summit. "No, no. I can't be king, even if I wanted to. All that pressure? I'd collapse into a pile of weeping goo." He held out his hand and The Watcher took it. "Jax's the name. Farming's my game."

"A farmer?"

"We can't all be kings and queens. Someone needs to tend the fields."

Jax had a shine to his onyx hair, paired with eyes so brown that they almost looked black. His facial features were nothing extraordinary. Rough skin, rounded chin, dimpled cheeks. He was an average man with an average build. Aside from the thin muscles and tan developed from working the lands, Jax was ordinary in every other visible way.

The Watcher shrugged, smiled, and asked, "I thought I was supposed to meet the leader of the Clovers?"

"Apparently, you're looking at him."

He cocked a brow. "Isn't that King Adam?"

"Nah. Adam just thought it'd be smart if everyone assumed it was him. We took a vote. They said it's me, but I haven't really done any 'leading' since." Jax placed his hands in his pockets and slacked his back, relaxing with a deep breath. Turning back to the kids below, he continued, "That's my daughter. She's dating the boy over there. Junior Vallertes. Miguel's son. Honestly, I'm kind of conflicted as a father. Junior's a good kid. Straight as can be. But I've always wanted to do that scene from *Bad Boys Two*."

The Watcher guessed, "Where Will Smith went bad cop on the boyfriend of Martin Lawrence's daughter?"

Jax smiled. "Yeah! I mean, that always looked cool. I wanted to try it once as a father and be the bad cop that goes, 'I will find you!'." He turned back to The Watcher. Jax noticeably retrieved two objects from his pocket and handed them over. "Anyway, here's what I wanted to give you."

The Watcher turned the items over. "A handheld radio and a playing card?" The walkie-talkie was more compact than most models he knew of, fitting into just half his palm and owning a sleek, polished white steel casing. The card itself was nothing extraordinary, save for the design on it being an artwork of a 3-leaf and 4-leaf clovers growing from a stalk. "I didn't even know radio worked here."

Jax laughed. "Neither did we. We spent about ten thousand a pop for these from some futuristic universe, then modified them ourselves. You charge them with magic or solar power, and they bounce the signal from any other of them within range. Put a little magic juice in them and they go far if there's nothing to block them. A lot less underground or in forested areas." He took out his own and spoke into it. His right arm glowed a very faint brown as he did so. "Hey, Tehir?"

A short moment later, a gravelly voice replied post-beep, "Yeah?"

"Dare you to get Cray to shoot a fireball out his window?"

Almost stoically and without question, the voice replied. "Sure, give me a moment."

Jax gestured towards the spire in the distant north that pierced the sky. A few seconds later, a flash of red flames lit up the top of the tower's eastern side. The two man laughed at the spectacle of using futuristic grade technology to pull-off what amounted to a game of dare with unimaginable powers that could burn the clouds themselves.

The Watcher pocketed the radio before asking, "And the playing card?"

"Homing magic. Courtesy of Miguel." Jax took his own card out which had what looked to be a three-leafed clover. He tossed it in the direction away from The Watcher. The card spun and floated along unseen currents of air and magic, gently moving away at the speed of a brisk walk. "It'll hover towards the next nearest card in the general direction thrown. Good to have, since there are no satellites in Tearha. This way, you'll be able to find one of us if you're ever in trouble."

Slowly, the card descended. The boy named Junior looked up as the card spun towards him. Just as he was about to catch it, the girl jumped in front of him and stole the card before dancing on her feet and throwing it back to her father.

"That boy..." The Watcher let out.

"Is a Clover," Jax confirmed as his card slowly returned. Once the card was back in his hand, he turned back to face the tree and The Watcher replicated his actions. "Not all of us can be old and cynical. Some of us needs to be young and hopeful."

"That's a good view to have."

Changing topic, Jax pointed to the plant and asked, "Do you know the legend behind this tree?"

"I had a fairytale of a tree back home. I wonder if it's the same."

"Shoot."

Smiling at memories of home, The Watcher began, "Back where I come from, there's this story that this tree on a hill would grant people with loyal friends and allies. Royals and armies sought it out, wanting to build an army of dedicated soldiers, but never found it. Only a little boy, a young squire, stumbling alone one day, found the tree out on an empty plane. Beneath the sunny sky, he met his first friend. The two went on to overthrow a corrupt queen, establishing peace throughout the lands for centuries."

The farmer chuckled. "Cute story. Do you believe it?"

"I was there."

Jax laughed. "Does the story have a name?"

The Watcher nodded. "The Tree of Crossroads, where Haven began."

"That's what we call it too." Jax turned to The Watcher, and a solemness took his eyes. "But there's another part to our legend. Want to hear it?"

Copying the former, he answered, "Shoot."

As if made for storytelling, Jax's voice smoothed over, dragging with a sing-song timbre. "Out of all the universe that exists, life takes different forms. Most of time, they resemble another life from another time in another world. And always are something different in a way. Except for this tree. In every universe, in every moment of time and fabric of space it appears in, it is a tree. It's never anything more."

He paused dramatically, looking to The Watcher in earnest. "Except in one universe. For one short moment of a lifetime, in all of the time-lines of all the universes, the tree is a human for only one lifetime. And it lived a remarkable life, filled with love, honour, and adventures." He looked to The Watcher with a smile. "In the language of the ancients, do you know what this story is called?"

The latter shook his head.

"*Tier*. It translates loosely to 'A Moment'."

The Watcher's heart skipped. An image of his brother's face came to mind. He wondered, if the story was indeed true, and that despite being in another universe with other possible versions of themselves, will there never be another Tier? Then, he looked to the tree, and a thought dawned on him. A small smile formed across his lips. *Watch over me, brother. I will find you everywhere.*

Jax grinned. "Miguel said you're looking for the meaning of the number one-three-nine. Has he told you what it is?"

"There was no need," The Watcher replied, clearing his throat. "I figured it out. It's just the speed of time here in tandem to the multiverse as a whole."

"Well, that's not entirely true." Jax waved his hands in dramatic explanation. "Universes are these large broiling concoction of energy. Every so often, they form into something coherent. The rest? Not so much. We wouldn't even be able to exist in those planes. So the real question is, what is the number one-three-nine?" Jax asked.

As if a bulb clicked in his head, The Watcher replied, "A prime number."

Their radios rang with vibrating beeps, but Jax carried on. "You came from world seven. I came from world three. I know a few people from world thirteen." You've been chasing the base code of a universe with recognisable physics. A prime numbered base that cannot be divided by anything but itself. My friend, welcome to one-three-nine. Welcome to Tearha."

The Watcher let out half a laugh, surprised at having missed a theory so obvious. He had crossed hell and high waters, drudging through time and space to find something that could have as easily been solved with a little math.

Pulling out his own radio, Jax finally accepted the call as The Watcher listened in.

From the other end, a female voiced, "Hey! Anyone near Rubicum? We've got a tear here and void creatures are pouring out. Class-C is holding, but we're being overrun."

A young male voice replied, "Ruby, this is Junior. Shion and I are on our way!"

The two adults turned to look downhill to see Junior materialising a wand in each hand.

Jax shouted, "Don't you dare!"

Junior smiled, and with a flick of his right wrist, white magic sigils blossomed in the air in front of him, with more taking form further towards the west. The girl called Shion ran up to him, taking his offered outstretched hand. With a wave back to their guardian, the young teens jumped into the first sigil and was propelled through the air towards the next one. They continued, bouncing across the plains on launchpads of magic.

Their radios beeped again, and a different female shouted through. "Jax! Did you let Junior run off again?"

"He's a pretty fast kid! I'm not going to be able to stop him with a stern stare!"

Miguel's calmer voice replaced the channel. "You're with The Watcher, right? Get him to teleport you there."

Jax whined back, "Come on! Junior's strong. He can take care of himself. I really wanted to get home and relax a little."

There was a subsequent period of radio silence. The two man on the hill exchanged shrugs, wondering if that was the end of the debate. Then, a beep rang out and a new voice replaced the previous group's.

Oozing with malice that they could feel seeping out of the receiver, a woman said with a light-hearted but malefic tone, "Jax, if you have the time, please go make sure our daughter is safe."

The Watcher heard his companion gulp audibly, before the latter replied, "Yes, my love." They kept their radio, and Jax let out a stressed sigh. The Watcher could not help but laugh, which only earned him a stare that begged for pity.

Wishing to refocus the topic, The Watcher asked, "What's with this tear thing?

"Well..." Jax began, before raising his hands to demonstrate wildly with simple words. "Big explosions. Loud noises. Giant monsters. Terrible danger."

Even after a thousand years of adventures, The Watcher could still feel his hair stand on the back of his neck at the sound of potential excitement. With a toothy grin, he replied, "What are we waiting for?"

Bonus Short Story
Three Questions and Time

The muddy clearing had not heard as much sounds of outside life since time began. Clanking of metal boots and worried chatter filled the air as the soldiers of the Queendom of Luutvin stood in the freezing misty weather, plated armours dipped in mud, and voices drowning in confusion.

"Make sure no one gets in or out without a say-so!" Lunamaria shouted.

"Yes, captain!" her soldiers replied loudly before dispersing to their duties.

Lunamaria adjusted the plates of her uniform armour. Chest, pauldrons, tassets, and finally sword. The operation around her ran smoothly, despite not knowing what would come next nor the exact details of the situation at hand. Military operations of course, were often simply organised chaos, always one wrong step away from failure.

As she surveyed the bog around her, that's when she saw him.

Dressed not in armour but in a coat, and wielding not a sword but a confident swagger, the man crossed the clearing with wide strides. His short, unhinged dark chocolate hair rustled with a cold wind's blow and his dark brown eyes grinned forward. Grey shirt underneath a black vest painted him closer to a scholar. The colour of his mud brown pants seemed almost repellent to the mud itself. No one else stopped him or even looked in his direction. It was as if he was suppose to be there, the man swaying minds from the sheer confidence of his groove. For a moment, even she questioned whether or not the man had authority to enter until she remembered that permissions were given by herself.

She crossed the field quickly and cut the man off midway. "Excuse me, sir! You're not suppose to be here!"

The man stopped and looked at her confused. "Oh. I really thought that would work."

Lunamaria stepped up to him and asked, "Who gave you permission to enter?"

"Um... nobody, actually. I just walked in here like I owned the place. It always worked in spy movies."

"Well, this isn't a spy... move-eee or, whatever it is that you're talking about. Care to tell me who you are and what you are doing here before I have you arrested."

"I'll be honest, I was arrested before. Did not really much took to it."

"Then I suggest you start talking."

The man puffed up his chest and thumped proudly. "I'm The Watcher!"

A period of quiet rested over them. A literal breeze whistled through the bog.

She asked, "Who?"

The man called The Watcher was taken aback. "The Watcher! I just saved the world? Stopped Lord Light? Protector of time?"

She raised a brow, questioning his earnest. When she realised he was serious, she let out a laugh. "You? I'm sorry, but I doubt a single man was the one who defeated Light, let alone someone as..." She looked him up and down. "Weird as you."

"I'm taking offence to that," he pouted like a child. Then his mood turned serious in a heartbeat. "But the fact that you, dressed so captainly aren't kicking me out yet means you want something."

"That depends. No mere man would dare walk by the Queen's Guards towards certain doom with such insouciant. Which to me means you're either extremely stupid or well acquainted with the breaking of laws."

He shrugged. "You're not wrong."

"On what count?"

He simply shrugged again.

She paused to think and sized him up with parting eyes. "First off, I still don't know what you're here for."

"What if I'm here for what you think I'm here for?"

"Then I guess we could work something out."

"Well, I'm going to need a name."

"Luna. Captain Lunamaria Falecon."

"Luna." He grinned and crossed her in one large step and continued walking on. "Tell me about this."

She followed on. "It appeared about ten days ago."

They walked together towards the giant sandstone statue in the middle of the marsh. With the face of a man but the body of a cat, the structure towered over them. Unlike the bog which, while damp, was filled with life, a radius around the statue held nothing but death. The carcass of animals and brown decaying plants littered the ground and with every passing second, the circle grows just very slightly larger, engulfing the world around it in the blackness of the deceased.

The zone's growth was barely noticeable. Every few seconds that passed had them squinting before spotting any major change in its size.

"The statue—"

"Sphinx," he corrected.

"What?"

"It's called a sphinx."

"What's a sphinx?"

"It's just a sphinx."

She waited for him to explain what a sphinx was but when seconds ticked by and she realised he had nothing else to add, she sighed and continued, "The sphinx," she emphasised. "Doesn't seem to move at first."

"At first? So there are circumstances where it does move?"

"When someone enters the area, yes."

He turned back to the monument, quizzical. Nothing surrounded it within the invisible barrier but a landscape of corpses.

With doubts, he asked, "Are you sure?"

She exchanged a knowing stare. "I did not say they survived."

"So what happens inside there? Do they start a party?"

"No," she answered matter-of-factly with a disgusted glare to him. "So far, only adventurers and a few of our soldiers have entered. Whenever they go in, they seem to... talk to the thing. After a while, they panic and one by one, they get..."

She stopped short of the explanation and simply looked skywards. He followed the gaze to a bird that soared carefree in the sky. Without seeing it, the avian flew into the invisible zone and they watched as it instantly began shrivelling, spiralling out of the air as it lost all its life energy and plummeted to the ground, exploding into a puff of dust as its decomposed body unable to even hold its shape together.

He exclaimed, "Did you see that?"

"Yes. Any living creature that goes inside the zone eventually dies."

"What? No!" he replied, confused. "That's not what I'm talking about. You didn't see it?"

"See what?"

"When the bird hit the sphere, the area grew by one point two five nanometres."

She threw her hands in the air. "How would I have possibly seen that? And besides, it's been growing since it first appeared."

"Yes, but it grew faster. That's the point." He placed a hand on his chin in ponder. "It's not growing over time. It's draining the life of its surroundings. Every single moment it takes a little more, grows a little bigger, and eats a little faster. I estimate that by tomorrow evening, this thing will be big enough to envelop half the planet."

"What?!" she exclaimed. "How? It's growth has been slow so far."

"Exponential increase. It gets faster the bigger it gets."

"But that means–"

"End of the world," he finished nonchalantly. "Unless we stop it here."

"How?"

"I don't know. It's a deadly phenomenon that no one has ever encountered before. My suggestion?" He paused, squinted, then smiled. "Let's go poke it with a stick."

"W–wait!"

But The Watcher was already walking confidently towards the sphere, leading her to chase after him.

"No time to wait," he eagerly stated. "If we want there to be a world left tomorrow, we're dealing with this today."

"This is too dangerous," she shouted after him. "Shouldn't we at least find out what's going on first?"

"And do you know what's the best way to figure things out? By trying it out! So don't dilly-dally, let's shilly-shally!"

She paused momentarily in her tracks, exasperated. "What does that even mean?"

They crossed the field, her mostly jogging after him with his long, inpatient strides. She thought he would stop at the edge of the invisible barrier and hesitate like everyone before. But instead, he simply continued walking, stepping into the zone of death without a second breath aside.

She wanted to slow down. She wanted to stop. She wanted to not have to follow him through for a slight part of her was afraid of dying, despite it just being her doing her job. But another part was fascinated by what The Watcher was doing. Her sense of adventure was tickled. She swore she felt that if she missed what happened next she would regret that decision for the rest of her life.

So she took a step forward and followed him into the zone.

Immediately, the drain began coursing through her. She felt as if every pore of her body was being sucked at. A constant shiver of goosebumps shook her. But the most disconcerting was the noise, or lack thereof. Silence had stolen the voice of the universe and the world was dead in its quiet.

"Ah! You followed," he looked all surprised, delighted, worried, and disappointed at the same time. "Now, if you want to survive this, do as you're told and don't ask any questions."

"But–!"

"Don't–!" He cut fiercely. "–ask any questions." He made a zipping motion across his mouth.

She stood at attention, confused as to his reaction. Then he turned and took a step towards the sphinx.

"Hello! I'm The Watcher."

"Interesting."

The sphinx moved its sandstone head, cocking it sideways in curiosity. But despite speaking, its mouth did not move. Instead, with each shift of its body, the sand of its skin crawled grain by grain. A million tiny white ants shifted to make the stone creature take on a new position every second. It was dizzying. Like watching water turning into ice.

The Watcher smiled. "If you think this is interesting, you've obviously not looked in a mirror."

"How did you know not to ask questions?"

"You're the sphinx. Asking questions is what you do. Not me. I'm suppose to provide the answer. And I'm guessing you're on a 'Answer my question and save the world' kind of deal. Probably with a limited number of questions as well. Something along the line of only being allowed one question or something."

"Three, actually. But very astute nonetheless."

Lunamaria piped up, "That was why you–" She stopped herself. Instinctively, she almost asked a question even though she found out the 'rules' for the 'game'. She re-toned, "That was why you told me not to ask questions."

"Correct, my dear Luna."

She paused again, running her next sentence through her mind. The Watcher noticed her thinking and smiled, patiently waiting. "You figured this out on our way here."

"No," he answered. "It was when we were talking."

"How–?" she tried to stop her inflection but it was too late.

The sphinx replied, "That is a question only The Watcher can answer. And now, captain, you are left with two questions."

She placed a hand over her mouth, a look of shock crossing her face. "I didn't–"

"Don't worry," The Watcher calmly stopped her. "See, that's the reaction. You told me the people who came in here started to panic. Now, if you were calm enough to enter into a dangerous, unexplainable situation willingly, you won't just panic. So something must have happened. For example, the sudden realisation that one of your chance at survival was unknowingly taken away by, you know, asking an innocent question."

Lunamaria had her mouth agape. He had deduced all that simply from an off-handed information she said. But beyond all, she was still having trouble not running her mouth off and asking unnecessary questions. Yet, between their short conversation and the walk into the zone, The Watcher had not just prepared his speech patterns, but made no mistakes following.

The Watcher continued, "Well, Mr. Sphinx. Tell me your game. I can't wait to find out what bullshit you have in stored for us."

With sand shifting into a solid, the sphinx replied, "Any questions asked will be answered with accurate truth. With three queries before the end of your lives, make me tell a lie."

"A reverse liar paradox. Interesting."

"Watcher," Lunamaria began but managed to stop before the question got asked. Instead, she awkwardly added, "Ask a question."

"Good, good," he replied immediately. "You're getting the game. It's a stupid game, but still..." He looked to the sphinx. "We've got to play it."

He stopped speaking and she could practically see the gears of thoughts whirring in his head. She took a quick look behind. The world outside them continued to turn. Some of her guards were lined outside the zone of death, fraught with worry. They looked in. A few caught her gaze and questioned what they should do. Lunamaria calmed them with a waving hand, telling them not to follow. She hoped she had convinced them she had the situation under control. In truth, she was just as uncertain as they were. She merely followed The Watcher in and was just waiting for the mysterious man to become the man with a plan.

Then, he spoke, "Lunamaria. I need to ask four questions, but I only have three. So you will have to ask one for me. But since I can't tell you the exact question to ask, you will have to figure it out yourself."

She was slower to reply, taking a pause to throw her inflections out. "Sure."

The Watcher did not seem to mind her lagging. In fact, he grinned happily as if impressed with her catching up to the situation.

"Don't worry," he added. "I'll make sure you get out of this alive. That's a promise."

She nodded. "Tell me what you need."

"The sphinx has not spoken since giving us his rules. I'm guessing it's by the laws of his 'game'." He turned to the sandstone creature which gave no reactions, affirming his theory. "I need to know if it will answer questions with a yes or a no only. You need to phrase that into a question that it cannot play around with. Its answer will determine how I question it later."

"No exits," she confirmed.

"Exactly."

It ran through her mind. She started small, beginning with how she would normally phrase the question. 'Will you answer yes or no questions?'

But that question could be answered in many ways. Answering yes or no doe not prevent the sphinx from giving more complex replies later on. And the creature could easily avoid it by giving a pivot, as do many politicians do. While she was looking at a way to prevent the enemy from finding a loophole, she thought perhaps a loophole itself was what she needed.

She looked to sphinx which stood unmoving, then to The Watcher who waited with a patient smile. "If you need help, just let me know."

"No," she replied. She was not sure why, but she wanted not to rely on him for this bit. "I can handle this."

The man was otherworldly. So much so she was sure The Watcher was not of Tearha. As much as she appreciated his help, she was responsible for the world they lived in. She was amongst monsters, as sure as day. On one side was the sandstone beast that saps away the life of its surroundings, threatening to eat the world in death. On the other was the man that walked up to it to say hello. Between them, she stood. A representative of the world at large in a battle between eternal entities.

"Answer in yes or no," she began. "Will you answer any questions the two of us asks exactly as we asks for them?"

"Oh," The Watcher grinned wide. "Very nicely done. Much more than I had hoped for."

Lunamaria tapped her chest twice in thanks of the compliment. "My pleasure."

The Watcher's grin widened as he turned back to the sphinx. "Now, this is getting fun. I noticed you're not answering. I guess you're thinking of how to get yourself out of this little hole my clever companion has dug you. If you do not give a yes or no answer, you've lied about answering accurately. If you do give a yes or no answer, you've pinned yourself to the entrance of a logic gate."

The sphinx wasn't replying. She felt that if its ever shifting sand for a face had expressions, she would likely see its nostrils flaring.

The Watcher joked, "I would say 'cat got your tongue', but you're already a cat."

The creature made a rumbling noise and the earth trembled with it. "Yes," it finally answered Lunamaria.

The Watcher's mouth stretched into a grin. She was not sure what was more terrifying. The world about to end or the man's strangely manic smile.

"Fantastic..." he said under his breath. "Three questions to save the world. Just me, the moon, and the giant talking cat."

The sphinx growled, "Who are you?"

"No no no. We're the players here," he replied. "We're the ones following your rules. You don't get to ask questions. Only give answers. Yes or no, is it possible for me to win this game?"

A slight pause. "Yes."

"Second question. Yes or no, will you ever lie to me?"

Another pause, much longer than the first. "No."

"Last question. Which of the two previous question did you lie about?"

The sphinx aggressively broke apart. Each grain of sand floated off and forming into a coagulated floating cloud. There was a roar of undeniable non-natural anger. The dust cloud balled together into a solid snaking fist that flew towards The Watcher.

Lunamaria jumped between the man and the attacking monster. "Watch out!" she shouted, drawing her sword in defiance of death.

But she knew they were going to die. The dust cloud was larger than both of them combined. The swirling mass that could envelop them a hundred times over was heading their way with the speed of a punch. Despite her years of combat training, she closed her eyes instinctively and prepared for death.

But nothing happened. The world around was quiet. She felt no pain. Then, she heard his voice.

"Very brave of you," The Watcher said. "That's what bravery is. Doing something in spite of being afraid."

She opened her eyes. Around her, the sand mass swirled, kept out of their way by a bubble of unknown energy. The sphinx punched, smashed, collapsed, wrapped, desperately trying to penetrate the shielding but could not budge through. The Watcher stood calmly, his entire body aglow with the purple sheen of his magic circuits.

He began, "I know what you are, you stupid cat. You're one of these 'gods' I've been hearing so much about. You, playing your games on this world, trying to conquer it, destroying the lives of all who lives here." Despite the steadied tone, there was anger in his voice that boiled. "You're just another player, trying to move the pieces in your favour. Well, too bad, you've lost. You lost because Luna and I are here to stop you today, and many more of us will be here to stop everyone else you send along the way."

His fists balled and his voice raised high. "I know one of you gods did it! One of you murdered Vashmir Commons! One of you brought my best friend into this universe to be killed! One of you orchestrated the end of two worlds. I know it's not you, God of Riddles, so I will send you back to tell them this message. Tell them I'm coming! I will find all of you playing your games, up to the one holding the high score! I don't know which god you are, but I will find you! And I will stop you! Because I am The Watcher, the God of Time! This universe is under MY protection! And you, are. In. MY. WAY!"

He pushed his hands outward and the world instantly cleared. No more sand. No more force field of death. The weight of decay lifted immediately off Lunamaria's shoulders. The world around was quiet. The land around them was still dead. But they were alive and the god was gone.

It seemed like it was their win that day.

Instantly, it occurred to Lunamaria that no one would know what really happened there. She would give her report to her queen. But knowing the power The Watcher held, she felt compelled to leave his involvement minimum, less the man be targeted by her country's love for power. She would likely get a promotion for her deed. A small, uncomfortable price to pay to keep The Watcher out of the hands of government and royals.

Her soldiers were running up to her from a distance. And by that time, The Watcher was already walking away.

"Wait!" she called after him. "Who are you?"

He half turned with a smile. "I'm The Watcher."

A gust blew through, carrying fresh leaves and swamp scent. A leaf fluttered across her vision. The man was gone. Magic. Alien powers. Whatever it was, the man was not a trick of her eyes. She turned to her soldiers, all of whom seemed not to have noticed his disappearance. She let out a happy sigh, despite dreading the report she would have to pen.

In it, there will be one line that echoed through the rest of history.

There are some questions only time can tell.

www.ingramcontent.com/pod-product-compliance
Lightning Source LLC
Chambersburg PA
CBHW030112180626
46812CB00002B/393